Praise for Susan Carroll's Dark Queen Series

"An intoxicating brew of poignant romance, turbulent history, and mesmerizing magic."

> —KAREN HARPER, author of *The Fyre Mirror*

"With a pinch of both the otherworldly and romance to spice up the deep look at the Medici era . . . Susan Carroll writes a wonderful historical thriller that will have the audience eagerly awaiting [the next] story."

> —*The Midwest Book Review*

"[A] riveting tale of witchcraft, treachery, and court intrigue." —*Library Journal,* Starred Review

"Utterly perfect—rich, compelling, and full of surprises. A fabulous, feminist fantasy from a masterful storyteller that's bound to be one of the best books of the year!"

> —ELIZABETH GRAYSON, author of *Moon in the Water*

"Enthralling historical detail, dark and intense emotions and the perfect touches of the paranormal. [Carroll] leaves readers to savor every word of this superbly crafted breathtaking romance."

> —*Romantic Times,* Top Pick!

The Huntress

The Huntress

A NOVEL

SUSAN CARROLL

BALLANTINE BOOKS · NEW YORK

A Ballantine Books Trade Paperback Original

Published in the United States by Ballantine Books,
an imprint of The Random House Publishing Group,
a division of Random House, Inc., New York.

BALLANTINE and colophon are registered trademarks
of Random House, Inc.

ISBN 978-0-345-49061-2

Library of Congress Cataloging-in-Publication Data
Carroll, Susan.
The huntress : a novel / Susan Carroll.
p. cm.
ISBN 978-0-345-49061-2 (pbk.)
1. Elizabeth I, Queen of England, 1533–1603—Fiction. 2. Great Britain—
History—Elizabeth, 1558–1603—Fiction. 3. Queens—Fiction. I. Title.

PS3553.A7654H86 2007
813'.54—dc22   2007006930

Printed in the United States of America

www.ballantinebooks.com

2 4 6 8 9 7 5 3 1

To the Monday ladies:

Gina Hinrichs, Sheila Burns, Trudy Watson,
and Stephanie Wilson.

For movies, Chinese food, and friendship.

Acknowledgments

I would also like to acknowledge both the Betten-
dorf and Moline public libraries for aid with re-
search and for providing me with a cozy corner
for writing. And a special thanks to all the staff
at the Moline Panera for nourishment and encouragement.

The Huntress

Prologue

THE COMET BLAZED AGAINST THE NIGHT SKY, BRIGHTER THAN any star, its ghostly head trailed by a streak of fire. It had hovered for the past week, like a sword suspended over the earth, spreading fear and wonderment across France.

The cluster of women atop the rugged Breton cliff all trained their eyes skyward, their forms concealed by flowing gray mantles, hoods pulled forward like monks shrouding themselves from the temptations of the world. Silhouetted against the leaping flames of the bonfire, the women presented a sinister aspect, the eeriness of the scene enhanced by the haunting rhythm of the surf pounding against the rocks far below.

The women drew in a collective breath as they stared

up at the comet, oblivious to the fact that they themselves were being observed.

Flattened on her stomach, Catriona O'Hanlon found what concealment she could among the sparse brush and straggling trees that rimmed the clearing. The Irishwoman was petite, but her size was deceptive, her slender frame imbued with a wiry strength, her tautly honed limbs clad in masculine clothing, fustian breeches and a leather jerkin that helped her fade into the darkness.

A strand of fiery red hair escaped from her cap, but she did not dare brush it aside for fear the slightest movement would betray her presence. Especially while the women she spied upon were so silent.

One of them spoke at last, her voice so low Catriona had to strain to hear.

"The comet is clearly a sign, my sisters. The omen we have all been waiting for."

Yes, a sign that your wits have gone a-begging, Catriona thought contemptuously. Like so many other superstitious fools trembling in awe of a great gob burning in the sky eons away.

True daughters of the earth should know better than to subscribe to such nonsense. Since the beginning of time, there had been wise women who struggled to preserve the light of learning in an ignorant world, especially the knowledge of healing and white magic.

But there were others who succumbed to the lure of the darker arts, seeking power instead of wisdom, more intent upon spreading chaos and superstition than knowledge. Such were the women that Catriona observed gathered about the bonfire. They called themselves the Sisterhood of the Silver Rose, fanatical to the point of being dangerous.

Catriona inched her hand toward the scabbard, fastened about her waist, her fingers closing over the hilt of her rapier, taking comfort from the length of steel strapped to her side.

She liked a good scrap as well as any of her countrymen, but if it came to a scuffle, she might be a wee bit outnumbered. Besides, the orders from her chieftain had been quite clear. Do not engage the enemy. Just discover who had resurrected the dread coven of the Silver Rose, the identity of their new leader.

Perhaps it was the taller one who now addressed the group from the depths of her cowl.

"Comets have always been portents of great change, the death of the old, the birth of the new." The woman gestured skyward with one white, graceful hand. "That one burns for our Silver Rose, heralding her glory, her long overdue triumph as she assumes her rightful place as the ruler of France and lands beyond."

"We have to find her first," someone demurred.

"And so we will." The tall woman rested her hand solemnly upon the shoulder of the one who had spoken. "I promise you that. I have finally discovered that our young queen was taken out of France."

"Out of France!" one of the coven wailed in dismay. "But that increases our difficulties of finding her tenfold."

"No, Megaera shall be rescued, I swear to you. And then we shall punish the rogue who dared snatch our queen away from us."

"Yes, death to the villain!" Other voices piped up in shrill agreement.

"Show the bastard no mercy."

"Make him regret he was ever born."

"Destroy the fiend who abducted our Rose."

"Death to the Wolf. Death to the Wolf!"

The chant swelled louder and louder until the first woman called for silence. She spoke again, but this time her words were too soft for Catriona to hear. Apparently some sort of command had been issued, for the group ranged itself around the bonfire. Catriona narrowed her blue eyes, straining to close the distance, obtain a glimpse beneath the leader's cowl.

The keenness of Catriona's sight even on the darkest night, combined with her agility and stealth had long ago led her own people to nickname her Cat. At least before her clan had cast her out and taken to calling her something else.

Witch.

Her banishment was mostly owing to the malice of Banan O'Meara, the man who had married Cat's mother. Cat wished she had her stepfather with her tonight. She'd show the great dolt what a real witch looked like.

As the leader reached up to draw back her cowl, Cat held her breath.

"That's right, darlin'" Cat coaxed the woman silently. "Take off that hood and give me a good look at your crazed, evil little face."

But as the woman's cowl fell back, Cat bit her lip to keep from swearing in disappointment. The woman's features were hidden behind a silk mask, the kind ladies wore to shield their complexions from the sun. Cat could make out little beyond the delicate line of her chin, the golden glint of hair pulled back in a severe chignon.

As the others drew back their hoods, they were likewise masked. Only one face was bared, a young girl with a mass of raven hair. She stripped off her mantle entirely, revealing that she wore nothing beneath except a white chemise. The chit was a novice to the order, about to undergo the ceremony that would proclaim her a full-fledged devotee of the Silver Rose.

Cat suppressed an impatient sigh, having no desire to witness some demented initiation. She already had a cramp in her left leg from lying immobile on the cold ground so long, but she had no choice but to remain where she was and hope when they'd finished with this blather, they'd get on with discussing their plans regarding the missing Rose. And perhaps when they were done and finally melted away in the darkness, Cat might get a chance to corral the leader alone, get a blade to her throat, force her to strip off that mask.

The woman was all but lost to Cat's view as the head of the coven bent down to heat a dagger over the fire. The rest of the group commenced a toneless chanting in what they probably imagined was some mystic tongue, but which was nothing but a load of shite, Cat thought derisively. She herself had been well-schooled in all the ancient languages, thanks to her old gran, and this taradiddle resembled none of them.

The dark-haired girl swayed in time to the chanting, a dreamy detached look on her thin face, perhaps the result of being drugged with some opiate or a healthy dose of brandy. For the girl's sake, Cat hoped that was the case, as she guessed what was coming.

Yet it was she who shuddered and not the girl as the novice calmly extended her hand, exposing the soft white skin of her forearm. Two of the witches laid hands on the girl, gripping her arm to hold her in place lest she change her mind as the leader approached wielding the hot blade.

Cat was not squeamish, having witnessed many gruesome sights in her twenty-seven years. But she lowered her gaze, bracing herself for the girl's inevitable screams, no matter how much poppy juice the poor fool had swilled.

But the sound that disrupted the night was the sharp crack of twigs snapping, the dislodging of pebbles beneath heavy boots. And it came from behind Cat.

She twisted around, startled. So absorbed had she been by the scene being played out atop the cliff, she had failed to realize she was not the only one tracking the witches.

Shadows loomed up around her, a large troop of men, a dozen at least charging up the path toward the clearing. Witch-hunters? Cat was tempted to shout out a warning. She loathed the idea of any woman falling prey to a witch-hunter, no matter how misguided or evil the woman had become. Daughters of the earth should dispense justice to their own kind, not some pompous priest or grubby mercenary who earned his bread through torture and murder.

But it was too late for any warning and unnecessary. The coven had already taken alarm, some of them emitting frightened cries. Cat caught a blurred impression of burly legs, thick boots, and the glint of drawn swords as the men surged past her hiding place. She rolled to one side, barely avoiding being trampled.

The women shrieked, falling back about their leader. Cut off from the cliff path, there was nowhere to retreat except for the sheer drop to the jagged rocks far below. Some of the women unsheathed knives and swords, but they were badly outnumbered, no match for these hefty brutes. Fearing she was about to bear witness to a terrible slaughter, Cat scrambled to her feet.

Cat unsheathed her weapon. Despite her chieftain's orders, she could not just stand aside and—

"Halt!"

The brusque command from the captain of the troop caused his men to freeze and Cat as well. She remained unnoticed in the shadows as the man stepped forward, the glow from the bonfire enabling Cat to make out his features. Handsome with a sandy-colored beard and softly curling hair, he was far more polished than his collection of rough-hewn men.

"Ladies," he said, sweeping the huddled women a courtly bow and flashing an amiable smile as though he were at a ball and intended to invite one of them to dance.

Cat experienced a shock of recognition. She knew that all-too-charming smile that masked a cold assassin's heart. Ambroise Gautier. He was no witch-hunter, but something far worse.

He continued, his silken voice sounding almost apologetic, "My dears, I regret I have to interrupt your little satanic rituals, but I am obliged to place you all under arrest. I have no wish to harm any of you, so I must request, most courteously, that you put up your weapons and come quietly.

"I am sure you can see you have but two options. Surrender or die."

One of the women gave a choked sob, the young noviate perhaps. But the leader of the coven appeared quite calm as she moved forward.

"You are mistaken, monsieur," she said. "There is a third choice. We can all simply disappear."

"Indeed, mademoiselle?" Gautier's teeth flashed in a grin as he inquired politely, "And how do you propose to do that? Leap onto your broomsticks and vanish into the sky?"

"No, in a puff of smoke." The witch whirled quickly and flung a handful of something into the fire.

The effect was startling and immediate, a loud boom followed by a shower of sparks that caused everyone to duck for cover, including Cat.

One glowing ember landed on her sleeve and she slapped it out. Whatever the witch had flung in the fire produced a cloud of black smoke that spread rapidly, fanned by the breeze.

Cat heard Gautier swear and command his troops to charge. Chaos erupted, the cliff top rapidly engulfed in an acrid haze of shouts, screams, choking, and cursing. Someone was down, but whether it was one of the coven or one of the men, Cat could not tell as her own eyes began to sting.

Clapping her hand over her mouth and nose, she sheathed her sword and beat a swift retreat back down the hill. Half running, half stumbling, she reached the place where she had left her mount tethered, relieved to find Red Branch still there, the roan gelding undiscovered by Gautier's men.

Gautier. Cat reeled from her recognition of the cold-blooded mercenary, but less from fear of the man than of the one who had sent him, the one Gautier served.

Catherine de Medici, the Dowager Queen of France, but better known to other daughters of the earth by a far different name . . . *The Dark Queen.*

As Cat untethered Red Branch and swung up into the saddle, she cast a frustrated glance in the direction she had come, where all hell was breaking loose. As far as diversions went, the witch's trick with her exploding powder had been a stupid one, the smoke enveloping her coven as well as the guards.

Cat would not have given good odds on all of those women escaping. Perhaps none of them would. If Gautier's men captured even one of the coven, hauled her back to face Catherine, if the Dark Queen learned the truth about the Silver Rose . . .

Cat's blood ran cold at the possibilities. Still, there was nothing she could do but hasten back to Faire Isle and warn her chieftain.

"The devil's in it now and no mistake," Cat muttered as she wheeled Red Branch about. Cat dug in her knees and raced off into the night as though the fate of the world depended upon her.

Chapter One

THE LADY OF FAIRE ISLE WANDERED THROUGH HER GARDEN, her slippered feet scarce making a sound as she followed the familiar path. Even the lark that nested in the old elm was not stirring at this early hour, the sky just beginning to lighten with the first hint of dawn.

The garden was as silent as the house that loomed behind her. With its ivy-covered walls, single square tower, and mullioned windows, Belle Haven conveyed a snug, solid appearance. The manor had been sanctuary to countless generations of wise women and home to the one heralded as the leader among them, the Lady of Faire Isle.

Ariane Deauville, the present holder of that title, was a tall, stately woman with masses of chestnut-colored hair and solemn gray eyes. Despite all of the danger and hardship she had faced during her thirty-four years, Ariane's countenance was usually marked with a regal serenity. But at the moment, her face was pale and drawn from lack of sleep.

After tossing and turning for hours, she had finally given up. Fearing to disturb her husband's repose, she had stolen from the warmth of their bed, flung a woolen cloak over her nightshift, and slipped outside the kitchen door.

Her gardens had always been a source of peace to her, all those well-tended beds of herbs she used in her healing arts a great comfort. But this morning her gaze turned in the same direction as so many others all across Europe— toward the sky, where that strange apparition disrupted the peace of the heavens.

Even as the sky grew lighter, the comet was still visible, lurking just beneath the pale disc of moon. Ariane stared, humbled and awed by the spectral phenomenon streaking the sky.

Since the dawn of time, folks had viewed comets as the herald of floods, earthquakes, plagues, famines, and the deaths of emperors and kings. Ariane knew she should be above such superstitious beliefs.

But she could not suppress the chill that worked up her spine. Lowering her gaze, she chided herself for entertaining such foolishness. There was trouble brewing in the world beyond her island, but she needed no comet's arrival to tell her that. The coven of the Rose was on the rise again, the order as mad and dangerous as the sorceress who had founded it.

Cassandra Lascelles had once attempted to assemble

an army, drawing into the Sisterhood of the Silver Rose those women who had fallen victim to the cruelties of the world. And there were far too many of them, Ariane reflected sadly. Abused wives, girls pregnant out of wedlock, aging courtesans discarded by their lovers. The impoverished, the disillusioned, the desperate, the insane had all flocked to the Silver Rose's banner.

Cassandra's intent had been to spread chaos throughout France, bring down the house of Medici so that she could place her daughter, Megaera, on the throne. The scheme might have been dismissed as pure insanity if Cassandra had not been in possession of the dread *Book of Shadows,* a compendium of all the most powerful, destructive, and darkest ancient science.

Ariane had been in Ireland at the time, driven into exile by false allegations of witchcraft and treason against the French king. By the time word had reached her regarding the Sisterhood of the Silver Rose, Cass's plot had already been foiled by Ariane's youngest sister, Miri, and the witchhunter, Simon Aristide.

With Cassandra Lascelles dead and Megaera spirited away by Martin le Loup, the girl's father, that had seemed to bring the dangerous matter to an end, or so everyone had hoped. But a few months ago, troubling tales had reached Ariane that the cult had a new leader and the witches were mounting a relentless search for Megaera.

Ariane was expected to possess the wisdom and strength to deal with this new threat. Unfortunately, she felt more tired, more fragile than she ever had in her life. She slipped her hand beneath her cloak, running her fingertips gently over the slight swell of her belly, the child growing there just beginning to make its presence known. A miracle after so many barren years . . .

A sound from the direction of the house interrupted Ariane's troubled thoughts. Candlelight spilled through the kitchen windows, the creak of hinges followed by the low slam of the door. Someone was coming in search of her.

Ariane half-expected it to be her husband. Finding her absent from their bed, Justice had no doubt flung off the covers with a low curse, grumbling and growling as he shrugged into his breeches and shirt.

When he found her wandering the gardens in the crisp morning air, he would be bound to scold.

"Have you taken complete leave of your wits, woman? Even the sun has enough sense not to be up yet. There is a peculiar habit some of us indulge in. It's called sleep and you need try it a bit more often, my wise Lady of Faire Isle."

Ariane's mouth quirked in a smile. Even after thirteen years of marriage, her great bear of a husband was notoriously overprotective of her. How much more so was Justice going to be when he learned about the babe? She could not conceal her condition from him much longer.

The thought caused her smile to fade. She was ashamedly relieved when she realized it was not her tall, strapping husband tramping down the garden path, although the diminutive warrior maiden who approached moved with Justice's same determined stride.

"Cat," Ariane murmured, the breath she released a mingling of trepidation and joy, glad to see the woman returning to her unharmed, apprehensive of what tidings Cat might bring.

Cat hesitated at the place where the path came to a fork, one way leading off in the direction of the orchards and stables.

"Ariane?" she called softly.

"Over here." Ariane stepped out of the shadows cast by the towering elm trees. As Cat headed toward her, Ariane moved eagerly forward to embrace her friend.

Before Ariane could prevent her, Cat dropped to one knee and carried Ariane's hand reverently to her lips.

"Hail to you, my Lady of Faire Isle. All honor and glory attend thee."

"Cat," Ariane chided, gently trying to disengage her hand from Catriona's calloused grip. "How many times must I beg you not to greet me thus? I am not a queen."

"You are to me." Cat tipped back her head. The sky had lightened just enough for Ariane to make out the smooth curve of her cheek, the fierce light burning in Cat's blue eyes.

"Ever and always, my lady, my queen, my chieftain."

Tugging at Cat's arm, Ariane urged the younger woman to her feet. "I would far rather you think of me as your sister and friend."

She enveloped Cat in a warm hug, an embrace that Cat returned awkwardly. Even though their friendship spanned a decade, Cat was still not comfortable with such tender displays. That was only to be expected, Ariane thought sadly. During the stormy course of her life, Cat had received little by way of love or gentleness. Even from her mother.

Drawing back, Cat regarded Ariane with gruff affection. "So how fares my chieftain?"

"Better, now that I see my gallowglass safe returned to me," Ariane replied with a smile, but she took worried note of her friend's appearance, the smudge of dirt on her cheek, the dust that coated her jerkin. The garment was torn at the shoulder and was that a burn mark on the sleeve?

"Oh, Cat, never tell me you have been fighting."

"Nay! Did I not promise you? I have not so much as had my sword drawn from its scabbard." Some of Cat's wounded indignation faded as she scratched her chin and confessed. "Well, only for a moment or two, but I sheathed it straightaway without so much as pricking anyone. As soon as I found those witches, I hastened back to make my report to you."

"Then you did find the coven?"

Cat drew herself up. "Did you ever doubt that I would?"

"No." Ariane had more hoped that Cat wouldn't, that all the rumors that had carried to Faire Isle would prove to be just wild tales and nothing more.

"And . . . and so?" she faltered.

"And so everything you feared is true. The Sisterhood of the Silver Rose still exists. Although there are not as many of them as before, they are recruiting new members. Unfortunately, I was interrupted before I could ascertain who leads them." Cat bit her lip, looking chagrined and frustrated by her failure. "The witches wear masks to their gatherings, but they've all taken to marking themselves, searing the emblem of a tiny rose onto their right forearms. They are as fanatically devoted to Megaera as ever and determined to recover her. Somehow, they have discovered she was taken out of France. It may be only a matter of time before they find her. Or someone worse does."

Ariane paled at hearing her worst dread confirmed. She closed her eyes, swaying a little as her head swam.

"My lady!" Cat cried. She slipped her arm about Ariane's waist, bracing her. She guided Ariane toward one of the garden benches, easing her down onto the cold stone.

Ariane bent forward, lowering her head, taking in long slow breaths until the garden began to stop spinning. Cat hunkered down in front of her, chafing her wrist, her voice full of concern.

"What shall I do? Can I get you some water? Or should I summon milord to carry you into the house?"

Ariane shook her head, straightening up as she recovered, feeling foolish over her display of weakness.

"No, it's nothing," she insisted. "I occasionally get these spells of lightheadedness. Quite normal for a woman in my condition."

Cat scowled, looking far from convinced. " 'Tis clear to me you have not been taking proper care of yourself. What were you doing out of your bed at such an hour? I am surprised himself would have allowed it, especially you being with child and all."

Ariane said nothing, but the guilty way she averted her face must have told Cat all she needed to know. The Irishwoman rocked back on her heels, groaning.

"Ah, by all the saints. You haven't told him yet. But isn't that a bit daft? Milord is bound to notice soon. I am surprised he hasn't already, himself being such a deep and clever one."

A half smile escaped Ariane at Cat's description of Justice. *Himself,* as Cat so quaintly called him, was indeed clever. Ariane was highly skilled in reading eyes, those windows to the soul. With her steadfast gaze, she could take the measure of someone's character and often read thoughts as well. But Justice was even better at it than she was, her husband having been schooled in the ancient art of mind reading by Melusine, his wicked old witch of a grandmother.

Ariane and Justice were as close as man and wife could be, but she could shield her thoughts from him if she had to, although she'd had little cause to do so until recently. Justice had to be aware that she was closing him out, but he hadn't pressed her, waiting for her to confide whatever secret she guarded so closely, trusting that she would.

Ariane sighed. "It has been very wrong of me to conceal the babe from Justice. But, oh, Cat! You know I had given up hope of ever conceiving again. Is it so selfish of me to want to quietly savor my joy awhile longer? Because I know Justice won't be able to share my happiness no matter how hard he will try to pretend. He's going to be so afraid for me."

"You'll pardon me saying so, but doesn't he have a right to be afraid?" Cat softened the reminder by pressing Ariane's hand, the woman's palm rough and calloused, but her touch comfortingly warm. "He almost lost you once."

"I suppose so," Ariane murmured, but after all these years all that she recalled of that time was not her own near death, but the face of her stillborn child. The devastating sorrow of gazing upon the small, wizened body of her daughter. The babe she had so longed for, a girl child to teach all the old wise ways, passing on the healing arts that Ariane had learned from her own mother, a daughter who might one day succeed her as Lady of Faire Isle.

The old pain of loss and grief threatened to engulf Ariane, along with her terror for the child she now carried, but she stemmed the dark emotions. She had resolved early on during her pregnancy that this babe would be nourished only by her life's blood and breath, her calm and strength. It would not be poisoned by its mother's apprehensions and fears.

"I will tell Justice soon, I promise you. But it's going to be different, this time, I know it." Ariane splayed her hand over her womb. "This babe is strong. I can sense that. This child *will* survive. You must believe me."

"If you say 'tis so, then 'tis so," Cat responded gravely. "But—"

Ariane squeezed Cat's hand firmly, anxious to bring the subject to a close. "Please finish what you were telling me. You said something about fearing that someone far worse might be hunting Megaera?"

"Did I?" Still looking worried, Cat straightened to her feet. Averting her face, she scuffed the toe of her well-worn boot against a thick tree root. "Well, you—you know me. Sometimes I get carried away, tend to exaggerate my tales. I daresay it is the Irish in me and—"

"Cat, don't."

The command in Ariane's voice obliged Cat to look at her.

Ariane continued, "I know what you are doing. My brief spell of weakness alarmed you and now you seek to spare me. As much as I appreciate your solicitude, I need you to make a full and honest report to me. Trust me. Whatever you have learned, I am strong enough to deal with it."

I have to be, Ariane thought grimly.

Cat blew out a gusty sigh. She withdrew the flask she kept tucked in her belt and fortified herself with a gulp of usquebaugh. How Cat could swallow such a potent whiskey before she had even breakfasted, Ariane had no idea. Her own stomach roiled at the very thought of it.

Cat corked the flask and hitched it back in her belt. She paced the garden path as she regaled Ariane with the rest of her story, her tale punctuated by many gestures and sweeping waves of her arms. Ariane had often reflected with some amusement that it would not be necessary to gag Catriona O'Hanlon to silence her. One would only have to bind her hands.

But she was not even tempted to smile as she listened to the rest of Cat's report. She did not want Cat fretting over her, but it was hard for Ariane to maintain a calm façade as Cat described the soldiers who had charged the cliff top.

". . . I recognized Gautier almost at once, which left little doubt who had sent him."

"The Dark Queen," Ariane whispered. As if this matter did not promise to be difficult and dangerous enough without the threat of Catherine de Medici's involvement. A shudder coursed through Ariane. She gripped her hands tightly in her lap to conceal the depths of her dismay from Cat.

Her voice was surprisingly level as she asked, "You are absolutely certain it was Gautier?"

"Aye, I marked the man well when I accompanied you to court the day you received your pardon from the Dark Queen, and like the most gracious of thieves, she restored everything she'd stolen from you. Gautier was the smirking bastard who stood behind the queen. Did you not notice him?"

"No," Ariane said ruefully. "I fear I saw no one but Catherine. That evil woman has cast a long shadow over my life."

"Quite a feat for someone so short. Gran used to fair give me the shivers with her chilling stories about France's Dark Queen. When I finally came face-to-face with the woman, I was disappointed." Cat wrinkled her nose with disdain. "She was so—so old and fat."

Ariane conceded that Catherine had aged considerably. The once-formidable Dark Queen moved stiffly and painfully, her hands gnarled with rheumatism, her jowls heavy, her chin sagging, her face deeply lined. Those penetrating dark Medici eyes that had once been capable of stripping the soul bare were rheumy and dim. And yet Catherine's mind had seemed as sharp as ever, just as disturbingly devious.

Cat went on, "It's possible that we are getting ourselves into a stew over the queen for nothing. Her power appears to be on the wane. After all, she was obliged to sign over control of the French army to the duc de Guise. By what I hear, he has the love and support of the people of Paris, not Catherine or that puling son of hers. Some say that the duc is in a fair way to become the ruler of France in all but name."

"And that only makes me fear Catherine the more," Ariane said. "Threats to her power have ever made her desperate and dangerous. I have no doubt why she sent Gautier to find the coven. She wants the *Book of Shadows*. She has probably never stopped searching for it."

"And do you think those witches still have it?"

"I wish I knew."

After Cassandra had died, the sinister book had never been found, although Simon Aristide had made every effort to locate it. Catherine had always been fascinated by the darker side of knowledge. If she ever got her hands on that book, she would have no scruples about using it. But now Ariane had an even more pressing worry.

"If Gautier captures any of those witches and forces them to talk, Catherine's going to learn the truth about Megaera," Ariane said. "Aristide managed to convince the queen that Cassandra was really the Silver Rose. Catherine believes that both she and her daughter drowned. If the queen discovers that Simon lied, her anger may well turn to him. He has to be warned."

Cat shrugged. "That's the least of our worries. Let the witch-hunter look to himself."

"Unfortunately, that witch-hunter is now married to my sister, and he is the father of Miri's child."

Cat frowned at the reminder. The marriage of Miribelle Cheney to the notorious witch-hunter Aristide had found little favor among the community of wise women. Ariane had found it painfully difficult herself to stand aside and allow Miri to wed the man who had once raided Faire Isle under the orders of the French king, forcing Ariane and her family into exile.

But she had to admit Simon had done his best to make amends. After he had saved the Dark Queen from Cassandra Lascelles, Catherine had offered him one favor and Simon had used it to see Ariane restored to Faire Isle.

Besides that, Miri truly loved him. She had always seen the good in Simon, insisting that he was but a man who was lost and misguided. And if there had ever been a woman good at healing wounded souls, it was Miri.

Their other sister, Gabrielle, had not been as understanding. Passionate and quick-tempered, Gabrielle had vented her feelings in a scorching letter to Ariane.

"What could you have been thinking of to allow Miri to wed that villain? You should have locked her up in the storeroom and thrown away the key. How could Miri be such a fool? I'll never forgive her for this. Never."

But in typical Gabrielle fashion, she had inked in the very next line, *"That bastard had best take excellent care of my sister. If she suffers any harm or unhappiness at his hands I vow I will flay him alive."*

This discord in her own family grieved Ariane deeply, but she was forced to thrust it from her mind, and focus on the far more pressing matter at hand.

Rising to her feet, she took to pacing in the garden herself. Steepling her fingers beneath her chin, she reached a difficult decision.

"There is only one thing to be done," she said. Squaring her shoulders, she turned back to face Cat. "Megaera must be found as soon as possible and fetched to the safety of Faire Isle."

Cat rarely questioned Ariane's decisions, but the woman

frowned. "Forgive me, but do you think that's wise? There is no guarantee we could keep her safe here and all she might succeed in doing is drawing down danger upon the island."

"I have considered that. But it is a risk we will have to take. The girl will be far safer here than out in the world with only her father to protect her. If the coven still has the *Book of Shadows* and they get their hands on Megaera as well, there will be pure hell to pay. And if Catherine finds the girl first, I have no doubt she will want the child destroyed."

"There are many of our kind, good women who would counsel the same thing. They fear that the girl is tainted by her mother's evil blood."

"Oh, Cat, surely you don't think—"

"Lord, no!" Cat gave a bitter laugh. "I've been called the devil's child enough myself not to be casting stones at anyone else.

"I'm only reporting to you what I've heard, even here on Faire Isle. Many find it troubling that a girl so young was able to do what older and more learned wise women could not. Translate the *Book of Shadows* and make use of its cursed spells, fashioning those lethal witch-blades, concocting such deadly poisons."

"Only because Cassandra forced the child to do so. I admit I have never seen the girl myself. Miri said that Megaera is extraordinary, clever and wise beyond her years, but there is also an innocence that shines from her eyes. Perhaps my sister will be able to convince others—"

"No offense to your sister, milady, but I doubt anyone is going to take much heed of a woman who had the poor judgment to marry a witch-hunter," Cat said bluntly.

Ariane winced, knowing Cat was right. She massaged the back of her neck, which tensed as it always did when she was feeling overwhelmed and stressed.

"There is little sense in worrying about what sort of welcome Megaera will receive on Faire Isle until we actually find the girl." Ariane glanced regretfully at Cat. "Someone must go in search of Megaera, and I fear it must be you, my dear friend. I am sorry to send you on another arduous journey so soon."

"Whist now with your apologies." Cat splayed her hands on her hips and struck an indignant stance. "Sure and who else should you be sending but your gallowglass?"

"No one." Ariane smiled. Exiled from her home, separated from her sisters, she had learned to depend upon the fierce little Irishwoman so much over the years. Next to her husband, there was no one Ariane trusted or relied upon more than Catriona O'Hanlon.

"You can't be after sending himself," Cat continued. "Not in your delicate state. You'll be needing your lord close by and you know me, milady. I'd march into hell itself if you so commanded."

"You will likely think it worse than hell when I tell you where to look for Megaera. By our last report, Martin le Loup took his daughter to England."

"*England!*" Cat didn't turn and spit as she once might have done. But she let fly an oath and groaned, "Were the man's wits lacking? Couldn't he have gone to ground in Ireland or Scotland or—or even Italy or Bavaria? Why the devil did it have to be England?"

"Is that going to pose a difficulty for you, Cat?" Ariane asked anxiously. "I know you have little love for the English."

"Only because the murderous bastards have been robbing and raping my country for years." Cat pulled a wry face and said, "Ah, no need for you to fret, milady. I have traveled among the Sassenach before and managed to contain my feelings. I had to. I ran out of spit.

"And there is at least one good thing about the English," she added grudgingly. "They brew a tolerable ale. So where did this—this Martin the Wolf take his daughter in that godforsaken country?"

"At one time, they had settled in Southwark. Martin used to keep Miri apprised of his whereabouts, but he stopped writing months ago around the time—" Ariane hesitated, reluctant to expose another's private heartache, but if Cat was going to go after Martin, she needed to know everything.

"Martin stopped communicating around the time Miri wrote him that she was with child. Wolf adored my sister for years. Despite the brave face he put upon it, he must have found her marriage to Simon Aristide very painful."

"So not only is this Wolf a fool, he's a lovelorn one. Wonderful." Cat shook her head in disgust. "I am sorry, milady. The man's love pangs be damned. It should have occurred to him that some of that coven might survive to come after Megaera. To cut himself off where no one can help protect her or even warn of approaching danger—it's pure lunacy."

"Martin believed he was acting in Megaera's best interests by just disappearing."

"Then he's an idiot. But what can one expect from a

man stupid enough to have ever bedded a demented witch the likes of Cassandra Lascelles?"

"He claimed he was seduced."

Cat snorted. "Isn't that what they all say? Ah, well, at least if he is such a lackwit, this Wolf shouldn't be hard for me to track down."

"Cat," Ariane admonished. "Please don't make the mistake of underestimating Martin le Loup. I'll admit the man can be a trifle rash and impetuous at times, but far from being a fool, Wolf is clever, bold, and resourceful. And from what Miri tells me, he is ferociously protective of Megaera.

"He can also be very stubborn and proud. It may not be easy to convince him to bring Megaera to Faire Isle."

"Oh, I am sure I'll find a way." Cat lovingly fingered the hilt of her sword.

"Catriona!"

"What? I was only referring to my charm, milady. I am Irish. I am blessed with an overabundance of it." Cat's lips tilted in an impish grin.

Ariane attempted to return her smile, but the tension in her neck had crept upward until it stabbed between her eyes. As she rubbed her temple, Cat's smile fled, the woman instantly repentant.

"Ah, I'm the one who's the idiot. Here I am making stupid jests when you have the weight of this trouble bearing down upon you." Cat crossed over to Ariane and rested her hand gently on her shoulder.

"Don't worry, milady. I'll take care of this matter for you, I promise."

A look of rare vulnerability crossed Cat's strong features. "Besides my grandmother, you are the only one who has ever believed in me. Please don't lose faith in me now."

"As if I could." Ariane attempted to smile despite the pain tightening her brow. "Justice and I could never have survived those years hiding in the Wicklow Mountains without your aid. We owe you our lives."

"And I owe you more than that. When my clan cast me out, I felt worthless. But you—you gave me back my pride." Cat swallowed and then said fiercely, "I'll find that wee girl and protect her as I would you, with the last drop of my blood. I'll fetch her safe back to you, milady. I swear it."

"Just make sure you fetch yourself back safe as well. Whatever would your chieftain do without her gallow-glass?" Ariane teased to avoid displaying how moved she was by Cat's devotion to her. Cat would be mightily disconcerted.

The Irishwoman had already withdrawn her hand, looking gruff and discomfited by all this sharing of emotion. To spare her friend any further embarrassment, Ariane insisted Cat go inside to rest and refresh herself. Later they could form a plan for Cat's search in more detail.

It took some doing to persuade the woman to return to the house without her, but Ariane succeeded at last. She needed a few moments alone to gather both her thoughts and her strength.

Long after Cat had vanished into the kitchen, Ariane lingered. The sun was fully up, bathing the garden in a white glow, the dew glistening on the grass, the larks twittering cheerfully. It promised to be one of those temperate days of early summer.

Ariane tried to enjoy it, suspecting this might be the

last moment of peace she would know for some time. But her throbbing head was already crowded with thoughts of all she needed to do. Prepare Cat for her journey, warn Miri and Simon of what had transpired, and consult with Justice about how to tighten the security of Faire Isle.

And no matter how much she dreaded it, tell him about the babe as well. Cat was right. Ariane could not keep her secret any longer.

Even now, she could feel her child quicken inside of her. Not like the fragile flicker of a butterfly but more like the strong beat of an eaglet's wings.

Ariane pressed her hand to her womb and tried to smile, but was surprised to find her eyes fill with tears instead. If—if only she did not feel so weak and tired all of the time, much more tired than she should be.

Almost against her will, Ariane's face turned skyward. The comet was no longer visible, but it was strange. She felt as though she could sense it hovering there, its fiery tail like a sword suspended over the thread of her life.

Her babe was indeed strong. It would survive the ordeal of childbirth. The Lady of Faire Isle was not as certain that she would.

Chapter Two

"AVANT, THEE WITCH," THE KNIGHT GROWLED, DRAWING HIS sword. "I'll see thee cast into hell ere I be tempted again by your evil conjuring."

The sun glinted off the weapon and his breastplate, bathing Sir Roland in a shining aura. His dark hair swept back from his brow, the rich sable waves offset by the scarlet of his doublet. A beard and mustache softened the blade-like aspect of his chiseled features, but his green eyes were fierce and compelling. He had such a commanding presence few noticed that he was not overly tall, his frame more wiry than strapping. But his shoulders were broad enough, his waist trim, and he had a handsome pair of legs, the brevity of his trunk hose revealing well-honed calves and a hint of muscular thigh.

More than half of the women in the audience were in love with him, the men awed to silence. Even the ground-lings in the pit, a raucous and noisy lot, were held spell-bound as Hecuba hissed and cajoled the bold Sir Roland.

Martin le Loup repulsed the hag with an angry gesture, roaring out his defiance in a series of spirited couplets. He strode downstage, reveling in his power to carry the audi-ence with him far beyond the confines of the theater. The crowded galleries and cramped pit with its stench of sweat, pipe smoke, and stale ale transformed into a midnight heath, the rushes that crackled beneath his boots turning to windswept grass.

"Love's fool I have been, but no more," Martin in-toned. "Traveling through realms of despair, my hopes wrecked upon a distant shore. Bartering my soul for one dark spell to win my beloved, never counting the cost. All to no avail, no magic strong enough to bind a heart that is lost."

His throat thickened, his voice vibrating with an emo-tion that Martin did not have to feign. All he needed to do was think of Miri Cheney, his lovely Lady of the Moon.

No, not his, never his, Martin reminded himself with a dull ache. She was Madame Miri Aristide now.

"Then here upon this cursed heath, let all dreams die," he cried hoarsely.

Somewhere in the audience, a woman let out a shatter-ing sob and more than a few sniffled as Martin continued.

"Sink all my desires into a deathlike sleep. I'll traffic no longer in your darkness, witch. Though my heart be lost, my soul I'll keep."

Hecuba sprang from behind her cauldron with a furious snarl. "Nay, Sir Knight. Break faith with me and 'tis thee who shall die."

The crowd gasped and a few called out warnings as the witch prowled closer, played to sinister perfection by Arthur Lehay, the old man a fine actor when he was sober. He made a repulsive crone in his rags and straggly gray wig, his chin sporting days-old bristle.

But it was not the witch menacing him on stage that caused Martin to stumble back a pace, but the one he spotted lurking in the audience.

He froze, his gaze riveted on a petite woman seated at the front of the first-tier galleries close to the left of the stage. Crushed between a plump matron munching an apple and a burly merchant, the woman might have gone unnoticed but for her flaming crown of hair.

A bright beacon and not the first time that day Martin had noticed those fiery tresses. He'd caught a glimpse of her earlier when he'd disembarked from the wherry at Southwark. And then again later in the marketplace down by the docks. Modestly cloaked, garbed in a plain spun woolen gown, the woman would have occasioned little remark except for that red hair.

Having once been a skilled street thief in Paris, Martin had too much of the hunter in him not to sense when he had become the prey. He had set a deliberately casual pace, the woman always earnestly inspecting the wares at some shop counter when he chanced to look behind. A pickpocket? Or someone more menacing, after a treasure far more valuable than his purse?

When he had finally lost her outside the Crown, Martin had exhaled in relief, dismissing his apprehensions as merely the product of that tension that always beset him before a performance.

But here the wench was again . . .

"An' you do not defend yourself, you shall die, Sir Knight," Hecuba all but shouted in Martin's ear. He started, realizing he had missed his cue to draw his weapon.

Even as he unsheathed his sword, Martin could not tear his gaze away from that gallery. Arthur spread wide his arms, roaring out a threatening incantation only to stop mid-curse, nonplussed when Martin darted past him.

There was more than one redheaded woman in London, Martin told himself. Mayhap he was mistaken. Mayhap it was not the same chit. He needed a closer look.

Ignoring the glares he was receiving from the stage manager, Martin stalked toward the left side of the theater. He stopped just short of colliding with one of those young noblemen who paid extra for the privilege of sitting at the edge of the stage. Edward Lambert, the Baron of Oxbridge, had more right to do so than most. His family's money had paid for the building of the Crown Theatre.

Ned Lambert grinned and playfully pelted Martin with a cherry pit. Martin ignored his lordship, his gaze honed upon the red-haired woman.

She leaned forward on the bench, bracing her hands against the gallery rail, her expression one of rapt attention.

Martin's stomach knotted. Mon Dieu. No mistake. It was her. She had an unusual face, the delicacy of her cheekbones at war with the strength of her chin. For a moment, her piercing blue eyes collided with his and he felt a strange connection sizzle through him as though he had just grasped the wrong end of a red-hot poker.

Stumbling back, his heart thudded. Who the devil was she? He could fathom no reason for her to dog his steps, except for one. She was one of *them*. She had to be. What he had long feared had come to pass. The coven had found him again and that meant his little Meg was in the gravest of danger.

Cold sweat broke out on Martin's brow. He was seized by a blinding panic, the urge to leap from the stage, race for home, and—.

And lead the coven straight to his daughter, which was likely what this witch hoped he'd do. Somehow the voice of reason quelled his alarm. If the witches had already located Meg, this flame-haired she-devil wouldn't be wasting her time stalking him. She would have simply killed Martin or tried to.

His lips tightened, his initial panic giving way to the wily calculation that had saved him and his daughter upon more than one occasion.

A shrill whistle and a few catcalls from the pit jarred Martin back to his surroundings. Aware of the restiveness overtaking the theater, he realized that Arthur was all but plucking out the ends of his grizzled beard in his frustration with Martin.

Martin managed to resume the performance as though nothing was wrong. He had been a consummate actor his entire life, playing at one part or another: soldier, spy, courtier, gentleman. There had only ever been one role where his glibness had failed him.

Father. The advent of Meg into his life had changed

everything. He'd die for his little girl . . . kill for her. If those witches threatened her again—

The thought sent such a feral surge of anger through Martin, he stopped just short of slashing down his fellow performer. Arthur yelped with fright, shook his fist at Martin, and then collapsed awkwardly into his death scene.

The applause that followed was deafening, but no more than a distant roar in Martin's ears, his mind busy with the trap he would lay for the red-haired witch.

Perhaps she was a member of the Silver Rose coven. Perhaps she was not. Whoever she was, she had best be prepared to give a good account of herself, or unlike the witch sprawled on stage at his feet, she wouldn't be getting up to take her bow.

᚜᚜᚜

LONG AFTER THE PLAYERS HAD EXITED THE STAGE, CAT REmained in her seat, feeling dazed. Like some hapless maiden lured off into a fairy wood, she blinked hard, groping her way back to the real world.

Never in all her travels had she seen anything like this vast wooden arena nor the performance that had taken place this afternoon. Three shillings of her scant store of coin it had cost her, but it had been worth every penny.

Cat had oft thrilled to the stories woven by the outlawed bards in her native land, but that had been magic spun out entirely in her head. Watching this play had been like seeing one of the tales of her childhood spring to life and that had been mostly owing to him—the handsome Sir Roland with his mesmerizing eyes and hypnotic voice.

When he strode toward her across the stage, she had

felt as though her heart might beat straight out of her chest. And when his eyes had locked with hers, she could scarce breathe, his gaze stirring in her memories of the wild young girl she'd once been. Her head stuffed full of romantic notions of legendary Irish heroes, how many nights had she lulled herself to sleep imagining herself lying naked in the arms of the mighty Cuchulainn or the bold Brian Boru and—

Cat stroked her throat, a flush of warmth spreading through her. She cast a nervous glance about her lest anyone else be aware of her foolish imaginings and was disconcerted to realize she was alone.

The gallery she occupied was empty and the rest of the theater as well. The audience was gone and perhaps the players too, including the man she had been so determinedly following for most of the day.

Cursing herself for being a moonstruck ass, Cat sprang to her feet and winced, numb from three hours on the hard bench. Rubbing her bottom, she walked stiffly from the gallery, making her way down the steps and through the corridor into the pit. The cobblestone floor was littered with orange peels, walnut shells, and a pungent dark stain where some drunken groundling had relieved himself.

Cat wrinkled her nose in distaste. The platform towered above her, vacant and silent, but she thought she heard voices coming from the backstage area, likely the actors changing out of their costumes, and, if she was lucky, Sir Roland still among them.

She would pay a high price if her moments of witlessness caused her to lose sight of Martin le Loup and after she had had the devil's own time finding the man in the first place.

Days of discreet and painstaking inquiries at the inns and lodgings in the quarters of the city where foreigners dwelled had yielded nothing. Only by the merest chance had she overheard a conversation at the tavern where she had broken her fast that morning.

Two actors had been lamenting the fact that their chief player had been laid low by a bout of dysentery. But fortunately Marcus Wolfe was familiar with most of Sir Roland's lines and could be persuaded to step into the role.

Cat's ears had pricked up. Marcus Wolfe . . . Martin the Wolf. The names were certainly similar. It might be mere coincidence, but it was more of a lead than she had uncovered thus far.

She had watched from a discreet distance as the two actors had greeted their friend when he had disembarked from the wherry. Cat's pulse had quickened with excitement. The man certainly matched Ariane's description of Martin le Loup, but Cat was still unsure.

This man sounded so . . . so English. Was it possible for anyone to so alter their accent, lose all trace of their mother tongue?

She could not be absolutely certain until she obtained a private word with this Marcus Wolfe, something she had been unable to do thus far. It was imperative that she corral the man before he left the theater and she had to begin her hunt for him all over again.

Hastening across the pit, Cat looked for a way to get backstage. She could see none except the two doors at the back of the stage itself. The raised platform would have been at eye level for an ordinary man, but was well above Cat's head.

If she hadn't been hampered by her damned skirts, she could have leaped up, caught hold of the railing, and hoisted herself over onto the stage. The curtained area below the platform held out the promise of an easier egress.

Lifting the heavy black fabric, Cat ducked inside. The area beneath the stage was stiflingly close, dusty, and dark. When her eyes had adjusted to the gloom, Cat spied a ladder leading up through the trap door. Hecuba had arrived on stage that way during the third act, supposedly ascending from the pits of hell.

Cat did likewise. Clambering through the trap, she let the door fall quietly back into place, and then made her way backstage.

She braced herself to be challenged, struggling to come up with some convincing lie to account for invading the private regions of the theater.

But it was unnecessary, her presence going unnoticed. The backstage appeared empty except for a couple in the far corner engaged in some sort of dispute.

An older woman, apparently the wardrobe mistress, was clutching a rose silk gown and heartily scolding a sullen-looking youth.

"And I tell you what, Alexander Naismith, if you continue to be so careless of your costume, I shall lodge a complaint with Master Roxburgh, that I shall. Do you think fine dresses like this shake themselves down from the trees?"

The boy's only response was a bored yawn, and in that

instant Cat was dismayed to recognize in him the fair-haired Belinda who had so completely broken Sir Roland's heart in Act Four.

The magic of the performance was further dispelled by some of the props left lying about. Hecuba's cauldron was no more than a rusty iron pot, and the magic mirror's glittering gold frame was merely wood gilded with paint.

Passing in front of it, Cat pulled a face. Definitely no magic there; the polished steel reflected all too truthfully a short disheveled woman wearing a dusty cloak, her red hair as usual defying her chignon to escape about her face in mad tendrils.

Licking her fingers, Cat tried to slick back some of the strands from her eyes. She froze in mid-swipe at the sight of the dark figure hovering some distance behind her. He had changed out of his costume, the red doublet and armor discarded in favor of tight leather breeches and a black doublet, the sleeves slashed to show the white linen of the shirt beneath. Both shirt and doublet were unlaced at the neck, revealing a glimpse of bare chest and crisp dark hairs.

"Sir—Sir Roland," Cat stammered, her pulse skittering. Feeling like a fool, she corrected, "I mean, Marcus Wolfe?"

But by the time she spun around, he was gone. Now where the blazes could he have disappeared to so quickly? As she peered round a pillar, she concluded there was only one way he could have gone. Back out on the stage. She thought she heard a footfall.

She darted after him through the center curtain. The late afternoon sun poised at just the right angle to blind her. Cat was obliged to shield her eyes as she walked downstage. A stage that was empty.

Puzzled, she frowned, glancing to the right and the left, wondering if he had somehow doubled back through one of the other stage doors when she spied a movement in the same gallery where she had been seated.

Wolfe lifted one hand to his brow in a mocking salute before melting back into the shadows.

"Wait. Please. Just one moment. I need a word with you. I—"

But he was already gone. Cat's jaw fell open, and then snapped shut as she realized the man was toying with her, playing at cat and mouse.

Stomping to the edge of the stage, she muttered, "Fine! But you had best be aware, Monsieur Mouse. This cat has claws."

Hiking up her skirts, Cat dangled her legs over the side of the rail. Between the short sword strapped beneath her cloak and the height of the stage, it was not an easy feat, but Cat leapt, landing on the balls of her feet.

She staggered a little, but quickly recovered her balance, racing toward the doorway that led to the galleries. By the time she got there, there was no sign of the man. At least not in that gallery.

He waved at her from the one on the opposite side of the theater. Swearing in vexation, Cat tore after him, chagrined to realize this mouse had one advantage. He knew his theater far better than she did.

Ten minutes later, she was hot, perspiring, short of breath, and short of temper. Finding herself back at the entryway to the galleries for the third or fourth time, she bellowed, "All right, you fool. I am not amused by this game. Enough of this nonsense."

"Oh, I entirely agree with you."

The voice was low and silky and so close behind her that Cat jumped. She whirled around. He stood a few risers up the gallery stairs, leaning against the wall, coolly studying her as though enjoying her discomfiture.

"You appear to be rather befuddled, my dear. Racing about in circles as though you'd lost something. Can I be of assistance?"

Cat released her breath, struggling to keep her temper, remind herself why she was there.

"That—that all depends," she said, annoyed that she sounded so breathless as he levered himself away from the wall.

He was even more handsome up close than he had been on the stage, although there was no longer any hint of the noble Sir Roland about him. He didn't move with the knight's heroic swagger. He prowled down the stairs, and as for the expression on his face—there was no other word for it. His countenance was decidedly wolf-like.

He halted a foot away from her. "Depends upon what?" he asked.

"If you are Martin le Loup." Cat had meant to be more subtle, more discreet, but her bluntness startled a reaction from him, the merest flicker of an eyelash, but it was enough.

"Alas, my dear, I fear you have made a mistake."

"I don't think so." It was all Cat could do not to crow with triumph. "You have led me on quite a chase, Monsieur le Loup, but I have found you at long last. My name is—"

"Completely irrelevant," he cut her off, looming so close Cat took an involuntary step back.

A mistake, for he now had her pinned against the corridor wall, one arm braced to either side of her as though to cut off her escape.

"As I've already said, you have made a mistake. But one that I might be willing to let you walk away from." He regarded her through narrowed predatory eyes that were the deep green of a primeval forest. Although his voice remained pitched low, there was an edge of danger to it. A danger that emanated from every pore of his taut frame and seemed to prickle along her skin in a way that was both exciting and disconcerting.

"You don't understand. If you will but let me explain. I have something for you—" Cat reached beneath her cloak for the letter of introduction Ariane had provided her. He prevented her, seizing her wrist in an iron grip.

"Whatever you're hiding beneath that cloak, you'd best keep it there, sweetheart. I have no interest in your wares, and as you can see, any other prospective customers are long gone. But you can find a bawdy house at the end of this street where—"

"A bawdy house." Cat's face flamed with indignation. "You take me for some common doxy?"

"No respectable woman would pursue a man through the streets as you have done me. If not to spread your legs for my coin, what other reason could you have?" His eyes both mocked and challenged her.

Cat didn't know whether she was more vexed with him for his insults or herself for being so clumsy that he had detected her shadowing him.

Wrenching her hand from his grip, she proudly lifted her chin. "It will be a frozen day in hell when Catriona of the Clan O'Hanlon ever sells herself to any man."

"Ah, give it away for free then, do you?"

"No!" Cat spluttered. "And certainly not to a spalpeen such as you."

She struck her fists against his chest, shoving him away from her. He staggered back, clearly caught off guard as most men were, surprised by her unexpected strength.

"Now listen well, you fool. I followed you because I had to be certain it really was you before I revealed myself. You are in very grave danger and—"

"Truly? I would say it is quite the other way around."

He prowled toward her again, but Cat ducked away from him. "We have no time for this nonsense, le Loup."

"Pay close heed to me, my dear. As I told you before," he said enunciating each word with exaggerated care as though she were some witless dolt. "You. Have. Made. A. Mistake. You. Have. The. Wrong. Wolf."

"One who apparently knows his name when it is spoken in French. By the way, it is astonishing how well you disguise your accent. I must commend you."

He cocked one eyebrow, much to Cat's annoyance. She had always envied people able to do that, convey scorn and skepticism with such a suave, simple gesture.

"Is that why you followed me? To extend your congratulations on my voice? Much as I would like to believe my charms are enough to send you trailing after me—"

"Ho! No doubt you would. I wager you are conceited enough for anything."

His lips thinned and he took a menacing step closer.

"Enough of these pleasantries. Tell me who you are and what you want and do it quickly."

"Haven't I been after trying to do so? If you would shut your mouth long enough to listen."

"Talk about the inability to keep your mouth shut! Stop nattering on about nothing and give me a straight answer, woman."

Cat folded her arms across her chest. "How observant you are, le Loup. Yes, I am a woman and one who does not tolerate being insulted or ordered about. Give me one reason why I should tell you anything until you start being more civil."

."Here's an excellent reason." He unsheathed his rapier and leveled it at her. "I have a sword with a very sharp point."

Cat sprang back, her hand flying instinctively to her own blade. She unsheathed it in one fluid motion.

"What a coincidence," she said with her sweetest smile. "I have a sword, too."

"Mine's bigger." His teeth flashed in a feral grin. "So you had best put yours away, little girl. I am as chivalrous as the next man, willing to cherish and protect the ladies. But when you draw steel on me, I consider you my equal and I'll treat you as I would any man."

"Your *equal*?" Cat all but choked. "I doubt anyone on this earth is your equal for arrogance, but when it comes to the foils, this *little girl* is more than a match for you or any other man."

As she struck a fighting stance, the man had the effrontery to heave a long-suffering sigh.

"God knows I have tried to deal with you reasonably." He shrugged. "Have at it then."

Their swords came together in a clash of steel, their initial feints and parries slow and deliberate. Cat realized he was doing the same thing she was, proceeding cautiously until she took her opponent's measure.

Her movements were hampered by both her skirts and the narrow corridor. She backed away, taking care not to trip over the hem of her gown, moving out into the open arena of the pit.

Between parries, she managed to undo her cloak and toss it aside. The bodice of her gown was tight, lacing up the front for ease in attiring herself. She wished she could have loosened it, but that was impossible. Not with him maneuvering around her like a wolf stalking its prey.

He was lithe and graceful, quick on his feet, she had to grudgingly admit. As they fought, circled, and clashed, it was like some glorious dance. Cat realized she was enjoying this far too much; it had been such a long time since she'd been involved in a good scrape. And she could tell that he was enjoying it as well, his green eyes glittering, his lips crooked in a languid smile, his movements almost playful.

Cat experienced a twinge of guilt when she thought of her chieftain. She knew that this would have been the last thing Ariane would have wanted, Cat clashing with le Loup straight off, actually dueling with him.

But blast the man. He had been the first to draw steel, and there was never any reasoning with any man once he got a sword in his hand. Perhaps after she had disarmed him, they could finally have a sensible discussion.

Cat saw an opening and lunged, but he swiftly blocked her and sprang back with a low laugh.

"*Bon.* You have some skill, mademoiselle," he said, his accent slipping as he swept her a mocking bow. "For an Irishwoman."

"You don't do so badly yourself," she crowed. "For a *Frenchman.*"

He grimaced when he realized how he had betrayed himself. He leapt back into the fray, pressing her hard, driving her back.

Cat countered his blows, swearing as her skirts tangled about her legs.

"I could do a damned sight better if it wasn't for this cursed gown," she muttered.

"Allow me to help you out of it then." With a lightning stroke, he broke through her guard, his blade slicing open the top lacings of her gown.

Cat glanced down at her bodice with dismay. "You idiot. This was my best gown. My *only* gown."

Furiously, she struck back at him, slipping past his defense, her rapier tearing a large rent in his sleeve. He twisted, deflecting her sword and swearing.

"Rot your hide, woman. Do you know how much I paid for this doublet? Several crowns."

"Then you wasted your—damn!" Cat cried when he retaliated, severing two more lacings and the top of her shift besides, revealing the soft swell of her décolletage.

Her cheeks fired when he attempted to stare down the front of her gown.

"And just what the devil would you be looking for?"

"I don't know." Again the tantalizing lift of that eyebrow. "The carving of a rose, perhaps?"

"That shows how much you know. The roses are always carved on the right arm . . ." Cat's voice faltered at the sudden and swift change that came over his expression. His smile fled, his eyes going hard and cold.

"Ah. So my first impression was right. You *are* one of them."

"Them?"

"The coven. You're a God-cursed witch."

"No, you bloody fool, of course not. I—" Cat's words choked off as he came at her with renewed vigor. It was all she could do to fend off several brutal strokes.

His face was suffused with anger, his eyes full of deadly intent. "What does it take? How many of you lunatics do I have to kill to convince you to stay away from my daughter?"

"But I'm not—if you would but listen—" Cat panted from the exertion of defending herself, realizing he was beyond heeding anything she had to say. All playfulness had vanished from their duel. She was fighting for her life and he had the advantage that men always did in battle— strength and endurance, while her chief skill rested in her speed, agility, and wits.

He was hammering her so hard she could already feel her energy flagging, her breath coming in short bursts. Unfortunately, his anger didn't make him careless, only more vigorous and determined. Her only hope lay in distraction, a trick that had often served her well in the past.

Deflecting a thrust that came perilously close to piercing her shoulder, she gripped her sword tighter. With her other hand, she yanked open her bodice, completely baring one breast.

His eyes widened, his attention wavering just for a moment, but it was enough. Cat thrust, catching the fancy guard on the hilt of his sword. She wrenched the weapon from his hand, sending it flying.

He leapt back, his boot skidding on an orange peel. His feet flew out from under him and he fell hard, landing on his back. Before he could recover himself, Cat was upon him, leveling her weapon at his heart.

Propped on his elbows, he glared up at her, his chest rising and falling, his expression dark with a mingling of defiance and despair. He truly expected her to kill him, Cat realized.

She ought to make haste to reassure him, but damnation, the man had just done his best to cut her down. Heart racing, she was so badly winded that she could hardly speak.

Yanking her bodice back over her breast, she panted, "Now, Monsieur le-le Loup. Perhaps we can—"

She broke off, gasping at the sudden sharp pain in her back. The assault from behind was so swift, so unexpected, she nearly lost her grip on her sword. But somehow, she managed to keep the blade leveled at le Loup as she twisted to peer behind her.

Her assailant skittered back in a rustle of skirts. A slender child, all elbows and wide green eyes startlingly like le Loup's. And she appeared possessed of his stealth as well for she had managed to take Cat completely by surprise, something that rarely happened.

"M-Megaera?" Cat faltered.

The little girl said nothing, her face pale, her chin thrust at a belligerent angle as she secreted the weapon she had stabbed Cat with back beneath her cloak.

A strange weapon that Cat had only ever heard tell of, never before seen with her own eyes until now. A witch blade, the stiletto of almost needle-like thinness, hollow, capable of delivering the most lethal of poisons.

Cat could already feel it rushing through her veins like wildfire, pulsing, causing her head to swim. She staggered away from le Loup, her sword wavering in her hand.

She blinked, fighting hard to still her panic, retain control of her senses, but the galleries of the theater shimmied before her eyes. She caught a blurred impression of yet another assailant, but could do nothing to defend herself against an old woman with thin white hair, skin like a dried apple, and an enormous nose.

The old woman let out a cackling shriek and swung her cane at Cat. The knobby end cracked hard against her brow, causing Cat to gasp with pain.

She swayed, fell to her knees, her sword falling from her hand. But it was not the old woman's blow bringing her down, Cat realized in despair. It was that deadly fire coursing through her body.

She cast a reproachful glance at the child and tried to speak. But her voice came out in a hoarse croak.

"You—you little witch. What have you done to me?"

Through the fog that had become her mind, Cat was aware that le Loup was on his feet. Thrusting himself in between Cat and his daughter, he snatched up Cat's sword.

"Don't—need that anymore," she tried to tell him, but the words wouldn't come as she sprawled onto her side.

Black webs danced before her eyes, her last thought what a great muck she had made of her mission, how she had failed her chieftain.

"Forgive me, Ariane," she whispered.

Chapter Three

MARTIN STOOD OVER HIS FALLEN OPPONENT, HER FACE pale, an ugly lump swelling on her brow where old Agatha Butterydoor had struck her.

The O'Hanlon witch had proved a skilled fighter, tough and strong. He would never have imagined she could be so easily felled by one blow from the cane of a scrawny old beldame.

Perhaps this was just another of her tricks like that outrageous stunt of flaunting her breast. Hunkering down, Martin cautiously examined her, feeling for the pulse at her neck. The witch didn't twitch so much as an eyelash at his touch.

Good, Martin thought. But that still left him with one devil of a problem. What in the bloody hell was he going to do with her? Weigh her down with rocks and toss her in the Thames? He wasn't capable of that, although in the past any chivalry he'd shown these witches had nearly proved his undoing.

Even if he could be that cold-blooded, it was still daylight, the streets teeming with people. He was damn fortunate this little scene hadn't already attracted someone's attention inside the theater.

He couldn't dispose of the witch, but he could hardly risk just walking away and leaving her here either. Before he could come up with a solution, Meg hurled herself at him, her small frame heaving with a mighty sob. Martin caught her in his arms, interposing himself between her and the sight of the unconscious witch. His daughter had borne witness to far too much violence and horror for her tender years.

"Oh, P-papa." Trembling like a leaf tumbled by the wind, Meg wept into his doublet. "I—I th-thought . . . terrible w-woman . . . k-kill you."

"Non. Hush, ma petite. It is all over now." Martin soothed, stroking her back, feeling the wings of her bones through the layers of chemise and silk. Although she had gained a little weight since being with him, Meg still struck him as being far too frail.

He eased Meg away so that he could hunker down in front of her. Stemming the flow of her tears with the pads of his thumbs, he managed to smile. "What! You thought your bold Papa could be bested by a redheaded midget? Moi? Martin le Loup? Why, even as you arrived, I had a cunning plan. I was preparing to—to—"

To be skewered like a chicken on a spit.

Martin faltered, annoyed to feel a tremor course through him. He had been in scores of duels, narrowly escaped with his life on more than one occasion, only to mop the sweat from his brow and laugh, his blood singing through his veins.

Never had he experienced such terror, such despair as when he had found himself at the witch's mercy. His one thought, Meg. He was about to die and leave his daughter unprotected. Becoming a father had given him an entirely new acquaintance with fear.

Thank God for Mistress Butterydoor and her cane, although Martin was not sure whether he most wanted to embrace or strangle Agatha, a familiar mix of emotions where the cantankerous old woman was concerned.

His anger won out. Giving Meg another fierce hug, he straightened and glared at the old woman.

"Explain yourself, Mistress Butterydoor. What demon possessed you to bring my daughter here?"

The old woman gave a haughty sniff, as usual unimpressed by Martin's growl. Before she could answer, Meg tugged at his sleeve. "Please, Papa. It was not Aggie's fault. I begged her to bring me to the theater. I so badly wanted to see you be Sir Roland, but Aggie was slow and then it took so long to find a boatman to bring us across from the city and we arrived too late."

Meg's shoulders slumped with chagrin. She asked wistfully. "Were you utterly magnificent?"

"But of course, ma chère." Martin grinned, only to sober immediately, striving for a graver tone. "But that is of no consequence, Margaret Wolfe. I told you before, this theater is too rough, too crude a place for a young lady."

"But Papa, I always used to watch you perform in the innyards when we traveled with Master Roxburgh's company."

"Those days are long behind us, Meggie. We are respectable folk now."

When Agatha snorted, Martin scowled at her. "As for you, Mistress Butterydoor, I engaged you to look after my daughter, not expose her to the dangers of the streets or the vulgarity of a theater."

"Oh, pooh! As if I am not fully capable of protecting my little poppet." The old woman brandished her cane with a fierceness Martin might have found amusing under other circumstances. "Besides, it is perfectly acceptable for a young girl to go to the market or the theater when accompanied by her maid."

"Meg is not just any young girl as you well know. The dangers that could threaten her—" Martin broke off, hating to speak of the dark forces from Meg's past in front of his daughter. "Her circumstances are . . . extraordinary."

Mistress Butterydoor looked somewhat chastened by his reminder, although she muttered, "It has been so long since we were troubled by any of those madwomen. How should I have guessed we would find you fighting tooth and nail with some demented hussy?"

She gave the inert witch a poke with her cane. "So who is she?"

"Some lunatic Irishwoman named Catriona O'Hanlon. One of that hellish Silver Rose coven."

"Sisterhood," Meg corrected him in a small voice. "Maman didn't like the word *coven*. She said we were a sisterhood."

Martin bit his tongue to avoid retorting that Meg no longer had to worry about what her mother liked. Cassandra Lascelles was dead. How many nights had he cradled his daughter, soothing her back to sleep when Meg had awoken screaming from nightmares about watching Cassandra sink to a watery grave in the Seine?

Better the evil woman's name never be mentioned. Better that Meg simply forget those terrible days when she had been forced to play a part in her mother's insane schemes. And far better that Meg was well out of this, tucked safely back in their snug house in Cheapside.

Tenderly stroking Meg's hair back from her brow, he said, "You don't need to worry about this particular member of the *sisterhood*. Your Papa will deal with her. You just go home and put all this out of your head. Mistress Butterydoor, I want you to escort Meg back to—"

Martin broke off, vexed to discover that Agatha was paying no heed to him. Hunching over, she examined the cloak that the witch had discarded in the midst of the duel.

Straightening with a grunt, Agatha produced something that looked like a rectangle of parchment.

"What have you got there?" Martin demanded.

"I don't know. Some sort of letter. That redheaded vixen must have dropped it." Agatha squinted at the paper she held. Not that it would do the old woman much good. She could not even read her own name.

"Give it here," Martin said. Striding over to her, he snatched the missive from her. "Now will you kindly do what I told you and take Meg . . ."

Once more his words trailed off, his gaze locking on the single inked line on the note.

Martin le Loup.

"What the devil?" he muttered, jolted by the sight of his own name, made even more uneasy by the fact that the elegant handwriting was vaguely familiar.

Meg crept to his side. "What is it, Papa?" she asked.

"Nothing of consequence, I daresay. Just something belonging to the witch. Her passport perhaps," Martin lied to reassure his daughter.

"More likely some sort of curse or wicked spell. Don't open it," Agatha advised.

But Martin had already broken the seal. The old woman sucked in her breath, and Martin found himself doing the same as he scanned the note's brief contents.

Mon cher Martin,

> *This letter is to introduce my emissary, Catriona*
> *O'Hanlon. A new trouble has arisen. I dare not say*
> *more. Cat will explain all. Trust in her as you would me.*
>> *As ever, your devoted friend,*
>> *Ariane Deauville*

Martin expelled his breath in a long rush, feeling as though he had been poleaxed. Ariane Deauville, the Lady of Faire Isle, sister to his beloved Miri, sending him some sort of warning? And the red-haired virago at his feet, the one that Agatha had rendered unconscious, the woman he had nearly killed, was Ariane's *emissary*?

"*Merde!*" Martin swore, crushing the note in his hand.

"Papa?" Meg pressed close to his side, her small brow furrowed with deep anxious lines. "What is wrong? The letter . . . is it about that witch?"

"She's no witch," Martin groaned. "At least not one of the evil ones. She was sent to bring me a message from the Lady of Faire Isle."

Meg's eyes flew wide, what little color she possessed draining from her cheeks. "A m-messenger from the Lady?" Meg cast a stricken glance in Catriona's direction. "Oh, Papa!"

"Odd sort of way to deliver a message," Agatha groused. "With the point of a sword."

"She was only trying to defend herself. I drew steel on her first," Martin admitted grudgingly. He dragged his hand back through his hair in frustration. As if his life was not already difficult enough without this fresh complication.

He glared at Cat, torn between regret and the desire to shake the woman even more insensible than she already was. Why the bloody hell couldn't she have shown him that letter at once? Maybe he hadn't given her much chance, but she could have tried harder instead of going all stubborn and belligerent on him. But there would be time enough for assigning blame later. Right now, the important thing was to get the woman looked after, get her out of here before anyone turned up asking awkward questions.

Kneeling down beside the unconscious Irishwoman, he attempted to chafe her wrists, hoping to rouse her. But her hand remained limp and cold, his touch not eliciting so much as a moan.

He felt Meg's small hand light upon his shoulder. "She—she's not going to die, Papa," she faltered.

"Of course not."

"But she will be dreadfully sick. And it's all my fault."

"Your fault?" Martin twisted round to peer at her. "How could you possibly be to blame, my angel? You weren't the one who thumped her on the head."

Meg cast him an odd guilty look, his daughter's reasoning as ever a puzzle to Martin. The girl had a tendency to take the blame for everything onto her own slender shoulders.

"This was all just an unfortunate misunderstanding. But we'll bring Mademoiselle O'Hanlon back to our house, mend her head, and then she'll be fine."

He gave Meg's cheek a reassuring pat, and then turned back to the O'Hanlon woman. But before he could lift Cat into his arms, Agatha let loose a loud shriek and rushed forward as if to prevent him.

"Lord save us, master. What are you doing? You can't mean to fetch this creature back to your house."

"What else would you have me do with her?"

"Turn her over to the constable. Or—or one of the charity hospitals."

Martin eased his arm beneath Cat's shoulders. "I told you. She's not one of the evil witches. She was sent by the Lady of Faire Isle."

"I don't know anything about this lady. But I know what *she* is." Agatha leveled an accusing finger at Cat. "And you can't have her beneath your roof."

"Why the devil not?"

"Because she's *Irish*. That's why not," Agatha spluttered. "And everyone knows they're nothing but a pack of bloodthirsty savages with their wicked Popish ways. Ignorant idol-worshipping barbarians who practice human sacrifice."

Martin rolled his eyes.

"It's true. They devour babes and little children."

Martin gathered Cat close to his chest, straightening carefully to his feet. "I doubt Mademoiselle O'Hanlon will have an appetite for much of anything for a while. Before she recovers, you'll have plenty of time to hide any stray infants in the larder."

"Jest if you will, master, but—"

"Enough! For once will you do what I pay you for and look to my daughter."

The old woman's mouth puckered. She subsided with an offended sniff, but not before she had the last word.

Wrapping her arm about Meg, she steered the girl toward the theater exit, flinging back at Martin over her shoulder. "You'll be sorry, master. Mark my words. That Irish creature will prove nothing but trouble."

Martin merely grunted, seeking to shift Cat into a better position as he followed. The woman was small enough, but her dead weight made her awkward to balance. Her head lolled against his arm, her hair spilling like a flame across the sleeve of his doublet. She seemed somehow smaller and more fragile cradled in his arms, but Martin was not fooled. Even unconscious, the woman had a damned truculent set to her chin.

Nothing but trouble. Martin grimaced. Hadn't he sensed that about Catriona O'Hanlon from the moment he'd first clapped eyes upon her?

ﻉﻉﻉ

CAT STRUGGLED TO OPEN HER EYES, BUT HER LIDS SEEMED FAR too heavy, as though they were weighted with tiny anchors.

She felt as though she was lost beneath a midnight sea, so peaceful she wished she could surrender, sink deeper into the soothing darkness.

But the warrior in her urged her to fight, strike her way back to the surface. She forced her eyes open, emerging into a world of crimson, fire, and pain.

Cat moaned, twisting away from the blinding light. She closed her eyes, burying her face deeper into the soft down of a pillow.

"Mademoiselle O'Hanlon? Catriona?" The voice that called her name was a low purr, as coaxing and seductive as the hand that brushed back her hair.

But even that light touch caused her to throb with pain. Cat groaned again. Her head . . . someone had whacked her with an axe. No. They had buried the blade in her skull. She lifted her trembling hand to her brow, terrified she would find her brain leaking out of her pate. Her fingers struck up against a thick wad of something. Her brain? No, a cloth of some sort, but before she could explore further, a warm calloused hand caught her wrist, easing her arm back to her side.

"Here. Let me," the deep voice murmured.

Let him what? She felt the cloth being removed and then replaced with another, damp and cool. The compress sent an initial shock through her. She shivered. But as the cold penetrated, it dulled the ache enough that she dared risk opening her eyes.

The world was still far too bright, streaming with sheets of fire. She blinked hard, trying to clear her blurry vision. The blazing light resolved itself into nothing more than a candle flickering upon a tripod table, the flames no more than bed-curtains of crimson damask.

Bewildered and alarmed, Cat looked around the unfamiliar bedchamber. Where—where the devil was she? What had happened to her?

She struggled to spring up, only to gasp as her head throbbed and swam, the room reeling around her.

Gentle hands eased her back against the pillow. "Careful, my sweet. You are going to be all right, but you had best take it slow. Here, drink this."

He lifted her head, pressing a cup to her lips. She sought to obey his command, although her tongue felt thick and unwieldy. She choked on her first swallow, the liquid potent and bittersweet. But her mouth was so parched she drank greedily, the brew soothing to her dry throat, sending a reviving surge through her veins.

Cat's lashes fluttered as she sought to focus on the man sitting on the edge of the bed, bending close to her. He at least was familiar. She knew that darkly handsome face, that trim beard, that lean blade of a nose, those vivid green eyes.

Wonderingly she reached up to touch his cheek. "Sir— Sir Roland?" she asked hoarsely. "Did you save me from the witch?"

"Alas, no, ma chère." He caught her hand and upturned it to plant a light kiss against her palm. "I fear I mistook *you* for the witch. My sincerest apologies, milady."

Cat frowned, trying to make sense of his words, trying to remember. The effort caused her head to pound, but she persisted until the events of the afternoon came rushing back to her.

Southwark, the quay, the crowded market, the Crown Theatre. Breathlessly watching the play and then—then fighting for her life in the theater pit. This man who had the temerity to kiss her hand was the same bastard who had tried to run her through. Not the noble Sir Roland, but Martin le Loup.

Cat jerked her hand away from him and cringed at both the pain in her head and the one in her lower back. The place was sore where Megaera had stabbed her with that cursed witch blade, sending a deadly poison through her veins. Or so Cat had thought.

Cat ran her hand over her face, testing for any sign of fever. None. She pressed her fingers to her neck, her pulse strong and steady.

"I—I am not dead," she marveled.

"No." He chuckled. "Why? Did you think you had awakened to find yourself in heaven?"

"Hardly. Not if you're here." Her palm still tingled where he had kissed her. She wiped it on the bedclothes and curled it protectively back to her side.

"And where exactly is *here*?" she demanded.

"*La Maison des Anges.*"

The house of the angels? Cat glared at him. "My head hurts far too much for any more stupid jests, le Loup. So if you don't mind—"

"Here in London, I go by Marcus Wolfe, mademoiselle, and I would thank you to remember that." He frowned as though recollecting himself. When he spoke again, he had ironed all trace of French from his accent. "And I made no jest. The houses in London all have names, and this particular one is called the Angel. And that is where you are, reposing safely beneath my roof, tucked up in my bed-chamber."

His house? Her gaze more focused, Cat took another look about the room, assessing her surroundings. For a simple player, Martin le Loup had done astonishingly well for himself. The walls were decorated with tapestries that appeared as costly as the richly embroidered bed-hangings. The carved oak bed was luxurious, with a thick feather tick mattress and linens finer than Cat had ever lain upon. The sheets were seductively soft against her bare skin.

Bare skin? Cat stiffened, and then stole a cautious peek beneath the coverlet. She was mortified to realize that not a stitch of her clothing remained. Not only was she ensconced in Martin le Loup's bedchamber, she was stark naked.

Gasping, she made a frantic effort to drag the covers higher, her efforts hampered by the fact that he was sitting on the bed.

"Get off!"

"Happy to oblige, my dear." He rose at his own languid pace. "Although I feel compelled to remind you that it is *my* bed you are tossing me out of."

Cat scowled daggers at Martin, but had to stop, the ferocious expression aggravating her headache. "You miserable wretch. What have you done with my clothes?"

"Me? Nothing. I had one of the housemaids undress you for your own comfort and, er, not to be disparaging, your garments were a trifle travel-stained for my bed linens. But given that little performance of yours during our duel, I didn't imagine that you suffer overmuch from modesty."

"One does what one must in the heat of battle."

"Even resorting to such a paltry trick as shoving your bare teat under a man's nose?"

"I would hardly call it paltry." Cat burrowed deeper beneath the covers until only her head peeked out. "That trick has worked every time I've ever used it, men being the lascivious simpletons that they are. Back when I used to spar with Rory O'Meara, that fool actually fell for my ploy three times."

Martin flung back his head and laughed. "You'll pardon my saying so, but I doubt this Rory was the one being fooled."

"You think he was only pretending in order to—to—."

"To get himself an eyeful? Why not? It's a lovely breast, well worth a second look or even a third."

The miscreant was laughing at her, but his twinkling green eyes seemed to invite her to share his amusement, his voice full of frank admiration.

Cat rarely allowed any man to fluster her, scorning any sort of flattery or flirtation. To her annoyance, she realized she was blushing.

"Remind me to box your ears later when I am feeling better," she said gruffly.

He chuckled and drew up a chair to the bedside. Placing it backward, he straddled the seat in boyish fashion, resting his hands upon the oak slats of the back.

"Let us declare a truce, Mistress O'Hanlon. I fear we have gotten off to a very ill start."

"For which I am sure you are sick with remorse, entirely blaming yourself."

His teeth flashed again in that devastating smile. "Not exactly. You might have spoken up and showed me this letter before matters got so far out of hand." He produced Ariane's creased note from inside his jerkin and tossed it down on the bedside table. "For a woman who likes to talk so much, it takes you a long time to come to the point."

"As though you were prepared to listen to anything I might have had to say."

"I tend to be a little edgy when I am followed and accosted by strange women. Since you are familiar with my daughter's history, you should understand why." His features took on a grim cast, and then softened as he added, "But I am sorry that you were hurt. Mistress Butterydoor is devoted to both Meg and me. She believed she was saving my life."

"Mistress Butterydoor?"

"Agatha. The old woman with the cane. She whacked you into oblivion and gave you that lump on the head. Remember?"

Cat remembered, but the blow of the cane was not what had sent her spiraling into oblivion. That was entirely owing to Megaera and her witch blade. Cat studied Martin through narrowed eyes. Did the man think to cozen her, protect his daughter from any possible repercussions of Cat's anger? Or was it possible he had not seen what had really happened?

His next words answered that question.

"I realize you took quite a painful blow, but I fear the one most hurt was my daughter. Meg was very distressed by what happened at the theater. She has already endured so much, one would not have expected her to be so upset. But my angel has such a tender heart. You cannot possibly imagine."

Cat winced, rubbing the small puncture wound in her back. Yes, she could imagine and apparently far better than he. From his fond smile and the protective light in his eyes, it was obvious le Loup didn't have the least notion what his daughter was capable of. Cat debated enlightening him, but decided to keep her own counsel. At least until she had had the chance to speak to Megaera herself.

"And now Mistress O'Hanlon," he began, but she interrupted him.

"Will you please stop calling me that? It makes me feel like some old woman." Her lip curled with distaste. "And an *English* one at that."

"All right then. Catriona . . ."

"Cat. Just Cat will do."

"Very well. *Cat.*" He smiled. "I can't imagine why Ariane dispatched you to track me down, but knowing the Lady of Faire Isle, I am sure she must have had an urgent reason. I hate to press you while you are still feeling so poorly—"

"No, no," she cut him off. "I am well enough and we have wasted far too much time already."

Clutching the covers to her, she made another effort to sit up and was annoyed when her head still reeled. She glanced longingly at the pewter cup he had set upon the table. "If you could just give me another drop of that— that—."

"Tisane." He leapt up to fetch the cup. "Agatha brewed it for you. She has some modest skill in the stillroom."

"When she is not breaking heads," Cat muttered. She removed the cloth from her head and gingerly felt the lump on her brow. She had quite a goose egg, but the swelling seemed to be going down.

Martin handed her the cup and would have helped her to drink, but she waved him off. What she really longed for was a swig of her usquebaugh, but she had left her flask along with her other meager belongings back at the inn she had frequented last night. The tisane did not pack quite the same fire, but she downed the mug and felt the better for it.

Propping herself up higher against the pillows, the coverlet tucked demurely about her shoulders, Cat started her tale with the revival of the Silver Rose coven and ended with the events on the cliff side that night.

She sought to keep her narrative simple, resisting her natural bent to embellish, to punctuate her words with many gestures.

Martin listened with his chin propped on his hands along the back of the chair, that remarkably intense face of his still for once, revealing little of his thoughts. When she had concluded her tale, he remained quiet and grave. The silence stretched out so long, Cat grew impatient.

"Ariane believes you and your daughter should come to Faire Isle. I am sure you must see the necessity of leaving England at once."

Martin stirred at last like a man awakening from an unpleasant dream. "No, I am afraid I don't see the necessity of that at all. It strikes me as being a hasty and foolhardy action."

"By the goddess Brigid! Have you heeded not a word that I said?"

"Yes, I heard you quite clearly." Martin raised his head, straightening in his chair. "Witches, bonfires, midnight Sabbaths, the Dark Queen's soldiers. It all sounds to me

like exactly what I left France to escape. All the more reason that Meg and I should stay right where we are."

"Where you are! Do you imagine you will be safe—"
Cat started, only to have him cut her off.

"Clarify something for me. You were obliged to break
off your surveillance at the cliff and flee, were you not?"

"Yes," Cat muttered. She was still chafed by the memory of her retreat without landing as much as a blow. "My
orders from Ariane were not to fight. I had to get back and
warn her, but I am no coward—"

"I never said that you were. My point is this. You have
no idea what actually transpired after you left. For all you
know it is possible that this Captain Gautier slaughtered
the entire coven."

"Or more likely he dragged one of those witches back
to the Dark Queen, and now she knows the truth about
your daughter."

"You have some proof of that? Before you left France,
you saw some sign of Catherine searching for my little
girl?"

"Well, no. But there was scarce time—"

"Then I see no reason to panic. It is possible that the
Dark Queen learned nothing at all and that the coven was
destroyed."

"And it is possible you are a complete idiot!" Cat
flared. "Are you willing to gamble your daughter's life on
possibilities? If Catherine has discovered that Meg was the
Silver Rose, I *guarantee* you she will leave no stone un-
turned to find her, if for no other reason than she still
wants the *Book of Shadows*."

"Then Her Grace will be wasting her efforts because I

don't know what became of that cursed book and neither does Meg." Martin shoved to his feet, pushing the chair away from him. "If the queen is truly after my daughter, I feel much safer with the English Channel between us."

"But on Faire Isle, Meg would have Ariane and her husband and a legion of vigilant wise women to protect her."

"She has her father for that. I have a done a fair job of protecting Meg thus far."

"No one is saying that you haven't," Cat began, only to break off in frustration as Martin strode away from her, unheeding. Damn the man! Could he never listen long enough to allow her to complete a sentence?

He stalked over to a window opposite the bed, drawing back the heavy brocade curtains to reveal diamond panes of glass. Cat blinked in some surprise as she caught a glimpse of night-darkened sky where she had thought to see the purple of twilight. She must have been out far longer than she'd supposed.

"Tell me," Martin said, nodding toward the window. "What can you see out there?"

Cat craned her neck only to stop when her head throbbed and the covers threatened to slip.

"Damned little," she grumbled. "Not without making my head explode or affording you a view of my bare arse. Even if I could drag myself out of bed, I don't imagine I'd see much beyond rooftops."

"The rooftops of a vast city."

"Dirty, noisy, crowded. Too full of bloody Englishmen."

"You are right." Martin smiled, but as he stared out the window, a dream-ridden expression stole over his face.

"But it is also a city teeming with energy, enterprise, and opportunity. A place where any man can make his fortune, bury his past, and lose himself in the future."

Cat regarded him with barely suppressed exasperation. "Is that what you believe you have done? Lost yourself? I admit it took me awhile to track you, and I have some skill at hunting. But so does the Dark Queen. If I could find you, so could she, especially with you strutting about on a public stage."

"That was a mistake, I grant you. But when our lead actor fell ill, I could not resist the temptation to—" He checked himself, a tide of color washing into his face. Letting the drapery fall, he turned away from the window. "I won't be so careless again."

"So you will what? Quit the company? How will you provide for your daughter if—"

"That is not how I provide for her *now*." Martin swept his arm in a gesture that encompassed the room. "Do you think I afford all this on an actor's wages? When we first arrived in England I might have been nothing more than a vagabond player, but my fortunes have risen greatly since then. I am actually an investor in the Crown Theatre, and I have powerful friends."

"Those actors?" Cat asked scornfully. "A grand help they would be with their fake cauldrons and blunted swords."

"My own blade is sharp enough, as you nearly discovered. And I have acquaintance beyond Master Roxburgh and the company. I have acquired a patron, a man of vast resources and influence."

"Who?"

"That's none of your concern," Martin snapped. He compressed his lips in a taut line, and then addressed her in a more moderate tone.

"Look, Mistress O'Hanlon . . . Cat. Don't think I am not grateful to you for coming to warn me. I realize that you did so at no little inconvenience to yourself. I shall see that you are generously rewarded."

"Rewarded! Why, you ignorant lout." Cat sat bolt upright, ignoring the ache in her head and the fact that she was close to giving Martin another eyeful. "I came because Ariane asked me to, and I serve the Lady of Faire Isle out of love and devotion, not for any reward or—or—."

"Forgive me." Martin flung up his hands in a defensive gesture to stem her flow of fierce words. "I have no wish to offend you or Ariane. I appreciate her offer of sanctuary, but even if Faire Isle was not so close off the coast of France, it would be the last place I would be inclined to take my daughter. As I told you before, I mean to bury the past."

"Whose past? The child's or yours?" Cat retorted.

When Martin arched one brow in haughty inquiring fashion, Cat knew she might do better to hold her tongue, but that had always been a wisdom she lacked.

"I know all about your relationship with Miribelle Cheney."

"Indeed?" Martin inquired politely, but his eyes flashed a strong warning.

Cat ignored it, rushing on. "Ariane told me how much you loved her sister. And that your heart was broken when she married Simon Aristide. I understand how awkward and painful the thought of seeing Miri again must be, but you needn't worry. She hardly ever comes to Faire Isle these days."

Martin frowned. "Why is that? Faire Isle was Miri's home. She loved it there beyond any place on earth."

"Yes, but her husband, the erstwhile witch-hunter, is not exactly welcome there."

Martin approached the bed. Curling his fingers about the newel post, he peered anxiously down at Cat. "So—so Miri is not happy then?"

"I didn't say that. Miri might have loved Faire Isle, but she loves her husband more. She is completely besotted with the man, more so than ever since the birth of their daughter and—" Cat checked herself at last, glancing rue-fully up at Martin. "I am sorry. This is likely the last thing you wanted to hear."

"No, it is exactly what I wanted to hear. I am glad that she is well and—and happy."

He truly meant that, Cat was astonished to realize. Lord knows she had not been so generous when Rory O'Meara had broken faith with her all those years ago, roundly curs-ing the man's name every time it was mentioned.

But Martin's voice had softened as he spoke of Miri, his eyes full of such tenderness and regret, it roused a strange ache of envy within Cat's bosom. She wondered if Rory ever still spoke of her with such fondness. No, she thought bleakly, very likely the O'Meara never spoke of her at all, never even spared her a thought. She was not like Miri, fey and gentle, full of feminine graces, the sort of woman a man would never forget.

Martin's gaze turned inward as though caught up in

some poignant recollection of the past. Then he gave himself a brisk shake.

"Miri and I parted as good friends. My reluctance to go to Faire Isle has more to do with Meg. When I rescued my daughter from that coven, I vowed to expel all witchcraft and magic from her life."

"You can hardly equate the women of Faire Isle and Ariane with those evil witches of the Silver Rose."

"I have nothing but the greatest respect for Ariane Deauville—"

"And so you had better," Cat said fiercely.

"But I don't see where studying this ancient knowledge ever did anything for Ariane except get her charged with witchcraft. I envision a far better, safer future for Meg. I intend to see her become a great lady one day, happy, prosperous, and well married."

Cat regarded him incredulously. "And you think what? That the past will all go away just because you will it so? From what I have been told, your daughter possesses certain gifts and abilities that she inherited from Cassandra Lascelles."

"That woman's name is not to be mentioned beneath my roof," Martin snarled. "Meg inherited *nothing* from her mother. Nothing. As far as I am concerned that part of her life is over and done with. Now where are the rest of your belongings?"

"My belongings?" Cat faltered, jolted by the abrupt change of subject. "I didn't have much, just a small saddlebag. I left it at the inn where I stayed last night. The Fighting Cock in Southwark, near the riverbank. But regarding your daughter—."

"I know the place. I will send one of my servants to fetch your pack." He strode toward the door.

"But Monsieur le Loup—I mean Master Wolfe." Clutching the covers and ignoring her aches, Cat tried to struggle to the edge of the bed. "Martin!"

He paused at the door, turning to look back at her. Something had shut down in his eyes, his expression so cold and forbidding, for once Cat was stilled to silence.

"Understand this, Mistress O'Hanlon. As a friend of Ariane, you are welcome to remain here until you are recovered. But there will be no further discussion of my daughter. When you are well, you will return to Faire Isle and convey to the Lady my compliments and thanks for her concern. But Meg is staying right where she is."

Sketching a civil bow, he swept from the room, leaving Cat staring openmouthed at a closed door. Then she flopped back down upon the mattress with a groan, frustrated and fuming.

She had been warned that Martin le Loup might be a trifle stubborn, but even Ariane had not prepared Cat for a man as blockheaded as this. She needed to get up, find her clothes, go after Martin, and pound some sense into his thick head. Even if she had to use old Agatha's cane to do it.

If only her own head wasn't still throbbing as though a hundred *bodhrans* were drumming away in her skull. She rubbed her temple. The futility of arguing with Martin le Loup had only aggravated her headache. She would just rest her eyes for a moment and recover some of her strength before she tackled the obstinate fool again.

Cat was on the verge of drifting off when she heard the

door creak. Opening her eyes, she saw the bedside candle flicker from a draft. Tensing, she realized someone had inched open the bedchamber door just far enough to peek inside.

Le Loup returning in a more reasonable frame of mind? Cat doubted it. He would have no reason for being so stealthy. She started to call out, demand to know who was there when she caught a glimpse of a ghostly figure clad in white, a pale face that was all enormous green eyes.

Shoving herself up onto her elbows, Cat said tartly, "Why don't you come in, Megaera, and take a closer look?"

The child froze like a coney caught in an eagle's sight. Cat half expected the girl to bolt. But after a moment's hesitation, Megaera stepped inside the room and closed the door.

She approached the bed with a dignified carriage a princess might have envied, her slender frame garbed in a night rail of the finest white lawn, her dark brown hair spilling about her shoulders. Her face was framed by a lace-trimmed nightcap that might have looked well on a plumper, prettier girl but only served to accent the sharpness of Megaera's features. Her dark brows stood out in marked contrast to her pale skin.

A child of light and shadow, Cat thought with an inexplicable shiver. She struggled upward and swung her legs over the side of the bed, draping the sheet over her shoulder like a chieftain donning his plaid.

Ridiculous, she thought, to be so wary of a wee slip of a girl, but she had already had a sharp taste of what this particular girl could do.

Megaera halted about a foot away, devouring Cat with her eyes. Cat stared back just as fiercely, squaring off with her small nemesis.

"My name is not Megaera," the girl announced with a stubborn lift of her chin. "It is Margaret Elizabeth Wolfe."

"And mine is Catriona of the Clan O'Hanlon. Would you care to be telling me why you were lurking outside the door, spying upon me?"

A hint of color crept into the girl's cheeks. "I wasn't lurking. I only wanted to see how you were faring."

"How kind of you," Cat replied dryly. "Aside from the hole you punched in my back and the hammering in my skull from whatever concoction you shot into my veins, I am faring just grand. I'd like another look at that witch blade of yours. I never saw one before and I confess I am curious."

Meg's lips tightened in a stony line. "I do not have the least notion what you are talking about."

"Don't you? Then perhaps we had best call your father and ask him."

"No!" Meg's hauteur vanished, her face suffused with something akin to panic. "Please, don't do that. Papa has no idea that I—I—."

"Go about stabbing folk with your witch blade?"

"It is not a witch blade. Its proper name is a *syringe* and I don't go about stabbing people. Not unless I have to and— and I can't show it to you because I don't have it with me."

"Truly? I thought you might have been sneaking in here to take another poke."

"No!" Meg cried again. "I wouldn't have poked you the

first time if I hadn't thought you were trying to kill my papa. Anyway it was only a sleeping draught."

"Only a sleeping draught?" Cat pressed a hand to her throbbing head. "I suspect much more of your sleeping draught and I might never have waked up."

The girl stiffened indignantly. "I know the right amount to use. Besides, if I had wanted to kill you, I could have just used poison. I am very skilled at brewing those, too."

"Oh, I don't doubt that you are."

"I would never want to hurt you, but make no mistake, to protect my father, I would destroy you or anyone else."

The warning look that Meg leveled at Cat was disconcertingly adult, woman to woman, warrior to warrior.

"I believe you would," Cat replied gravely.

Meg regarded Cat belligerently for a moment, then her lip trembled and she whispered in a voice that was that of a child.

"I love my papa. He is everything in the world to me, all that I have."

"I can understand that," Cat admitted. "I felt the same way about my father." Against her will, Cat was carried back to that summer when she had raced desperately through the heather after the brawny man whose fire-colored hair was so like her own.

"Da! Wait," she had panted, her small legs pumping hard to overtake his great strides. Tiernan O'Hanlon had turned to wait for her and she had flung her arms about his waist, tears streaming down her cheeks.

"Da, you must not go to fight today. Gran has had one of her visions. She—she says you'll not return if you go."

Her father had merely let loose his booming laugh and scooped her up in his burly arms. "Whist now, ma chroi. You'll not be after listening to the rantings of that foolish old woman. Be a good lass, my Cat. Run home and wait for me. I'll be back before the sun sets with many a fine tale to tell you."

Her father had kissed her cheeks, dried her tears, but in the end pried away her small arms and set her from him. Because nothing or no one stayed an Irishman when his blood ran hot and the war drums were calling, Cat reflected bitterly.

She had returned to their cottage and waited . . . and waited. But as usual her grandmother's vision had proved true. Long after the sun had set, her father's stool by the hearth remained empty and Tiernan of the Laughing Eyes came no more.

A timid touch on her arm drew Cat back to the present. She was startled to find Meg standing right in front of her. The girl peered up at her with intent sad eyes.

"You lost your papa when you were very young, didn't you? I am sorry."

Cat stared at the girl. It could have been a good guess on Meg's part or the girl just might be adept at the ancient wise woman's art of reading the eyes.

Cat had always kept her hurts and grief buried deep in the dark corners of her heart, wounds too tender to bear the light of day. Clutching the sheet like protective armor, Cat inched warily away from the little girl.

"That was all a long time ago," she said. "Besides, we weren't talking about my father. I believe we were discussing yours."

Meg bit down upon her lower lip. "So are you going to tell my father about me? He wouldn't like me having the syringe or brewing potions. He wants me to forget everything I learned when I was with Mam—I mean, from the old days. Papa would be so disappointed in me if he knew what I did today."

Cat frowned. Martin le Loup definitely needed to have his eyes opened where his daughter was concerned and yet as Cat studied Meg's downcast face, she felt an unwilling empathy. She well remembered those days when one disappointed look from Tiernan O'Hanlon had been worse than a blow.

"Perhaps it might remain our secret for now."

Meg brightened only to blanch with consternation when Cat added, "But you'll have to surrender that witch blade to me."

"Oh, no, please, I can't. I always carry the syringe with me when I go out. To—to protect Papa. And if the sisterhood is still after me as you claim, or even the Dark Queen, I'll need my weapon more than ever."

Meg sank down in front of Cat, begging. "Please, Catriona . . . Cat, please. Let me keep the syringe. I'll be careful how I use it and my potions. I swear it. Just please promise you won't tell Papa any of this."

Cat thought she would be an idiot to agree to any such thing or to make such a promise. But as she gazed down at Meg, she could not steel her heart against that earnest young face or those great pleading eyes.

She blew out a gusty sigh. "Oh, very well."

Meg reached up to touch her hand. "No, you must really promise."

"What on earth do you want, girl? An oath in blood?"

Meg regarded her gravely. "Promise me upon your sacred honor. I know that's a vow you'd never break."

And there was only one way Meg could know that. The little witch could read eyes and she had raided Cat's mind again.

"All right. I promise you upon my sacred honor," Cat said, then added sternly, "but you must promise me. No more practicing that little trick of yours upon me."

Meg rose slowly to her feet. "What trick?"

"You know full well. You are dealing with another wise woman here, not your gullible papa. I am very familiar with the practice of reading eyes."

"Oh. *That.*" Meg looked sheepish. She solemnly held up one hand. "I promise I won't do it anymore. Upon my honor."

But as she lowered her hand, her lips twitched with the hint of a smile. "But I *am* very skilled at it, aren't I?"

"Yes, you are, minx."

Meg's smile widened and it was astonishing how the expression transformed her grave little face, giving it a hint of Martin le Loup's roguish charm.

"I am good at other things too, like brewing potions." She gestured to the empty cup on the bedside table. "That tisane I fixed for you should make you feel perfectly all right soon. If not, I can make you some more."

"*You* brewed the tisane?" Cat asked. By the goddess Brigid! Was Martin le Loup aware of anything that went on beneath his own roof? "Your father told me it was Mistress Butterydoor who made the posset."

"Aggie? She knows nothing about such things. Besides, she said she would not give you so much as a cup of her piss."

Meg offered Cat an apologetic glance. "I am sorry, but Aggie doesn't like Irish people. She says you'll crunch my wee bones the first chance you get."

"And you believe her?"

"Of course not. I am not some naive child," Meg replied with dignity. "Aggie is a kindhearted woman, but sometimes she can be a trifle . . ."

"Superstitious and ignorant like most of the English?"

"I was going to say unlettered and untraveled. She has never been farther from London than Southwark. She has not had my experience of the world."

It was an absurd claim for an eleven-year-old girl to make. Anyone but this one, Cat thought. But studying Meg, she glimpsed something sad and weary in the girl's green eyes, so very like her father's and yet so very different.

Martin's eyes sparkled with a youth and vitality the man would likely possess if he lived to be a hundred. But as for Meg, an expression passed over her face that made her look as though she were already a hundred years old. There was a very old soul haunting that child's eyes.

Cat was rarely subject to maternal impulses, but she brushed her fingers through a strand of Meg's silky brown hair, smoothing it over the girl's shoulder.

"Since you are so good at reading eyes, you must have some idea why I came to London."

"You think I am in danger. I overheard you talking to my papa."

"Ah, listening at the keyhole, were you?"

Again there was that trace of an impish smile, but Meg

immediately sobered. "It is wrong of me, I know, but I have to. Papa doesn't always tell me the things that he should. He tries too hard to be protective."

Papa wasn't the only one, Cat was tempted to retort, but she kept the observation to herself.

"If the sisterhood or the Dark Queen still threatens us, I need to know these things." Meg shuddered. "I met her once . . . the queen. In the gardens of her palace in Paris. She is very old, but still quite powerful and frightening. There—there is a terrible darkness in her."

"Which is why I came to fetch you to Faire Isle."

Meg cocked her head to one side, considering. "Would I be entirely safe there?"

Cat hesitated over her answer, but was unable to lie to the girl. It would have done no good with Meg anyway. The child was far too wise for that.

"No, Margaret. There is no place on this earth entirely safe, but I think you would be safer there than in this infernal city."

"Is Faire Isle a pleasant place? Who lives there?"

"The island is inhabited mostly by women because their husbands and sons are often away, making their living upon the sea as sailors or fishermen. Consequently, you will find many women employed in trades you would not elsewhere, blacksmiths, carpenters, brewers, shopkeepers, and—"

"And wise women?" Meg interrupted eagerly.

"Most certainly wise women. Faire Isle has long been a refuge for those seeking the ancient knowledge, herbalists and healers. The isle is small, but lovely like a gem set in the sea, with rugged cliffs and shell-strewn beaches, and at the heart of the island, a deep dark wood with trees too old to imagine. There's a beautiful, wild spirit that inhabits Faire Isle, even more ancient than the ones that dwell in my own country."

Or at least used to dwell there, Cat thought sadly. She had long felt that the spirit of Ireland was dying, being driven out by the invading English and the folly of her own countrymen.

"And what about the Lady of Faire Isle?" Meg asked.

"She is as wise as she is good and very learned. She could teach you a great deal more about the healing arts and the ways of the earth."

"It sounds wonderful." Meg looked wistful for a moment, and then sighed. "But Papa will never agree to go there. He likes London and he has great ambitions for me. He wants me to become a grand lady, admired, beautiful, and accomplished in music and dancing and—and fine needlework. I am not sure I can be all he wants me to be, but I have to try."

"You talk a great deal of what Papa wants. But what about Meg?" Cat asked. "What does she want?"

"To please my papa. It is my duty. The clergyman at St. Barnaby's preached just last Sunday how important it is for daughters to be obedient."

Cat took the little girl's smooth hand between her own calloused ones. "There are other kinds of daughters, Meg. Daughters of the earth, which is what you are. First and foremost a wise woman learns to be true to herself."

"I—I remember. My first nurse, Prudence Waters, was just such a wise woman. She tried to teach me—" Meg broke off with a sorrowful shake of her head. "But I need to forget all of that. It is what my papa desires."

"It is not that easy, Meg, forgetting the past, trying to deny who you really are deep in your bones, striving to be what someone else wants you to be. Trust me. I know."

But the girl drew her hand away. "It was interesting talking to you, Catriona of the Clan O'Hanlon. But I agree with my papa. You should rest and then go home."

Meg bobbed a quaint curtsy, her shuttered face a mirror image of what Martin's had been. "I wish you a safe journey back to Faire Isle."

The girl whisked from the room and once more Cat found herself staring at a closed door. She sprawled back upon the mattress with a disgruntled sigh.

Go home? She wished she could take Meg's advice, but it had been a long time since Cat had known exactly where that was. As for the journey to Faire Isle, she would have been glad to embark on the next tide.

She had hoped to accomplish her mission swiftly and return to Ariane as soon as possible. For all of Ariane's assurances about how well she was doing, Cat was deeply worried about her friend. Not that she was of much use when it came to the mysteries of childbearing, but if anything went wrong, she wanted to be there at Ariane's side.

But this mission was proving to be more difficult than Cat had ever dreamed, navigating the shoals between Martin le Loup and his equally obstinate daughter a near impossible task.

Cat didn't blame Meg. For all of her wisdom, she was only a little girl desperate to please her father. Martin, on the other hand, ought to know better than to risk his daughter in this fashion. But the man was too blinded by his own ambitions to see what was best for his child.

Well, it was up to her to teach Monsieur le Loup the error of his ways. She would get Meg safely back to Faire Isle even if she had to snatch the girl out from under her father's nose to do so.

Chapter Four

MARTIN STRODE THROUGH THE SILENT CORRIDOR, SHIELD-ing his candle from the draft, the rest of the household long abed. It was not the first time he had found himself stirring while the rest of the world slept. From his days as a thief in Paris to when he had acted as an agent for the king of Navarre, much of his business had been conducted under the cloak of darkness.

His hooded cloak fastened about his neck, sword and dagger tucked in his belt, he prepared to steal from the house for a late-night meeting with his patron. But not before he checked to see that all doors and windows were barred, and he looked in on his daughter. For the third or perhaps the fourth time. That wild Irishwoman with all her dire warnings had alarmed Martin far more than he cared to admit.

Easing Meg's bedchamber door open, Martin tiptoed inside. She was like a princess lodged in a tower, with her room situated at the highest point of the house. Martin had run up considerable debt refurbishing the chamber in regal fashion, the ceiling trimmed with gilt moldings, the walls papered with heraldic devices. An arras hung from one corner to shield the room from drafts that came from the north, the heavy tapestry depicting Meg's favorite creature, a blue-green dragon with his wings tricked out in iridescent threads.

The chamber was crowded with everything a doting father could bestow upon his daughter, trunks stuffed with lovely gowns, a golden harp, a workbasket overflowing with silken skeins of thread, shelves crammed with books, a small writing desk.

Martin set the candle down atop the desk, the surface littered with ink, quill, and parchment where Meg had been busy translating some passage of Latin into English. Never much of a scholar himself, Martin was proud of his daughter's achievements, although sometimes the hunger of her mind worried him.

His friends the Cheney sisters would no doubt be ready to roast him alive for harboring such an opinion, but Martin feared it was not always a good thing for a woman to be too clever. Certainly, Meg's mother had benefited little from—Martin compressed his lips, blocking out all thought of Cassandra Lascelles.

He stepped closer to Meg's bed, taking great care not

to wake her as he drew back the Indian silk bed-curtains. His daughter looked small and fragile, a mere babe curled up in the center of the huge feather tick mattress.

He was relieved to see that she was fast asleep, her brow smooth and untroubled. He had been afraid that the events of the afternoon might trigger some of her bad dreams. It had been a long time since Meg had been tormented by any of her nightmares and Martin was determined to keep it that way.

She had fallen asleep as she often did, poring over the contents of her treasure box. The small chest inlaid with mother of pearl lay open on the mattress near her. Martin carefully eased the small coffer away, lest Meg roll over on it and hurt herself in her sleep. He smiled over her tiny hoard of treasures, a shell from the beach at Dover, a bird's feather, the strand of pearls he'd given her for her tenth birthday, and a large oval locket that stirred other memories.

Hooking his finger around the silver chain, he drew the locket out of the box and dangled it in the candlelight. The oval surface was adorned with the portrait of a wolf baying at the moon. The pendant opened to reveal a cunning miniature clock and the etched words *Yours until time ends.*

The necklace originally had been a gift for Miri Cheney, a prelude he had hoped to a betrothal. He remembered all too well the night he had discovered Miri was no longer wearing it. They had been walking in the moonlight by the pond on Simon Aristide's farm.

"I have the locket safe," Miri had said. *"I meant to give it back to you the next time we met."*

"I won't take it," he had cried. *"What, my Lady of the*

Moon? After stealing my heart, do you mean to try to rob
me of all my hopes and dreams as well?"

"My dearest friend." Miri had touched his cheek, her
eyes full of sadness and regret. "I should have known years
ago that I could never be what you want me to be."

Very likely he should have known it as well, Martin reflected. If he hadn't been so blind, he would have seen that
Miri would never be his, that she had long been in love
with Aristide.

Martin placed the locket back in the chest and closed
the lid. The pain of losing Miri had dulled to a bittersweet
ache. They had parted friends, and she had given the locket
to his daughter the day that he and Meg had left for England.

There were times late at night when the house was too
quiet, when he kept his lonely vigil over his daughter, that
he still missed Miri. Mon Dieu, how he had adored the
woman, or so he had believed.

Miri had often accused him of treating her like some
distant goddess, of pursuing her the way he lived his life,
as one grand romantic adventure. Likely she was right.
Sometimes he felt as though he had not known what it
meant to truly love another human being until he had become a father.

Placing the chest back on the shelf, Martin returned to
Meg's bedside. He tucked the coverlet up over her thin
shoulder and stroked back a tendril of her silky brown hair.

Meg stirred at his touch, nestling deeper into her pillow, and Martin swelled with such love for his child, it was
nigh painful. He had not even known of Meg's existence
for the first nine years of her life, but how swiftly she had

burrowed her way into his heart until she was knit into his very blood and bone. He loved her so much, it frightened him.

If he ever lost her, he knew he would run stark mad. Perhaps he was as much of an idiot as Cat accused him of being for not heeding Ariane's warning. Perhaps he would be wiser to scoop Meg up and run. But to do what and to go where?

To Faire Isle with all its strange mystical influence and the lure of the ancient knowledge and ways of the daughters of the earth? Magic, even the most benevolent kind, could lead to darkness and danger. Martin had striven far too hard to exorcise all of that from Meg's world.

And as for simply taking Meg and trying to disappear . . . He had inflicted enough of a fugitive existence upon his daughter when they had first come to England and he joined Master Roxburgh's traveling company of players. Struggling to shield Meg's innocence in a world of low taverns and lewd talk, often obliged to flee from some puritanical vicar determined to keep his town free of the pernicious influence of rascally actors. Pursued by dogs, constables, aldermen wielding pitchforks.

Such a madcap existence might have suited Martin just fine. He was used to it. He felt as though he had spent most of his life running from or running to something. But it would not do for his little girl.

No, Martin thought, his jaw hardening with resolve. He had worked too hard, risked too much to secure a better future for Meg to panic now and throw it all away.

He would simply have to be more vigilant, hire an extra servant or two, burly men to patrol the garden and keep watch over the house. And he'd threaten to switch Agatha Butterydoor within an inch of her hide if the old woman ever took Meg out of the house alone again.

He *would* succeed. He'd give his daughter the kind of life he had never known, secure, contented, and respectable, even if he had to hazard his soul to do it.

Martin's mouth twisted ruefully as he thought of the man he was leaving to meet tonight. Sell himself to the devil? Sometimes Martin feared that he had already had.

Bending down, he brushed a kiss upon Meg's brow. He retrieved his candle and slipped from the room.

The figure hiding behind the arras waited long minutes after Martin had left before emerging from her hiding place. Cat moved as quietly as she could, awkward in a pair of Martin's boots, the toes stuffed with extra stockings in a vain effort to make them fit. His breeches threatened to fall to her knees no matter how tight she cinched the length of cord about her waist, and she had to keep shoving up the sleeves of his shirt to keep them from falling over her hands.

Not exactly the kind of garb to render one stealthy, but unable to locate her own clothing, Cat had had to make do with whatever she could find, rummaging through Martin's wardrobe. It felt disturbingly intimate to be wearing the man's garments, the clothing carrying a hint of his musky, masculine scent.

Martin's removal of the candle had plunged the bedchamber back into darkness. With only the moonlight filtering through the window to guide her, Cat banged her shin against a leg of the writing desk.

Suppressing an oath, she cast an anxious glance at the

bed. Meg stirred and Cat froze. But the girl only rolled over, tunneling deeper beneath the bedclothes. Releasing her breath, Cat bent to rub her aching shin, grateful that such a simple action no longer caused her head to reel.

Meg's tisane had done its work, just as the girl had promised. Feeling much better, Cat had soon grown restless lying in bed. Having reached the unhappy conclusion that it might be necessary to abduct Meg back to Faire Isle, Cat had decided the sooner she implemented her plan the better. When she had thought the household asleep, Cat had stolen from Martin's bedchamber to study the house and its environs. What she had discovered was a trifle daunting.

The Angel was but one house in a row of buildings crowded together on a narrow street. A street that was bound to be bustling with people and carts by day. By night it was patrolled. Cat herself had heard the watchman intoning the hour.

"Eleven o'clock and a fair night. All is we-ell."

As for the rear of the house, the Angel had a small garden, but it was surrounded by a very high wall. Cat had to concede that Martin had chosen well when he had selected this house to rent. It would not be easy to spirit his daughter out of here unseen.

Cat had been creeping about upstairs, checking for the possibility of an egress to the roof, when she had been surprised by Martin le Loup and forced to take refuge behind the arras in Meg's room.

Surprised by the man? Cat frowned, thinking it a poor word to describe the tumult of her feelings as she had watched le Loup bend over his sleeping child.

Cat had set him down as an arrogant, swaggering knave. But as he had drawn the coverlet about Meg, the rogue's face had been so open and vulnerable, Cat had felt half-ashamed to be spying upon him.

His expression had been such a mingling of tenderness, love, and fear that it had taken Cat back to those times when her own father had tucked her in. She remembered grumbling in a sleepy voice.

"You don't need to do that, Da. I can tuck myself in. I am not afeard of the dark anymore. I am not a babe."

"Alas, no, you aren't," her father had replied in a *strangely melancholy voice. "I look in upon you at night to appease my fears rather than yours."*

"Yours, Da?" Cat had peered up in wonder at her bold warrior father. "What could you ever be afraid of?"

Tiernan of the Laughing Eyes had skated his rough broken knuckles along her cheek. "Of losing you, my wee lass. You are such a great treasure, I am afeard some dark night the sidhe *might have a mind to steal you away from me."*

Cat's lips curved in a wistful smile at the memory. The *sidhe.* Martin le Loup certainly had more substantial fears for Meg than Tiernan's worry that the little people might snatch his daughter.

Tonight there was only one bad fairy creeping about the house and that was her, Cat thought guiltily. As she gazed at the girl innocently asleep, Cat abandoned all thought of abduction.

Not because of the difficulties of carrying out such a scheme, the layout of the house, the crowded streets, finding a way to get Meg alone—Cat was confident she could surmount all of that.

What stayed her was the thought of that little girl whose father was everything to her and the look on Martin's face when he had kissed his daughter good night.

No matter how badly she wanted to get back to Faire Isle and Ariane, she would not be stealing anyone's child. That left her with no other choice than to remain in London and guard Meg until she persuaded Martin to change his mind.

Quietly exiting the room, Cat stretched herself across the threshold to begin her watch.

　　　　　　　　　　✼✼✼

WHITEHALL SPRAWLED OVER TWENTY-THREE ACRES OF LONdon, a city within a city. The palace was a haphazard jumble of architectural styles, a warren of fifteen hundred rooms where Queen Elizabeth's courtiers jostled, fought, and intrigued for scraps of the royal favor.

But neither queen nor court were in residence, Elizabeth preferring her palace at Richmond during the summer months. As Martin followed his escort through a maze of corridors, their footsteps echoed in silence through empty halls. Many of the walls were bare, the costly tapestries taken down and removed with the queen, but some of the portraits remained, particularly those of the late king, Henry VIII. It was as though Elizabeth was determined that no one should ever forget whose daughter she was.

Martin's usher was a laconic young man who looked bored, as though it was mere routine to be escorting dubious characters to meet with the principal secretary of the realm at such a late hour, and very likely it was. Sir Francis

Walsingham was rumored to employ a legion of shadowy men, of whom Martin feared he was but one more.

The page left Martin waiting in a small antechamber while he announced Martin's arrival to Sir Francis. The small room was occupied by a clerk with a yellow beard and a face pitted from a bout of smallpox. He labored wearily with quill and ink over some parchment. Glancing up with tired, red-rimmed eyes, Thomas Phelippes acknowledged Martin's presence with a curt nod before returning to his work.

Phelippes's taciturnity left Martin nothing to do but pace and wish himself elsewhere, back home with his daughter. Once, the kind of furtive dealings he had embarked upon with Walsingham would have been like a heady wine to Martin, but his taste for such intrigue had begun to pall.

"We are respectable folk now," Martin had told Meg, but that was not true and never would be while he continued in Walsingham's secret employ. He hoped that the information he had recently acquired might suffice to bring his service to an end.

The page returned to inform Martin that Sir Francis would receive him now. Martin followed the young man into a study crammed with books. Sir Francis was said to be fluent in at least five other tongues besides his own, and the volumes lining the shelves represented a diversity of languages as well as interests.

There were books on history, law, politics, castles and fortifications, as well as treatises on training militia and tactics of war and ledgers of the expenses for the queen's many households and estates.

It made Martin's head throb just to contemplate it all. He often wondered how Sir Francis coped with such a staggering array of detail and information, to say nothing of the locked cabinet containing more-secret matters, to which only Walsingham had the key.

One could hardly see the man seated behind his desk, the surface was piled so high with copies of treaties, correspondence from ambassadors, maps, and haphazardly stacked paperwork.

Somewhere in the midst of this avalanche, Walsingham set his seal to a letter he had just completed. Absorbed by his task, he barely looked up as Martin entered.

Sir Francis was a man of lean stature and long narrow countenance. His pointed black beard and sallow complexion had led the queen to dub him "the Moor." Attired in simple dark clothing, he could have easily been mistaken for a clerk himself instead of what he was, Elizabeth's principal secretary and a powerful member of her privy council.

He handed the letter off to the page, commanding, "See that this is dispatched at once."

As the young man hurried off on his errand, Walsingham beckoned to Martin, indicating he should be seated. "Your pardon for the delay, Master Wolfe."

"I am entirely at your disposal, Mr. Secretary." Martin sketched a bow, reflecting that that was far truer than he liked. "I would hardly expect to take precedence over some urgent matter of state."

"Matters of state," Walsingham grimaced. "Yes, there is always an endless supply of those. I have been besieged of late by letters from justices throughout the country, complaining of riots owing to that infernal comet."

"The comet?" Martin arched one brow as he settled himself into a chair opposite the desk.

"That fiery object that has been hovering in the sky this past month," the secretary replied dryly. "I trust you have noticed it."

"It would be impossible not to, but I can find enough trouble right here on earth without concerning myself with a celestial disturbance a million miles away."

"Regrettably, you are one of the few with the sense to realize that. I vow that the rest of the country seems to have run a bit mad, panicked citizens paying out good coin to mountebanks for protective charms, preachers ranting on street corners about the end of days. Most recently, I had this letter from a justice of the peace regarding an agitator in Surrey who has been spreading untold alarm."

Walsingham picked up a sheet of parchment and read,

"This wild-eyed vagrant hath stirred up much unrest in my district by preaching that the comet is a manifestation of the wrath of the Almighty, the fiery orb forged of the sins of mankind rising like a noxious gas into the heavens."

Martin laughed. "Good Lord. If that were the case, we'd be plagued by comets every day of every year."

"Precisely. Unfortunately, this madman has managed to stir up a great deal of hysteria. The justice planned to hang him. I, however, recommended the poor fool be confined to St. Bethlehem's Hospital for the insane. That will just as effectively put an end to his agitation."

Locked up in Bedlam, likely never again to see the light

of day. Martin repressed a shudder, thinking he would have by far preferred the rope.

Walsingham tossed the letter from the justice atop a stack of other papers and rubbed his eyes. There were some who referred to the secretary as the man who never slept and Martin could almost believe it.

There was something preternatural about this dark, gaunt man who tended to keep his own counsel in a court noted for its wit and gossip. Martin often reflected how Sir Francis must stand out in his somber clothing amongst the bright silks, jewels, and furs of the courtiers, like a raven amongst peacocks.

Or perhaps, and far more likely, he simply faded into the background, a silent shadow, ever watchful. Watching and waiting—it was what Walsingham did best.

Leaning back in his chair, he folded his hands across the front of his dark robes and trained his penetrating gaze upon Martin.

"The hour grows late, Master Wolfe, and I have many more matters that require my attention. So let us get down to business. What have you to report to me? Some good information at last, I trust."

"I have information. I don't know how good you will find it," Martin replied. "The man who has been frequenting the Plough Inn near the Temple bar and styling himself Captain Fortescue is an imposter, just as you suspected. He is really a priest by the name of John Ballard."

"Indeed." Walsingham leaned forward eagerly. "You are sure of this?"

"I attended a mass celebrated by Ballard at the house of Sir Anthony Babington." A forbidden rite that could get a man clapped into prison or worse. Martin made haste to add, "I did so purely for the purpose of establishing my bona fides as a fellow recusant. It was not all that difficult. I—"

Martin checked himself on the verge of revealing that he had spent part of his youth in Paris amongst friars after he had been abandoned on the steps of Notre Dame by his mother.

Walsingham was only familiar with Martin as a former agent for Henry of Navarre. Martin had first crossed paths with the secretary two years earlier when Martin had journeyed to London in an effort to raise much-needed funds for the beleaguered Protestant king.

That was all that Walsingham knew of Martin and he preferred to keep it that way. He had no desire to have the secretary looking too closely into his past, especially not the parts regarding his daughter.

"I am familiar enough with the forms of the old faith to pass myself off as a Catholic."

"Indeed." Walsingham's countenance was impassive, his voice noncommittal, but his shrewd gaze never left Martin's face. "Another fine performance by you, I have no doubt."

"Passable." Martin hunched his shoulders in a modest gesture. "But not good enough to convince Babington and Father Ballard to take me fully into their confidence.

"I have been able to learn more by lurking about the Plough Inn of an evening. Young Babington and his friends often repair there for supper and are not always cautious when deep in their cups."

Martin paused and went on grimly, "There is definitely some plot afoot to get rid of Queen Elizabeth and place her cousin, Mary of Scots, on the throne. I overheard Babington asking Father Ballard if it would be wrong to kill Elizabeth."

"An assassin with a conscience. How admirable." Walsingham sneered.

"Ballard assured him it would be no sin. The Pope has declared Elizabeth a heretic and would absolve Babington. And yet he still sounded loath to act. Truly, for all of his bold talk, Babington does not strike me as much of a threat. He's an indecisive and dream-ridden young fellow. I believe he has resolved to write to the Queen of Scots herself, asking for her blessing before he proceeds any further."

Martin's lip curled contemptuously. "How the young fool thinks he will manage that, I know not. Everyone knows the Scottish queen is guarded too closely at Chartley to receive any communication from the outside world.

"Oh, the lady shall receive his letter." Walsingham gave a rare smile, so cold it chilled Martin's blood. "I will relax the guard and see that she does."

Martin regarded Sir Francis in astonishment. "Your pardon, sir, but hadn't you better arrest Babington and this priest at once? Wouldn't it be dangerous to let Elizabeth's enemies correspond and plot against her?"

"Dangerous, but necessary." Walsingham was not a forthcoming man, seldom explaining himself fully to anyone, even his queen.

He surprised Martin when he steepled his fingers together and continued gravely, "I have dealt with many of these Catholic conspiracies against Her Majesty. In the past I always moved too swiftly, never rooting out the dark heart of the matter. But this time I mean to end these plots once and for all. To do that I must entrap the Scottish Jezebel herself and offer Queen Elizabeth incontrovertible proof of her cousin's guilt."

Walsingham sighed. "While Her Majesty can be as astute as any man I have ever known, she is very much a woman in this respect. She has no stomach for execution, especially when it concerns another anointed queen."

"Mayhap the queen has good reason for her reluctance," Martin ventured to suggest, "considering the tragic way her own mother died."

"I wouldn't know. The queen never speaks of the Boleyn woman and there is great wisdom in that. She has had her legitimacy challenged too many times to remind the world that she is the daughter of a woman beheaded for treason and adultery. But regardless of what ghosts haunt her, the queen must set aside her private feelings.

"While Mary lives, neither this realm nor Elizabeth will ever be safe. If I can get a letter from Mary's own hand, endorsing Babington's plot, Elizabeth will have no choice this time. She will have to have her cousin tried and executed."

"But will Mary really be foolhardy enough to answer a letter from Babington?" Martin asked.

"Oh, I rather think she might. She believes herself safe, writing her messages in code, but I have a cryptographer capable of deciphering anything. The woman has never been noted for her wisdom."

"And so the Queen of Scots will lose her head for indiscretion." Martin nearly added, "Poor foolish woman." But he thought better of it.

It was just as well because Walsingham eyed him sternly. "She will lose her head for treason and plotting the murder of our sovereign queen."

"Er—amen to that," Martin said. Elizabeth was a clever and able ruler, but he felt a certain pang of sympathy for the deposed Scottish queen. Part French herself, Mary had once been wed to the king of France, made a young widow the year Martin was born.

He had grown up hearing many of the romantic legends of *la petite Marie.* They still drank toasts in the taverns of Paris to *la belle reine,* although it had been a long time since Mary had sat on any throne. She had been a prisoner of the English for the past twelve years. It was understandable she would plot to regain her freedom.

Martin tapped his fingers restively upon his knee, frowning over his own thoughts. He might have suppressed his accent and anglicized his name, but he feared that at heart he was still a Frenchman. Elizabeth's conflict with her Catholic subjects struck him as an English problem, little to do with him.

As for Walsingham, the secretary was playing a dangerous game in more ways than one. Queen Elizabeth possessed a formidable temper and Martin doubted she would thank Walsingham for forcing her to deal harshly with her cousin, or favor anyone who aided the secretary in his maneuverings.

All this plotting could only end in blood and tears. More heads than one were going to roll and Martin wished himself well out of the business.

He was therefore greatly relieved when Walsingham

said, "You have done very well, Master Wolfe, but I have in my employ a man who actually once studied at the Jesuit seminary in Douai. I think him better suited to wangle his way into the confidence of both Babington and the Scottish queen and act as conduit for their letters."

"Excellent," Martin agreed heartily, rising from his chair. "If you have no further need of my services, I shall—"

"Not so hasty, sir. Sit down."

When Martin hesitated, Walsingham repeated in a firmer tone. "*Sit down.* I find your report to me incomplete."

"I know not what you mean." Martin settled uneasily back into his chair, fearing that he knew what was coming, questions he had hoped to avoid.

Walsingham studied Martin through narrowed eyes. "In your discussion of all these treasonable activities, I notice you make no mention of your young friend, Edward Lambert, Lord Oxbridge.

"That is because there is nothing to tell," Martin replied coolly.

Walsingham frowned, his brows knit with displeasure. "I didn't go to the expense of setting you up in your own household and furnishing you a more respectable veneer merely to have you lurk about in taverns. Your main assignment, in case you have forgotten, was to insinuate yourself into the baron's graces and discover how far gone he might be in this treason against the queen."

"And I have done so," Martin said with a trace of asperity. "I will admit that Ned—I mean Lord Oxbridge—is at times reckless and foolish as any young man of twenty may be. But even though he is a Catholic, I have found nothing to suggest he is anything other than loyal to the queen. Certainly I have uncovered no connection between him and this Babington plot."

"Perhaps you haven't looked hard enough."

"What do you mean by that?"

"I mean that you might find it inconvenient for the man who helped fund your precious theater to be guilty of treason."

"Actually, it was not Oxbridge's money that paid for building the Crown, but his sister's."

Martin regretted the words as soon as they were out of his mouth, because Walsingham pounced upon the remark like a dog at a bone.

"*Ah!* So we come to the heart of the matter, the Lady Jane Danvers. She is reputed to be a lovely woman."

Martin shrugged, trying to appear indifferent. "I reckon she is comely enough."

"And a wealthy widow, still young enough to require a new husband in her bed."

"I have no idea what the lady requires. I would hardly dare to raise my lowly gaze to the sister of a baron."

"Oh, I think there is little you would not dare, Master Wolfe."

Martin squirmed. Walsingham was said to have a gaze that could strip a man's soul bare, and at the moment the secretary was peering uncomfortably close into Martin's.

Of late, his thoughts *had* strayed to Lady Danvers more often than they should. She was a sweet, gentle woman, at times a little too solemn for Martin's taste. But he could not help considering how marriage to the lady would advance his fortunes, and Jane would make a good mother for Meg.

Walsingham continued to regard Martin through narrowed eyes. The secretary knew how to wield silence like a weapon, often prodding another man into injudicious speech.

When Martin refused to be goaded, Walsingham continued, "We are living in a unique age here in England, when a man of ambition and abilities can rise far above what his father was. You strike me as such a man, Master Wolfe. You are also something far more dangerous."

"And what would that be?"

"A man who acknowledges no master, no ties or loyalties to anyone."

"How strange," Martin drawled. "I had the peculiar impression that I was bound to your service, Mr. Secretary."

"Certainly you take my coin and carry out the assignments I give, but I have never been fool enough to consider myself your master. After six months employing you, I know little more of you than I did at the outset."

"I might say the same of you, sir," Martin retorted. "You have the reputation of being a man who says little, but sees everything."

"And you are a man who speaks much, but reveals nothing. I am not even entirely certain where your religious convictions lie."

"I attend the Protestant services regularly every Sunday."

"So do a great many men, if for no other reason than to avoid the fines imposed upon those who abstain."

Martin smiled. "My relationship with the Almighty is fairly uncomplicated. When I was a boy, God spoke to me. He told me, 'Martin, my lad, I have far more important things to worry about than you, so you had best look to yourself.' "

Walsingham gave a dry laugh, but Martin could tell he had offended the stern Puritan with his blasphemy. He became more serious as he added, "As for this conflict between Catholic and Protestant, I have seen firsthand the misery and suffering it causes. France has been torn apart for years by civil war—men, women, and children cruelly slaughtered. And all for what? I think your own queen put it best. Didn't she say, 'There is only one Jesus Christ; the rest is disputes over trifles.'? I tend to agree with her."

"And yet you once served the Protestant king of Navarre," Walsingham prodded.

"Because I genuinely liked the man and he made it worth my while to do so."

"And that is exactly what concerns me about you. That your liking for Lord Oxbridge's sister and her purse has led you to be less than zealous in your investigations of the baron."

Martin vented an exasperated sigh. "Why you are so certain Oxbridge is inclined to treason?"

"I have outlined my reasons to you before. The Lamberts are one of the last great Catholic families from the north. They have an unfortunate history of rebellion against the crown. The present baron's grandfather ended up with his head mounted upon the Tower. The father would likely have shared the same fate had he not tumbled from his horse and broken his own neck while fleeing from justice."

"But you yourself just assured me it is a new age in England. That a man need not be what his father was."

Walsingham looked nettled to have his own words turned against him. "I have other reasons as well. Oxbridge and his sister were fostered by the Earl of Shrewsbury when Sir Anthony Babington was a page in that household. They all lived under the same roof at the time when the earl had custody of the Queen of Scots."

"Coincidence," Martin scoffed. "Just because they were all known to one another in the past does not mean there is any present connection. I have seen nothing to suggest that either Lord Oxbridge or his sister—"

"Then I suggest you look more closely, sir," Walsingham snapped. "Lest I be obliged to employ someone else to scrutinize the baron and your loyalties as well, Monsieur le Loup."

Martin steeled himself not to show how badly such a threat shook him. "I shall do my best."

"That is all I require. Now I am sure you are anxious to return to your daughter." The secretary rose to walk Martin to the door. "And how fares young Margaret?"

"She does well," Martin replied cautiously. He studied Walsingham, trying to perceive if any sort of threat lay behind the question.

But something had softened in Sir Francis's usually cold eyes. "It has been six summers now since I lost my youngest daughter, my little Mary.

"She is with God now. Treasure your days with your daughter, Master Wolfe. Our children are often lent to us for all too brief a time. And in the end it is not kingdoms or power that matters. It is only God and family."

The secretary spoke simply, no pious cant, but straight from the heart. And for a moment it was as though they were but two ordinary men, one father addressing another.

Then Walsingham's mask settled back into place. "Do you plan to call upon Lord Oxbridge and his sister soon?"

Martin nodded reluctantly. "I have been favored by an invitation to a great banquet to be given at Strand House tomorrow eve. The queen herself is expected."

"Not if I can dissuade her. Given all these plots swirling, it is hardly the best time for Her Majesty to be dining in the houses of known recusants."

Walsingham rested his hand upon Martin's shoulder. "Help me defeat this conspiracy against my queen and I will see you rewarded. A coat of arms and respectability can be bought. There is no need for you to court danger by wooing a woman whose family may be steeped in treason.

"Serve me well, and you may rise to great heights. But remember, it is possible to fall just as hard. Good night, sir."

Martin had no difficulty perceiving the threat this time.

⁂

AS SOON AS WOLFE HAD DEPARTED, PHELIPPES ENTERED. THE clerk jerked his head toward the door. "Do you entirely trust that Frenchman, sir?"

"As much as I trust any of you," Walsingham replied. "I find there are very few men who don't bear watching. How goes the translating?"

"Well enough. Or at least most of it." Phelippes scratched his beard. "I was certain I had cracked the code, but part of this message reads so strangely, I am not certain this can be right."

"I am sure it is. You are the best cryptographer I have ever employed. Who is the letter from?"

"It is from the Scottish queen's factor in Paris, Thomas Morgan."

Morgan had been acting on Mary's behalf for years, working to gain her release and drum up support for a French invasion to free her and set her on the English throne. To retain good relations with England, the French king had finally been persuaded to arrest the man. But Henry III had been reluctant to hand Morgan over to the English government.

Morgan was locked up in the Bastille, but that certainly had not kept the man from continuing his activities on the captive queen's behalf.

"What is it about Morgan's letter that troubles you?" Walsingham asked.

"He recommends Babington to Mary as a man to be trusted."

"All to the good."

"But it is the rest that is so strange. Morgan feels all means should be tried to free the queen this time. Including witchcraft."

"What!" Walsingham reached for the parchment and scanned Phelippes's translation.

"And though Your Majesty is a woman of great piety, I must beg you to consider that even the forces of darkness might be harnessed for a holy cause. I have heard

rumors of a powerful sorceress living in England whose
skills might be channeled to your deliverance . . ."

Walsingham scowled with contempt. "It sounds as
though Master Morgan has been incarcerated too long. His
brain is going soft."

"You place no credence in witchcraft?"

"If I believed in magic and superstition, I would be a
papist. But much damage can be wielded by those who ad-
vocate such dangerous beliefs. We can ignore no threats,
no matter how far-fetched."

"What do you wish me to do then, sir?"

Walsingham massaged his temple, considering for a
moment before ordering, "Seal up the letter and see that it
reaches the Scottish queen along with the correspondence
from the French ambassador. I will write to instruct our
own agents in Paris to see if they can learn more about this
witch. What is she called?"

Sir Francis took another glance at the translated parchment.

"The Silver Rose."

Chapter Five

CAT CURLED UP OUTSIDE MEG'S DOOR, THE MORNING LIGHT soft upon her face, beguiling her into pleasant memories of booleying time. Pillowing her head upon her arm, she dreamed she was bedded down beneath a wickerwork shelter, drowsing upon a bed of moss and rushes. She could hear the lowing of the cattle in their summer pasture and the soft footfall of her gran fetching Cat a lovely breakfast of buttermilk and black bread.

It was not her grandmother's melodic voice that awakened her, but an ear-splitting shriek like the cry of a banshee.

"Papist witch! Irish she-devil!"

Cat's eyes flew wide. Her warrior's instincts prompted her to roll just in time to avoid the heavy cane that threatened to crash down upon her skull. Scrambling to her feet, Cat found herself under siege. Not only from Agatha Butterydoor, but also from a scrawny housemaid armed with a broom.

Cat flung up her arms to shield herself from the blows. "What the devil! Are you insane, old woman? Stop that— ow!" Cat yelped as the cane cracked against her elbow. She twisted away from Agatha, caught the broom handle, and wrenched it away from the maid.

Gripping the broom with both hands, Cat wielded it like a staff, blocking Agatha's wild swings. The terrified maid retreated behind the old woman's black skirts and screeched at the top of her lungs.

"Will you quit?" Cat grated between thwacks. "And cease that caterwauling before you wake the little girl."

Panting, her drooping bosom heaving, Agatha retreated a few steps down the corridor. "I pray my poppet can still be waked. What have you done to her, fiend?"

"Nothing, you old fool—"

"Maude! Run below stairs and fetch the master at once," Agatha ordered the cowering housemaid, but it was an unnecessary command.

Martin le Loup came thundering up the stairs, sword drawn. Barefoot and bare-legged, he was clad only in a white shirt that came to mid-thigh. Wild-eyed with alarm, he looked very much like a man who had just been rudely startled from his sleep, his dark hair tousled about his bearded features.

Taking the stairs two at a time, he roared, "What's happened? Is it Meg? Has someone—"

He broke off, coming to a halt at the top of the risers. He blinked as he took in the scene, his gaze first traveling over Cat clad in his clothes, and then flicking to the old woman with the sniveling housemaid clinging to her skirts."

"What in thunder is going on?"

"Oh, master, I warned you!" Agatha cried. "That Irish witch was skulking up here—"

"I was doing no such thing, you silly wench," Cat interrupted.

"Skulking and plotting to steal the silver and murder us all."

"I was asleep, you damned fool—"

"—and I fear she already must have devoured the little mistress." The old woman's eyes glinted with tears. "Because she—"

"Oh, for the love of heaven! Woman, you have the wits of a flea."

"Quiet!" Martin bellowed, glaring so fiercely even Cat felt compelled to subside. Raking his hand back through his unruly cap of hair, he stepped in between Cat and Mistress Butterydoor. He used the flat of his sword to force the old woman to lower her cane.

"Now will someone please explain—one of you at a time," he added as both Cat and Agatha drew breath. "You first, Mistress Butterydoor."

"Well, master, poor Maude was about her morning chores when she spied that nasty papist sprawled in front of Mistress Meg's door. Gave the poor girl quite a turn it did and she ran immediately to fetch me. Only she could not find me all at once. I was out in the garden—"

"Yes, thank you." Martin cut her off. "I am sure Mistress O'Hanlon has some reasonable explanation." Despite his disheveled state, he was still able to arch his eyebrow in that cool, aggravating fashion.

"I already told you," Cat growled. "I was sleeping."

"And what was wrong with the bed I provided you?"

"Nothing, except it was too far away from Meg. I was doing what Ariane sent me here to do. Keeping watch over your daughter."

He frowned in astonishment, rendered momentarily speechless. Cat took advantage of his silence to snarl at Agatha. "And I am no papist."

"There, Mistress Butterydoor, you see—" Martin began, but Cat peered round him at the old woman, informing her with wicked relish.

"I was never baptized into any Christian faith. I follow the old ways, honoring only the good mother earth."

Cat's announcement sent both the old woman and the maid into fresh cries of horror. "A heathen! God save us all."

Martin clutched his head and groaned as Meg's bed-chamber door opened. Everyone froze as the girl took a tentative step into the corridor, her brow knit in consternation.

"Papa? What is everyone shouting about?"

"Nothing, Meggie." Martin glanced down and flushed, for the first time seeming to notice his half-clad state. "It is only a small domestic disturbance. Papa will deal with it. You—you just stay in your room."

He shooed Meg back into her chamber and closed the door, leaning up against it. As he did so, the neckline of his shirt pulled even farther open, revealing an expanse of hair-darkened chest.

Cat could not help staring, her gaze roving from that masculine chest on down to the taut calves and glimpse of muscular thigh. She realized she was not the only one gaping. Mistress Butterydoor gawked at her master, the little housemaid craning around the plump old woman for a better look.

Martin scowled and adjusted his shirt. He straightened away from the door with amazing dignity for a half-naked man being inspected by three women.

"Ladies, it is far too early in the morning for a man to be plagued with these hysterics. Maude, get back to your chores. Mistress Butterydoor, fetch Meg some bread and honey, and some hot water to bathe, now that you all have awakened the poor child.

"And *you*—" He leveled a dark look at Cat. "Come with me."

Without waiting to see that she complied, Martin strode toward the stairs. The chastened housemaid mopped her tearstained cheeks, and even the sullen Agatha prepared to obey.

Cat was the only one who bridled, unaccustomed to being ordered about by any man. But she felt chagrined to be caught by Martin in the midst of such a ridiculous fray. Scornfully flinging the broom down in front of the quaking housemaid, Cat followed Martin down the stairs.

She stalked after him as best she could in the overlarge boots, grumbling, "I may be many things, Wolfe. But I am no man's *domestic* disturbance."

"What you are is pure chaos. A disaster waiting to happen." Opening a door to the left of the stair, he jerked his head, indicating she should precede him inside.

Cat flounced past him into a small study, sparsely furnished, the walls dark with linenfold paneling. It was obviously where Martin had spent the rest of the night, a makeshift pallet of pillow and blankets piled before the hearth.

Martin closed the door and picked his way past the disordered pile of bedding to where he had abandoned his breeches.

Hopping upon one leg, he jammed the other into the dark woolen fabric. In all maidenly modesty, Cat supposed she should have averted her gaze. But it had been a long time since she had been a maiden.

She watched, obtaining a flash of flat hard buttocks as he eased the breeches over his hips. Only when he caught her staring at him did she reluctantly train her eyes elsewhere.

While Martin tucked his shirt around his privates and buttoned up the breeches, Cat studied the polished surface of the desk and the bookcase. The shelves were empty except for a few books that appeared to be gathering cobwebs. Cat hazarded a guess they had been left by the house's previous tenant. Martin didn't strike her as a man who gave himself over to study and quiet contemplation.

Curious about the titles of the abandoned books, Cat took a step in that direction, only to have her loose boot shift beneath her. She stumbled, nearly twisting her ankle.

"Damn!"

When Martin regarded her quizzically, she complained, "It's these bloody boots of yours. They are too big. I'd have been better off going barefoot."

"How remiss of me not to have my boots fashioned to

fit your dainty feet," he drawled. "Remind me to speak to my bootmaker about it."

He flung himself down in the chair behind his desk and proceeded to don his stockings. "Would you care to tell me what the devil you were doing raiding my wardrobe in the first place?"

"You left me little choice. Not after you made off with my clothes."

"I passed your things off to the laundry maid for washing and mending. If you had remained abed resting as you should have done, your lack of garb would not have been a problem. Er—would you mind?" He indicated another pair of boots lined up before the hearth, shabbier than the pair Cat had borrowed.

Cat gave him a disgruntled look, but stomped over to fetch them. As she lifted the well-worn boots, she noticed what appeared to be fresh mud caked on the heels. It was also splashed upon the hem of a cloak tossed carelessly over a stool. The same cloak he had worn when he had crept in to check upon Meg last night.

Cat frowned. The significance of Martin's attire should have struck her much sooner. He had gone out after tucking Meg in. But what reason would a man have for venturing abroad at such a late hour in a dangerous city like London? Gaming? Carousing? Wenching?

Cat could easily imagine Martin engaging in such pastimes but for one thing—the tender, protective way she had seen him hover over his daughter. A rogue he might be, but Cat doubted Martin would have risked leaving Meg at night unless he had a compelling reason. But what the devil could it be?

"Uh—Mistress O'Hanlon? Cat?"

Martin's voice jarred Cat from her contemplation of his boots. He addressed her, all silken politeness, "I am of course entirely at your leisure, milady. You may hand me the boots anytime you feel ready. But I beg you, before I age another day would be good.

"My sincerest thanks," he said when she plunked the boots down in front of him.

Cat scowled. "My chieftain did not send me here to act as your valet."

"Your chieftain?"

"Ariane. The lady honors me by considering me her gallowglass."

Martin choked, struggling to hide his grin. He chuckled as he worked on his boot.

Cat clenched her hands into fists. "One of these days, Wolfe, your tendency to laugh at me is going to get your skull broke."

"I wasn't laughing at you. Only at the notion of the Lady of Faire Isle, the epitome of peace and feminine grace, being anyone's chieftain and hiring an Irish mercenary."

"I already told you. I serve the Lady for love, not money. And it has been a long time since there was peace to be had for the Lady or anyone else. These are dangerous days."

"Yes, they are." Martin's smile faded. He finished donning his boots and then levered himself to his feet. "And in light of that, and as you appear to be fully recovered, you had best journey back to your chieftain with all haste."

"I have no plans to be going anywhere without you and the girl."

"I believe we settled this matter yesterday."

"All that we settled was how stubborn you are. Until you change your mind about taking Meg to Faire Isle, I am staying right here to protect her."

"Don't think I am not grateful for your offer or the pleasure of your company. I have not enjoyed myself this much since my last bout of dysentery, but I think it best if you sail on the next tide, Mistress O'Hanlon."

Cat folded her arms across her breasts. "No."

"No?" His smile was soft as his voice, but his eyes glittered as he rounded the desk, prowling toward her.

Cat braced her legs apart, digging in her heels. "Don't think to intimidate me. You tried that yesterday at the theater and you ended up on your arse with my sword at your throat. Oh, I suppose you could attempt to toss me out of your house and into the street. You and the half dozen other men you'd require. But I'll only come back, camp on your doorstep if I have to."

"God's death, woman, I would not treat a dog with such discourtesy, let alone a friend of the Lady of Faire Isle. But there is no necessity for you to remain here."

"Yes, there is if you persist with this folly of remaining in London. If the coven or the Dark Queen comes after Meg, you are going to need me. Who is there to help you look after her, that ignorant old woman with her cane? A housemaid with a broomstick? Whereas I, as you may have noticed, am a fair hand with a sword."

"More than fair," he surprised her by conceding.

"And I will guard your daughter as I would my own chieftain. I will defend Meg with my very life."

Martin peered intently into her eyes. Something softened in his features as he brushed his fingertips over the bruise upon her brow, the place still a little tender.

"By God, I believe that you would," he murmured. "But that is hardly to the point. You have not been beneath my roof for twenty-four hours and you've already set my household into an uproar, to say nothing of the fact that you're wearing my breeches."

"So send one of your servants to the Fighting Cock Inn to fetch my things. Then I'll have my own breeches."

"Actually, I sent Jem to do that yesterday evening." Something about the way Martin avoided her gaze made Cat uneasy.

"Then where is my saddlebag?"

Martin grimaced and confessed, "Your belongings are gone."

"What!" Cat's heart lurched. "What the devil do you mean *gone*?"

"Someone appears to have made off with them."

"Everything?"

"I am afraid so."

"All my clothes? My jerkin and breeches and—and my boots?" Cat paced up and down, her anger and dismay increasing with every step. "My saddlebag and all of my coin? Except for what I took to pay my fare into the theater, I left the rest hidden inside my stocking."

"That was hardly the best idea."

"It seemed far safer than carrying it on me and running the risk of footpads or—or pickpockets."

"Safer at the Fighting Cock?" Martin rolled his eyes. "It is not exactly the most reputable establishment."

"Where else in hell do you think I could stay? The better places would never welcome a woman traveling alone with no husband or maid. Especially an Irishwoman. I am fortunate I didn't have to bed down with swine.

"But I would have been better off with the pigs," she raged. "How I hate this damned country. 'Tis peopled by no one except villains and thieves."

Storming by Martin, she punctuated her words with fierce gestures.

He reared back to avoid being flailed by her fists. "You have no thieves in Ireland?"

"Yes," Cat snapped. "The goddamned English."

She took another furious turn about the room, realizing that she was carrying on like a lunatic. But it was easier to give vent to her anger than think about the one beloved object among her missing belongings, the one thing she could not bear to lose.

When her rage finally burned itself out, she sank down despondently upon a wooden stool, her fists balled in her lap. Martin hunkered down in front of her.

"I am sorry," he said gravely. "So what did you lose that is of such great value?"

"Nothing. What makes you think—"

"Because you don't strike me as the sort of woman to weep over lost clothes or a pocketful of coin."

"I am not weeping!" But to her horror, Cat felt her eyes prickle. She twisted her head away from him, but he caught her chin, forcing her to meet his gaze.

His eyes were far too sympathetic. It had been a long time since any man had looked at her thus.

"Tell me what you lost. I'll get you another."

"You c-can't." She thrust his hand away from her face.

But he persisted, curling his fingers over her fist, coaxing her with the softness of his eyes, the kindness of his smile.

"It was nothing. I am merely being stupid, fretting over the loss of an old leather jack that I keep filled with usquebaugh."

"You are grieving over the loss of your *whiskey*?"

"Not the whiskey, damn it." Cat swallowed hard. "But the flask . . . it belonged to my da. It—it was all I had left that was his."

Martin pressed her hand. "You still have your memories and for that I envy you. I have no idea who my father was. I am the illegitimate offspring of a Parisian whore."

"Bah, there is no such thing as *illegitimate*. Not in Ireland." She added sadly, "At least not in the Ireland I once knew. Under the old Brehon law, everyone is considered legitimate because we are all born with souls. It has nothing to do with our parents being married."

"What a fine and sensible law," he remarked wistfully. "Unfortunately, there is nothing I can do about your father's flask. But I can buy you clothes—a new gown, shoes, stockings, corsets, anything you need."

"You'll do no such thing!" Cat cried, drawing her hand away. She felt mortified enough to have nearly dissolved into tears in front of Martin without compounding her humiliation by accepting his charity. She leapt up from the stool.

"Your pardon. I don't mean to seem ungracious, but I have never yet been reduced to accepting gifts from any man as though I were his—his mistress."

"My mistress? Hardly!" Martin straightened to his feet. "No, consider the new gown as—as merely a courtesy to a friend of Ariane's. And besides," he smiled. "At some point, I would like my breeches back."

"Fine. You can have them now. And the shirt as well." Her lips thinning into an obstinate line, she started to undo the ties at her neckline.

Martin seized her hand to stop her. Looking torn between vexation and amusement, he demanded, "Are you always this infernally proud and stubborn? Be reasonable, Cat. Even if your clothes hadn't been stolen, you can't tramp about London in boots and breeches. This isn't Faire Isle. Some Puritan preacher would have you arrested for indecency. Whether you like it or not, I have to furnish you with a proper gown—"

"Indeed you won't," Cat said, pulling indignantly away from him. "I have a gown. As soon as your laundress sees fit to return it to me."

"That shabby thing. I wouldn't rub down my horse with it. If you insist upon remaining here and being part of my household, you must be respectably attired."

"A plague upon your respectability." Cat jabbed her finger against his chest. "Let me make one thing plain, le Loup. I won't be part of your household. I am not here in your service, but to protect Meg. And I will be the one to decide what I wear. I have never—"

She gasped as he seized her shoulders and stopped her mouth with a hard kiss. His lips were warm and rough, sending a shaft of heat through her.

Cat sprang back as though she'd been scalded, for a moment unable to catch her breath, let alone speak.

Martin likewise leapt back, looking stunned by his own action.

"What—what the devil did you do that for?" Cat demanded.

"I—I am damned if I know," he blustered. "It was your fault. Always arguing about everything. You drive me to distraction. It was the only way I could think of to get you to shut your mouth."

He expelled a loud gust of breath. "Besides, it was nothing, merely an—an English custom. Men here often buss women by way of—of friendly greeting."

"Well, I am not English and neither are you. So you had best be remembering that." Cat wiped her mouth on her sleeve. "Try that again while I am here and your friendly lips will be too swollen to be *bussing* anyone."

"Don't fret yourself, mademoiselle. I'd sooner kiss a hedgehog. They are a good deal less prickly." Martin glowered. "And I never agreed you could stay."

"If I had asked for your agreement, I'd be sore troubled about that."

Cat would have liked to have raised her eyebrow after his own cool fashion, but the best she could manage was a proud toss of her head as she strode to the door. But her dignified exit was marred by those damned large boots causing her to trip again.

Swearing after a fashion that would have blistered a sailor's ears, Cat stormed from the study, slamming the door behind her.

Martin stood stock-still for a moment, uncertain whether he wanted to roar with laughter or bang his head against the wall.

He sagged down into the chair behind his desk, rubbing eyes that still felt bleary from being rudely jarred awake. Not that he had gotten much sleep after his meeting with Walsingham last night. He had tossed and turned for hours, cursing the day he'd ever let himself be caught up in all this damned English intrigue.

It had seemed like such a golden opportunity when he had first agreed to work for Sir Francis. Just acting as a courier, delivering messages, picking up a little gossip here, acquiring a little information there. Nothing too dangerous.

He had never expected to find himself entangled in plots to assassinate one queen, intrigues to entrap another, and, worst of all, obliged to spy upon people whom he liked and felt indebted to.

As if that was not complication enough, now he had this firebrand Irishwoman to deal with. God knows what had ever impelled him to kiss her. He preferred his women soft and gentle, with figures that were tall, willowy, and graceful like Miri's. Catriona O'Hanlon was such a tough, fierce little thing.

Martin's lips curled in a mischievous smile. It might be worth kissing her again just to see the sparks fly from her eyes. They were like twin blue flames. But a man who was sitting on a powder keg had no business lighting fuses.

Martin dragged his hand wearily over his beard. He was beginning to feel like an acrobat he had once seen juggle knives at a fair in Paris. One blink, one misstep on his part could spell disaster.

If anything were to happen to Martin, mayhap it would be a good thing to have Cat here, someone strong and resourceful enough to look out for Meg. Martin had no doubt that Cat was all of that, no matter how much the woman exasperated him.

He had been strangely moved to discover that Cat had spent the night curled up in front of Meg's door. Bruised from the blow she had received yesterday, it had to have been damned difficult for Cat to drag herself from a comfortable bed and keep vigil on a hard floor.

Nor could he forget the intent look in Cat's eyes when she had declared, *"I will defend Meg with my very life."*

Martin had swaggered enough in his youth to know the difference between a boast and a genuine vow. Cat had meant what she said. She would die to protect his daughter, just as he would.

If only he and Cat could refrain from killing each other, perhaps it would be a wise decision to allow her to stay.

Allow her? Martin pulled a wry face, wondering when the last time was that any man had ever *allowed* Catriona O'Hanlon to do anything. Likely never.

It seemed that Meg had acquired herself a gallowglass.

Chapter Six

CAT LACED UP THE BODICE OF HER NEWLY LAUNDERED GOWN and gasped at the sharp prick against the tender skin of her breast. Swearing under her breath, she delved inside the woolen fabric and drew forth a pin left by whoever had mended the gown.

Another *accident,* she would no doubt be assured if she complained. Just as her portion of the pork served at the noontime meal had been accidentally oversalted and burned. Or her cup of ale had a crack in it and nearly leaked all over her.

She seemed to be having an extraordinary run of bad luck today, Cat thought wryly. Ever since Martin had announced to his household that Cat would be staying with them for an indefinite period of time, and she was to be accorded every respect.

Agatha Butterydoor had received the command in fuming silence, biting her lower lip nearly raw. The old woman had been waging covert war ever since. And she had the rest of the household from the maids to the kitchen boy ranged on her side.

Ah well, let them do their worst, Cat thought with a shrug. The only one who concerned her was Meg. The girl had not spoken a word to Cat since she had learned that Cat was not leaving. Meg had merely stared, her eyes wary, obviously not welcoming the presence of someone privy to her secrets. This made Cat wonder what other secrets Meg might be harboring. Cat was determined to protect the girl, even if that meant protecting young Mistress Margaret from herself.

As Cat finished lacing up her gown, a soft breeze wafted through the open window of the small maids' room where she was changing. Voices carried from the back of the house, one of them Meg's. Cat strolled to the window and peered into the garden below.

Enclosed by a high brick wall, it was a small plot of land containing a modest vegetable and herb garden, a pair of apple trees, an apiary, and a rabbit hutch. The Butterydoor woman knelt picking turnips while Meg sat nearby, her legs dangling off a stone bench. The girl presented the picture of a quaint little gentlewoman, clad in a pink silk gown with a starched white ruff encircling her slender throat, her soft brown hair smoothed back beneath a bon grace cap.

She leaned forward a little, listening intently as the old woman regaled her with some tale.

". . . and I entered the bedchamber where the poor man was laid out, all stiff and cold. His eyes were wide and staring straight at me, his face twisted into a terrible rictus as though he'd been snuffed out in the middle of a horrible scream.

"Yet when I examined him, I could find no sign of any disease or injury. But it was clear to me what had killed him, as obvious as the nose on your face, Mistress Meg."

"What, Aggie?" Meg asked breathlessly. "What killed him?"

The old woman lifted her trowel and pronounced in sepulchral tones. "He died of an evil thought."

Cat expected that Meg would shake her head at such nonsense, but there was still too much of the child in her. She shrank back, her face blanching so white, she looked as though she might be ill.

Rot that garrulous old fool to be filling the girl's head with such horrors, Cat thought. Her mouth set in a grim line, she marched off to put a stop to it.

As Cat hastened down the stairs, she tiptoed past the closed door of Martin's study, then stopped. Assuming her regular stride, she berated herself for a fool. She had no notion if Martin was even in the study and she could hardly avoid the man forever, not if she was going to be living in the same house.

But that was exactly what she had been trying to do all day and she well knew the reason for it. That blasted kiss. The realization made her so disgusted with herself, she stomped the rest of the way through the hall.

It wasn't as though she were some innocent maiden to get all flustered over a stolen kiss. The embrace had meant no more to her than it had to him. For her, it had been merely an irritation, not all that good . . .

Cat's mouth twisted ruefully as she headed toward the back of the house. No, in all honesty she had to admit, the kiss had stirred in her a sweet ache, a flood of memories.

It had been such a long time since she had experienced such intimate contact. The last man she had kissed was that Irish rebel she had helped hide from the English. Banished from her stepfather's clan, Cat had been living a rough existence herself, hiding and hunting in the Wicklow Mountains.

What had that rebel's name been? Ciernan? Conner? They had spent an entire night taking comfort in each other's arms before going their separate ways at sunrise. It saddened Cat that she could not remember his name or even his face.

But she could remember how he had made her feel, passionate, alive, reassured that she was a woman still despite her rough woolen breeches and calloused hands. If only for one night.

She sighed. Martin's fleeting kiss had reminded her that at seven and twenty, she was not an old woman yet. She still had the need for a man's touch, desires that as a daughter of the earth she knew were perfectly natural.

Desires she would not be indulging anytime soon and certainly not with a rogue the likes of Martin le Loup. But damn the man! He could be disconcertingly kind and gentle when she least expected it.

His expressive eyes had been warm with sympathy when she had grieved over her stolen things, nearly blubbering like an idiot over the loss of her da's flask. The memory of that embarrassed Cat far more than the kiss.

It had been nothing but a cheap leather jack, but to Cat, it had felt like one more piece of her past slipping away from her, and she had lost so much already.

Still, it was not the way of Catriona O'Hanlon to go all weepy in front of any man. Le Loup and his sympathetic eyes be damned. She'd not be letting him past her guard again.

By the time Cat emerged from the kitchen door, Meg was nowhere in sight. Only Agatha remained, kneeling over the vegetable plot. She paused long enough to give Cat a baleful glance before returning to her labors, shaking the dirt off a large turnip she had just plucked.

Cat strode over to her, skirting past the basket Agatha was filling and a small wooden cage occupied by a plump, speckled toad.

Cat nudged the cage with the toe of her shoe. "If you are planning to slip that between my sheets, I should warn you you'll be wasting your time. I've had far worse in my bed."

"I don't doubt it." Agatha gave a scornful sniff. "I have more important uses for that toad than frightening you, mistress. My cabbages are full of grubs."

"And you expect to get rid of them with a *toad*?"

The old woman looked up at Cat and shook her head in disgusted disbelief. "Do you receive no education over there in Ireland? Everyone knows the best way to get rid of grubs is to tie a string around a toad and drag it around the garden three times forward, three times back."

When Cat snorted a laugh, Agatha glowered. "Find that amusing, do you? You don't believe it works?"

"I believe you'll succeed in annoying the toad just fine and I daresay the grubs may find it entertaining."

"That shows all you know," Agatha muttered. "And an ignorant wench like you thinks to replace me, looking after my little poppet, trying to win her favor away from *me*." She forcefully yanked up another turnip.

"I am not trying to win Meg's favor from anyone."

"You're plotting something nasty, of that I am sure. You may have fooled master, but you haven't fooled me." Agatha shook her spade threateningly. "But I warn you. I have my eye on you, wench."

"You'd do better to keep your eye on young mistress, which is what I plan to do. Believe it or not, we have the same interest, Mistress Butterydoor, and that is Meg's safety."

"No one could care for the young mistress better than I do."

"Then you might show some sign of that caring and not terrify the girl with tales of dead men who died of evil thoughts."

"You were spying on me?" The old woman cried, her chin wobbling with indignation. "What passes between me and Mistress Meg is none of your concern."

"Everything to do with Meg concerns me." Cat hunched down, draping her arm across her knee. "I won't tolerate you or anyone else frightening her."

"As if I would! Mistress Meg is right fond of hearing tales of my days as a searcher of the dead."

"A *what*?"

"A searcher of the dead." Agatha lifted her head proudly. "Before I came to Master Wolfe's employ, I was a woman of some importance here in Cheapside. It was my duty to examine anyone who died and report on the cause. The parish paid me two pennies a body."

Cat was hard-pressed to believe the foolish old woman could have been of much use at such an occupation. Unless she had seriously underestimated Agatha and she was more of a wise woman than Cat would have ever supposed.

Or more of a witch. Cat studied the old woman intently. Was it possible she had been gulled into overlooking a threat to Meg that was right under her very nose? Cat's gaze traveled over the old woman. She wore an apron to protect her dark woolen gown, but she had not bothered to shove back her sleeves. A curious thing, considering the warmth of the afternoon and the fact that the woman was grubbing in the dirt.

"Roll up your sleeves," Cat commanded.

"What?" Agatha scowled.

"You heard me. I have already checked the housemaids' arms. Now I want to see yours. Roll up your sleeves."

"I'll do no such thing."

Cat did not wait for her compliance. She tried to shove back the fabric on Agatha's right arm. But the woman fought back like a tigress, slapping, punching, and scratching until they both tumbled into the cabbage patch. Cat landed half on top of the fierce old woman.

"Get off. Get off, you mad heathen," she shrieked, pummeling Cat with both fists.

Cat persisted until she had thrust back one sleeve and then the other, exposing . . .

Nothing. No scar burned in the shape of a rose, only pale flaccid skin.

Agatha was nearly weeping with outrage, her withered cheeks mottled bright red. Cat drew back.

"I am sorry, Mistress Butterydoor," she apologized. "But I had to be sure—"

"How dare you suspect me of being one of those evil creatures!" the old woman cried. "Me who has been Mistress Meg's most devoted nursemaid for all these m-months."

Agatha groped for her cane. Cat sprang up to help her but the old woman smacked her hands away. Somehow Agatha managed to get to her feet.

"Irish savage," she choked.

"Mistress Butterydoor. Please, I truly am—" Cat broke off with a sharp intake of breath when the old woman thwacked her in the shin.

Gathering up her basket and her toad, Agatha hobbled toward the house, vanishing through the kitchen door. Cat watched her go, pricked with guilt, feeling like a wretched bully.

She might argue it was her duty as Meg's protector to scrutinize every woman who came near the girl. But she could have handled her suspicions a trifle more diplomatically and gently.

She winced and bent down to rub her throbbing shin. She was going to have another spectacular bruise thanks to Mistress Butterydoor, but this time she deserved it.

She reminded herself that she wasn't here to win friends or spare anyone's feelings, but she sank down on the bench, despondent all the same. The light was fading. It would soon be time for supper and Cat was not looking forward to another burnt meal with the rest of the household drawing away from her as though she were afflicted with leprosy.

She shrugged, telling herself it didn't matter. She had endured far worse in her stepfather's house, the haughty O'Meara clan full of nothing but scorn for the "dirty little O' Hanlon pagan."

Cat had survived snubs and taunts, to say nothing of her stepfather's frequent thrashings. But what had hurt the most had been her mother's indifference to her daughter's misery.

"You would get on much better if only you would try to be more pleasing, Catriona," Fiona had scolded. "Act like a proper young lady, instead of some half-wild savage. Agree to be baptized in the holy Catholic faith."

"But my father was never baptized," Cat had protested. "Most of the O'Hanlons follow the old ways and you never seemed to mind it when we still lived with Da in Gran's cottage."

"Your father is dead and that life is well behind me now."

And as she had looked in her mother's cold eyes, Cat had realized that Fiona had already forgotten her great love for Tiernan of the Laughing Eyes and that she would have liked to forget the daughter she had got by him as well.

Cat was annoyed that the memory of those childhood days had the power to wound her still. She shook off the hurt, telling herself she was only the tougher for all the cruelty she'd endured amongst the O'Mearas. Too tough to be daunted by the snubs of a few puny English.

And it was a fair summer's eve, the sun spreading its

last golden light over the garden, a fat bee setting up a pleasant drone near the clover, wrens chirruping in the apple tree.

She thought wistfully that right about now she should be with Ariane and Justice in the garden at Belle Haven, sipping wine, watching the sun go down. Cat had felt set adrift ever since her father had died and she had been torn away from her beloved grandmother. But at least with Ariane and the other wise women of Faire Isle, Cat had experienced some sense of belonging. A borrowed home and a borrowed clan perhaps, but she expected that it was all she would ever know.

She wrapped her arms about herself, suddenly feeling isolated and alone.

᛭᛭᛭

MARTIN STRODE THROUGH THE KITCHEN, STRUGGLING TO fasten his fashionable new cloak to the shoulder of his doublet. Jem looked up from turning a haunch of venison upon a spit and Maude left off cutting up turnips to gape at him.

But Martin was feeling far too harried to spare a jocular word for his servants as was his usual custom. He was already running late, readying himself for the banquet at Strand House this evening. Having to take time to soothe Agatha's ruffled feathers certainly hadn't helped matters.

Anticipating another fiery confrontation with Cat as well, he felt as though he would like to stitch both women into sacks and consign them to the next ship embarking for the New World.

As he stalked into the garden, he expected to find Cat ready to square off after her usual belligerent fashion. He was surprised to see her slumped down upon the bench, her chin propped on her hand.

At least she had obeyed his command to surrender his breeches. But her appearance was decidedly dejected and her worn-out horror of a frock was much to blame. Mon Dieu, but he would like to strip that rag off her back and burn it.

Martin sucked in his breath and checked the wayward thought, the notion fraught with the memory of what lay beneath Cat's frayed bodice, that soft white breast with its delectable rosy crest. Scarcely an appropriate thought to be entertained by a man striving to be more respectable.

Besides, it was more than that miserable gown making Cat appear forlorn. She had attempted to fasten her hair back with a leather thong, but strands had escaped to straggle about a face pale with melancholy, her eyes dark blue wells of sadness. Absorbed by her own unhappy thoughts, she did not even notice Martin's approach.

Cat was such a ferociously proud woman. It tugged at Martin in some way he could not explain to see her looking so lost and vulnerable. His vexation forgotten, he experienced a strange urge to draw her onto his knee and croon, *"What troubles you, cherie?"* An action that would likely earn him a swift clout to the ear. He contented himself with lightly touching her shoulder.

"Mistress O'Hanlon? Cat?"

Cat started at the sound of Martin's voice. Jarred out of her unhappy musing, she glanced up and nearly tumbled off the bench at the sight before her.

The late afternoon sun struck full upon him, bathing

him in a golden blaze that made him seem far too handsome to be real, like a hero from one of his plays, some
great and noble lord.

He was clad in a scarlet doublet with slashed sleeves
and matching trunk hose, a short dark cape swirling off
one shoulder. A black toque sporting a white feather was
perched on his head at a rakish angle. His taut muscular
legs were encased in ivory hose, shoes with silver buckles
upon his feet.

He was the epitome of the charming prince in fairy stories and she was gawking at him like a beggar maid. Cat
staggered to her feet, conscious of her disheveled condition from her recent tussle with Agatha in the cabbage
patch.

She tried to brush the dirt from her skirts, her mortifi-
cation complete when Martin plucked a stray leaf from her
hair.

"Ah, I see that another epic battle has taken place."

Cat flushed hotly. Smoothing her hair back, she squared
her shoulders. "I suppose Mistress Butterydoor has been
talking to you."

"At great length," Martin sighed. "Cat, I appreciate
your zeal in wanting to protect Meg, but if you had any
doubts about Aggie, you should have come to me. Do you
really think I would not have thoroughly checked anyone I
engaged to look after my daughter?"

"I am sorry. I—I made a mistake. But the woman
roused my suspicion by refusing to let me see her arm and
all her strange talk about having been a seer of the dead."

"A seer?" Martin appeared puzzled, but then his brow

cleared. "Oh, a *searcher* of the dead. Has Aggie been boasting about that again?"

He smiled and shook his head. "The parishes of London regularly hire old women to examine corpses and report the cause of death. It's a service no one else wants to perform for fear of contagion. The local officials don't even particularly care how skilled or educated these searchers are. Poor and desperate seem to be the only requirements."

Cat nodded, but she was having difficulty focusing on what he was saying. She found herself distracted by the pearl that dangled from Martin's left ear. A fashion that might have appeared effeminate on another man, but only offset Martin's darkly masculine looks, giving him a piratical appearance.

". . . and I realize Agatha can be a cantankerous old wench. But she is devoted to Meg and she hasn't exactly had the easiest life, beginning with the day she was born. She was abandoned by the buttery door of Christ's Hospital."

Cat blinked, dragging her fascinated gaze from the earring. "Oh. Buttery door. That would explain the oddity of her name."

"Charity institutions don't show a great deal of imagination when naming orphans."

"So that would mean what? That you were found amidst a pack of wolves?"

He laughed. "No, the priest who baptized me didn't trouble to give me a surname. I was merely christened Martin after the saint. When I was old enough, I dubbed myself le Loup, and as soon as the good fathers realized there was more of the wolf than the saint about me, they were glad to see the back of me. The streets of Paris became my home."

Cat had thought parts of her own childhood unbearable, but at least she'd had the memory of her father, of being part of the Clan O'Hanlon. She could not imagine what it must have been like for Martin growing up alone, no claim to any kin.

"That—that must have been a very perilous existence," Cat observed almost shyly.

"I survived. But perhaps that is why I feel a certain kinship with Mistress Butterydoor. Both of us orphans, never knowing any father or mother."

"It is possible to feel orphaned and still have a mother—" Cat broke off uncomfortably.

"Your mother is still living?" Martin asked so gently that Cat nodded.

"But like your priests, my mother was quite happy to be shed of me. I think she wished I had never been born." Cat attempted to shrug as though it were of no great matter. Once more she had been beguiled into revealing too much of herself. She was relieved when the door to the kitchen flew open and Meg burst out into the garden.

Meg lifted the hem of her gown and raced breathlessly to her father. "Papa! You are still here. I was afraid I had missed you and I so wanted to see you in your new clothes before you left for the banquet."

Martin grinned and turned about for his daughter's benefit.

Meg clapped her hands together with a delighted sigh. She started to touch the hem of his cloak only to draw back as though fearful of marring his finery.

"Oh, you look so handsome and—and very grand."

"Humph! I'd rather be in rags if the prettiest girl in England refuses to embrace her poor old father for fear of creasing his doublet."

He bent down to her level, holding wide his arms.

"Papa! What nonsense you talk," Meg said, but she dimpled and flung her arms about his neck.

Martin's roguish gaze softened as he kissed his daughter's cheek. Meg's eyes glowing with adoration, her grave face transformed until she truly was pretty.

Watching the two of them, Cat shifted her feet awkwardly, feeling like an intruder and at the same time oddly wistful.

Meg drew back, smoothing out his sleeve and giving it a small pat. "So you are off to dine with Lord Oxbridge. And the queen—she will be there?"

"So I am told."

"The queen?" Cat let out a low whistle of surprise. "You are after keeping some grand company, Master Wolfe."

Her wariness of Cat momentarily forgotten, Meg beamed up at her. "My father has many important friends, particularly the Baron of Oxbridge, who is greatly indebted to him. Papa saved the life of his lordship's sister, Lady Danvers. He is quite the hero."

"Now who is talking nonsense?" Martin playfully pinched his daughter's nose.

Meg made an impish face at him, then rushed on, "When you return, you must tell me everything about the queen. What her gown and jewels were like, what she eats, what she says to you, and—"

Martin interrupted her with a laugh. "Despite your exalted opinion of your father, I will be of little significance among such noble company. I will be seated well below the salt and go quite unnoticed by the queen or anyone else."

Cat doubted that. She could not imagine Martin le Loup ever going unnoticed anywhere, but Meg looked crestfallen for a moment. She angled a speculative glance at her father.

"Well, I have been thinking . . ."

"That sounds dangerous," Martin teased.

Meg gave him a dignified frown and continued. "Why could I not see the queen for myself? Agatha could take me down by the river so I could see her barge arriving and—."

But Martin was already shaking his head. "No, mon ange. We've already discussed this. There will be no more of these jaunts about town with Agatha, especially not in light of the Lady of Faire Isle's warnings."

"I suppose *she* might come and bring her sword." Meg stole a shy glance at Cat. "Being a visitor to London, I daresay Mistress O'Hanlon would like to see the queen as well."

"I daresay *she* wouldn't," Cat said. "I'd hardly risk taking you abroad with night about to fall just to catch a glimpse of that Tudor she-devil."

Meg gave an affronted gasp. "That is no way to speak of your sovereign queen."

"Yours perhaps, but not mine, sweetling. Elizabeth and her cursed governors have inflicted nothing but misery upon my country, thieving, burning, and killing."

"Well, the queen would not have to be so harsh if—if you Irish were not always rebelling."

"Ah, so it is rebellion now to try to protect your home from invasion and hold onto what is yours?"

Meg compressed her lips, clearly having no answer for that. "Very well. Don't come then if you feel that way. I am sure Aggie would not wish to have you along, anyway." Turning her back on Cat, she appealed to her father, "I am sure Aggie and I would be safe enough if—."

"No, Meg," Martin said. "Cat is right. You should not be leaving the house this near to nightfall. You may see the queen another time."

"You have been promising me that ever and forever!" Meg cried. "I don't see why I can't—"

"Because I said no, Margaret, and there's an end to the matter."

Cat doubted that Martin had ever spoken so sternly or refused his daughter anything. Meg looked stricken, her lower lip quivering. She spun on her heel and dashed toward the house.

Martin made no effort to stop her, but he vented a regretful sigh as Meg vanished inside.

"I am sorry," Cat said. "I didn't mean to upset Meg, but it is nigh impossible for me to hold my tongue whenever that Tudor woman's name is spoken."

"It is all right. I understand, and it is more my fault than yours. For some reason, the child has conceived a strange fascination with the queen of England. I did promise Meg that somehow I would arrange for her to see Elizabeth. But it is a promise I never should have given. I don't want Margaret to draw any undue attention to herself until—until—"

"You have succeeded in burying her past and turning

her into a proper Englishwoman? You seem well on the way to achieving that."

Martin must have sensed the disapproval in her voice. He stiffened. "Meg has always been more English than French. She spent the first five years of her childhood in a cottage near the sea in Dover. She still speaks of it. I believe that despite her mother, Meg was happier during those days than—" Martin paused, then finished bleakly. "Than she is here with me. My little girl really doesn't care much for city life."

That would be the daughter of the earth in her, Cat thought, but she wisely kept the observation to herself.

"Someday if all goes well, I mean to buy a small parcel of land and a manor somewhere along the southern coast," Martin said, a hard determined light in his eyes. "But my fortunes may well be lost on the tide if I don't hie me off to Strand House and be about my business."

"Business?" Cat's gaze drifted over his finery. "You look more like a man about to go a-wooing."

It was none of her concern, but she couldn't refrain from asking, "So, is she very fair? This Lady Jane Danvers who fancies you such a hero?"

"Oh, quite fair, hair like goldenrod, the eyes of a dove, but as to my being her hero . . ." Martin's lips twisted wryly. "I fear that I rescued the lady as much for my daughter's sake as her own."

When Cat gave him a puzzled look, he explained, "Jane Danvers fell off her brother's barge into the river. Meg and I were passing by in a wherry at the time and you cannot imagine the horror in my daughter's eyes. That is how Meg's mother died, drowning in the Seine."

"I know. Ariane told me."

"And Meg witnessed it. She used to have such terrible nightmares about Cassandra's death. Watching Lady Danvers drown would have been more than Meg could bear. So I was obliged to rescue the lady."

"And if Meg had not been there, you would have let Lady Danvers drown," Cat challenged.

"The Thames is full of currents and can be very treacherous. I don't know if I would have taken the risk."

"I do. You strike me as exactly the sort of chivalrous fool unable to resist a damsel in distress. I am sure this Lady Danvers must be brimming over with gratitude, ready to fall into your arms."

"Hardly. She is a gentle and noble lady, as far above me as the stars in the heaven." Whether the man realized it or not, his voice took on a softer note as he spoke of the lady.

Mother Earth defend him, Cat thought. Martin had found himself another Miri Cheney and would likely end with his heart just as broken. The sisters of barons were not noted for surrendering their hands to nameless rogues, no matter how handsome.

Arching one brow, Martin regarded her quizzically. "You, of course, would never have need of being rescued."

"Hah. I'd be more likely to have to rescue you. I prefer to fight my own battles," Cat grimaced. "And speaking of which, I suppose I'd best *hie* myself off to the kitchen lest I end up being served roast toad for my supper."

As Cat headed for the house, Martin fell into step beside her. "I suspect that my household has been giving you a difficult time. I will speak to them all again, making it clear to everyone, including Meg, that when I am absent, your authority is absolute. Anyone questioning your orders will answer to me."

"That will really endear me to everyone. I'd prefer to handle things my own way, but I promise I'll do it without breaking heads. And as for Meg, she will be safe while you are gone, so don't worry."

"Strangely enough, I am not. For some reason I can't begin to fathom, you inspire confidence, Catriona O'Hanlon." He stopped just short of the kitchen door and gazed at her, his eyes warming.

He took her hand. Cat was so surprised by the unexpected gesture she let him.

"I know nothing of your mother, so I can't presume to speak of her feelings. But as for myself, I am glad that you are here."

Damned if the man didn't sound as though he meant it. Perhaps that was why Cat was unable to snatch her fingers away. He carried her hand to his lips, saluting it as though she were some great lady and not a dispossessed Irishwoman in a worn frock.

The brush of his lips was light, but her skin tingled. He flashed her a smile that set her heart to racing.

Cat was disconcerted to realize she was blushing. Ah, the rogue had charm in abundance, she was obliged to concede that much. If he smiled at his Lady Danvers in that way, belike he would win the woman's heart.

This was nothing in the least to do with her, Cat told herself fiercely. But she was hard-pressed to explain why the thought gave her such a pang.

Chapter Seven

MARTIN LEANED BACK IN THE BOAT, WHILE THE WHERRY-
man plied his oars, cutting through the murky waters of
the Thames. The river was by far the fastest way of moving
through the city, the streets too dirty and narrow, jammed
with carts, horses, and pedestrians.

But tonight the Thames was heavy with traffic, the river
teeming with boats and barges sporting their square sails.
Even at this hour, the docks were a forest of masts, cargo
still being unloaded—wine, timber, herring, and wool. The
evening reverberated with the sound of rough English
voices, laughing, swearing, singing, and arguing, and the
perpetual cries of the boatmen soliciting customers.

"Westward ho! Eastward ho!"

The bustle, the noise, and the dank smell of river life were all familiar to Martin from the days of his youth. If he closed his eyes he could almost imagine himself back on the banks of the Seine. Londoners were a hardheaded, insular lot, contentious and suspicious of any foreigners, which meant anyone who hadn't been born in the city. Although Martin did not despise the English as much as Cat did, he missed the lyrical voices of his own countrymen, the fine wine to be had in the taverns, the passion and verve for life that was Paris.

He was seized by a rare sense of longing for his native soil and did his best to shake it off. Shielding his eyes from the last glare of sunset, he watched the rays streak the water with a red glow, as fiery as Catriona O'Hanlon's hair.

An involuntary smile touched his lips at the thought of the fierce Irishwoman. Despite his final stern admonitions to his servants regarding Cat, he had sensed their simmering resentment. But he had no doubt Cat would be able to hold her own, and more important, she would keep Meg safe.

A comforting thought, the only one that gave him any ease of mind about this evening. He tensed as the boat neared that part of the city where palatial houses loomed above the Thames, their lawns and gardens stretching down to the water. The kind of grand homes where Martin would not even have been able to press his nose against the windowpanes during his youth, for fear of having the dogs set upon him.

He had risen far in the world to be attending a banquet at Strand House as an invited guest. But the satisfaction that he should have felt was marred by the sobering realization of his true purpose tonight, not as a guest, but as Walsingham's spy.

There was to be a fine supper, music, dancing, a play presented by the Crown Theatre's company, and fireworks, all in honor of the queen. Ned Lambert had gone to no little expense, arranging all of this entertainment, but Martin would be able to enjoy none of it.

He would spend the evening on tenterhooks, feeling like a treacherous bastard himself as he awaited his opportunity to steal away from the festivities and search the house. But search for what? Evidence of treason that he was certain was not there to be found.

He wondered, in frustration, how he could ever convince Walsingham that Lord Oxbridge had no part in any of these plots swirling about Queen Elizabeth. It was so much easier to offer proof of a man's guilt than his innocence.

Resting his elbow upon his knee, Martin propped his chin glumly on his hand as the boatmen steered the wherry toward the landing below Strand House. It was a massive stone manor with a wealth of diamond-paned windows. Windows that appeared, for the most part, strangely dark for a house hosting a vast gathering. Nor did there appear to be much activity along the path or in the gardens leading up to the manor.

Martin frowned, sitting bolt upright. He feared he might be a trifle late, but there should have been some sign of other guests arriving. As he gazed up at the silent house, his gut clenched with the sense that something was very wrong.

He scarce gave the boatman time to make the dock before climbing out of the wherry. Tossing a coin to the man, Martin headed away from the landing. The shrubs, the towering oak trees, and the tidy borders of the elaborate knot garden were lost in shadow as darkness descended.

But a torch flickered on the path ahead. A small group of men marched down from the house. Martin stepped beneath the shelter of a tree until he ascertained who they were. Their modest attire along with the viols and lutes they toted marked them as the musicians engaged to play for the fete. They were closely followed by a young lady in a silk gown draped over a farthingale.

No, not a lady. Martin recognized the familiar boyish stride of Alexander Naismith, the youthful actor who assumed the role of the female leads at the Crown. As he came down the path, Alexander hiked up his skirts, revealing the breeches he wore beneath.

As the musicians streamed past Martin's place of concealment, he stepped out of the shadows and caught Alexander by the arm. The boy started a little at Martin's sudden appearance.

"Master Wolfe."

"What's amiss, Sander? What's happened?"

"Not our performance, that's for certain," the boy replied in disgruntled tones. Although nearly sixteen, his face was still smooth from lack of beard and his voice had a high pitch. His heavily rouged cheeks looked even more garish as he stripped off his black curling wig.

Sander's own chin-length blond hair had been pinned up out of the way, revealing an ugly stump where his left ear should have been. The boy was usually self-conscious about the deformity, taking great pains to conceal it, but at the moment he seemed too vexed to care.

"Everything's off, the banquet, the entertainment, the fireworks, all because our most gracious sovereign has declined to put in an appearance. At the last moment, the queen sent her regrets. I don't know why."

But Martin did. Walsingham. The secretary must have managed to sway the queen and convince her not to attend.

"His lordship must be extremely disappointed," Martin mused.

"Disappointed?" Sander gave a shrill laugh. "Mad with rage would be a better description. He threw a bloody tantrum, overturning the banquet table, hurling stools, bellowing at all the guests to get out. Poor Lady Danvers was near to tears apologizing to everyone as they were hustled out the door.

"Our company was in the low parlor chamber, readying ourselves to perform after supper. When the fracas broke out, the rest of them took to their heels. I was the only one who dared linger in hopes I might still be recompensed for this evening."

That hardly surprised Martin. Sander Naismith was a bold lad and something of a protégé to Lord Oxbridge, who had introduced him to the Crown Theatre's company.

"It looks like I shall be heading home with an empty purse," Sander groused. "And I am nigh desperate for a few crowns."

"Ah, you young fool. You have doubtless been hazarding too much at the dice again."

"No, sir!" But the boy's sheepish smile belied his words.

"Never mind. I am sure Lady Danvers will see that you all are paid when she is less distressed." Martin clapped the boy on the shoulder. "If she doesn't, I will."

Sander looked heartened by Martin's promise. But as he continued on down the path, he called back over his shoulder, "I wouldn't go up there if I were you, Master Wolfe. Ned—I mean his lordship—is roaring drunk and it isn't doing much to improve his disposition."

Scooping up his skirts, Sander disappeared into the darkness. Despite the boy's warning, Martin continued on his way, much troubled by Sander's tidings.

Martin knew that Ned Lambert had been looking forward to entertaining the queen, had been boasting about it for weeks. Like any other ambitious young nobleman, he frequently haunted the halls of Whitehall in hopes of currying the royal favor.

Hampered by the fact that he was a Catholic and by his family's unfortunate history, Ned had been frustrated in his efforts, obliged to rub elbows with the common petitioners in the outer court at the palace. But queen Gloriana was very fond of presents. A costly gift of a jeweled pin in the shape of a peacock had finally gained him admittance to the Presence Chamber. His handsome face, much flattery, and a song composed in Gloriana's honor had won·him greater favor still, the queen graciously agreeing to attend the banquet to be held at Strand House.

Martin could well imagine Lord Oxbridge's chagrin and humiliation at the queen's absence this evening. But it was the extreme fury of his lordship's reaction that disturbed Martin.

Ned Lambert tended to confine his recklessness to the hunting fields, a breakneck rider who had brought more than one fine stallion to grief. He was far more temperate in his drinking habits than most of his friends. When he did imbibe too much, he became quiet and morose until he tumbled off to sleep. Martin had never known the young man to fly into a drunken rage. He hoped that the savagery of Ned's disappointment did not have its roots in some sinister cause. Such as an assassination plot thwarted by the queen's failure to appear . . .

No, it would be hazardous to the point of lunacy for Ned to risk bringing harm to the queen beneath his own roof. Martin could not believe his lordship would be that foolish, especially since it would also put his sister at risk. Although Jane was nearly ten years older than Ned, the pair was very close.

He couldn't believe that Ned could be involved in any plots at all. Couldn't believe it or didn't want to, a voice in his head demanded, sounding remarkably like Walsingham's.

"You find it inconvenient for the man who helped fund your precious theater to be guilty of treason. Your liking for his lordship's sister has led you to be less than zealous in your investigations."

The secretary's accusations nagged at Martin as he entered the inner court. He did his best to thrust them from his mind.

The household was still in enough turmoil that he made it as far as the great hall unannounced. Glancing about him, he was dismayed to see that Sander had not exaggerated.

The dining parlor looked like it had been invaded by a

troop of marauding Turks, tables, chairs, and stools over-turned. The rushes were littered with the remains of what had promised to be the setting for a fine supper. Damask napkins, salt cellars, silver plates, and trenchers were scattered everywhere, the white linen table covering stained with wine from shattered crystal.

Servants clustered in the doorway leading from the kitchen, whispering in hushed voices, clearly uncertain what to do next, but leery of the man sprawled in the chair before the hearth.

Lord Oxbridge had his back to the entryway. All Martin could see of him were his long, elegantly hosed and shod legs stretched out before him. One arm dangled over the side of the chair, the tapering white fingers of his hand bejeweled with rings. Ned's rage had finally spent itself or he had passed out. From his vantage point, Martin could not tell which.

His sister hovered nearby, a ghost of a woman in her ecru silk gown draped over a farthingale, her fine blond hair confined by a net caul seeded with pearls. She was the first to notice Martin's arrival.

When one of the pages would have ventured across the parlor to attend to Martin, Jane Danvers waved him aside. She approached Martin herself with her hand out-stretched.

"Marcus. I—I mean Master Wolfe."

"Lady Danvers." Martin bowed. He took her hand and brushed a light kiss against her cheek in the customary greeting for one's hostess.

A hint of color crept into Jane's pale cheeks. She usually

had the serene countenance of a Madonna, but her smooth brow was furrowed, her dove gray eyes full of distress.

"I—I am sorry. I regret to tell you we have been obliged to cancel. That—that is the queen did not—and—and my brother is not quite himself. He—he—."

"It is all right. I know what happened." Martin squeezed her hand gently.

The simple action was enough to cause Jane's eyes to fill with tears, but she blinked them back. She might not possess Cat's fierce pride, but Lady Danvers had a quiet dignity of her own.

"Is there anything I can do?" Martin asked.

"Find me a nice quiet convent where I can hide?" Jane made a wan effort to smile. "Ned's behavior has been so scandalous I will scarce dare to show my face in London or at court for weeks."

Her lashes swept down. "Not that Ned or I were very welcome at Whitehall before."

"Wolfe, is that you?" A slurry voice called from across the room. Lord Oxbridge roused himself, staggering up from the depths of the chair.

He lurched toward Martin, his gait unsteady, the candlelight winking off the jeweled buttons of his blue silk doublet. Ned Lambert's hair was slicked back from his brow, the blond strands lighter than his sister's, but his gray eyes were a shade harder. Unlike most fashionable men, he went clean-shaven.

Handsome in an arrogant sort of way, tonight his lean countenance was stained an ugly shade of red from too much wine. His eyes still glittered dangerously. Even though his temper was banked, Martin sensed it would not require much by way of tinder to flare up again.

Martin sketched a bow. "Good evening. How fares my lord?"

"Ill. Cursed ill." Oxbridge stumbled a little and braced himself, resting one hand heavily on Martin's shoulder. "The old bitch didn't come."

"Ned, please—" Jane began, starting toward him.

But her brother righted himself, waving her off with a contemptuous gesture.

"Oooh, my older sister scolds me. Mustn't speak disre-spectful of my sovereign queen even though she made a bloody fool of me. Sending a message round sayin' she was in-indisposed. Phfft!" His lordship made a scornful noise through pursed lips, poking Martin in the chest. "Did you ever hear the like, Wolfe? Old bat's never sick a day in her life. She'll live forever even though we'd all be better off if she up and—"

"Edward!" Jane cried, shooting her brother a warning look that he was too far gone to see. Her hands fluttering nervously, she appealed to Martin, "Please. You must par-don his lordship and myself. We are in no fit state to be re-ceiving guests. I must beg you to leave."

"Certainly. I understand, my lady," Martin said. He had already heard far more than he wished.

But Ned slung his arm around Martin's shoulders. "No, stay." He glowered at his sister. "Mustn't be rude to Wolfe, Jane. He's a fine fellow. Saved your life, y'know."

Leaning heavily on Martin, he said, "Come and have a cup of wine and com-commiserate with me."

"Ned, you've already had far too much," Jane said, but

Martin gave her a warning shake of his head, realizing that all of her pleas were doing nothing except aggravating her brother.

"Excellent idea, my lord." Martin added in a softer voice to Jane, "More wine might help him to sleep."

Jane's eyes widened, then she nodded in comprehension.

"Who the devil wants to sleep?" his lordship growled, overhearing. Peeling himself off of Martin, Ned managed to make it back to his chair on his own. Tumbling into it, he bellowed for more wine.

A dignified servant wearing the Lambert scarlet and black livery appeared swiftly, bearing two flagons on a tray. Swilling his own wine, Ned didn't even notice that Martin placed his cup atop the mantel, untasted.

Martin realized he was in a cursed difficult situation and he needed a clear head. This was exactly the opportunity Walsingham would expect Martin to take full advantage of. Pry out what secrets he could while Ned's tongue was loose with drink.

But Martin could scarce tear his eyes from Jane. Her gentle face was so distraught, rousing all of Martin's most protective instincts.

The servant caught her attention and asked in an undertone, "Your pardon, my lady, the cook was wondering. What is to be done with all the food prepared for the banquet?"

Ned's copious drinking didn't seem to affect his hearing. He snarled, "Fling it into the streets. Let the dogs and kites have it."

Jane frowned, remonstrating with her brother gently.

"Surely, my dear, it would be much better to distribute the food among the poor."

Ned took another gulp of his wine, scowled, and then shrugged. "Oh, very well."

While Jane quietly imparted her instructions to the servant, Ned brooded over his wine cup and intoned, "The poor will be with you always. Especially nowadays. No place for the poor buggers to go for alms. Damned Protestants didn't think of that when they were closing down all the monasteries and convents, did they, Master Wolfe?"

"No, I daresay they didn't," Martin replied uncomfortably. Both the Lamberts had always been so discreet about being Catholic. Martin knew Jane wore a simple crucifix but she kept it tucked beneath her gown, only the gold chain visible. As for Ned, Martin had never heard him mention a word on the subject of religion until now.

Jane returned in time to hear her brother's latest ravings. She rested her hand on his shoulder.

"God expects all of us to be charitable, Ned. Not just the holy men."

"You are charitable enough for both of us. M'sister's a saint, Marcus. Did you know that?"

Martin smiled at Jane. "Certainly she is a noble and virtuous lady."

"No! I am telling you she's a saint," Ned said. "A goddamned saint!"

"Edward!" Jane admonished, squeezing his shoulder. She cast Martin a rueful glance. "I assure you I am not."

Ned gave a sloppy grin, reaching up to pat her hand. His expression darkened almost immediately. He startled both Martin and Jane by suddenly flinging his wine cup into the empty hearth.

Doubling over, he buried his face in his hands and groaned. "What am I going to do? What am I going to do? I thought by licking the queen's boots I could obtain some fat post at court. I should have known better. She gives preference only to Protestants, dark-skinned gypsies like that old fart Leicester. He used to be the queen's lover, y'know. They plotted together to murder his wife."

"Ned, for the love of heaven, I beg you. Talk like that could get you thrown into the Tower." Jane cast an uneasy glance at Martin.

"Don't fret, my lady," he hastened to assure her. "I am familiar with all the old gossip. I take little heed and certainly would not repeat it."

"Why not? Everyone else does," Ned muttered, and then went back to moaning. "I am ruined. I've near bankrupted myself on this s-supper. Do you have any idea how much money I spent? Jane's money."

Jane rubbed her brother's back soothingly. "It doesn't matter, dearest. I don't mind."

"But I mind, damn it." Ned jerked his head up. "I don't want to spend the rest of my life tied to m'sister's apron strings."

"It is a woman's duty to look out for her family."

"That's our father talking," Ned sneered. Peering up at Martin, he asked, "Did you know Jane was bartered off twice to repair our family fortunes? Once to a sickly boy and then to an old man with gout. Poor little cow."

When Jane lowered her gaze in embarrassment, Martin

longed to give the young man a good clout to the ears. An unwise idea in Ned's current inebriated state. It would only lead to fisticuffs or a duel, distressing Jane further.

Ned twisted in his chair to blink owlishly up at his sister. "Never again, Janey. Next time you'll wed to your own fancy, some handsome lusty fellow who will bed you proper. I'll make our fortunes. I'll be the wealthiest and most powerful man in England, if all goes well."

As he turned back to Martin, a sly expression played over his lordship's flushed face. He laid one finger dramatically over his lips and said, "Shhh. Wolfe, old man, can you keep a secret?"

No!

Martin managed a stiff smile. "I try to be discreet. But I don't think this is a good time for your lordship to be sharing confidences. Not when your judgment is impaired."

"Nothing wrong with my judgment." Ned struggled upward, swaying a little. "I want to show you something."

"Ned, no!" If Jane had looked uneasy before, she was now white with alarm. "I am sure Marcus would have no interest—"

"Sure he would. He might even want a share in my enterprise."

Jane clung to her brother's arm, but he shook her off roughly. Beckoning Martin to follow, Ned lurched off toward the kitchen.

Martin looked uncertainly at Jane. Although she cast him a pleading glance, she spread her hands in a helpless gesture. Martin had no choice but to follow Ned, but he did so with his stomach in knots.

Goddamn the irresponsible young fool. Was it possible

that Walsingham was right about Ned being involved in Babington's plot? Was the drunken idiot about to serve up Martin the evidence the secretary needed on a silver platter?

As Ned staggered into the kitchen, the servants skittered back like frightened shadows. Ned snatched up a candle.

"This way," he slurred, leading Martin through a door with a rough stone stair winding down to the cellars. Martin picked his way carefully after him, Jane rustling behind.

Martin offered his hand to aid her down the worn narrow steps. She clutched at him with an almost frantic grip as though she wanted to draw him back. But Ned was the one she needed to stop, damn it, Martin thought.

Unsteady on his feet, Ned nearly lost his balance weaving down the last step. Martin wrenched the candle away from him before the drunken fool set the entire house ablaze.

Light flickered over a storeroom filled with casks of wine and barrels of ale. There was a heavy oak door at the far end. Weaving his way toward it, Ned fished inside his doublet and produced a large iron key.

This couldn't be good, Martin thought. A door to some mysterious room at the bottom of the house to which only his lordship had the key.

And whatever lurked inside had his sister looking ill with apprehension. Some terrible secret that Jane obviously feared Ned revealing to anyone.

So why the blazes didn't she do something besides wring her hands? Why didn't she stop Ned? Cat certainly would have done so if it had been her brother. She would have knocked him unconscious before ever allowing him to betray himself.

As Ned swore, making repeated jabs with the key in his drunken efforts to get it into the lock, Martin surreptitiously wiped a bead of sweat from his brow. He didn't know why he was even thinking of Cat at such a moment, comparing her to Jane.

Perhaps because he felt a trifle desperate, dreading whatever Ned might be about to show him, perhaps evidence of treason, something Martin might feel obliged to report to Walsingham.

He half hoped that Ned might break the blasted key off in the lock. But there was a loud click. Ned tugged on the heavy door and it swung open with an ominous creak. Leaning up against the jamb with a foolish smug smile, he indicated Martin should precede him inside.

Jane made a soft sound. When Martin glanced at her, her hands were folded, her lips moving silently. Damnation, was the woman actually praying? What the bloody hell was in that room?

A cold lump in his stomach, Martin squared his shoulders and stepped over the threshold. But nothing could have braced him for the sight that met his eyes.

Holding the candle aloft, his mouth fell open in total shock.

Chapter Eight

NIGHT SETTLED OVER MEG'S BEDCHAMBER WINDOW LIKE A warm dark blanket, signaling the time for sleep. But the girl was wide awake. Her night rail fluttering about her bare legs, She opened the casement. Leaning out the window as far as she dared, she raised the magnifying device to her eye.

She had fashioned it herself, following the instructions the best she could, fitting the convex glass into the metal tube. Like everything else described in the *Book of Shadows,* the device was intended for a sinister purpose, spying upon one's enemy, gaining the advantage in war.

But the only enemy that Meg longed to conquer was the one that lurked in her own heart. She trained the spyglass upon the darkened heavens, her breath catching in her throat as she studied the comet. Each night, it seemed a little brighter, blazing as though it would burn a hole in the sky.

A harbinger of evil. Both astrologers and holy men agreed on that. The comet signaled some cataclysmic change, some dark destiny. Meg only prayed it wasn't hers. She lowered the spyglass and settled back on the window seat, releasing her breath with a tremulous sigh.

Her destiny . . .

"From the moment of your birth, nay, even before, you were singled out for greatness. The daughters of the earth will topple thrones and strip all men of their power. You are the one fated to lead us to this new age of glory, Megaera. A queen among queens, the most powerful sorceress the world has ever known."

Meg drew her knees tight to her chest and pressed her face against them, clutching her hands over her ears to shut out the memory of her mother's voice.

"Forget, forget, forget," she chanted. It was what Papa wanted her to do above all things. Well, next to becoming a proper English gentlewoman who knew nothing of poisons, syringes, or the *Book of Shadows*. She longed so desperately to please him, but why did it seem to be getting harder instead of easier to do all that he asked?

"It is not that easy, forgetting the past, trying to deny who you are deep down in your bones. A wise woman learns to be true to herself," Cat had told her.

But what if who you truly were was evil, someone predestined to be a dark and powerful sorceress, *the Silver Rose*?

Meg shivered, feeling a surge of anger against Cat. She

and Papa had been doing just fine before that Irishwoman had ever turned up here with all of her unwanted advice and dire warnings.

Now Maman's voice was back in Meg's head again. And Papa was so worried, Meg doubted he'd ever let her set foot out of the house. It was all Catriona O'Hanlon's fault, and to add insult to injury, that upstart Irishwoman had dared criticize Meg's good and gracious Queen Elizabeth.

She wished Cat had never come here. She wished the sea had opened up and swallowed Cat before—

No. Meg checked the thought with a tiny whimper. Peering past the top of her knees, she glanced about the room, fearing some malevolent spirit might have overheard her wish.

"I take it back. I take it back," she whispered fiercely, trembling as she remembered Aggie's story about the poor man who had died of an evil thought.

Just like Maman . . .

A light knock at the door startled Meg, her heart banging against her ribs. She scrambled off the window seat. She had barely enough time to hide the spyglass in the folds of her night rail before Cat entered the room.

Cat hesitated on the threshold. Ever since Martin had left for his banquet, the girl had avoided Cat, even taking her supper in her room. Cat had allowed her to do so.

She was so exhausted by the hostility of the rest of the household, she had not been up to the task of dealing with a sullen Mistress Margaret as well. Cat had hoped to find the girl asleep, not hovering by the window like a phantom child who had just drifted in from the night, her eyes as wild and wary as a badger trapped in a thicket.

"May I come in?" Cat asked, closing the door behind her.

"Looks like you already did," Meg grumbled. "Papa said this is where you are to sleep so you can keep watch over me without scaring the servants. He doesn't want to be waked by any more broomstick battles."

With a long-suffering sigh, the girl pointed to the pallet that had been arranged for Cat before the hearth. "I doubt you will be very comfortable."

"I have slept under worse conditions in caves and under thickets, in cattle byres and abandoned clochan huts."

Cat's remark raised a brief flicker of curiosity in Meg's eyes as Cat had intended. But the girl suppressed it, a stony expression settling over her face as she marched over to her bed.

"I learned to be more comfortable on the hard-packed earth than on the finest feather bed." Cat leaned up against the mantel. As Cat removed her shoes, Meg made a great show of drawing back the counterpane and plumping her pillow.

Cat added casually, "Although I admit, I'd rest a sight easier tonight if I knew what it was you were trying to hide under your pillow."

Meg froze and then gave a scornful toss of her head. "It's not the *witch blade* if that's what you are worrying about."

"It's good to know what it isn't, but perhaps you had better show me what it *is*."

Cat strode toward the girl and held out her hand. Meg regarded her defiantly for a moment. Cat held her gaze with steady patience until Meg surrendered.

Meg delved under the covers and produced a metal cylinder that she slapped against Cat's palm.

Cat studied the object, her brow creasing in puzzlement. "What is it? Some sort of wee cudgel?"

"No! Is everything some sort of weapon to you? It's a looking device. You have to hold it up to your eye."

As Cat raised the cylinder, she saw that there were pieces of curved glass fitted into either end of the hollow tube. Cautiously she lifted one end to her eye. Squinting with the other eye closed, she looked through the tube.

The bedchamber flipped upside down, the dragon woven into the tapestry seeming to fly at her in a dizzying rush.

"Holy Brigid!" Cat gasped and yanked the tube from her eye. "What devilment is this?"

"It's just a spying glass," Meg said impatiently. "Only I couldn't figure out how to make it work so things are right side up. But it doesn't matter if you use it to look up at the heavens." She gestured to the window.

Cat walked over to the open casement. Lifting the tube to her eye, she risked another look, training the spyglass on the waning moon. To the naked eye, it looked as though half of it had gone missing, cleaved in twain by some gigantic sword.

But with Meg's device, Cat could see the part of the moon lost in shadow and the entire surface was pitted like a round face marred by the pox. Her breath catching in her throat, Cat shifted to observe the rest of the sky, the stars so brilliant and close, she half-reached out with her other hand to touch them.

And the comet . . . Seen through the lens, it was even

more awe-inspiring and terrifying, a burning sphere trailing behind it a dragon's breath of fire.

Cat lowered the tube and sank down upon the window seat, staring at Meg in amazement. "This thing is incredible. And you say that *you* made it?"

Meg gave a cool nod. But as she came to reclaim her possession from Cat, her pride in her achievement would not allow her to remain silent.

"I read about the spyglass in—in a book somewhere. I told a friend—well, Aggie, what I needed and she made the purchases, giving the glassmaker my *particular* instructions about the lenses. But once I had the parts, I had to fashion the device all by myself."

"How clever of you."

Meg's smug smile revealed that she thought so too.

Cat handed the spyglass back to Meg, doing her best to conceal her troubled thoughts. There was only one ancient text that she knew of that detailed such unusual devices and powerful weapons, knowledge that had been long lost to the present world.

The Book of Shadows. Martin was adamant that neither he nor his daughter knew what had become of the text after Cassandra's death. Cat believed Martin didn't. She was not as sure about Meg.

While Meg was busy, returning the spyglass to the trunk at the foot of her bed, Cat strolled past the shelves that held Meg's collection of books, scanning titles. They were a strange mixture of scholarly works and whimsy, the esoteric and the practical. Books such as Plutarch's *Lives* rested side by side with texts such as *The Gardener's Labyrinth* by one Didymus Mountaine. Meg's hungry mind seemed to range in all directions, devouring anything in its path.

The spine of one book looked more battered and well-worn than the rest. Cat tried to ease the book out to examine the title, but it was wedged firmly between two larger tomes.

As Cat tugged at it, she was arrested by the sound of Meg's voice.

"If I did have the *Book of Shadows,* I would hardly leave it about in plain sight."

The girl cocked one brow in such an imitation of her father, Cat nearly smiled in spite of herself. She folded her arms across her breasts and reminded Meg, "You promised upon your honor not to be reading my eyes."

"And what if I don't have any honor?"

"Then I suggest you acquire some."

Meg glowered at her and then gave a disdainful shrug. "I did not have to read your eyes. Your face is like a looking glass, reflecting everything you are thinking.

"You can search my entire room if you like, but you won't find any *Book of Shadows.* It was lost in Paris and I am glad of it. As for that book you are eyeing so suspiciously . . ." Meg stalked to the shelves and yanked the volume free, tapping one short blunt finger upon the title.

The Secrets and Wonders of the World.

Cat winced. It was not a comfortable thing when an eleven-year-old girl was able to make you feel like a bit of a fool. She took the volume from Meg to examine it more closely.

"This book is very lovingly worn," Cat remarked. "It must be your favorite."

Meg hunched her shoulders but as Cat flipped through the pages, she was unable to maintain her indifference. She crept closer, gesturing to the illustration of a dragon in flight.

"The book says that the dragons in Ethiopia are very amiable."

"I have always believed so." Cat smiled.

Meg leaned closer still, turning the pages herself to one that she had dog-eared . . . the sketch of some monstrous huge creature with tusks and a tail at either end, one of them long and thick, extending where its nose should have been.

"Oliphants, on the other hand, are quite fierce. Have you ever seen one, Mistress O'Hanlon?"

"Thankfully, no."

"Apparently, the only way you can fight them is to tie their tails together so they trip each other."

"I'll remember that," Cat replied solemnly. Meg glanced up at her, half-starting to smile before recollecting herself.

She snatched the book from Cat. Leaping up on her bed, she tunneled under the covers and propped herself against the pillows with her book.

Cat followed, perching on the edge of the bed. Holding the book in front of her face, Meg studiously ignored her.

"So you are not liking me all that much, I'm thinking," Cat remarked.

Meg risked a peek over the top of her book. After a moment she replied, "I like your voice. It has music in it."

"Well, that's something at least."

Meg disappeared behind her book, turning another page. "Papa used to have music in his voice too. Before he started trying to be English."

"You don't approve of that?"

"I am fiercely proud of him," Meg blazed, but after a moment she admitted, "but I liked it better when we first came to England and we traveled about with Master Roxburgh's company. Papa laughed more then and he made every day seem so exciting, like a grand adventure. But everything changed after Finette found us."

"Finette?"

"She was one of the sisterhood. She was a nasty, sly, dirty creature who smelled bad. I never liked her. I don't know how she was the one who managed to track me and Papa. She was never all that clever."

"But somehow Finette found you," Cat prompted when Meg fell silent. "What did she want?"

"What all of the sisterhood want. Me," Meg said in a sad little voice. "They all expected such unreasonable things of me. That somehow I would possess the magic to make them all beautiful, wealthy, and powerful. That I would be able to bring back people who they had loved and lost from the dead."

Meg shrank down farther. Cat was tempted to reach for the book. She wanted to be able to see the girl's face. But Meg seemed to find it easier to speak of such painful things from behind the shield of her book.

"Finette was—was a complete madwoman when she overtook us on the road. She was so angry with my papa. She said that when he took me, he had stolen away all the sisterhood's hopes and dreams. She tried to stab Papa with the syringe. They wrestled and Finette ended up sticking herself. She died from the poison."

The girl fell silent again.

"And then?" Cat asked gently.

"Finette was buried in a pauper's grave in this little village near York. No one knew who she was or how she died, except Papa and me. He hugged me so tight and said we both must forget it had ever happened, never speak of it again. He got rid of the syringe, threw it in the pond near where Finette had attacked us. But the water wasn't as deep as Papa thought and I was able to fetch it later. I thought we might need it for protection.

"It was after Finette that my papa changed. He started acting like the world was full of oliphants and they were all after me."

Meg heaved a huge sigh. "And now that you have brought us this warning from the Lady of Faire Isle, I'll probably never be able to leave the house again. I'll never see the queen."

She shifted her book enough to steal a resentful glance at Cat. "Not that *you* would understand or even care."

"I'd like to be able to understand," Cat said, resolutely suppressing her loathing for Elizabeth Tudor. "What is it you so admire about the woman?"

Meg studied Cat suspiciously as though unsure her interest was genuine. Whatever she saw in Cat's face must have satisfied her because she said, "There is a great deal to admire about Her Majesty. She is so wise and accomplished. She can speak six different languages and she plays the lute and the virginal. When she was a girl, she barely managed to survive. She had so many enemies who wanted to destroy her and just as many who wanted to use her just like—like . . ."

"Like you?" Cat filled in.

Meg disappeared behind her book. Her voice dropped so low, Cat had to lean closer to hear.

"Queen Elizabeth also had a mother that everyone thought was evil and she can't ever speak of her."

"You can speak of your mother to me."

"Papa wouldn't like it."

"Then it would have to be another one of our secrets." Cat plucked the book from Meg's hands and set it aside. "Your papa is a good man who only wants to protect you. But I don't think he understands that if you keep some memories trapped in your heart too long, they can swell in importance, become darker and worse than they actually are."

Meg swallowed hard, the girl's huge green eyes hungering with the need to express thoughts she'd buried for so long. Still she hesitated before confessing, "Sometimes it feels like my heart is going to burst."

"We would never want that to happen." Cat touched the girl's cheek. "So tell me about your maman."

Meg lowered her gaze and curled her fingers into the bedclothes.

"I know that most everyone thinks my mother was truly wicked and she did do many evil things that I don't even like to think about." Meg's lip quivered. "Anyone who ever opposed my mother just disappeared, like my first nurse, Mistress Waters. Maman destroyed her enemies, using the poisoned roses and the syringe described in the *Book of Shadows.* Things that I helped her to make."

The girl's voice dropped to a whisper. "I didn't want to, but Maman could be terrifying when she was angry. She knew how to use her power to hurt me.

"She lost her eyesight when she was young, but it was the darkness in her heart that frightened me. She could see into a person's soul with a touch of her hand. But she was never able to see me, never really touch me. All she saw was the Silver Rose."

A wistful look crept into Meg's eyes. "That was why it was so amazing when Papa found me. For the first time, I had someone who really saw me.

"But I don't think he does anymore, only the lady he hopes I will become. Someone noble and gentle like Lady Danvers. I am not sure I can be that."

"You are a daughter of the earth. You should not have to be anyone but yourself." Cat rested her hand over Meg's. The girl didn't draw away, but she tensed beneath Cat's touch.

"What if that means being someone truly evil? Maman said I was destined to become a sorceress so powerful, the entire world of men would tremble and bow down before me."

"Your mother was wrong, Meg. Your destiny is in your own hands."

The girl looked up at Cat, the longing in her eyes showing how desperately she wanted to believe that. She gave a sad shake of her head. "It was the great seer Nostradamus who told Maman about me."

"That isn't possible, sweetling. Nostradamus has been dead for years."

"Maman raised his spirit. I watched her do it."

Sweet heaven! Cat shuddered. Was there no end to the horrors Cassandra had inflicted upon this poor child?

"And if I am not destined to become this sorceress,

why am I the only one who has ever been able to read and understand the *Book of Shadows*?" Meg asked.

Cat hesitated, hardly knowing how to answer. She was troubled by Meg's uncanny ability, as were many other true daughters of the earth. But the girl looked so apprehensive herself, Cat squeezed her hand.

"It—it just means you are extraordinarily clever. But what you choose to do with that cleverness is entirely up to you. I know you would never want to harm anyone."

"I already did," Meg whispered, hanging her head. "I killed my mother."

"Merciful heavens, child! Where did you ever get such a notion? Cassandra fell into the Seine and drowned. It was no fault of yours."

Meg looked up at Cat with great haunted eyes. "Yes, it was. I—I wished her gone."

The girl looked far too young, too fragile to be carrying such an enormous burden of guilt. Cat's heart ached for her. Stroking her fingers back through Meg's hair, she said, "Oh, Meg, no matter what you have been told, people don't die from evil thoughts. If that were so, my own mother would have shriveled up and turned to dust."

Meg tipped her head to one side, regarding Cat with wonderment. "You—you did not get on well with your mama either?"

"I was the bane of my mother's existence. Irish ladies are supposed to be sweet of speech, skilled with the needle, and full of feminine wisdom. I could curse with all the fluency of my da, was far more adept at hunting than I was at sewing, and the only wisdom I possessed was the lore of the earth that I had learned from my old gran. My mother hated and feared all of the ancient learning, as did my step-father. When he accused me of being a witch, she never said a word in my defense. She just turned away."

Cat spoke in a matter-of-fact tone, as though it were of no consequence, but the pain of her mother's betrayal still rested heavy upon her heart. Meg curled her fingers around Cat's.

"So your mother despised you for being a witch and my mother hated me because I was not enough of one. Isn't that strange?"

"I suppose 'tis. But there comes a time when we must grow past the need for our mother's love and approval."

"When, Cat? How old do you have to be for that to happen?" Meg asked anxiously.

"I don't know," Cat admitted ruefully. "I'll tell you when I get there. Now perhaps we had best be getting off to sleep."

Meg nodded, nestling deeper under the covers. Cat blew out the candles. She readied herself for bed, stripping down to her chemise. As she was about to stretch out on the pallet, Meg called out.

"Cat?"

"Yes?"

"Sometimes I have trouble falling asleep. Not that I am afraid of the dark," she added hastily. "It is just that some nights my head is too full and—and it would be nice if you rested on my bed beside me. Just for a while until I fall asleep. If—if you wouldn't mind—"

"I wouldn't mind at all."

Cat groped her way to the bed, lying down beside Meg. The girl nestled closer by degrees until her head rested against Cat's shoulder. Cat wrapped her arm about Meg, glad that the darkness concealed her worried expression.

What a confused girl Meg was, trying to sort out the tangled emotions about her mother, struggling with questions about her destiny and fears regarding her abilities that would have taxed a far older and wiser woman.

The child needed the guidance of a daughter of the earth like Ariane; if Cat could only persuade Martin of that.

As Cat stroked the girl's back, she could feel the tension in her thin shoulder blades. "If you are worrying about the Dark Queen coming after you, don't be. You have both me and your da to protect you."

"I am more afraid of the sisterhood than I am of the Dark Queen. That they'll find me and drag me back to France to be their Silver Rose."

"I would die before I'd let that happen."

Meg sucked in her breath. "Don't say that, Cat, please. It—it is what my followers used to promise, to live and die for me."

"I am not one of those daft women, Meg. I will be your *fianna*."

"What is that?"

"The *fianna* were warriors of old in my country, the special protectors of the high kings."

There was silence as Meg considered this. She murmured, "I would rather you would just be my friend."

"I think I can manage that as well." Cat brushed a kiss atop the girl's head.

Meg sighed. Relaxing a little, she melted closer.

"Tell me more about the high kings."

Cat smiled and began to speak of the high kings, the mighty Cuchulainn, Brian Boru, and the Red Branch knights, the same stories her father had spun out for her on many a starlit summer night. Taking comfort herself from the tales, Cat wove the old magic until both she and Meg fell asleep.

卅卅

THE GOLDEN CROWN PRESSED DOWN UPON MEG'S HEAD, CUT-*ting into her temple. The ermine robes weighted down her shoulders until she could scarce take a step. She struggled desperately to escape the hands that clutched at her, the sea of pleading eyes and whining voices.*

"Oh, great queen, restore my youth."

"I beg you, mighty sorceress, smite the man who betrayed me."

"Please, Your Grace. Raise my sister from the dead."

Meg shoved their grasping hands away. She twisted in a frantic effort to escape, only to have her path blocked by another of her devotees kneeling before her.

The girl looked up at Meg, her bead-like eyes glistening with all the avidity of a hungry rat.

"See what I have done for you, Your Grace. I lay at your feet my sacrifice."

She placed a small bundle in front of Meg and started to undo the wrappings.

"No, please," Meg whispered.

The blanket fell away from the shriveled form of the dead infant. It stared up at Meg with hollow, accusing eyes. When Meg recoiled in horror, the girl cooed, "Nay,

do not be distressed, my Silver Rose. It was only a worth-
less male babe."

"No! No." *Meg shrank away, tears streaming down*
her cheeks. "I am not your Silver Rose. Leave me alone.
All of you, just leave me alone!"

But as she stumbled back, a cold hand fell heavily
upon her shoulder. Meg gazed fearfully up to find her
mother looming over her. Cassandra's long black hair was
wet and tangled with reeds from the river, her lips blue, her
white skin etched with veins. Her dark sightless eyes
pierced Meg clean through.

"We will never leave you alone, Megaera," Cassandra
rasped. "Did you think to elude us so easily? You might
have been able to deny me, wish me dead, but you will
never be able to escape your destiny."

"No," Meg whimpered. She squirmed out of her
mother's grasp, fighting her way out of the darkness of her
dream. Her eyes flew open and she gave a shuddering gasp,
her first instinct to cry out for her papa. But she remembered that he had gone out, leaving her with . . . Cat.

Meg groped the mattress beside her and found it empty.
Raising her head, she realized that Cat had moved to her
pallet before the hearth. With the moonlight streaming in
the window, she could just make out Cat's slumbering form.

But either the woman was a light sleeper or Meg had
cried out more loudly in the throes of her nightmare than
she had realized.

Cat stirred, calling out sleepily, "Meg? Are you all
right?"

No, Meg longed to sob and beg Cat to return to her bed

and cradle her close again. But she was ashamed, feeling as though she had already behaved like enough of an infant for one night.

So she held herself very still, forcing herself to breathe regularly and feigning slumber until Cat rolled over and went back to sleep.

Realizing her face was damp with tears, Meg dashed them aside. She didn't doubt that Cat would have been kind and consoling if Meg were to tell her about the dream. But Cat was so brave and bold, she could never be brought to understand.

"Your destiny is in your own hands," she would insist.

How Meg wished she could believe that. But she feared that she would never be free of her nightmares unless she could find a way to peer into the future herself and see that her mother was wrong.

Shifting onto her other side, Meg squinted through the darkness toward the shadowy outline of the great dragon tapestry. The arras concealed the loose panel in the wall, Meg's most secret hiding place.

She had lied to Cat, Meg thought with a twinge of guilt. Another legacy from Maman. Avoiding her mother's constant probing, Meg had learned how to distort the truth and mask her emotions.

Although in this instance she had not so much lied to Cat as omitted telling her everything, Meg consoled herself. When she had described the encounter with Finette, Meg had neglected to mention that there was one other thing she had acquired from the demented woman besides the syringe.

The *Book of Shadows.*

Tucked in its hiding place behind the arras, the ancient volume seemed to call to Meg, whispering of all its dread secrets for parting the veil between the living and the dead. If she could conjure up Nostradamus the way Maman used to do . . .

She recalled the ritual with the black candles, the ghostly face rising from the mists in the copper bowl, the sepulchral voice of the old man's spirit, so angry at having his peace disturbed.

Meg trembled, knowing she lacked the courage to attempt such dark magic. At least not yet, when there was a less terrifying, less dangerous way of peering into her future if she was clever and skilled enough.

But she would require a certain object and for that she must rely upon the same person who had helped her before, procuring the materials she had needed for her spyglass. Not Aggie, as she had told Cat. That had been an outright lie. Meg winced, but her conscience was soothed as she thought of her particular secret friend, his voice and his face like those of an angel.

Closing her eyes, she conjured up an image of his golden hair and his handsome visage. Her heartbeat quickened and her cheeks warmed as she murmured his name softly to herself.

"Sander."

Chapter Nine

"*MERDE!*" MARTIN BREATHED, ENTIRELY FORGETTING HIM-self. He nearly dropped the candle, hot wax spattering his hand as his gaze roved about the chamber. The candlelight flickered, casting eerie shadows over rough stone walls lined with shelves holding jars and bottles filled with all manner of murky liquids.

By far the most alarming was the table in the center of the room, the oak surface draped with a bloodred cloth gilded with stars, pentagrams, and other mysterious-looking symbols.

The objects placed atop the table were equally disturb-ing, a mortar and pestle, a dusty old book, a set of scales, and a small iron cauldron.

Martin's blood iced in his veins. "What the devil is all of this?"

Ned staggered into the room. He clapped Martin on the shoulder and smirked.

"Magic, my good man. *Sorcery.*"

Jane stood on the threshold, refusing to come any farther. She looked pale with fear, rapidly making the sign of the cross, and Martin didn't blame her.

It had been years since he had blessed himself but he did so now. During his youth he had possessed a healthy fear of all things supernatural, often fashioning himself charms for protection against witches.

After he had met the Cheney sisters, he had learned more of the true nature of wise women, how much of the so-called ancient knowledge could be good, Ariane's gift for healing, and Miri's extraordinary ability to communicate with animals.

But he had also seen the darker side of magic through Cassandra Lascelles, with her seductive perfumes and cursed medallions, her hellish skill in conjuring the dead and drawing out a man's thoughts with but a chilling touch of her hand.

He had experienced much that he never wanted to experience again or for Meg to, either. Especially not Meg. And now he was surrounded by everything he had tried to protect her from, everything he had sought to cut out of her life.

His hand shaking a little, Martin set the candle down upon the table, his eyes drawn to the dust-covered tome. He had been told there was only one *Book of Shadows,* one compilation of the worst of the ancient knowledge. But there were other old texts that could be dangerous enough.

Martin looked at the book and shuddered, unable to bring himself to crack the cover. Anger flashed through him and he spun around, seizing Ned by the front of his doublet.

"You damned young idiot. Do you have any idea of the kind of dark power you are meddling with? How cursed dangerous all this stuff is?"

Ned blinked, momentarily stunned by Martin's assault. He scowled and struck Martin's hands away.

"There is nothing dangerous or sinister about my workshop. Bigod, you—you sound just like m'sister."

"It is true," Jane spoke up in a distressed voice. "I have tried to warn him so many times—"

"Bah! You'll both sing another song when I succeed."

"Succeed? Succeed at what?" Martin demanded.

Ned swayed on his feet, stealing a drunken glance around him as though the walls possessed ears. Leaning closer to Martin, he whispered, "The philosopher's stone."

"What?"

"I am trying to create the philosopher's stone, so I can turn lead into gold. I nearly did it once. When I do, I'm going to be fab-fabulously wealthy."

Martin stared at him, choking back an outbreak of hysterical laughter. That was what his lordship was doing down here?

Turning back to the table, he flipped the cover of the book open, reading the title.

The Art of Alchemy.

The book might be dusty, but it wasn't old, just one of

those cheap texts that could be picked up for shillings at the Leadenhall Market.

Martin expelled a deep breath. No treason, no witchcraft, no sinister plot to use dark arts against the queen. Only a bored young nobleman playing at being a magus. If there was one thing Martin's acquaintance with the ladies of Faire Isle had taught him, it was how to tell the difference between true magic and utter nonsense.

He closed the book, feeling so giddy with relief, he had to suppress an urge to scoop Lady Danvers up and give her a reassuring hug.

The poor woman still hovered in the doorway, fingering the gold chain of her crucifix and looking sick with apprehension.

Martin smiled at her. "Your brother is right. He is not doing anything dangerous."

"Haven't I told her that many times?" Ned rocked back and forth on his feet. "She's like a frightened rabbit. But women don't understand about magic. They've got no head for—for—"

Ned trailed off, his complexion turning a greenish hue. "Ohhh. Think I'm going to be sick."

Jane's timidity vanished. She darted past Martin and fetched the cauldron in time to prevent Ned from retching all over his elegant shoes.

※※※

JANE DREW THE COVERS ABOUT HER BROTHER, RELIEVED TO have Ned tucked up in his bed at last. His valet worked quietly in another part of the room, folding His Lordship's discarded finery into the wardrobe chest. Timon was a solemn, dependable man and a good Catholic. Jane valued him for his discretion. She wished she could be as sure of all her other servants.

It had been so long since Ned had flown into one of his rages. Jane could usually recognize the warning signs and defuse her brother's temper. But the message from the queen had caught her unawares. If only she could have intercepted the queen's messenger first and relayed the bad tidings herself. She could have softened the blow.

Jane tenderly stroked Ned's brow. Poor boy. Her Majesty had so cruelly disappointed him. Ned stirred beneath her touch, his face waxy and pale. His eyes opened to narrowed slits and he whispered, "Sorry, Jane. So sorry. I disgraced you tonight."

A tear leaked from his eye. "Such a worthless scoundrel. All I bring you is heartache."

"Nay, hush, Ned." She feathered away his tear with the tips of her fingers, just as she used to when he was a small boy.

"Butterflies, Neddie. Butterflies come to drink away your tears."

"You are as ever my one joy," she assured him. "None of this was your fault."

"But—but you must be vexed with me for showing Wolfe the s-secret room."

"I wish you hadn't done that," she said softly. "But I daresay it will all come right. I will see to Master Wolfe. Now you must try to sleep." She bent and brushed a kiss against his brow.

"Dear Jane. So kind. Like a mother, always looking out for me," Ned mumbled, his eyes drifting closed.

"And so I always shall, little brother," Jane vowed silently, compressing her lips in a steely line. Leaving her brother to Timon's care, she tiptoed out of the room.

When she reached the top of the stair, she could see Marcus Wolfe waiting for her in the hall below. He paced restively, his cape swirling off one strong shoulder. The candles' soft glow played over his rich sable hair and trim beard.

To Jane's dismay, she felt her heart miss a beat. She was far too old to go all fluttery over a man she knew little about except that he had saved her life and had once been an actor. Hardly a reputable occupation, but it would not be the first time she had been charmed by a rogue.

Would she ever be able to escape the memory of her past sins, the grand folly of her youth? She'd been but fourteen when she had become wildly infatuated with the handsome young groom in the Earl of Shrewsbury's stable.

"Your passionate nature will lead you to disaster, child," her old nurse had scolded. And Marie had been right. The evidence of that lay buried in an obscure church-yard, a little girl who had mercifully been stillborn.

If all the religious orders had not been dissolved in England, Jane supposed she would have bundled off to a convent. The only other alternative had been a respectable marriage.

Ned might deplore the fact that she had been forced to wed a sickly boy like Richard Arkwright, but Jane herself had been made to see the sense of it. A callow youth would be much easier to deceive into thinking his bride still a virgin.

Poor Dickon, Jane thought. He had never noticed much

beyond his constant ailments and complaints. He'd perished from a bout of tertiary fever during the first year of their marriage. By the time she had wed her second husband, the wealthy wine merchant, Sir William Danvers, Jane had been a different woman entirely. Sober, sensible, dutiful, the fires of passion and rebellion long forgotten until recently . . .

Taking a moment to compose herself, Jane lifted the hem of her skirts and traipsed solemnly down the stairs. Wolfe glanced up at her approach. He stepped forward to greet her at the foot of the risers and smiled. Not his roguish grin but that warm expression that threatened to melt even the most resolute woman inside.

"Is everything all right?"

"Yes, my brother is asleep at last. He is well, or at least he will be until he wakes tomorrow with—"

"I misspoke myself. I meant to ask, are *you* all right?"

Unaccustomed to having anyone inquire after her welfare, Jane scarce knew how to answer. All she could do was nod.

He reached out to take her hand. She should not have allowed him such liberties. But it felt so good, her skin clasped against his warm hard palm. She let her fingers linger in his grasp a moment longer than she should have before drawing away with a nervous smile.

"Oh, Master Wolfe, I can't imagine what you must be thinking—."

"I think nothing except that your brother had too much to drink, something that can happen to any of us."

"Thank you for being so understanding, but I could see how disturbed you were by Ned's strange pastime down in the cellar. I have long been troubled by his interest in—in sorcery."

"Trust me, there's nothing for you to worry about. I have heard that many young noblemen dabble in alchemy, hoping to discover the secret for turning lead into gold. It is harmless nonsense."

"Nonsense that can result in accusations of sorcery. The queen's own astrologer, Dr. John Dee, was obliged to flee abroad for taking his studies too far, trying to raise the spirits of angels to speak to him."

Jane fingered the gold chain of her crucifix. "My faith teaches me that it is all very wrong. God never meant us to pursue such forbidden knowledge."

She gave a wry half-smile. "Ned likes to tease me. He said if I had been the woman in the Garden of Eden, the apple would have remained untouched."

Wolfe smiled, daring to touch her cheek. "Then there would have been no fall from grace and that would make you an angel."

Jane shook her head, thinking how little Marcus Wolfe knew her. Nor did her own brother. "Ned should not say such blasphemous things. He really needs to make confession."

She spoke before she thought, a rare thing for her. She searched Wolfe's face for some sign of disapproval of the Catholic rite, but his expression was merely grave as he asked, "It is hard for you, being denied the practice of your faith?"

"It is hard for a good many Catholics. But I survive, quietly praying my rosary at night where there is none but God to see."

She sighed. "The men in my family have never been as sensible. You—you are no doubt aware of our unfortunate history. My grandfather lost his head fighting for the Catholic cause. My father was killed as well.

"And Ned . . ." She fretted her lower lip. "He is not exactly the most pious of men. But he is young and ambitious, longing to make his mark on the world. That is why I was glad when he became a patron of your theater. It gave him an interest in something besides that horrible alchemy. I dread that one day he too may do something rash and end up in the Tower."

"That he will not! Not if I can help it."

Jane's eyes widened at his impassioned words. Wolfe looked a little taken aback himself by his rash promise, but Jane could not help feeling grateful to him for it.

Impulsively, she rested her hand upon his sleeve. "What a good friend you have been to both of us."

He gave a dry, mirthless laugh, his eyes going strangely dark. "I would be honored to call myself your friend, but I dare not presume. I fear I am nothing but a common rogue."

"No, you are very far from common, Marcus Wolfe," she said softly. Her hand seemed to move of its own volition, caressing his arm.

His eyes flew to hers in surprise. Their gazes met and locked for a long, intent moment. Then he leaned forward and brushed a kiss across her lips.

Jane should not have welcomed the kiss, but the warmth of his mouth stirred in her an unexpected hunger, a longing to bury her fingers in his hair and taste him more fully, feel the hot thrust of his tongue.

She shrank back, flushing. It seemed the fires of her youth had not been entirely reduced to cold ash. One spark remained and Jane did her best to douse it as she bid Wolfe a breathless good night and fled back up the stairs.

⁕⁕⁕⁕

MARTIN LOUNGED IN HIS BREECHES AND SHIRTSLEEVES, HIS feet propped on the desk in his study. He sipped at a flagon of wine, his thoughts so grim he wished he could follow young Ned's example and drink himself insensible.

It was not an indulgence Martin had allowed himself for a long time, not since the advent of Meg into his life. But his daughter was fast asleep, and if there was ever a night for imbibing too much, this was it.

Consume enough wine and it just might wash the taste of guilt from his mouth, Martin thought, taking a huge swallow and grimacing. An English wine, too heavy, too sweet, and it hadn't been properly strained.

Not that it mattered. He doubted there was enough wine in all of London to ease his conscience or erase from his mind the memory of Jane Danvers's trusting eyes.

"What a good friend you have been to us."

Oh, yes, Martin reflected bitterly. About as good a friend as the Grand Inquisitor was to heretics. He pressed the cool pewter flagon against his heated brow.

He was going to have to report what had happened at Strand House tonight to Walsingham. If he didn't, someone else would. Ned had made such a spectacle of himself, ranting about the queen. God knows what the other departing guests might have heard. At least Martin might be able to soften the account, convince the secretary it was nothing more than the ravings of a young man drunk with wine and disappointment.

As for Ned's secret room, Martin saw no reason to speak of that at all. It was but idle foolishness, nothing to do with any conspiracies against the queen, but Walsingham might seize upon it as a pretext to arrest Ned. The secretary was so convinced Lord Oxbridge might be a threat to the queen. If Walsingham could not convict Ned for treason, sorcery might do just as well.

How grieved Jane would be, her worst fears coming true, the last remaining member of her family dragged off to the Tower.

"Not if I can help it."

Martin winced, wondering whatever had induced him to make such a rash promise. He feared Catriona O'Hanlon had been right when she had accused him of being the kind of romantic fool who delighted in rushing to the aid of a damsel in distress.

Jane Danvers was so sweet, so gentle. Seeing her serene face pale and distraught with worry had stirred all of Martin's most chivalrous impulses. He would have promised anything to ease that troubled look from her soft gray eyes.

How refreshing it was to meet a woman content to simply be a *woman,* no interest in acquiring any powerful, forbidden knowledge, sensible enough to perceive the dangers in it.

She truly would make the perfect wife and mother. Martin had not been certain that he stood much of a chance with her until now. She had surprised him when she had dared caress his arm, that warm come-hither look springing to her eyes.

When he had kissed her, unlike Cat, she hadn't threatened to break his head. Jane had blushed adorably, going all soft and breathless with ladylike modesty.

She truly was an angel—.

Martin's thoughts were disrupted by a faint sound coming from the outer hall. The candle flame wavered as though disturbed by a draft. Someone was cautiously inching open the study door. Martin tensed, preparing to swing his legs off the desk and spring into action when he saw who it was.

Cat peered in at him, her tousled red hair spilling about her shoulders as though she had just been roused from her sleep. It scarce surprised Martin to see that she was armed with her sword.

He relaxed back into his chair. "Come in, Mistress O'Hanlon. If you are looking for another chance to run me through, have at it. I entirely lack the ambition to defend myself."

There was a pause and then Cat entered, looking a little sheepish. "I heard someone moving about down here and I wasn't certain who it was."

"So you rushed down, sword drawn, without the damnedest notion of what awaited you? Did it never occur to you that it might be wiser to bar yourself in my daughter's room and allow me to be the first line of defense?"

She scowled, her stubborn chin tilting up. "It is not my habit to cower behind locked doors. Besides, I didn't know that you had returned."

"Now that you are awake, you may as well come in and

join me in a cup of wine. The flagon is over there on the little tripod table. Help yourself."

Cat hesitated before closing the door behind her. Martin didn't know what had possessed him to extend the invitation, but he heartily regretted it as Cat moved into the candlelight.

She was clad in nothing but her chemise, the fabric so worn as to be almost transparent with the candle's glow behind her. Martin could clearly see the outline of her breasts, enough to tell that the other one was just as full and ripe as the first, which he had seen during their duel. The threadbare linen hinted at other charms as well, the curve of her hips, the intriguing dark delta between her legs. And the entire effect of her appearing near naked was made strangely more erotic by the fact of her being armed with that damned sword.

Martin felt himself go instantly hard and shifted position to conceal the fact. Lowering his legs from the desk, he sat upright, complaining, "Mon Dieu, woman! That old shift of yours is a disgrace. Your pride be damned. You are going to have to let me at least furnish you with a decent night rail."

"It would be a waste of money. I prefer to sleep naked," she replied with blithe unconcern as she propped her sword near the hearth. "Of course, I realize I can't do that here. It would be a little awkward if I did have to do battle with an intruder."

"I thought bare-breasted was your preferred method of attack."

"It does not do to start out that way. One loses the element of surprise." As she poured herself a cup of wine, she provided him with a tantalizing rear view, the thin chemise clinging to shapely buttocks. Martin gritted his teeth, grateful when Cat settled herself upon a stool away from the candlelight.

She took a sip of her wine and pulled a sour face. "This is swill."

"I know." Martin stared morosely into his own cup. "But I can't always afford the imported wines."

Cat ventured one more sip, shuddered, and set her cup aside. She leaned back against the wall, yawning and stretching her legs out before her, flexing her bare toes.

She did have astonishingly dainty feet. Martin marveled that she had ever been able to wear his boots. She had trim ankles too, to say nothing of her supple white calves. Martin squirmed in his chair, focusing his gaze on his cup.

"So I gather from your hangdog look, the evening was not a success," Cat said. "Did your Lady Danvers not smile upon you?"

Martin swirled the dregs in his flagon. "Her ladyship was in not much humor for smiling at anyone. The queen sent her regrets and the entertainment fell rather flat without Her Majesty present."

"Meg will be disappointed. She was counting upon hearing all the particulars."

"So has my daughter forgiven me for playing the role of harsh papa?"

"Meg would forgive you anything."

A certain edge in Cat's voice drew Martin's gaze sharply back to her face.

"You sound as though I have done something dreadful I need forgiveness for."

"Not intentionally." Cat caught her lower lip between her teeth. "If I tell you something about Meg, will you promise not to eat me?"

Martin winced. An unfortunate choice of words on her part considering his aroused state.

"I'll do my best not to sprout fangs."

Cat rose to her feet to begin pacing. Martin had already noticed that it was difficult for the woman to hold a conversation while sitting still. But as she paraded before him, he unfortunately noticed other things as well.

"For the love of God, Cat," he said. "Tell me anything you wish. But I beg you to do it sitting down and away from the candlelight."

She paused to regard him with a puzzled air. But as her gaze flicked from the candles back to herself, she suddenly seemed to realize all she was revealing.

"Oh." She gave a wry laugh. Without seeming particularly embarrassed, she returned to the stool.

She folded her hands together, drew in a deep breath, and announced in a rush, "I had a long talk with Meg this evening about this scheme of yours to turn her into a proper little English miss. She's so unhappy, it's nearly killing her."

Martin frowned at Cat, her words about Meg dousing any lust more effectively than a dunk in the Thames.

"You had no right discussing anything with my daughter."

"The child needs to talk to someone since you won't allow her to do so with you. What you have been asking of her is completely unreasonable. To forget she is a daughter of the earth, forget everything she ever learned about the ancient magic—" Cat paused and continued defiantly. "And most of all to forget her own mother."

"What good can possibly come to her from remembering?" he asked.

"Memories are not always good. But even the worst of our past is part of who we are. You have to allow Meg to grieve, to deal with her wounds."

"Wounds are better left healed, not ripped open."

"But the scars remain, Martin. Cassandra's legacy—."

"There is no legacy. Her mother left her nothing."

"Don't be so blind, man," Cat said impatiently. "Everything Cassandra ever taught her, every word she ever spoke about Meg's destiny as the Silver Rose, is lodged in the girl's head."

"Meg is wise enough to know that everything Cassandra said was complete rot."

"Knowing it in her head and in her heart are two different things. Meg is a clever girl, almost terrifyingly so. She is the only one who was ever able to translate the *Book of Shadows.*"

"Because Cassandra forced her and it no longer matters, because the cursed book is gone."

Why did Cat have to keep harping about this? In his agitation, Martin shoved to his feet, as though by pacing he could somehow escape Cat's unwanted opinions.

But the woman was as persistent as a gadfly. Leaping up herself, she trailed after him.

"Meg has an astonishing memory, Martin. I fear she recalls a great deal that she learned from that infernal book. It would be hard for the wisest of women to resist the power of the *Book of Shadows,* let alone a young girl."

Cat darted in front of him, her blue eyes fierce and earnest. "Your daughter is so confused. She needs guidance, someone to teach her the true ways of the daughters of the earth. She needs Ariane. If you would only have the good sense to take her to Faire Isle—"

"Not that again! You accuse me of being blind, but I think you are somewhat hard of hearing. I have already told you no, blast it, and I don't want the subject mentioned again."

He strode over to the window to escape her lest she see the truth. That beneath his anger, his stubborn resolve, ran a current of fear. So much of what she said about Meg struck him in a raw, secret place in his heart.

He could scarce admit to himself that there had been times he had studied Meg anxiously, dreading that he might see in Meg some trace of Cassandra, some hint of the witch's dark influence.

But it wasn't there, he told himself fiercely. Meg was all that was good and innocent. And given enough time she would forget about her mother. She *would.*

Martin stiffened when he heard Cat's footfall behind him.

"I am sorry," she said. "I tend to be too blunt sometimes. My gran used to say it was a fault in all the O'Hanlons. We make far better warriors than diplomats."

She touched his sleeve tentatively. "I know how much you love Meg and she adores you. But she worries about you, too. She told me you've lost the music in your voice."

"I expect she means my accent. Although she is more adept at the English tongue, for some inexplicable reason, my daughter likes me to speak French."

"Perhaps because you *are* French. All this pretending to be English, scheming to become some—some fat country squire in your snug manor house is no better for you than it is for Meg. What of the Martin le Loup who used to find life such a grand adventure? Will you be losing him entirely?"

"No great loss, I assure you," Martin said with a sad smile. "He was never anything much."

"Your daughter would not agree."

"She's only a child. There is much she doesn't understand." Martin angled an indignant glance at Cat. "Besides, who said I would end up fat?"

"Fat," Cat repeated with wicked relish. "And gout ridden."

He tried to glower at her, but ended up giving a reluctant laugh. He became serious again. "There is some wisdom in what you say. Meg does need a woman's guidance. Not that of a daughter of the earth, but of a mother. A proper one who would teach her the gentler arts, music, needlework, and—and managing a household."

"Someone like your saintly Lady Danvers?" Cat asked, her nose wrinkling with scorn.

"Yes, if she could be persuaded to have me."

And if he could keep her wretched brother off the scaffold and Jane from being implicated in any of Ned's folly, Martin thought grimly.

Cat folded her arms, her mouth puckered into a frown. Then she shrugged. "I wish you success in your courting. I

only hope this Lady Danvers has a drop of strength somewhere in the midst of all the sweetness flowing through her
veins. She'll be needing it, I'm thinking, to keep you and
that clever girl of yours in order.

"Heaven knows, I certainly can't stay here forever looking out for the pair of you. I already hoped to be on my way
back to Faire Isle because of Ariane. She—"

Cat broke off, her expression clouding over.

"What about Ariane?" Martin demanded.

"She's with child. Didn't I tell you that?"

"That's wonderful," Martin began eagerly, but as he
recollected what he knew of Ariane's history, he asked
more doubtfully, "Isn't it? Is she faring well?"

"She says so. But you know Ariane. The woman could
be dying and she'd put on a brave face just so . . ." Cat's lip
trembled, and she bit down hard to still it.

Martin grasped her hand in a comforting gesture. "I am
sure Ariane will be well. No one knows more of healing
than the Lady of Faire Isle. She has always been so good at
looking after everyone."

"Everyone but herself. Her confinement will be sometime early this winter. I—I would like to be there."

"I see no reason why you should not be, especially if
Ariane's warning comes to nothing. If all remains quiet
here—"

"I'll be going nowhere unless my chieftain orders me to
do so," Cat said stubbornly.

"Then write to her and ask her. I'll see to it that your
message gets delivered."

Cat frowned, considering, obviously torn by what she
saw as her duty to her chieftain and her concern for her

friend. What an intriguing study in contrasts the Irish-woman was, Martin thought.

So tough, so independent, so solitary, in many ways just like a cat. But when she chose to love, Martin imagined that she did it with a fierce devotion and no one could have a more loyal friend.

As Cat stood in the shadows by the window, her hair fell about her shoulders like dark flame. He resisted a longing to wrap one strand about his fingers and test its silky texture. Under other circumstances, he might have been tempted to do more than that, to draw her into his arms, to coax her lips to part for him, to see if he could find his way to the softness of the woman hidden deep beneath Cat's tough façade.

"All right." Cat's abrupt agreement jarred him out of his dangerous musings. "I should send word to Ariane if for no other reason than I don't want her fretting about me. Perhaps by now she will have learned more about the coven and the Dark Queen and she'll agree with you."

As Cat fetched her sword and headed toward the door, she paused to give him a wry grin. "Then we'll share another cup to celebrate being shed of each other. Although I'll expect something a little better than that dross you offered me tonight."

"Oh, only the finest Bordeaux will do for a grand occasion such as that," Martin said, matching her light tone. He swept an exaggerated bow as she exited the room.

His smile fled as soon as the door closed behind her. As grateful as he was for Cat's help in protecting Meg, he would not be sorry to have the Irishwoman gone. His life was already complicated enough.

For a man who had made up his mind to marry an angel, it wouldn't do at all—this attraction he was feeling for a woman with the devil's own temperament, but all the warmth of heaven in her blue eyes.

※※※

LONG AFTER WOLFE HAD LEFT AND THE REST OF THE HOUSE-hold was silent, Jane stole from her bedchamber. Her elegant gown of cream silk discarded, she was attired as soberly as a nun, wearing a simple dark gown beneath a long black cloak. For once she took no pains to hide her crucifix, the gold cross resting against her bodice.

She did not risk lighting a candle. Relying on memory alone, she picked her way through the dark house and out into the garden. Her soft-soled shoes whispered across the grass as she made her way to the rose arbor.

All was so still and silent Jane feared that he might have failed her because he had been discovered and arrested. She breathed a sigh of relief when a dark figure emerged from the shadows.

He was also cloaked and she could make out little beyond a pale flash of his face and the gold braid that adorned his doublet.

But she did not even bother with the pretense of addressing him as Captain Fortescue.

"Father Ballard," she whispered. "I am so glad you have come."

Chapter Ten

"*G*reetings.
*All honor, respect, and affection to my chieftain. I
have located the girl but do not look for . . .*"

Do not look for what? Ariane squinted at the scrawl on
the page and rubbed eyes tired from straining to read Cat's
message. Ever cautious, Cat had coded her letter by writing in an ancient tongue recognizable only to other daughters of the earth. Ariane was familiar enough with the
language. It was Cat's penmanship that made the translating difficult.

The Irishwoman was far more adept at wielding a
sword than a quill. The barely legible words, the many
blots staining the parchment spoke clearly of Cat's impa-

tience and haste. Ariane smiled, imagining how Cat must have fidgeted as she had labored over the letter, scarce able to keep still long enough to complete the task.

Ariane struggled her way through another paragraph before she was obliged to set the letter aside and stretch. She was finding it difficult to sit still for long periods herself these days.

Pressing a hand to her aching back, she flinched as she rose to her feet, her abdomen swelling with its precious burden. The child within her was thriving. She could sense that and it gave her much comfort, enabling her to ignore her own aches, her often overwhelming sense of fatigue.

Drawing away from her desk, she took a turn about her bedchamber, pausing by the window seat where she had left her workbasket. A small garment rested atop the other clothing she had been mending. Ariane ran her fingertips lightly over the tiny smock she had fashioned, all the stitches set with loving care.

Made of the finest lawn, the fabric would softly caress her babe's skin, surrounding the child with tangible evidence of a mother's love even if Ariane could not be there to hold—

Blinking back her tears, Ariane suppressed the thought. Faith, but she wept too easily these days, she thought with disgust. She had promised herself she would stop harboring these dark thoughts.

She had attended many women through childbearing. Some of these heightened emotions and fears were natural. But she would have scolded anyone else for entertaining the morbid fancies that she allowed to plague her.

But she could not seem to help herself. Knuckling the

small of her back, she gazed out the open window. The sun spilled warmly over the gardens below and the orchard. The sky was so brilliant a blue it dazzled the eyes, and the comet . . .

Ariane caught her breath. The comet was now visible by daylight, a phantom streak appearing to hurl on a collision course with the sun. An evil omen? She *knew* better than to give way to such superstitious nonsense. But even if such a thing were true, there was no reason to believe it had anything to do with her.

Despite the fact that she was the leader among the daughters of the earth and acclaimed as the Lady of Faire Isle, Ariane had always accounted herself a modest woman. Had she really grown arrogant enough to believe that the heavens would spew forth a comet to announce her death?

What folly! But all superstition aside, she could not ignore the sobering reality. Childbirth always involved a risk for a woman, and with Ariane's history, her odds of surviving were worse than most. She could very well die and there was so much she had left undone. One responsibility in particular weighed heavy upon her shoulders.

She had designated no one to carry on the traditions of the Lady of Faire Isle. Her youngest sister would have been the logical choice, but since Miri had married the witch-hunter, the community of wise women would never accept her.

Since her return to Faire Isle, Ariane had begun working with some of the women, teaching them her skills in healing, all that she knew of the old lore. Carole Moreau showed promise, but the girl was still very young.

Ariane knew full well why she had been so lax in this

important matter of choosing a successor. She had so hoped that one day it would be her own daughter. The possibility that she might actually give birth to a girl and not live long enough to teach her—. No, the thought was too unbearable to contemplate.

She would have to deal with the question of the next Lady eventually, but not today, Ariane thought wearily, massaging her temples. She had enough other matters clamoring for her attention, foremost Cat's letter.

She returned to her desk to finish transcribing Cat's message. Cat's tidings, unfortunately, brought little comfort to her already troubled mind.

Frowning, Ariane folded up Cat's letter and went in search of her husband. Justice was not difficult to find these days. Ever since Ariane had told him about the babe, he was either in the stables venting his worries by grooming his hunters or else in the yard chopping wood. Ariane feared by the time their child was born, all the horses would be curried bald and the entire island denuded of trees.

As soon as Ariane emerged from the house, she could hear the steady thwack, thwack of the ax. She sighed. At least the poor horses were being spared at the moment.

Passing through the garden, she moved toward the barn, the woodpile grown so alarmingly high she could scarce see her husband, and Justice Deauville was a formidable man, well over six feet of large bones and hard muscle.

Creeping around the woodpile, she peeked at him as he wielded his ax. Sunlight glinted off the silver strands mixed in his golden-brown hair, his linen shirt damp with sweat and clinging to his powerful frame. Clad in fustian breeches and work-worn boots, he looked like what her sister Gabrielle often teasingly called him, a great peasant.

Despite being nobly born on his father's side, Justice had always been more rooted in the simpler ways of the earth that he had inherited from his mother's people. He usually took great pleasure in vigorous physical tasks and hard work that broke a sweat upon his brow.

But the set of his mouth was grim as he swung his ax, splintering the log with a force that made Ariane flinch. Tossing it aside, he quickly set up another in its place.

Unseen, Ariane watched him wistfully. He had taken the tidings about the babe badly, but not in the way she had feared, hovering over her every moment. Instead he had gone quiet and distant, even drawing away to the opposite side of the bed each night. He had scarce touched her since she had announced her condition and she ached for him to do so.

They had always been so close, knit into each other's very bones, their thoughts and desires often coming as one. It hurt to have him so distant, the event that should have brought them closer together driving them apart.

Ariane went to fetch him a cup of water from the well before making her presence known. She stood back as he cleaved another log, sending splinters flying.

"Justice?"

He glanced up in mid-swing and then suspended his activity, burying the blade in the log. Justice would not have been considered a handsome man by most standards. His lantern jaw and battered nose, coupled with his massive size, gave him an alarming appearance. But when he gazed at Ariane, his harsh features usually softened with a tenderness that caused her heart to beat faster.

As she handed him the cup of water, there was more wariness than warmth in his hooded green eyes. He took several large swallows and splashed the rest over his face. "Merci, but shouldn't you be resting? I thought we agreed you would conserve your strength by napping in the afternoon."

"I needed to decipher Cat's letter." She touched his hand and added, "Besides, I—I missed you."

His thick brows arched upward. "Missed me? I haven't gone anywhere. I am right here."

No, you are not, Ariane bit back the urge to retort.

He handed the cup back to her and mopped his face with his sleeve. When he reached for the ax, Ariane clutched at his arm to stop him.

"Don't you think you have cut enough wood? There is enough here to supply the entire island." She attempted to infuse a teasing note into her voice, but her words came out sharper than she intended.

"It promises to be a cold autumn," he replied.

"I daresay it will be if you continue to look at me that way."

"What way is that, ma chère?"

"As though you think I am going to die. And if you are not looking at me as though you expect to be burying me tomorrow, you regard me with resentment as though I had betrayed you by getting with child."

Ariane had not meant to be so blunt. But there, it was out now. She had said it and perhaps it was just as well, even though Justice's brows knit in a mighty scowl.

"Don't be ridiculous," he muttered.

"I am not. You are angry with me and it would be better if you just admitted it."

His jaw locked in a stubborn line for a moment. "All right, yes. I am a trifle vexed. You know how dangerous it is for you to attempt to have a child. You also know enough of the old wise woman ways to have prevented this. If I had realized you were going to be so reckless, I would have taken precautions myself."

That was no idle threat. Justice had learned to brew a potion from his old witch of a grandmother that could render a man's seed temporarily infertile. He had used it years ago without Ariane's knowledge. She had forgiven him for the deceit, but only because he had promised never to use the potion again.

"Why would I want to prevent a blessing I had long given up hoping for?" Her fingers clamped down on the empty water cup and she vented a bitter sigh. "I wish I had never told you."

"It would be a rather difficult secret to keep." Justice raked his gaze over the bulge beneath her gown. "Did you really think I needed telling? I have lain beside you every night these past thirteen years, made love to you more times than I can count. I know every curve, every nuance of your body as well as I do my own. Did you think I would not notice the changes in you?"

"You never said anything."

"I was waiting for you to confirm my suspicions, hoping—hoping—"

When he clamped his lips together, Ariane finished for him in a flat tone. "Hoping you were wrong."

Justice regarded her with frustration and dragged his hand through the damp strands of his hair. "It has been so many years since you last conceived, I thought we were finally past the possibility of you bearing a child. I believed that you were content with my love, that it was enough for you to be just the two of us."

"I *was*. I am," Ariane cried. "But don't you see after all this time what a miracle this is?"

"No, all I see is the prospect of losing you. Mon Dieu!" He flung up his hands in an angry gesture. "You have always known that is my greatest fear, but you are so bent on having this child, you don't care if you live or die in the process."

"Of course I care," she shouted back at him. "If you were as good at reading eyes as you think you are, you would see how terrified I am. But for your sake I have pretended to be braver than I am. The least you could do is pretend a little for me, feign s-some joy . . ."

She choked off, furious to feel the ever-present tears spring to her eyes. In a rare display of temper, she hurled the cup at him. Justice was too astonished to dodge, but the cup glanced harmlessly off his shoulder.

Blinded with tears, Ariane stumbled away from him. She heard him call her name, but she kept going until she reached the edge of the orchard. Bracing one hand upon the trunk of a tree, she sought to contain the sob that shook her.

Catching her breath, she angrily dashed her tears aside. She stiffened as she became aware that Justice had followed her. He placed his hands on her shoulders. "Chérie, forgive me."

She blinked, refusing to look at him. "Forgive me," he repeated in a voice even more tender that nearly dissolved her into tears all over again. Wrapping his arms about her, he drew her back against him, breathing a kiss against the nape of her neck.

"You don't have to pretend to be brave for me, though it is small wonder you fooled me. You always have been the courageous one. I am the coward. The thought of losing you terrifies me. But I vow I will do better. I will be strong enough to see you safely through this. Both of you."

He splayed one large hand protectively over the region of her womb. Ariane melted back against him, closing her eyes, breathing in the sharp tang of his masculine scent, his warm, hard body bracing hers. It seemed so long since he had touched her like this and it was the first time he had embraced the prospect of their child.

She wanted to savor the moment, but there was another fear she had left unacknowledged and she could no longer contain it.

"If something did happen to me—" she began hesitantly.

"Hush, chérie. It won't." Justice rained fierce kisses along her temple and cheek.

Ariane tipped her head, exposing the curve of her neck to his tender assault. She persisted, "But if it did, you would still love our child?"

Justice paused, his lips halfway down her neck. "What kind of foolish question is that?"

Ariane turned to face him. She cupped his face, peered up at him anxiously.

"I would not want you to be so grief-stricken that you

would blame our babe for my death. Promise me that you will not, that you will love and protect our child no matter what."

Justice looked hurt, but his voice held more blame for himself than her as he replied, "Oh, chérie, have I truly been such a monstrous ogre that you feel you must demand such a vow? Of course I promise. I will do my best to care for our babe, nurture and teach her as you would have done."

He captured one of her hands and brought her palm to his lips. "But it will not be necessary, because you will be there to guide her yourself."

"Her?" Ariane smiled tremulously. "You are so sure then it will be a girl?"

Justice placed his hand on her swollen belly and made a great show of concentrating. To Ariane's delight and his, the child inside her stirred.

Justice grinned. "Mon Dieu. Most definitely it is a girl. I can already sense her, how strong she is, this little daughter of ours."

"She will be just like her papa."

Justice grimaced. "For her sake, let us pray she looks more like her mama."

Ariane laughed. For the moment, all fears and doubts were forgotten as Justice pulled her closer for a long passionate kiss. It was many breathless moments later before she recalled why she had sought him out in the first place.

Reluctantly drawing away from him, she said, "I finished translating Cat's message."

Justice gave her a searching look. "By the expression on your face, I would judge the tidings she sends are not good."

"Not entirely. Martin and his daughter are well and safe for the moment and I thank God for that. But as I feared, Martin stubbornly resists the idea of coming to Faire Isle. He has made a successful life for himself in London with many fair prospects. He wishes to close the door on Meg's past, sever all connections with the old learning and daughters of the earth."

Ariane pulled a rueful face. "Cat is considerably frustrated by his attitude but I cannot entirely blame him. There are times when I myself have longed for a life more ordinary. How much easier and safer our lives would have been if I were not the Lady of Faire Isle and versed in the ancient magic. I would never have been charged with witchcraft. We would never have spent all those years in exile and you—you would still be the Comte de Renard."

While Catherine had restored Ariane to Faire Isle, she had informed Ariane in tones of silky regret that it was impossible to reinstate Justice. Both the Deauville estates and title had been granted to one of the king's mignons, those painted fops who were Henry's constant companions, truckling for his favor. Henry would never consent to deprive any of his favorites of the toys he had bestowed upon them.

Ariane had been deeply aggrieved, but she minded the loss for her husband far more than he did himself.

Justice shrugged at her words. "Bah, you know how little I valued my grandfather's estates and title. Gabrielle was right when she accused me of being a peasant at heart. And you seem to forget you are not the only one guilty of being versed in the ancient knowledge. I learned quite a bit from my own wicked old grandmother."

Slinging his arm about her shoulders to guide her back toward the house, Justice continued, "Chérie, you are far too wise and clever of a woman to ever be ordinary and content with ignorance. And from what I have heard of this petite fille of the Wolfe, I suspect young Margaret may be the same."

"I fear you are right," Ariane said. "Cat intends to remain in London and guard the child until I order her to do otherwise. But I can tell she longs to be delivered from a city that, to quote Cat, 'reeks of Englishmen.' "

As Justice chuckled, Ariane added, "And to own the truth, I miss my gallowglass."

"Until Wolfe can be persuaded, I do not see what else there is to be done. I am astonished he would put his daughter at risk this way."

"Martin does not see that Faire Isle would be any safer."

"Then you must write and tell him of all the precautions we have taken," Justice said. "I have posted sentries at the causeway leading from the mainland and have men patrolling every secluded cove including the far side of the isle. No one will make a landing unseen. And we have friends along the coast of Brittany prepared to light signal fires should any of the Dark Queen's soldiers be spotted approaching. Faire Isle is safer than it has ever been."

"I will certainly inform Martin of that, but I fear it will do little good. He believes we might have overestimated the danger and refuses to be panicked into abandoning his life in London."

"He could be right, ma chère. You must admit it has been very quiet and peaceful since the night Gautier broke up the coven's meeting. If the Dark Queen had learned anything, she would have surely descended upon us by now like an avenging fury."

Ariane wished she could comfort herself with the thought of Catherine's ignorance, but she shook her head. "The queen might be quietly biding her time. That woman has always had the most subtle and tortuous mind."

"But by all reports she has enough trouble managing her half-mad son and preventing the duc de Guise from completely assuming all power in France." Justice gave Ariane's shoulders a bracing squeeze. "If things remain this calm, if we hear no more reports of the coven, I see no reason why Cat should not return to us by Christmastide."

"I worry more about Catherine than those witches."

"She is getting old, ma chère, and she is not immortal." Justice brightened, adding cheerfully. "Even the Dark Queen cannot live forever."

CATHERINE DE MEDICI SWEPT INTO THE AUDIENCE CHAMBER, head held high. The black silk of her gown, the veil trailing from her bon grace cap, lent a severity to her appearance. Her thinning silver hair, heavy jowls, and lined countenance revealed every one of her sixty-seven years.

Nonetheless, she moved majestically to the throne, acknowledging the curtsies and bows of her courtiers with a regal nod. None but she knew what the effort cost her. Her joints, inflamed and swollen with rheumatism, throbbed with pain that would have confined a lesser woman to her bed.

The strength of her will alone kept Catherine on her

feet, that plus a grim determination to display no weakness in front of an enemy. And Catherine had few enemies greater than Henry of Lorraine, the third duc de Guise.

Her sight had grown dimmer with the passing years, but she would have had to be near blind to overlook the duke's presence. He stood out from all the other courtiers, a tall handsome man, his dark hair waving back from a high forehead, his lean face sporting a neat mustache and beard. A scar bisected one cheek, a souvenir from battle that only enhanced his reputation as France's premier warrior.

His costly attire was elegant but simple, reflecting his desire ever to present himself as a soldier, the champion of the Catholic cause. At the age of thirty-seven, he was in the prime of his life. His very health and vigor seemed an affront to Catherine's aging and aching bones.

She would have enjoyed ignoring his presence, keeping him waiting until she had dealt with even the humblest of the petitioners, but that was not possible with de Guise. The other courtiers fell back like a flock of witless sheep scattering before a sleek mastiff.

His blue cape swirling off one shoulder, the duke dropped to one knee before her, a grand gesture, merely for protocol's sake. She no longer had the power to bring this arrogant nobleman to his knees, and what was worse, everyone present knew that.

She kept him kneeling before her as long as she dared. A petty victory, but the only one she seemed able to gain over the haughty duke.

"Your Majesty."

"Monsieur le duc." Catherine summoned a taut smile

that he affected to return. They might well have been figures in a masque, their false smiles but a thin disguise for their mutual loathing.

Catherine had been in a struggle for power with the upstart de Guise family ever since the death of her husband. The present duke had once thought to advance himself by marrying Catherine's own daughter, the Princess Margot. Catherine had thwarted that ambition by wedding Margot to the King of Navarre. De Guise had never forgiven Catherine for that.

Not deigning to offer him her hand to kiss, she touched his shoulder and bid him rise. "This is an unexpected pleasure. I did not know you had returned to Paris."

A lie and they both knew it. Catherine made sure that her spies kept her well informed of this dangerous man's every movement.

"I returned only yesterday and made all haste to wait upon Your Grace."

"Pining for my presence all that much, were you?" Catherine drawled.

"I am sure Your Grace knows full well how much I delight in your company," de Guise replied in an equally silky tone. "But actually it was the king I hoped to address on a matter of some concern to me."

"Indeed?" Catherine wished that her eyes still had their old power to peer into a man's gaze and strip his mind bare.

What could possibly be of such concern to him that he would seek audience with a king he despised? De Guise had already wrested control of the army from Catherine's weak son. He had won the adoration of the people of Paris and was acclaimed a hero wherever he went. He had wealth, vast estates, power. What more could the man possibly desire?

The answer rested behind her, the gilt-trimmed throne beneath its canopy of state.

Not while there is any breath left in my body, Catherine vowed. She deliberately lowered herself onto the seat, a painful process, her knee joints protesting, her hip flaring with a spasm of pain. She gave no indication of it beyond a tightening of her lips.

"Regrettably, the king is indisposed this morning." Catherine suppressed a scowl as she thought of Henry still lolling abed, groggy with the aftereffects of too much carousing with his mignons. But that was preferable to those times when the king suffered from a fit of religious zeal, flagellating himself to the point of collapse.

She continued smoothly, "Rest assured that any petition you present to me will immediately be laid before the king."

A flicker of annoyance crossed the duke's face. Clearly he had hoped to deal with her far more weak-willed son. But he had to know well that any request of his would reach her ears anyway. There had been a time when Catherine's son had attempted to rebel and shake off her influence. But with his kingdom torn apart by civil war and on the verge of ruin from his extravagance, Henry had grown more dependent upon his maman, ready to hide behind her skirts at any hint of approaching disaster.

The duke frowned for a moment and then gave a fatalistic shrug. "My concern is for Thomas Morgan, the man who acts as agent here in Paris for my cousin, the unfortunate queen of Scotland."

"I know full well who the man he is."

"Then why has he been thrown into the Bastille?"

"Because Monsieur Morgan has been a very busy little man, weaving plots, seeking French support for a scheme to free Mary and to assassinate Queen Elizabeth."

"Surely that is something that all devout Catholics should wish for." The duke crossed himself, assuming that look of false piety that always made Catherine want to slap him. She was further annoyed when agreement rippled amongst some of the courtiers present.

"The Tudor witch has falsely imprisoned my poor cousin for over ten years." The duke added sternly, "I hardly need remind Your Grace that our pretty little Mary was once your daughter-in-law."

Catherine pursed her lips. No, she needed little reminder of the pert chit who had once been wed to her sickly first son, Francis. Mary Stuart had had all the hauteur of her French de Guise relations. Those had been bleak and frustrating days for Catherine. In the wake of her husband's death, she had watched the de Guise family and Mary gain ascendancy over Francis, usurping the power and influence that should have fallen to Catherine as the boy's mother and dowager queen of France.

When Francis had died after his brief reign of two years, Catherine had been all too glad to send her impertinent daughter-in-law packing back to her native Scotland. What a willful, passionate creature the young woman had been, ruled by her emotions. It had little surprised Catherine when Mary had come to grief, not only losing her throne in Scotland, but ending up in an English prison.

Masking her indifference behind a bland look of concern, Catherine said, "I am of course as aggrieved as you over our pretty Mary's fate. Alas, I am told that she has grown quite old and fat in her captivity."

"A fate that has overtaken many of us," the duke retorted, raking his gaze over Catherine's corpulent form. One of Catherine's ladies-in-waiting gasped at his insolence.

Catherine chose to ignore it, although her fingers tightened imperceptibly on the arms of the throne.

"Monsieur Morgan is my cousin's good and faithful servant. I must demand his immediate release," the duke said.

Catherine's voice was a shade colder as she replied, "Regrettably, that is a *request* I am certain the king will deny. The arrest of Monsieur Morgan was necessary to placate the English."

"Since when does France need to placate English heretics?"

"We cannot afford to offend any foreign power. Not while both our treasury and army are depleted by civil war." Catherine leaned slightly forward. "A war that as yet you have failed to bring to a successful conclusion."

The duke scowled. "It will only be a matter of time until I crush the Huguenot rebels."

"So you have been assuring me for over a year. Forgive me if I don't order up the fireworks in celebration anytime soon."

De Guise reddened. A low murmur of sympathy for

him and indignation against Catherine buzzed about the chamber. Catherine ground her teeth, realizing she might have gone too far. In the eyes of many Frenchmen, de Guise was the hero and she had long been stigmatized as the villainess. The Dark Queen, the Italian witch, the Florentine upstart who had never been considered good enough to wed into the French royal family. How little had changed since she had come to France as a young bride so many years ago. Nothing except that she had grown older, weaker, and less able to hold her ground against her enemies.

Although it nigh choked her to do so, Catherine assumed a placating tone. "I am sure you will soon triumph over the Huguenots. Then you may don your armor, sail to England, and rush to Mary's aid yourself."

"Be assured that I shall do so," de Guise snapped.

Catherine smiled, entertaining a blissful picture of the duke being pierced by a hundred arrows fired by a troop of enraged English yeomen. There was the chance that he might succeed in putting Mary on the English throne and thus increase his own power and influence, but Catherine doubted it. She was confident that Elizabeth Tudor would never allow that to happen. Like Catherine herself, the Tudor woman was a survivor, tough, wily, and clever.

Wiping the smile from her face, Catherine continued, "In the meantime, I can assure you that Monsieur Morgan is lodged most comfortably in the Bastille and can receive what visitors he pleases. His confinement appears to have in no way curtailed his intrigues on your cousin's behalf."

The duke frowned, not pleased by her response to his demand, but he did not press her further. He had not yet grown powerful enough to entirely bend Catherine and the king of France to his will.

But as the duke made his bow and strode arrogantly from the chamber, Catherine feared that it was only a matter of time.

She heard a few more petitions, but scarce paid heed to what was being said. She'd once had remarkable powers of concentration, but exhaustion seemed to claim her far too easily these days. When she was informed that the English ambassador had arrived, pleading for an audience, Catherine refused, knowing what Sir Edward Stafford wanted. Not satisfied with Thomas Morgan's arrest, the ambassador was insisting that the Scottish queen's agent be turned over to the English government for trial.

Catherine was heartily sick of the entire situation. She wished she could have dispatched the entire lot of them, the troublesome Morgan, the importunate ambassador, and the arrogant de Guise.

Especially the duke. When she had been younger, at the height of her power, she would have known how to deal with such an insolent man after her own subtle fashion. A suitable accident arranged, a little morsel of something deadly slipped into his cup. Had the duke truly grown so powerful she did not dare lift a hand against him or had she merely declined into a weak, elderly woman afraid to act?

How old age makes cowards of us all, she thought with a sigh. Refusing to hear any more petitions, Catherine left the audience chamber, her ladies trailing in her wake.

Her footsteps lagged as she wound her way through the corridors of the Louvre, longing for the peace of her apartments, a comforting tisane to ease some of the pain in her joints.

She encountered the king emerging from his own chamber, as usual surrounded by an entourage of his painted sycophants. She thought sourly that Henry was looking remarkably fit for a man who had declared himself far too weak to deal with any matters of state or petitions.

Once Catherine had desired to have the reins of government entirely in her own hands, but Henry's increasing avoidance of his duties as king was becoming a source of concern and aggravation.

Henry looked little better pleased to see her than she was to see him. He strode toward her, his long black hair flowing back from his sallow complexion. He was attired in a saffron-colored doublet sharply nipped in at the waist, his ballooning trunk hose making his legs appear far too thin, almost effeminate. A painful contrast to the bold, vigorous duke who had so recently swaggered out of the audience chamber.

Although he was younger than de Guise, Henry's face was so carved by lines of dissipation, he appeared the far older of the two.

Catherine forced her knees into a stiff painful curtsy as Henry dutifully saluted her cheek.

"I'm glad to see you looking so well, my son," she replied, making no effort to hide her sneer.

"Well enough for a man with death hovering over his shoulder," he replied peevishly.

Catherine suppressed a wearied sigh. "What ails Your Grace now?"

"What ails me? *What ails me?*" His voice rose a little

with each syllable. "Have you not troubled to look outside this morning?"

Not giving her a chance to reply, Henry gripped her arm and all but dragged her over to the nearest window. Catherine gritted her teeth as her bones protested in pain.

"Look out there," he insisted.

Catherine's heart skipped a beat in spite of herself. Conditions in France had grown so bad these past few years, a succession of droughts and poor harvests spreading famine and desperation. Many had been driven from their homes and taken to begging upon the roads.

She half dreaded to find a discontented mob converging upon the palace. But all she saw was the expansive lawn sloping down to the peaceful waters of the Seine, the lovely gardens and fountains that she had designed herself.

Shrugging free of her son's grip, she said, "I see nothing beyond the fact that the roses require pruning."

"Not there," Henry snapped, seizing her chin, forcing her to gaze upward. "*There*. In the sky."

Catherine squinted until her eyes watered, but she could make out little beyond the faint streak set against the pale blue sky. But she well knew what was agitating her son, the same object that had been sending all other weak-minded fools across France into a panic. That damnable comet.

She fought to curb her impatience. "I have told you before, Henry, it is nothing, only a comet."

"But it is getting closer, Maman."

"No, it is heading toward the sun and will soon disappear entirely."

"What will that matter? It has already delivered its terrible curse. You know what the comet means as well as I do. Some great man is going to die."

And what has that got to do with you, my son? Catherine thought, but she patted his arm. "Surely Your Grace is too clever to be troubled by such nonsense."

"Nonsense? It is a matter of historical fact that a comet appeared to herald the death of Julius Caesar."

"You are hardly a Caesar, Henry," she said dryly, but in his agitation, he ignored her, drumming his fingers against the windowpane. His slender hand was so weighted down by costly rings Catherine often marveled that he was able to lift it.

"And what of the Emperor Nero? From what I have been reading, he most certainly understood the dangerous significance of comets."

"Ah, yes, Nero. What a fine example of reason and sagacity he was."

Her sarcasm was clearly lost on her son because he jerked his head in agreement.

"The emperor was wise enough to consult his astrologers about how to avert the disaster from himself. Do you know what they advised him to do?" Henry leaned closer, dropping his voice to a whisper. "Kill some of the nobles of his court as a sacrificial offering."

"What a fine idea. Why don't you begin with some of those friends of yours who are bleeding the treasury dry?"

Henry glowered at her. "I was thinking more of the duc de Guise."

Catherine froze, peering up at her son in dismay. Even with her dim eyesight, she could not miss the dangerous glitter that had sprung to Henry's eyes. Despite his lethargy, at times Henry could bestir himself to take action, but it was usually of the most rash and disastrous sort. And he loathed the duc de Guise to the point of madness.

With a nervous glance at her ladies-in-waiting and her son's friends, Catherine clutched at Henry's hand and drew him farther out of earshot. She spoke to him in a low urgent voice.

"We've discussed this before. We will deal with de Guise at a more favorable time, but not now. He is far too powerful at the moment. If anything were to happen to the duke and it could be attributed to us, all of Paris and most of the Catholics in France would rise up in revolt against us. We would be lost. It would be the end of everything."

Henry's face twisted into an expression that frightened her, one she had seen too often of late. For a moment he appeared beyond all reach of reason, on the brink of madness.

"It is too late already. I have known that for some time. Our end is written in the sky, Maman. In another year, you and I will both be dust and long forgotten."

For a man speaking madness, his expression was chillingly sane.

※※※

CATHERINE HUDDLED ALONE BENEATH A SHAWL, HER CHAIR drawn up close to the large stone hearth in her private apartments. Even the blazing fire was not enough to drive the cold from her bones. Yet another consequence of her advancing years, she thought dourly. There were times when she could not seem to get warm, an unpleasant presage perhaps, to that other vast cold that awaited her, the chill of the grave.

In another year, you and I will both be dust and long forgotten.

Catherine shivered at the memory of her son's prediction. She could have dismissed it as the ranting of a madman if it had not struck to the heart of her most secret dread. Dying, ceasing to exist. She feared the notion of a great nothingness far more than she did being called to account for her sins before some mighty Creator.

Daughters of the earth considered death a natural process, a fitting end to the cycle of life, being restored to the bosom of Mother Earth, becoming one with the rich soil. But Catherine found nothing comforting about the prospect of maggots stripping away her flesh until all that remained was a pile of moldering bones.

She cringed, shrinking down in her chair. In a fit of self-disgust, she forced herself to straighten. No, she was not ready to become worm food yet, her son's insane predictions be damned.

At least she had managed to placate Henry for the moment, turn him aside from taking any rash action against the duc de Guise. But she would have to watch her son more closely, perhaps slip some sort of powder into his food that would guarantee he remained in a state of lethargic calm. Surely she retained enough skill in brewing up potions to accomplish that.

Kneading her aching shoulder, Catherine sighed. As if Henry's erratic behavior and the duc de Guise's ambitions were not enough to plague her, another problem had returned to haunt her, one that she believed she had seen the end of when that Lascelles witch had drowned in the Seine.

But the legend of the Silver Rose lived on and apparently so did the sorceress herself. Not the Lascelles woman, but a mere child . . .

Catherine stirred as her ladies moved about the chamber lighting candles. Lost in her dark musings, she had scarce noticed the day fading into evening. When one of her ladies tiptoed closer to announce that Captain Gautier had arrived, seeking an audience, some of Catherine's flagging energy returned.

Flinging off her shawl, she struggled painfully to her feet, determined that even before someone as insignificant as her own mercenary, she would appear as a queen.

As the captain entered, Catherine dismissed her attendants. The business that brought Gautier to her was of far too private and secret a nature for any ears but her own. As the door closed behind her ladies, Gautier dropped to one knee before Catherine.

The candlelight played over his sandy-colored beard and curly hair of such thick silken texture many a woman would have envied him. He possessed a genial and smiling countenance, a valuable asset in a cold-hearted assassin.

Carrying Catherine's hand smoothly to his lips, he murmured, "How radiant Your Grace appears this evening. May I be bold enough to say—"

"No, you may not." Catherine snatched her hand away. "I have had my fill of overbold men and pretense for one day. Just make your report and be brief about it."

Undaunted by her rebuke, Gautier swaggered to his

feet. "Very well. It is done, Your Grace. The last of the witches that we captured in the raid have been executed."

"And the warder of the Bastille was discreet about it?" she asked anxiously. Bad enough that all these wild stories were circulating abroad about a sorceress destined to destroy the Dark Queen. Catherine did not need the execution of these witches lending any more credence to the legend of the Silver Rose.

"We were as discreet as it is possible to be when hanging nearly half a dozen women. One of them attempted to cry out 'Long live the Silver Rose.' " Gautier's teeth flashed in a broad smile. "But she was swiftly silenced when the rope snapped her neck. In any case, there was none but myself and the warder present to hear."

"Good." Standing still for too long was difficult for Catherine. She paced off a few steps in a vain attempt to stretch some of the stiffness from her joints. "So not one of those women was inclined to accept the reprieve that I offered in exchange for more information about the Silver Rose?"

"Alas, no. For some reason, they placed little faith in Your Grace's promises of *mercy*." The man had the insolence to smirk. "Nor was any form of torture able to loosen their tongues. We tried everything, the rack, the boot, thumbscrews. We learned little beyond what I told Your Grace before. The Silver Rose is actually the daughter of Cassandra Lascelles, a girl who goes by the name of Megaera, and these women worship her to the brink of insanity."

Catherine shook her head, still barely able to credit

that her dread nemesis was nothing more than a girl. She had actually had the child within her grasp that summer the Lascelles witch had attacked Catherine on the grounds of her own palace.

If Catherine had not been so distracted, so obsessed by the tantalizing prospect of obtaining the *Book of Shadows* from Cassandra Lascelles, would she have taken more heed of Megaera? If Catherine's powers of perception had been as sharp as in her youth, would she have noticed something strange and remarkable about the child?

Even now she could scarce remember the girl. She had been such a plain, scrawny little thing, all fearful wide green eyes.

"Those witches went to their graves without revealing the girl's whereabouts," Gautier said. "Myself, I am inclined to believe the wenches have no idea what happened to their precious Silver Rose."

"Perhaps because they were no more than ignorant lackeys like yourself," Catherine replied. "If you had not bungled that night on the cliffs and allowed the leader of the coven to escape, perhaps we would have learned more."

"I did my best." Gautier shrugged. Unlike other mercenaries who had served her in the past, the captain never stammered excuses for his failures. Perhaps because he was such a bold rogue or far more likely, Catherine reflected bitterly, because the Dark Queen was not as fearsome a figure as she used to be.

"Despite the trick the sorceress played upon us that night, only two of the witches escaped me," Gautier said. "The leader of the cult and the red-haired woman who was seen galloping away."

Gautier preened, stroking the ends of his mustache. "I have since learned that the flame-haired wench was likely an Irishwoman named Catriona O'Hanlon who works for Ariane Deauville."

Catherine frowned. Yes, it made sense that the Lady of Faire would have also heard the rumors of the coven's revival and sent someone to investigate. A surge of anger coursed through Catherine at Ariane, her sister Miri, and that damned witch-hunter, Aristide.

What a fool they had made of Catherine, deluding her as to the identity of the Silver Rose. But taking vengeance upon them was a distraction she could not afford at the moment. All that mattered was locating that child, finding out what had become of the *Book of Shadows*. Then there would be time enough to deal with Ariane's duplicity.

Catherine could sense that Gautier had more to reveal. The man rocked on the balls of his feet, gloating like a tomcat about to deposit a plump mouse at the feet of his mistress.

"What else have you discovered?" Catherine demanded. "I have already told you I am in no humor for games, Gautier. Whatever you have learned, spit it out."

"I have placed spies on the mainland, keeping close watch over the comings and goings from Faire Isle. It seems that the Lady sent the O'Hanlon woman off to find Megaera."

To protect the little dear no doubt, Catherine thought scornfully, the Lady of Faire Isle as usual being tenderhearted and nobly predictable.

"Quite recently a messenger arrived. I have no way of confirming the fact, but I believe that the tidings were from

Mademoiselle O'Hanlon. One of my men was able to track the messenger, ascertain that he embarked for—" Gautier paused dramatically, having the temerity to prolong Catherine's suspense.

"Embarked for where? Damn you, where?"

"London," Gautier replied with a grand flourish of his hand. "I believe that is where the child is to be found. I intend to send some of my men to begin the search—"

"You will send no one," Catherine interrupted icily. "You will go yourself. This matter is far too important to me. You will find that girl and get the book from her if she has it."

"And the little girl herself?"

"You need even ask me that? There is only one way to end the legend of the Silver Rose and that is to nip this flower in the bud. Do you have a problem dispatching children, Captain?"

Gautier smiled, his hand fingering the hilt of his sword. "If King Herod had had me for his lieutenant, you would not be plagued by these present religious wars."

"You are a blasphemous dog, Gautier, and a braggart. I don't want boasts. I want results."

"And you shall have them." The captain swept her a suave bow. "I shall not fail Your Majesty."

"I would advise that you don't, monsieur," Catherine replied coldly. "I may not be the woman I once was, but I assure you: The Dark Queen is not dead yet."

Chapter Eleven

CAT SHELTERED BENEATH THE OVERHANG OF THE UPPER STO-ries of the Angel, the din of the street assaulting her ears. The clatter of hooves and the creak of cart wheels mingled with the shouts of vendors, milkmaids, and bakers plying their wares.

"Any kitchen stuff, maids?" An elderly refuse buyer shrieked at the top of her lungs, struggling to be heard above a pair of tailor's apprentices who were engaged in a noisy brawl.

Accustomed to spending most of her life out of doors, Cat sometimes felt the need to escape the narrow confines of Martin's town house, but even after a fortnight, she had yet to accustom herself to the perpetual dirt, noise, and stench that was London.

But at the moment it was preferable to the racket taking place within the house. Meg was having another of her music lessons and, bless the wee girl's heart, she had no aptitude for it, being all but tone-deaf. Listening to Meg attempt to pluck out a tune on the lute was about as pleasant as hearing someone rip out a cat's claws.

Cat had stepped outside, seeking a brief moment of respite. But she was obliged to shrink back against the black-and-white timbered frame house as some noble lord and a troop of his retainers trotted past, flinging up mud and refuse and sending a trio of kites who had been feeding off a dung heap squawking and fluttering up onto the eaves.

Cat gritted her teeth. By the lady Brigid, how she hankered for the peace of the deep forests and rugged coves of Faire Isle, all swept clean and sweet by a brisk sea breeze. She comforted herself with the message she had recently received from Ariane.

All seemed quiet on the island, nor were there any dire tidings from the mainland of France regarding the Dark Queen and the coven. Ariane had been in communication with her brother-in-law. The witch-hunter Aristide intended to cautiously investigate the matter further. If it became evident that they had overestimated the danger to Megaera, Ariane saw no reason that Cat could not return to Faire Isle by next Christmas.

By Christmas . . . nearly five months away. The prospect would still have filled Cat with bliss except for one thing. She would be going alone, leaving Martin to pursue his mistaken dream of transforming himself and Meg into a proper English family. But she had to remind herself fiercely again and again, it would no longer be any of her concern.

The sound of someone cursing carried to Cat's ears above the usual cacophony of the street. Rob Nettle, the lad who delivered fresh water to the Angel, emerged from the rear of the house. Laboring under the large stave strapped to his burly shoulders, his amiable countenance was flushed bright red.

He was one of the few Englishmen Cat had taken a liking to, a well-spoken, civil lad. But instead of his usual cheery, "Good morrow, Mistress O'Hanlon," he merely grunted in reply to her greeting.

Shielding her eyes from the sun, Cat stared at the tall conical container balanced on Rob's broad back. She blinked in astonishment, for a moment imagining she was seeing things.

"Your pardon, Master Nettle," she called. "But did you realize that um, er, there appears to be an *arrow* lodged in your water carrier?"

Rob cast a disgruntled look as he trudged by. "It bloody well is and I count myself fortunate it didn't end up in my back."

"But who on earth—"

"Your lunatic of a master, that's who!"

"Wolfe shot at you?" Cat frowned, too startled by Rob's reply to correct him as she usually did, indignantly declaring that Martin was not her master. Rob was already too far down the crowded street to question him further. As Cat started around the house to investigate for herself, she heard Rob bellow out.

"I wouldn't be going back there if I was you, mistress. Not unless you don some bloody armor!"

Ignoring him, Cat threaded her way through the narrow passage between the Angel and the neighboring house, heading for the back gate.

Cat usually avoided the garden in the morning, that being the time of day when Agatha did her weeding and pruning. Although Cat had finally succeeded in winning the respect of the other servants, the friction persisted between her and Mistress Butterydoor. For the peace of the household, Cat tried to avoid the old woman as much as possible.

But as she inched open the garden gate, she saw no sign of Agatha. Nor would anyone else have ventured into the garden who had any regard for their skin, Cat thought.

A target had been set up near the apple tree, but the ground before it was peppered with arrows sticking up at odd angles in the dirt. The fence and the trunk of the tree were likewise pierced. Only the target itself remained unmolested as the frustrated bowman nocked his arrow for another try.

Despite the crispness of the day, the dark strands of Martin's hair and his white linen shirt were both damp with sweat, testifying to the vigor of his efforts.

Raising the longbow, he clenched his jaw with determination as he drew back the string. Cat frowned at his awkward stance, the stiff positioning of his left arm only begging for trouble.

She was tempted to call out a warning, but it was too late. Martin released, the bowstring whanging against his arm with a force that made Cat wince. The arrow sailed off wildly, imbedding itself in the beleaguered apple tree.

Martin flexed his battered arm and swore, forgetting his English accent. He cursed in French with a Gallic fluency Cat could not help but admire.

Closing the gate behind her, Cat entered the garden, calling out, "Oh, well done, monsieur. But I think you may hold any further assault. I doubt that tree will dare threaten us again."

Perhaps it was not the wisest thing to taunt a man armed with a longbow and a quiver of arrows belted around his waist, but Cat was entirely unable to resist.

Tensing at the sound of her voice, Martin swung round to glower at her. "If you don't mind, I—"

But he broke off whatever sharp retort he had been about to utter. His scowl easing, he rested the tip of the longbow against the ground and subjected Cat to an intense scrutiny that caused her to bury her hands in the folds of her new gown.

She had been obliged to swallow her pride and allow Martin to order a few garments to replace her stolen wardrobe. Her only other choice would have been to continue wearing the same worn frock and chemise day after day until she became as odiferous as the English, who had a marked prejudice against daily bathing.

The gown had arrived from the dressmaker only that morning. Although cut on the simplest lines, it was a bright shade of blue and the softest wool Cat had ever owned. With an apron knotted about her waist and her fiery hair confined beneath a linen coif, Cat figured she must present the image of a proper maidservant in a fine household.

But she felt like a bit of a fool when Martin commanded, "Turn about for me, please."

She frowned, but realizing she was indebted to the man, whether she wished to be or not, she reluctantly complied.

Martin's eyes twinkled as he took her in from hem to head. His gaze lingering on the demure lace-trimmed cap, he grinned.

"Why Mistress O'Hanlon, you look positively ador—"

But when Cat folded her arms and glowered, daring him to say it, he amended, "Respectable. You look most respectable."

"Thank you," she muttered. "It would have been far better if you had chosen a more sensible and darker fabric. Brown perhaps."

She was only too happy to draw the attention away from herself by gesturing toward his bow. "So what are you doing with that besides slaughtering a poor tree that never did you a lick of harm?"

His grin fading, Martin regarded the bow as though it were some sort of alien object he clutched in his hand. "What the blazes does it look like I am doing? I am trying to learn how to use this damnable thing, but I think there is something wrong with it. It doesn't work at all the way the book said it should."

"Book?"

Martin indicated a volume he'd left lying open facedown upon the garden bench. Cat picked it up and scanned the title. *Toxophilus.* Cat leafed through a few pages, slammed the text closed, and tossed it contemptuously over her shoulder.

"Cat!" Martin protested as the book hit the dirt. "That was written by Roger Ascham, a noted scholar and tutor to Queen Elizabeth—"

"I don't care if it was written by the queen herself. You will not be after learning how to use the bow from any book, especially not one written by an *Englishman*. Such skill is acquired only from years of practice. Happily for you, my da placed my first bow in my hands when I was but six years old."

Striding toward Martin, she said, "All right. Let's have a look at what you are doing wrong."

Martin arched one brow in haughty fashion, but she ignored him, tugging on his hips herself to pull him into correct position.

"Keep your side square to the target. Stand straight. Weight evenly balanced. Feet a little farther apart." Cat kicked at his boot until he gave up resisting her with a disgruntled sigh.

He opened his stance and allowed her to position his hands, bend his elbow to the proper safe angle. "Keep your elbow down. Relax your hands. One finger above the arrow, two below."

To her frustration, he shifted. Placing one hand against his back, she slid the other one around the front of his hips and forced him back into correct position.

"Now draw the string back slowly and concentrate."

"Uh, that's a little difficult. With you grabbing hold of my bollocks."

"Oh. Sorry." In her eagerness to help, she had not realized how far her hand had slipped. Feeling him stir against her, she snatched her fingers away.

"I was only trying to arrange—" She stammered, breaking off when he cast her a wicked look. She retreated a step, folding her hands awkwardly in front of her.

"Just—just take the damn shot already," she growled.

Martin complied, sending another arrow into the fence. And then another. Cat watched as long as she could from a safe distance, her fingers twitching with impatience as she called out more advice. But when another arrow thudded into the dirt before the target, she could no longer bear it.

Her embarrassment forgotten, she pounced on him again, tugging, arranging shoulders, elbows, hips, but taking a little more care where she put her hands this time. She wished she could have helped him with his draw and aim, but it was difficult being so much shorter than he was.

When Martin finally succeeded in nicking the edge of the target, she said, "Better. But let me show you something."

When she reached for the bow, he protested, "This is not a child's toy. You'll never even be able to draw the string."

Cat snorted and wrenched the bow from his grasp. She subjected it to a critical inspection.

It was a fine bit of weaponry, although a little fancy for her taste with its ivory nocks. She held it up and tested the string, estimating the bow to have about a hundred-pound draw. A little heavy for her, but nothing she could not handle.

She extended her hand, demanding an arrow. Martin gave her one with an indulgent shrug of his shoulders. As she fit the arrow into the nock, Cat pulled a face. "Peacock fletching? You'd be better off with plain gray goose feathers. They wear better and are more accurate."

Squaring off to the target, she attempted to line up her shot only to find the strings of her cap in the way. She paused to untie it, impatiently tossing the cap down on the stone bench.

Raising the bow again, she flexed her back muscles, drawing back the arrow and taking aim the way her father had taught her. It had been a long time since she had done any hunting, but the bow felt good and right in her hands, as familiar as caressing a longtime lover.

She took aim, relaxed her draw hand, and released, the arrow piercing the center of the target. Wolfe let out a low whistle of admiration. Cat did her best to bite back a smug smile.

"Now I want you to stand behind me as I take my next shot. Place your hands on my back and feel how I use my muscles."

Martin moved very close, his hands warm on her back as she drew back the string. She could feel the heat of him even through the fabric of her gown, an overwhelmingly masculine presence, all musk and sweat. Carried away by her enthusiasm for her teaching, Cat realized perhaps this had not been the best idea.

Her voice was a little unsteady as she tried to take aim. "You—keep relying on the strength of your arm. But you'll end up sore and tired before you ever complete a morning of hunting. You have to put your entire body into the task."

"Oh, I always prefer to do so," he murmured, his voice rife with suggestion, his breath tickling her ear.

Cat shivered and loosed the worst shot she had ever

taken in her life, even when she was six. The arrow careened wildly through the branches of the apple tree, shredding leaves.

She bit her lip in irritation as Martin crooned, "Bad luck, m'dear. Perhaps you needed to concentrate a shade more."

He seemed solemn enough, but as she twisted away from him, she saw that his eyes held a roguish twinkle.

"There is no such thing as luck with a bow, only skill," she said sternly and shoved the bow back into his hands. She strode off to retrieve the arrows, resolutely ignoring his chuckle.

She spent the next hour putting him through his paces, as merciless as any drillmaster, forcing him to fire off arrow after arrow. Martin's chief problem was similar to what hers had been when learning the bow. Impatience.

"Wielding a bow is not like rushing in with a sword, my wee Cat. It is a far more deliberate art." Her father's voice echoed through her mind, the memory warm and poignant.

Her throat thickened. She swallowed, focusing her attention on Martin. To her delight, he finally achieved a creditable shot, hitting the target near the center.

"Well done," she cried. "What a remarkable man you are."

"Why?" he laughed. "Just because I managed to stop slaughtering the tree?"

"N-no." A little embarrassed by the enthusiasm of her outburst, Cat traced her shoe in the grass and continued almost shyly, "Because you have endured me bullying and hectoring you. There are few men I know who would tolerate being instructed in anything by a woman."

Martin rested his bow against the bench, pausing to wipe a bead of sweat from his brow. "I have the greatest respect for your abilities, Catriona."

Catriona. Something about the way he said her name nearly brought a blush to her cheeks until he added with a mischievous smile: "And besides, it would not have been nearly as enjoyable being *arranged* by a man."

She did blush then.

"Why, you—" she choked, launching herself at him, intending to give him a swift box to the ears. But he laughed and caught her fist easily, pinioning first it and then her other hand to the small of her back.

Cat glowered, but she was all too aware of the mock quality of her outrage. She was enjoying this tussle far too much and not fighting nearly hard enough to get away.

Her heart skipped a beat as Martin drew her tighter against him, her breasts pressing against the taut wall of his chest. He peered down at her through the thicket of his dark lashes.

"Blue was the right choice," he murmured.

"I—I beg your pardon." She was feeling oddly breathless. Perhaps that was why his words made no sense.

"*Blue,*" he repeated. "It was the correct choice for your gown. It suits you."

Cat attempted to give a scornful sniff. "Oh, I suppose you are going to hand me some rot about it being the same shade as my eyes."

"No. I could have searched all of London and I would

never have been able to find that fierce and brilliant a blue."

Damn the man for sounding so sincere and for drawing her closer still. Her heartbeat sped from trot to full-out gallop. It was not the first time she had experienced this heat, this tug of attraction between them. Often during these past weeks, she felt as though it was always there, just pulsing below the surface.

A purely physical impulse and natural enough, she assured herself. She'd been a long time without a man and she suspected Martin also suffered from imposed celibacy. She doubted that the virtuous Lady Jane was servicing his masculine needs.

Yes, a completely natural and understandable attraction, but that didn't make it any the less wrong. A dangerous urge that could only complicate matters between them.

Martin was staring far too intently at her mouth. Cat caught herself moistening her lips in involuntary response. As he bent closer, she retained enough wit to duck her head.

Martin's grip tightened on her for a moment, then he appeared to come to his senses. He released her. They sprang apart, both of them concentrating on retrieving arrows with an energy and focus far greater than the task required.

She needed the use of Martin's knife to dig out one deeply imbedded in the apple tree. He handed it over, scarce looking at her. As she hacked away at chunks of bark, Cat desperately sought for a topic to ease the tension between them.

"So what inspired this sudden urge to take up the bow?"

"It is required of me by law."

"What!"

Yanking arrows out of the target, Martin explained, "Ever since the days of Henry the Eighth, every Englishman under the age of sixty is required to own a bow and know how to use it."

Ah, so that was what all this earnest practicing was all about, just more of Martin's endeavors to transform himself into a respectable Englishman. She wished she could give a derisive laugh at the notion, but she found it all too sad. As sad as that little girl in the house, plucking her fingers raw on that lute in her efforts to learn music "like a proper lady."

Cat knew by now the uselessness of remonstrating with Martin about his plans for himself and his daughter. She contented herself with muttering, "Trust the English to take the joy out of a fine sport by passing a law about it."

"The English don't regard skill with a bow as mere sport. They have no standing army. Should there ever be an invasion, the country relies on all the parishes mustering to the defense."

"With bows and arrows against cannon shot and gunpowder?" Cat could not resist, adding provocatively, "Alas, the glorious days of Agincourt are long behind us."

"Agincourt?" Martin snapped, his reaction exactly what Cat had hoped. He looked ready to spit. "Mon Dieu! There was nothing glorious about that battle. In the first place, Henry the Fifth had no right invading France. And in the second, the French had the English badly outnumbered. It was merely a matter of luck that the English were able to—"

Martin broke off, looking irritated, whether with himself or Cat, she was hard-pressed to tell.

She finished working the arrow out of the tree and strode over to hand it to him. As he thrust it into his quiver, Cat bit down on her tongue. But she was unable to stop herself from saying softly, "You're never going to be able to do it, Martin le Loup."

"Do what?"

"Turn yourself into an Englishman."

He compressed his lips into a stubborn line. "Yes, I will. Like the bow, it just wants more practice."

"And if you do succeed, what then? What if an invasion did come and it was the French?" she challenged. "Could you really become English enough to fire on your own countrymen?"

"From what I have heard, the English are far more likely to suffer an attack from Spain. But if it was France—" Martin paused, an expression shadowing his face that was at once grim and sad. "It wouldn't be the first time I have had to draw steel against someone from my own land. France has been plagued by civil war for years. I was in service to the Protestant king of Navarre, stood shoulder to shoulder in battle with my good friend, the Huguenot captain, Nicholas Remy.

"And I was there in Paris on that Saint Bartholomew's Eve when the streets ran with blood. People slitting one another's throats over who regards the wafer as the holy body of Christ and who thinks it's nothing but a bit of bread.

Frenchmen slaughtering Frenchmen. I daresay you wouldn't understand—"

"Oh, yes, I would. The Irish have been after killing one another for centuries longer than you French. That is how I lost my father."

Martin shot her a curious look. "Meg told me your father perished in battle when you were young, but I assumed it was the English . . ."

Cat gave a swift sad shake of her head. "No, it was in a skirmish with the Dunnes. The two clans had been feuding over who knows what for generations, a dispute over land, a bit of poaching, the theft of a goat perhaps."

She shrugged and gave a brittle smile. "'Tis the curse of my people, short tempers and long memories. I have no idea what set off the hostilities again. I was only eight at the time. All I know is that at the end of that day, my da never came home again."

Her voice grew husky with emotion. She made haste to turn away from Martin but he caught her hand. Another man might have chafed her raw, trying to offer some comforting platitude.

All Martin did was carry her hand to his lips. She trembled at his touch, finding these moments of empathy far more difficult to handle than those times when heat flared between them. Passion she could easily deal with. It was tenderness that undid her.

She yanked her hand free, saying with a false briskness, "I had best be getting back to the house. Meg has been as hard at her music lessons as you with your bow. Someone needs to rescue the poor girl."

Or more accurately rescue Master Naismith and the

rest of the household, Cat thought, but it would not do to make such a jest to Martin. The man was as willfully blind about Meg's musical abilities as everything else.

Striding back across the garden, Cat bent to retrieve the coif she had discarded. She was astonished when Martin reached out to snatch it away from her.

"Don't wear that thing. I gave it to you only in jest, to ruffle your feathers. I never really thought you'd put it on."

"I thought it was necessary, to complete my disguise of being a respectable member of your household."

As though to emphasize her point, one strand of her untamable red hair straggled across her face. Martin tucked it back behind her ear.

"The cap doesn't become you at all." His mouth twisted in a teasing smile. "There is such a thing as trying too hard to be respectable, Mistress O'Hanlon."

Cat tried to think of a clever retort, but any words seemed to lodge in her throat, her heart flooded with a strange ache. Perhaps because she wished so much she could convince him of that very same thing.

※※※

MEG FLEXED HER SORE FINGERS AND FETCHED A DESPONDENT sigh. Her tutor said that in time, her fingertips would become tougher, inured to the lute strings. Perhaps he was right. But what was never going to change was her ability.

In tune or out of tune, the difference between one note and another . . . she simply couldn't hear it. She was miserably conscious of being a failure and a great disappointment. Not just to her father, but to the golden youth who occupied the parlor window seat beside her.

Sunlight filtered through the window, haloing Alexander Naismith's smooth handsome face and wavy blond hair. Stretching his arm around Meg, he patiently readjusted her fingers upon the lute strings for about the dozenth time.

"There now, Mistress Margaret. Try it again. Just the first few bars of the song."

Meg nodded, scarce able to look up at him. Sander's mere presence, let alone his touch, was enough to make her feel all fluttery inside.

Drawing in a deep breath, she gripped the frets of the lute and assailed the instrument again. But no matter how hard she tried to imitate what Sander showed her, all she produced was the most dreadful twanging.

She stilled her hand, letting the last awful note vibrate to silence. A tear welled from the corner of her eye, cascading down her cheek.

"Here now. What's this?"

Sander crooked his fingers beneath her chin, trying to coax her to look up at him. But she ducked her head, allowing her hair to fall forward as she struggled to contain herself.

"I—I am hopeless, Sander."

"Nonsense, milady. You are much improved." Sander bent down, parting her cascade of hair to peer at her. "Why, you have not broken a single string today."

His grin was teasing, but warm as well, eliciting a chuckle from Meg in spite of herself. She tensed at the sound of snoring from across the room.

Sometimes she forgot that she and Sander were not alone. Agatha sat in a chair, plying her needlework, ostensibly to act as chaperone for her young mistress during the music lesson. But she tended to nod off from time to time.

Her head bobbed lower and lower until her chin all but rested atop her sagging bosom and then she straightened with a mighty jerk. She blinked owlishly at Meg and Sander, then gave a foggy smile before returning to her needlework. She set a few stitches before her eyelids grew heavy and the process began all over again.

Sander leaned closer to whisper in Meg's ear, "Sometime I expect Mistress Butterydoor's head to entirely drop off and go rolling across the floor."

Meg clapped her hand to her mouth to stifle a giggle.

"I cannot even begin to fathom how she can sleep that way," Sander added.

"Especially with the horrible noise I am making," Meg replied in a low voice. "Perhaps she puts cotton wadding in her ears the way Maude and Jem do." She turned her attention back to the lute positioned on her lap and added indignantly, "I overheard Jem laughing and telling Maude that you make far more melodic music with one ear than I will ever be able to with two—"

Meg broke off, horrified that she had been insensitive enough to repeat such a cruel jest. "Oh, S-Sander, I am so sorry—"

"Nay, don't you fret a moment about what that rapscallion says. I vow I will box both his ears if he dares to speak so disrespectfully about my young lady again."

His lady? Meg's cheeks warmed and she stared fixedly down at the lute.

"As for myself, I pay no heed to such stupid jests. I am accustomed to them." There was no bitterness in Sander's voice, but Meg felt his arm move and she did not even have to glance up to know that he smoothed his hair over the severed stump of his ear. It was a frequent gesture of his.

Meg tried not to think of it, but sometimes her mind could not help painting terrible pictures of Sander being dragged to the block, his beautiful head forced down upon the rough wood, the sharp glint of the jailer's knife . . .

She shuddered and stole a timid peek up at him. "It was a very cruel thing that was done to you."

"'Tis a cruel world, young mistress." He tapped his slender graceful fingers on the neck of the lute. "But music makes it a much sweeter place."

"Not the kind of music I make," Meg replied glumly.

Sander studied her for a moment before slowly shaking his head. "You have the most astonishing memory of any-one I've ever met. You can recollect the lyrics of every song I have ever taught you, even after you heard them only one time."

Meg brightened a little. "I can," she said eagerly. "I can also hold entire passages of Latin and Greek in my head, nay, entire books . . ."

She trailed off, cringing, realizing it was a dull accomplishment for a girl to boast of, certainly not the sort of thing a lively young man like Sander would find captivating.

"You are a very intelligent girl, Meg." He tapped her playfully on the nose. "So why can't you keep all the music notes in that clever little head of yours as well?"

"Because I don't *understand* the notes. They make no sense to me."

"Well, never mind. Perhaps you will prove more gifted in other arenas."

Sander craned his neck in Agatha's direction as though satisfying himself that the old woman truly was asleep. Leaning closer to Meg, he murmured, "I brought you the object you asked me to purchase."

Meg tensed, stealing a nervous glance at Aggie herself. But the woman continued to snore softly as Sander delved into the pack in which he carried his sheets of music.

He produced a crystal orb the size of a small melon. Before he would hand it over, he said, "Now you've got to promise you won't tell your father about acquiring this. I consider scrying a harmless diversion, but I know Master Wolfe doesn't hold with any sort of magic. I wouldn't want to get on his bad side."

"Oh, I promise," Meg whispered, setting the lute aside. Her fingers quivered as she took the orb from him. She had heard much of scrying balls but had never actually seen one before. It felt cool and heavy in her hands, the glass sparkling in the light pouring through the windows.

Because of her blindness, Cassandra Lascelles had never consulted a scrying ball, although she did not scorn the device.

"A gazing globe can be useful if one possesses the natural ability of a seer," she had told her daughter. *"Perhaps in time we will test if you possess such skill. But for now I want you to keep your mind to the task of translating the* Book of Shadows."

The memory of her mother's voice was enough to send a chill through Meg. She had been forced to master the book and had dreaded that Maman might one day teach her the arts of raising the dead. Even the prospect of a scrying ball had sounded a little frightening. She had never had any interest in acquiring one until now . . .

Holding the orb up to eye level, Meg peered into it, wondering if she did possess the ability to divine the future. She saw nothing except Sander's image distorted by the glass.

Lowering the ball, she realized he was regarding her curiously.

"What a mysterious girl you are, Margaret Wolfe. I still have never figured out what you wanted with those odd curved lenses you had me order from the glassmaker."

Sander thought her mysterious. Meg rather liked that. She summoned up what she hoped was an elusive smile. "Mayhap someday I'll show you."

"At least I know what a scrying ball is for, although I cannot begin to fathom what you mean to do with it."

Divine my future and hope that my mother was wrong, that I am not destined to be this evil Silver Rose.

Meg hunched her shoulders in an effort to appear nonchalant and not desperate to discover the truth about herself. "I just thought it might be amusing to—to play with a scrying ball, see if it really is possible to see into the future."

"You don't need a ball for that. I can tell you your destiny."

"You—you can?"

Sander plucked the scrying ball from her grasp and set it on the window seat. He turned one of Meg's hands palm upward and examined it. Her fingers looked depressingly short and squat compared to his long, graceful ones.

Meg squirmed, her skin tingling as Sander traced the lines on her palm.

"Ah!"

"What do you see?" she asked anxiously.

He squinted at her hand and intoned in a voice of mock solemnity. "I see you grown up to be a dazzling beauty, about to be married to some rich merchant or even a knight in a ceremony so grand, the queen herself will attend. And I shall be obliged to play the lute at your wedding, gnashing my teeth in envy of the bridegroom."

"Oh!" Meg's shoulders slumping in disappointment, she drew her hand away. Sander was only teasing her. He had to be. He was a handsome boy of sixteen while she was only a girl of eleven, scrawny and small for her age at that.

Still, she could not help wondering what he really did think of her. Cat said it was rude to read eyes, invade the privacy of another's thoughts. Meg had been seeking earnestly to curb her ability and it was usually easy with Sander. She was so bashful in his presence, she hardly dared raise her gaze to his.

For once the temptation was too strong for her. Overcoming her newfound scruples and her shyness, she tipped back her head and peered intently into his eyes. They were the softest shade of blue, fringed with pale lashes.

Meg delved deeper and deeper into his mind, groping for his thoughts.

"She is so young, still just a little girl."

Meg's heart sank. Mortified, she nearly broke off contact.

"But what a beautiful woman she promises to be

someday. Eyes like emerald fire, a neck as white and grace-
ful as a swan."

Overcome, Meg dropped her gaze back to her lap. He
hadn't been jesting. Sander really believed she would be
beautiful. Meg pressed her hand to the bodice of her gown,
wishing Aggie had not laced her corset so tight this morning. She could hardly breathe.

As Agatha jerked awake again, Meg barely had time to
spread her skirts over the gazing globe. She and Sander
were obliged to resume the lesson, but Meg found it more
difficult to concentrate than ever.

She was far too conscious of both Sander's presence
and the treasure hidden beneath the folds of her gown. Her
mind wandered, imagining peering into the globe and finding a future as delightful as the one Sander had described.
A grand wedding and herself tall and graceful, attired in a
lovely gown, the queen nodding in approval as Meg joined
hands with a handsome bridegroom who looked a great
deal like Alexander Naismith.

But the wonderful daydream faded, swiftly overshad-
owed by a darker vision, that of Cassandra Lascelles, her
raven hair thrown back, her sightless eyes gleaming with
derision as she laughed all of Meg's wistful hopes to scorn.

Chapter Twelve

C AT EDGED HER STOOL CLOSER TO THE HEARTH, RELYING ON the fire and the glow of a branch of candles for light as she labored over her task. Stripping the peacock feathers from Martin's arrows, she fletched them with far more sensible ones of goose.

She didn't approve of his reason for learning to use the bow, but if it was that important to Martin, she might as well do what she could to help. It wasn't as though she had anything else to occupy her this evening other than watching Meg flit restlessly about the bedchamber.

Meg usually had her nose buried in a book or badgered Cat for more tales of Ireland at bedtime. It was not the girl's habit to be so restive, but Meg had not been herself.

At the supper table, she had fidgeted in her seat, toying with the food on her plate, which she had scarce tasted.

Martin was usually able to jest and tease Meg out of her solemn humors, but he had been too distracted. Cat had frequently observed such edginess in Martin when he was about to disappear on one of his mysterious nighttime errands.

His excuse this evening had been a flimsy one. He needed to meet with Master Roxburgh to go over some accounts for the Crown Theatre. At this time of night? Cat had longed to demand. Some men might go all urgent and tense over totting up figures in a ledger, but Cat doubted that Martin was one of them.

Cat had divided her time at the supper table between studying Martin and his daughter. Both were quick to avert their eyes when they caught Cat staring. While Martin was able to maintain a smooth mask, Meg was too young to do other than start in a guilty manner that filled Cat with unease and made her wonder.

What might Mistress Margaret be up to now? Considering the girl's abilities and knowledge, the possibilities were endless and alarming. Martin's affairs were his own province and none of Cat's concern, she was forced to remind herself. On the other hand, Meg very much was.

But when they had retreated upstairs to the bedchamber, Cat had refrained from the urge to hammer the girl with questions. A friendship had blossomed between her and Meg over these past weeks, but it was a most tender shoot. Cat was loath to trample over it by forcing confidences from Meg.

Although it was difficult, she held her peace. Pretend-ing to be absorbed with the arrows, she watched Meg's pacing out of the corner of her eye.

The girl stopped in front of the looking glass sus-pended over the washbasin. Meg tended to avoid gazing at her own reflection, almost as though she feared to find some great flaw. But she leaned in close to the glass, study-ing herself earnestly.

She widened her eyes and craned her neck, shifting her face to one side and then the other, examining her profile. Her expression alternated between hope and despair as she tugged on her night rail. Pulling the linen fabric tight against herself, she stared down at her chest and emitted a deep sigh.

Cat's lips twitched with a smile, part amusement and part relief. At least now she had some inkling what might be ailing Meg and for once it was nothing so disturbing as wrestling with dark memories of her mother or questions of destiny.

How often as a girl had Cat done the same thing, stud-ied the flat planes of her own body and despaired of ever looking like anything but a half-starved urchin. Of course, she had been a few years older than Meg when she had vexed herself with such thoughts, but Meg was nothing if not precocious.

When Meg caught Cat observing her, Cat swiftly bent back over her work. The girl sidled over to her. She stood before Cat, twisting her hands in the folds of her night dress.

"Cat, may I ask you something?"

"Anything you wish, sweetling."

"How old were you when you grew one?"

"One what?"

"A—a bosom." Meg stared fixedly at her bare toes, her cheeks coloring a fiery red.

Cat bit back another smile. "I don't entirely remember. Fourteen, I believe."

"Fourteen!" Meg cried. "So old?"

"I was quite in my dotage, wasn't I?" Cat replied dryly. "I remember thinking that I was fated to remain as flat as a shield forever and then one summer my breasts erupted like melons ripening on the vine."

"Truly?" Meg stole a hopeful peek down the neckline of her gown.

"Don't be in such a hurry to grow, my wee friend. Acquiring a bosom can be a mixed blessing."

"How so?"

Cat smoothed the tip of a feather as she fitted it onto the arrow. "Well, my new protuberances certainly increased the admiration of the lads. But my bosom also got in the way and diminished my skill with the bow. I was a cursed poor shot until I learned to make adjustments."

"I have no interest in learning to use the bow."

"And what about catching the eye of a certain lad?" Cat teased.

"Don't be foolish," Meg replied. But her color deepened, confirming Cat's suspicions that the girl might be in the throes of her first infatuation and Cat had a fair idea with whom.

But she said nothing as Meg drew up another stool to sit beside her. The girl picked up one of the discarded peacock feathers and played with it.

"How was your music lesson?" Cat ventured.

"I am sure you must have heard."

"Ah, er, no, I was out in the garden for most of it."

"With your hands over your ears, no doubt. It takes a great deal of effort to strangle a lute, but I succeeded in the end."

Cat chuckled. For such a solemn little thing, Meg occasionally evinced a flash of humor.

"If your music lessons are making you so miserable, I will try to speak to your father about it," Cat suggested slyly. "I am sure he loves you enough to—"

"No. No!" Meg cried out in alarm. "I—I am very fond of my lessons."

"Or at least fond of your music master."

"That's ridiculous." Meg snapped. She threaded the peacock feather between her fingers. "Although Master Naismith is very handsome, isn't he?"

"A little too pretty for my taste."

When Meg glowered at her, Cat hastened to add, "I daresay I am too old to appreciate the charms of such a young man."

"He *is* charming and—and clever. He plays the lute and the tabor and has a voice like an angel. I am sure he must be one of the finest actors in all of London, although I have never seen him perform."

"I have. He is very good. In fact, the lad is far better at playing the woman than I am."

Meg crinkled her nose. "I shouldn't like to see Sander pretending to be a lady. He ought to be given a more dashing role, like that of a soldier or a knight."

"His voice isn't deep enough and I wager the boy has more skills with a fan than a sword."

"Why would you say that?" Meg asked indignantly.

"If the lad was any good at fighting, my sweet, he'd likely still be in possession of both his ears."

"It wasn't Sander's fault he lost his ear," Meg cried. "It was an act of the greatest injustice and cruelty. He was arrested for stealing and carted off to Newgate—"

"Alexander Naismith used to be a thief?" Cat interrupted sharply.

"He couldn't help it. He was young and poor and starving. All he took was a loaf of bread!"

Or at least so he had told Meg. Cat wondered if Martin was aware of Alexander Naismith's disreputable past. She would have liked to give the boy the benefit of the doubt, but there was something about the young actor that didn't sit quite right with her.

At times, his eyes could be a trifle too bold, too calculating. He was obviously an ambitious lad and how better for an actor to advance himself than by flattering and cajoling the daughter of the man who was part owner of the Crown Theatre.

Meg was very young and Cat doubted that Naismith was rash enough to seriously trifle with her. But her tender little heart was certainly capable of being bruised.

Brushing the feather against her cheek, Meg peered dreamily into the fire and murmured, "I have heard that sometimes girls are betrothed very young and their bridegrooms wait for them to be old enough to wed."

"That is true, but it is usually for the sake of ambition, for joining great estates, acquiring wealth or a title."

"My papa has ambitions for me."

"True, but he loves you far too well to barter you off so

young." Cat added gently, "And I don't think his dreams include seeing you married to a penniless music master who was once jailed for thieving."

"I know." The light in Meg's eyes dimmed. "Sometimes I don't think I shall ever marry at all."

Cat wrapped her arm about Meg's shoulders and gave her a bracing squeeze. "Of course you will, but—"

"No, I won't." It was not the melodramatic wail of a young girl, but a quiet pronouncement. That unnerving far-too-old look crept into Meg's eyes.

"Sometimes I believe I am fated to be alone."

"Oh, sweetling." Cat cupped the girl's cheek. "You haven't been fretting over your mother's predictions again?"

"This has nothing to do with Maman, at least not entirely. It is just something that I sense about myself. That I will never have a husband or children. That I will remain solitary like—like—"

"Like your great heroine, the Virgin Queen?" Cat filled in with a grimace.

"No, like you." The girl gazed up at her, her eyes glowing with a respect and admiration that caught Cat by surprise.

"Me?"

"You are so strong, brave and independent as women are rarely ever able to be, not even daughters of the earth. You need no one."

"I would not precisely say that, but—"

"And you are happy, are you not?"

"Certainly I—I am content," Cat faltered, as disconcerted by the question as she was by the almost-worshipful look in the girl's eyes. "But being independent is often just another word for—for—"

"For what?"

"For being alone." Cat tucked a stray wisp of hair back behind Meg's ear. "I am no one's hero, child, or example to follow. You must find your own path."

Meg wrapped her arms about Cat's waist and nestled her head against her. "That's what you keep telling me. But it's very hard and confusing."

"I know, babe." Cat dropped a kiss atop Meg's head. "Fortunately, you don't need to find anything tonight. It's been a long day. I think we had both better be getting off to bed before Mistress Butterydoor scolds us for wasting candles."

Meg nodded her agreement, allowing Cat to lead her over to the bed and tuck her beneath the covers. The girl was so tired Cat had scarcely gotten halfway through recounting a stirring tale of Grania, the pirate queen, before Meg was asleep.

Long after the girl had nodded off, Cat prowled about the room, tending to small domestic chores she usually left to Mistress Butterydoor or Maude. Picking up Meg's discarded gown and petticoats and folding them into the wardrobe chest, she continued to be haunted by Meg's question and her own reply.

"You are happy, are you not?"

"Certainly I am content."

Cat had always believed that she was. It had been a long time since she had given up hoping for anything different from her life, a home of her own, a husband and children. After Rory O'Meara had broken faith with her, after she had been cast out of the clan, she had had to learn to fend for herself, to be solitary and independent.

And she had more than learned; she had fiercely reveled in her freedom, her only fetter her friendship with Ariane Deauville. Even that had been a bond that she had embraced cautiously, tenuously.

Love anyone too much and the risk of losing them was too great, the pain of the loss unbearable. Meg fancied her to be so brave, Cat thought with a rueful twist of her lips. In truth, she was the veriest coward.

Tiptoeing back to the bed, Cat arranged the covers more snugly about Meg's shoulder and smoothed her soft tangle of hair back from her brow. The sight of the sleeping girl, so tender, so vulnerable, stirred an ache in Cat's heart that was alarming.

She had grown fond of Meg, too fond perhaps. If she had ever had a daughter— Cat was quick to check the wistful thought. Backing away from the bed, she reflected that December could not come soon enough. She was in great danger of becoming far too enmeshed in the lives of Martin le Loup and his daughter.

Retiring to her own pallet, she flung herself down only to spring up almost immediately, smothering an oath. Some object, small and hard, had jabbed against her spine. Rolling off the pallet, she caught a gleam of something silvery and the white outline of a piece of parchment.

Snatching up the note, she held it closer to the glowing embers of the fire and was just able to make out Martin's brief scrawl.

Here is something else I thought you might require.

Cat scowled. Now what the devil had the man had the impertinence to buy for her? Impatiently she groped through the bedclothes until she seized upon the object.

Holding it close to the firelight, her jaw dropped open when she realized what it was. A small silver flask and from the weight of it, it was obviously filled with some liquid.

Cat uncorked it and sniffed, cautiously tipping the flask to her lips. The Irish whiskey flowed over her tongue and down her throat, flooding her with warmth, burning her with memories of peat fires and heather-covered hills, of her father's booming laugh and her gran's wry wisdom. Tears stung her eyes.

"Damn you, Martin le Loup," she whispered.

What right did he have to be giving her a gift such as this? One that was bound to . . . to touch her heart. No, she assured herself fiercely, wiping her eyes. That was not why she was shaken.

It was the extravagance of the gift that appalled her. The silver flask and the whiskey had to have cost more than her new gown, petticoats, stockings, and shoes all put together. How could Martin afford such things?

Cat frowned, realizing that was a question that had been vexing her for some time. Only a short year ago, Martin had been a fugitive, nothing more than a vagabond player. Now he owned a share in the Crown Theatre, a fine town house staffed with servants, to say nothing of Meg's lessons, her books, her wardrobe. How did the man afford any of this?

MARTIN DELVED INTO HIS PURSE AND PRESSED SEVERAL guineas into the landlord's outstretched palm. It was a great deal of money for one night's supper, but one could scarce haggle over pennies, he thought grimly. Not when entertaining men he might end up sending to the gallows.

The meal paid for, Martin elbowed his way back through the taproom, pipe smoke, the tang of stale ale, and sweat thick in his nostrils. The Plough Inn was far too crowded and noisy for such a hot summer night, but the landlord had placed a screen, separating Martin's company from the rest of the men thronging the rough wooden tables and chairs.

As Martin stepped behind the screen, several of the inn's servants bustled about the table, removing empty platters and trenchers, refilling the cups. Keeping the sack and ale flowing just as Martin had instructed. Some of Martin's guests already evinced signs of having enjoyed his liberality by imbibing too freely.

Father Ballard's face was flushed and Sir Anthony Babington peered dreamily into his cup. John Savage slumped in his chair looking mellow . . . well, as mellow as the bumptious little man ever looked. The only one who still appeared clearheaded was Robert Poley. Bright-eyed as always, Poley gnawed enthusiastically at a turkey leg.

As the servants retired, Ballard beamed up at Martin, "Ah, Master Wolfe. There you are."

The priest raised his cup. "Gentlemen, we have yet to drink to the health of our generous host this evening. To Marcus Wolfe."

"To Marcus Wolfe," the others chorused, flourishing their cups.

"Or should we say Monsieur le Loup," Poley added in a stage whisper with a sly wink at Martin.

Martin forced a smile as the men drank to him. "Thank you, er, *merci*." He had worked so hard to train the French out of his voice, it was hard to remember to lapse into his native accent.

But he had only managed to ingratiate himself with these conspirators by inventing an entirely fictitious history, convincing them he had once been equerry to the duc de Guise, the Scottish queen's cousin.

As he drew back his chair, he flinched as a sharp spasm of pain gripped his shoulder. Licking the grease from his fingers, Poley stared up at him curiously.

"Touch of rheumatism, monsieur?"

"Non." Martin gritted his teeth as he eased down into his chair. "I, er, took a fall today, slipped on some refuse in the street."

His remark set off a spirited conversation among his companions, deploring the sad state London had fallen into, roundly condemning the current Lord Mayor and his council. During the discussion, Martin managed to surreptitiously empty his wine cup into the rushes, something he'd been doing most of the evening. He needed his own head clear if for no other reason than to keep track of all these lies he was telling.

Trying not to draw too much attention to himself, he kneaded his aching arm. Cat had warned him he would get sore if he didn't pay more heed to what she was telling him about the proper way to draw the bowstring. But how the blazes was he supposed to attend her instruction when he had been far too conscious of her hands *arranging* him and the brush of her breast against him?

Considering the direction his thoughts had strayed,

Martin reckoned his aching arm and shoulder was a fitting punishment. He had no business lusting after the woman who was here to protect his daughter.

He tried to rotate his shoulder to ease the pain, but it only seemed to make it worse. Mon Dieu, how much he would have given to forget about all these cursed conspiracies and assassination plots. Rest his aching bones at home tonight. Prop his feet up before the fire, sip some mulled wine, and listen to Cat weave some of those stories that so enthralled Meg and the servants. Martin was as bad as the kitchen boy, perching on the edge of his seat all goggle-eyed as Cat told tales of the Red Branch knights or the Hound of Ulster.

The Irishwoman had a lyrical voice and a genuine flair for drama, knowing just the right place to pause, how to paint images with her hands. Pity it was against the law for women to perform on the stage. What a magnificent addition she would have made to the Crown's company of players.

Not that it would have mattered if the laws were different. Cat could not wait to shake the dirt of England from her boots. If no threat from the Dark Queen or the coven materialized, Cat would be gone before the end of the year.

Martin was surprised at the pang that thought gave him, but he shrugged it off. The woman was proving too much of a distraction as it was, one that he could ill afford if he meant to navigate his way through all these treacherous waters and secure a solid, safe future for his daughter.

"Our good Wolfe no longer appears to be with us."

Martin was snapped out of his musings by Father Ballard's voice. He glanced up from his empty wine cup to find the priest regarding him quizzically.

"Your pardon, mon père," he murmured. "It is the fault of the heat and the wine, making me a little sluggish."

"Usually it is Sir Anthony whose wits have gone a-begging." John Savage sneered, tugging at the ends of his mustache.

"Nay, I p-protest!" Babington cried. The handsome young nobleman blinked owlishly. "My wits are—" He hiccuped. "—are quite well funded tonight."

"Or well floundered," Poley chimed in, invoking far more laughter and table thumping from the others than his weak jest merited.

To anyone peering around the screen, they would have looked like any other party of gentlemen sharing a convivial evening, a little too far gone in their cups. Instead, they were an unlikely band of conspirators, more desperate than dangerous.

Ballard, a priest with visions of glory; Savage, a braggart pretending to be far more fierce than he was; Babington, the romantic, more inclined to philosophize than take action; and Poley, an amiable fellow who just seemed to enjoy weaving plots over a good supper.

And then there was himself, Martin reflected wryly. The Judas in their midst. A French adventurer passing himself off as an English Protestant who claimed to secretly be a French Catholic. He felt like an actor with too many parts crammed into his head, confused about what lines were needed for each particular performance.

And to make matters worse, he knew his patron did

not entirely approve of this current role. Walsingham would have far preferred Martin continue to investigate Lord Oxbridge.

Just as Martin had feared, tales of Ned's behavior the night of the banquet and his angry mutterings against the queen had reached the secretary's ears. Walsingham had been more suspicious than ever that Ned was involved in the conspiracy.

Distasteful as it was to him, Martin had been forced to shadow Ned's movements, but he had uncovered nothing more damning than the fact that Ned gamed far too much and kept a mistress. Martin hoped he had finally convinced Walsingham of that, but he doubted that the secretary would ever believe in Ned's innocence until Martin managed to uncover all those who were guilty.

The servant returned, filling wine cups again. As soon as the man retired, Father Ballard proposed another toast.

"To our good and gracious queen."

"To the queen," the others echoed. A harmless-sounding toast but all the sly smirks and raised brows indicated it was not Elizabeth who was meant.

Martin tightened his fingers on his cup, suddenly weary of all this posturing and pretense. He raised both his cup and his voice a fraction.

"To our queen. La belle Marie."

The others drank, but uneasy looks were exchanged, nervous glances taken over shoulders.

"You are being a shade reckless, my son," Ballard admonished.

"Our kind of enterprise was never achieved by faint hearts."

"No one can accuse me of that," Savage bristled. "Did I not vow upon my sword years ago to rid England of its heretic queen?"

"And yet she still lives." Martin flashed a goading smile. "Unless of course Elizabeth takes some contagion from the heat of your breath."

"Damn you." Savage made a great show of struggling to his feet, clapping his hand to the hilt of his sword.

Martin didn't even bother reaching for his, knowing that Savage would be prevented. The man would wait until he was. Babington yanked Savage back to his seat, an easy enough task as the man swayed drunkenly.

Plopping down, Savage contented himself with twisting the end of his mustache and glowering across the table at Martin.

"Peace, gentlemen," Father Ballard soothed. "We cannot afford any division among ourselves. Not when our plans are so close to fruition."

"Are they? I see little sign of that," Martin retorted.

"Because you don't know everything," Savage growled.

Sir Anthony smiled apologetically. "I fear you are too new to our group to be trusted with all our secrets."

"I don't trust him at all," Savage muttered.

Father Ballard rested his hand atop Martin's sleeve. "You must learn to be patient, my son."

"I am patient enough." Martin affected a shrug. "I just wonder how long we intend to sit around discussing this revolt."

"It is not a revolution to take what belongs to our rightful and good Catholic queen," Sir Anthony reproved.

"*Très bien.* Then when do we *restore* our queen?"

Babington was drunk, but not so befuddled that he did not turn toward Father Ballard as though seeking permission. When the priest nodded, Babington leaned closer to Martin and said, "We only wait for Queen Mary's blessing. Her last letter to me was brief, but she has promised to write more in a day or two."

"Your pardon, Sir Anthony, but it will take more than the queen's blessing for this dangerous uprising to succeed."

"We have been promised help from Spain," Father Ballard said in a low earnest tone. "Perhaps as many as thirty thousand troops will land as soon as we have freed Queen Mary."

"And how are the mere five of us to accomplish that?" Martin demanded. "Are there no other English Catholics who will help us?"

Martin leaned back idly in his chair, giving no indication of how eagerly he awaited the reply.

"There are . . . others," Sir Anthony replied cautiously.

"Who?"

"You'll know when the time is ripe," Savage snapped.

"You are so curious about the English, monsieur," Poley said. "I for one would like to know what help the French mean to provide."

"I have been in communication with the duc de Guise. He pledges to come himself with . . ." Martin paused. If he was going to invent an imaginary army, he supposed he might as well outdo the Spaniards.

"Monsieur le duc will bring fifty thousand troops."

"Fifty thousand!" Babington exclaimed.

Martin wondered if he had gone too far with his lies,

but a ripple of excitement spread around the table, even Savage was grudgingly impressed. Putting their heads together, they were all soon lost in low earnest conversation of how these troops could best be deployed.

Leaning back in his chair, Martin was hard-pressed not to shake his head. What a pathetic parcel of fools they were, willing to believe anything, men more drunk on hope and desperate dreams than they were with wine.

Walsingham had more than enough reason to have them all arrested, but like Babington, he too was waiting for that next letter from the Scottish queen. The one that might give Walsingham the evidence he needed to achieve his true goal, the death of Mary.

These conspirators were little more than the means to an end. Martin could not but wonder how dangerous Babington or any of his friends would have been if Walsingham had not secretly encouraged them, allowed them to communicate with the imprisoned queen. Drawing them all ever tighter into his net, ever closer to the gallows.

Walsingham would have had Ned Lambert there too if he could. During his last meeting with Martin, the secretary had made a most insidious suggestion.

"So you have never seen Lord Oxbridge at any of these conspirators' meetings? You might offer to take him."

"To what end?" Martin had exclaimed indignantly. *"To lead him into treason?"*

"An honest man cannot be lured into anything."

No, but a weak one might be tempted even to his doom. Martin was certainly surrounded by enough evidence of that, he thought as he surveyed the flushed faces of his companions.

He took a swallow from his cup, but the wine left a sour taste in his mouth—or was that his conscience? He had supped with dead men tonight and he had little stomach for the part he had played in their doom.

"Captain Fortescue?" A servant poked his head around the screen to inquire.

Martin started to say there was no such person present when he remembered the priest's assumed identity.

"Yes?" Father Ballard replied with a trace of impatience at being interrupted.

"There is a gentleman here asking for you, sir." The servant leaned closer to whisper something in Ballard's ear. A subtle change came over the priest's face. He gravely excused himself, following the servant from the table.

The others were too deep in their cups and plots to pay much heed, but Martin was instantly on the alert. Mumbling an excuse about the need to relieve himself, Martin left the table and tracked the priest through the crowded taproom.

He followed Ballard out into the alley behind the inn. Hanging back near the shelter of the doorway, Martin observed the priest in urgent conversation with a tall thin man, his features obscured by the night and a dark cloak.

Strain as he might, Martin could only catch snippets of the exchange. The tall stranger clutched at the priest's sleeve.

"Please, father . . . must come."

"Impossible . . . not tonight. Already took grave risk . . . the first time. Will try tomorrow."

"That may be too late."

"I am sorry." Ballard shrugged free of the man, heading back to the inn.

Now what the devil was that all about? Martin wondered. And how did it figure in with all these plots against
the queen?

As Ballard bore down upon him, Martin hastily pretended to be doing up his breeches. The priest looked a trifle disconcerted to encounter him, but he recovered with a
jocular greeting, slinging his arm about Martin.

Martin stole a frustrated glance toward where the
stranger had evaporated into the darkness, longing to follow him, learn his identity. But with Ballard's arm about
his shoulders, urging him forward, Martin had no choice
but to return to the inn.

❧❧❧

CANDLES BLAZED, ILLUMINATING THE MAKESHIFT ALTAR IN
Jane Danvers's private closet, both the crucifix and the
statue of the Blessed Virgin brought out of hiding. Several of the household maids knelt and prayed, Adela and
Hilarie fingering their ave beads, young Louisa with her
head bowed, tears streaking her cheeks.

Only a single candle lit the adjoining chamber where
Jane hovered over the dying woman. Jane had tucked up the
elderly servant in her own bed, doing what little she could
to bring some comfort to Sarah Williams's final hours.

Her old nurse had oft seemed such a formidable figure
to Jane during her childhood. But the tumor gnawing away
at her stomach had reduced Mistress Williams to little
more than a hollow shell.

Sarah looked like a mere waif, swallowed up in the
vastness of Jane's tester bed. The old woman's white hair
was stretched thin across her pink scalp, her withered

cheeks sunken in. Her eyes were feverish as Jane lifted her, coaxing Sarah to take a sip of laudanum in a vain effort to dull the pain.

The old woman could scarce swallow, let alone speak. Nonetheless as Jane lowered her back to the pillow, Sarah rasped, "Has—has he come yet?"

Jane took the old woman's withered hand between her own, wanting to tell Sarah she had no need of a priest just yet. She was not going to die tonight. But the time for such soothing lies had passed.

"Father Ballard will be here soon, I promise you. I sent Timon to fetch him. There will be time enough . . . time enough." Jane faltered over the last words, her eyes stinging with tears.

"Nay, don't be sad for me, milady." Sarah squeezed Jane's hand as another spasm of pain shook her. "I—I will be well as long as I can confess my sins."

"Oh, Sarey, what can you possibly have to confess?"

"We are all sinners, child." The old woman smiled wanly. "But I have fewer regrets than most. I only reproach myself for leaving you now when—you need me most."

"Hush, Sarey. You must not fear for me."

"But I do. I always have. So passionate, so headstrong."

Jane pressed the old woman's hand to her lips. "Nay, I'll be meek as a lamb if only you will stay with me." She attempted to smile as she echoed the promise she had always made as a child when she had been banished to her chamber for letting her temper fly. But the words stuck in her throat and her tears spilled over, splashing against Sarah's hand.

Though it appeared to cost the old woman great effort,

she stroked the back of her frail fingers against Jane's cheek.

"D-don't cry. You have always been so brave, too brave, taking such risks. I should not have allowed you to take this one for me, summoning the priest. I am not afraid to die. Only if . . . if . . ." A look of terror crept into Sarah's eyes.

"I must be forgiven my sins, must have the last rites or I'll never reach the gates of heaven. I—I will go to the fires of hell, never to look upon the face of God."

She clutched at Jane's hand with a strength born of desperation. "I want to see God, milady."

"You shall, Sarey, I swear to you," Jane said. She glanced over her shoulder, wondering what was keeping Father Ballard.

She was relieved when Louisa crept into the room to whisper of Timon's return. Easing her hand from Sarah's grip, Jane bade Louisa stay with the old woman.

As Jane hurried out of the bedchamber, she reflected that she was glad Ned was not at home. Usually, she worried much when her brother was abroad so late, fretting over what he might be doing, but this evening, it was a mercy that he was absent.

Ned was far too impulsive, reckless enough on his own without Jane embroiling him in these secret matters of hers. She even regretted the necessity of employing Ned's valet for her errand. But Giles Timon was a good Catholic, a brave sensible man, and by far the most reliable servant in the household.

Jane spied Timon waiting for her at the head of the stairs and her heart sank. Timon's expression was extremely grave, and worse still, he was alone.

Jane rushed toward him. Not giving the valet a chance to speak, she demanded, "Where is Father Ballard?"

"He was unable to come, milady."

"Un-unable to come?"

"He said he was needed elsewhere tonight. And he feared he might be followed. He thought it might prove too great a risk to both him and your ladyship—"

"The devil take his risk and mine," Jane cried fiercely, not caring that she caused Timon's mouth to fall open in shock.

Jane stole a frantic glance back toward her bedchamber. Her jaw hardened with resolve. "Very well. I shall just have to go fetch the man myself."

"Milady, you can't. You mustn't." Timon trailed after as she stormed back to her bedchamber. "Father Ballard said he will try to come tomorrow."

"Tomorrow will be too late."

But as Jane crossed the threshold, she realized it already was. Her maids knelt by the bedside, weeping and praying. Sarah was lying so still, her sightless eyes staring upward at the canopy.

Jane's breath left her in a rush. Part of her wanted to scream, beat her fists against the wall in anger and frustration as she cried out, "No! I promised her. I promised!"

The other part of her was too numb to move, to speak. She could not even bring herself to close the old woman's eyes, too fearful of the expression she might find there. Not peace, but stark terror.

Louisa approached Jane, clutching her ave beads, her slender frame shuddering as she suppressed a sob.

.   "Oh, m-milady! Mistress Williams is gone and s-she died without a priest." The girl gulped and whispered, "Is she in hell?"

The other two maids turned to Jane, even Timon gazing at her as though they somehow expected her to be able to answer that question. As mistress of the household it was her place to guide her servants, offer them spiritual wisdom. But never had Jane felt less able to perform her duty.

"No," she managed at last. "We tried to fetch a priest to Mistress Williams. It was not her fault that she died without being shriven. I am sure God will understand."

At least Jane hoped that He would, because *she* didn't. Why did such a good blameless woman as Sarah Williams have to die not only in agonizing pain but in mortal terror for her soul? Why was it considered such a crime against the realm merely to consult a priest?

What harm could it have done anyone for a poor old woman to be eased into death, comforted by the rituals of her faith?

When Elizabeth Tudor had come to the throne, she had vowed to be a good queen to all her subjects, Catholic and Protestant alike. But over the years she had yielded to the pressure of her parliament and councilors like Lord Burghley and the infamous Sir Francis Walsingham, passing increasingly repressive measures against the Catholics.

Jane had once believed the queen had done her best to remain tolerant. But Elizabeth had not tried hard enough. The queen had failed her Catholic subjects, making it hard to remain loyal to such a woman.

When Jane's father had died, rebelling against the new edicts, Jane had wept angry tears. Wondering how her father could have risked everything, his life, his family, his estates, adding more disgrace to the Lambert name by being branded a traitor. But now she understood, Jane reflected grimly.

And for the first time in her life, her own path seemed clear.

Chapter Thirteen

MARTIN PACED BEFORE THE WINDOWS IN WALSINGHAM'S chamber at Whitehall. He could see the flare of torches in the dark courtyard below, hear the clatter of hooves as messengers came and went. Wearied servants still bustled about the halls, cleaning, sweetening rushes, airing linens and hanging tapestries, all preparing for the imminent return of the queen.

Even the indefatigable Walsingham showed signs of exhaustion, deep circles rimming his eyes. He leaned back in his chair, listening gravely as Martin concluded the report of his evening at the Plough Inn.

"And when I left them, they were still dreaming over their ale, discussing what rewards they might expect from Queen Mary. Savage hopes to be knighted, Father Ballard looks to be made a bishop. Babington . . ." Martin gave a tired, mirthless laugh. "I think all that young romantic fool longs for is to kneel at Mary's feet and be allowed to kiss the hem of her gown. As for Robert Poley, I have no idea what the devil he expects for his part in all this. I have not yet been able to take his measure."

"And what of the stranger who demanded to see Father Ballard?"

"It was too dark and I was too far away to make out the man's features or clearly hear what was being said." Martin hastened to add, "But it was not Lord Oxbridge, if that is what you are suspecting. I am sure I would have recognized his voice or stature. I know Ned Lambert well enough for that."

"Do you indeed?" Walsingham murmured.

"Yes, I do. I am sure his lordship spent tonight in the arms of his mistress as he usually does."

Walsingham pursed his lips in an expression of disapproval. "Though I cannot condone such behavior, keeping a mistress is the usual practice of many noblemen and his lordship does not have a wife to betray. Why then is Lord Oxbridge so furtive about his amours?"

Martin gave an impatient shrug. "There is no great mystery in that. Ned's woman appears to be a rather low sort of creature. He steals off to meet her in some ramshackle lodging in the stews of Southwark. I can well understand why he would wish to keep such a liaison a secret, especially from his sister. Lady Danvers is a very proper and pious woman."

Martin wondered how a sinner like himself would fare if he were to wed the virtuous Lady Danvers. Well enough, he hoped. He did not love Jane in the way that he had adored Miri, but he respected her. He would try to be all that she would require in a husband, staid, somber, and reliable. That is, if he ever managed to extricate himself from Walsingham's service.

He could not tell if the secretary was satisfied with his current report or not. Walsingham shuffled through some documents on his desk, a faint dent between his brows.

"So what would you have me do next?" Martin asked. "Perhaps I should try to find out more about this Poley."

"No, there is no need for you to do that."

"Why not?"

"Because the man also works for me."

Martin's mouth fell open in shock. "Oh, thank you," he said acidly. "How good of you to inform me of that fact."

"I am not here to inform *you*, Master Wolfe. It is you who are supposed to be keeping me informed," the secretary replied with a cold look. "There was no need for you to know anything about Robert Poley if you had concentrated on Lord Oxbridge as I ordered you to do."

"I did," Martin snapped. "I discovered everything about Ned Lambert there is to know."

"You think so?" Walsingham arched his brows in haughty inquiry. "Then I am sure you are aware that Lord Oxbridge recently applied to my secretary for a passport."

Martin frowned, shifting uncomfortably.

"No, I didn't."

"It seems his lordship suddenly feels a pressing need to travel to France. Now why is that, do you think?"

"Because he'd like to drink some decent wine for a change?"

When Walsingham scowled at his flippancy, Martin amended his tone. "I realize that you are all business and duty, but there are some men who might be inclined to travel for the mere joy of it and there is no more pleasure to be found anywhere than in France. Belike his lordship has friends there—"

"Friends like Thomas Morgan, for instance? Busily weaving plots on the Scottish queen's behalf from his cell in the Bastille? Or Mary's cousin, the duc de Guise?"

"You have no proof that Lord Oxbridge is acquainted with either of those men."

"No, perhaps France is merely the fashionable destination this summer because Lord Oxbridge is not the only one seeking a passport. Sir Anthony Babington has as well."

Martin wanted to dismiss the actions of the two men as mere coincidence, but found that he could not. What if Walsingham was right and there was a connection between Babington and Lord Oxbridge? What if Ned was somehow involved in the conspiracy and Martin was too blind to see it? He hoped not . . . for Jane's sake.

"I am sorry," he said. "It would seem I have not been as vigilant as I thought."

He expected Walsingham to be vexed with his incompetence. The secretary regarded Martin in a fixed manner, but there was a surprising hint of sympathy in his gaze.

"You have served me well enough in the past, Master Wolfe, but I fear you have made a mistake fatal for one in your line of employment. You have allowed yourself to become attached to the object of your surveillance. If not Lord Oxbridge, then certainly his sister."

"You can't suspect Jane is involved in any of this. She is completely innocent."

"I believe she is. But did you ever consider that by proving Lord Oxbridge guilty, you might actually save Jane Danvers from being caught up in his treason? With her brother gone, the lady would perhaps turn to you for comfort."

"Oh, yes," Martin said bitterly. "There is nothing more likely to endear a man to a woman than helping to place her brother's head on the block."

"Lady Danvers need never know of your part in this affair."

"I might be capable of a great deal of deceit, Sir Francis, but that would be one lie even I couldn't stomach. I would have to tell her ladyship the truth and she would hate me. As well she should."

Martin raked his hand wearily over his beard. "This is a wretched affair and I wish it was over with. The only reason I ever entered your service was because of my daughter."

"To secure Margaret a better future."

Martin smiled sadly. "I would do anything for my little girl. Give her the world if I could, with the moon and stars for her rushlights."

Sir Francis drummed his fingers on the desk, frowning. "I realize you find this an ugly business. Believe it or not, so do I. But the end is in sight."

He plucked a document from his desk, hesitating as though debating something within himself. "I am going to risk showing you something and I hope my confidence in you is not misplaced."

Walsingham extended the parchment toward Martin, who accepted it warily.

"What is it?"

"It is the latest letter from the Scottish queen to Sir Anthony Babington. The message was coded as were all the others. That is Phelippes's translation of the original text."

Martin lowered his gaze to the document, his stomach knotting with dread. A dread that was not unfounded. The Scottish queen pressed Babington for particulars of the plot, how many English Catholics would rally to the cause, the number of forces expected from abroad, what ports would be used for the invasion.

But the most damning paragraphs came at the end.

"The forces being thus prepared both within and without the kingdom, then shall it be time to set the six gentlemen to work to procure my release. Before this can happen, it is imperative that Elizabeth be dispatched. Otherwise if the attempt to free me should fail, my cousin will imprison me forever in some dark hole from which I shall never escape if she does not use me worse.

"Fail not to burn this present letter quickly . . ."

And with those words, Martin realized the Scottish queen had flitted straight into Walsingham's web and signed her own death warrant. Phelippes had even embellished his translation with a tiny sketch of a gallows.

Poor foolish woman . . .

"Congratulations," Martin said flatly, handing back the letter. "It seems you have the Scottish queen's head at last and the others as well. I assume you will begin issuing arrest warrants."

"Not quite yet."

When Martin regarded Sir Francis in surprise, Walsingham explained, "I still do not know the identity of all of these six gentlemen the queen mentions. I intend to let her letter go through to Sir Anthony with a forged postscript imitating the queen's hand, asking him to name all his conspirators."

"And if your ploy does not work?"

"Then I shall arrest the men you supped with tonight and be obliged to resort to cruder methods."

Martin shuddered. "Torture, you mean."

"Certainly it is an extreme measure I would deplore and one you might help avert. Perhaps with a little more diligence and ingenuity you can discover the rest of the names."

"I will do my best to get you the list, sir."

"Even should Lord Oxbridge chance to be one of the names on it?"

Martin hesitated a fraction too long before nodding. He feared that Walsingham might have noticed, but the secretary appeared absorbed by some papers on his desk. Bowing, Martin made haste to take his leave. He tensed when he was stayed by the sound of Sir Francis's voice.

"Martin?"

He glanced back in surprise. It was the first time the secretary had ever addressed him by his Christian name.

"When the arrests are made, take care to keep your distance so that you are not also detained."

Martin frowned. "But I work for you, sir. Surely you would be able to vouch for me."

"I would, but this matter will no longer entirely be in my hands. If you were implicated in the plot, it might be awhile before I could extricate you. You could be imprisoned for months, perhaps years. It would be most distressful for your daughter.

"So . . . so just take care," Walsingham concluded, dropping his gaze back to his paperwork. "Good night, sir."

LONG AFTER MARTIN HAD LEFT, SIR FRANCIS STARED OFF INTO space with a troubled frown. He employed many spies and agents, trusting none of them entirely and liking them even less.

But something about Martin le Loup had touched him in a way none of the others ever had. Perhaps it was the man's devotion to his daughter or perhaps it was because Martin possessed something the others lacked—a conscience.

Such scruples were not a desirable attribute in a spy, but Walsingham could not help respecting Martin for it. Unfortunately, it also meant that Martin could no longer be relied upon, especially with regard to Jane Danvers and her brother.

But Walsingham had learned early on in his career never to depend entirely upon one source for accurate information. Just as he had learned even the most upright men could be turned to his use if the right bribe were offered, the right pressure applied.

The tall man who crept into Walsingham's office kept

his head down, his eyes trained upon the floor as though he was deeply ashamed to be there.

Walsingham smiled reassuringly, addressing his new informant in the most gentle of tones.

"Good evening, Master Timon. I was hoping to hear from you tonight."

MARTIN DUCKED BETWEEN TWO HOUSES TO AVOID AN EN-counter with the watch. He would have had to come up with a good excuse for being out after curfew and he felt that even he had exhausted his store of lies for one night.

Trudging down his street, he could see his rented lodging silhouetted by moonlight, the Angel's sign creaking slightly in the night breeze. The black-and-white timber frame house with its overhanging upper story was little different from any other house on the street.

But to a man who had been a vagabond most of his life, the Angel was like a castle, a fortress whose simple wattle-and-daub walls had kept his daughter safe from the dragons that menaced her.

It was a bleak thought that the dangers that now threatened Meg might be of his own making. As Martin crept to his front door, the meeting with Walsingham continued to churn through his mind. The secretary's questions, demands, and warnings buzzed like a nest of angry wasps in Martin's head. Especially Walsingham's parting words.

Take care.

Had that been kindly advice or a threat? The secretary was so soft-spoken, it was not always easy to tell the difference. Despite his quiet Puritan demeanor, Sir Francis would be a dangerous and ruthless man to cross.

But Martin needed no warning from Walsingham to realize the precariousness of his situation. If he played his role as spy half-heartedly, he risked detection from Babington and his cohorts. Foolish they might be, but they were also desperate men, their own lives at risk. Arouse their suspicion and Martin could end up dead.

If he played his role well, Martin might succeed in gaining the information Walsingham wanted, the names of those six men. But if Ned Lambert was indeed one of them, Martin would expose him as well and thus break the gentle Lady Danvers's heart.

And if Martin played his part *too* well, he risked being mistaken for one of the conspirators and being cast into prison himself . . . if not worse.

Martin swore softly under his breath. What a damnable coil. Why had he never realized before how appallingly vulnerable he was? He was but a bit player in this great drama and his exit from the stage would be of importance to no one except Meg. His daughter would be left an orphan.

No, Martin thought, his jaw hardening. He would not allow that to happen. He was merely being morose because he was tired and there was something cursed depressing about creeping home at such an hour to a dark, unwelcoming house. All the world snug asleep except for him.

As Martin eased open the front door, he was startled when it was wrenched from his hand. Cat confronted him, holding her candle aloft. A petite dragon in a night rail and bare feet, her blue eyes flashed fire, her red hair a wild tangle.

"Ah! So 'tis himself come creeping home at last," she snarled.

Martin was momentarily taken aback and then he tensed with alarm. Crossing the threshold, he closed the door, demanding, "What's amiss? Has something happened to Meg?"

"Meg is fine other than the fact that she possesses an idiot for a father. Where the devil have you been? Do you have any idea what time it is?"

"Yes, and the rest of the household will as well if you don't keep your voice down," Martin hissed. "What the blazes are you doing out of bed?"

"Wearing a hole in the floor, waiting for you. Picturing you arrested by the watch or—or set upon by footpads, beaten to a bloody pulp and left lying in a gutter." Cat punctuated her words with furious gestures, regardless of the candle she held. "Do you have no sense? No idea of the dangers you risk traipsing alone through the streets at this hour?"

Martin reared back when the candle flame flared close to his cloak, spattering him with wax. "The only danger I am in at the moment is of being set afire."

He seized the candlestick from her. Grabbing her by the arm, he hustled Cat inside his study before she roused the entire house with her tirade.

"Cat, I am sorry if I worried you—" he began, but she wrenched herself free of his grasp.

"Worried me? Not a bit. I was only concerned for Meg's sake. I am sure I don't care a damn if you get your fool throat slit in some dark alley."

But she *did* care. Beneath all her furious bluster, Martin could see traces of her fear still shadowing her eyes, the small furrow carved into her brow. Despite his own exhaustion, Martin couldn't help breaking out into a grin.

"Mon Dieu! You really were concerned about me."

"No such thing," she spluttered. "I told you. It was because of Meg. I didn't want the poor wee thing fretting over her da."

"Oh? Did Meg notice I was gone? Is she also up pacing?" Setting the candlestick atop the mantel, Martin made a great show of looking about for his daughter, even peering under the desk.

"No, damn you! She's sound asleep just as I should be." Cat advanced upon him, shaking her fist. "By the goddess Brigid, I'd love to kick you square in your arse."

"Have at it then. It will save me the bother of trying to do it myself. I apologize if I alarmed you with my absence, but I thought you'd have been long abed."

"I waited up only because I have a vexing matter to discuss with you."

Martin's grin faded as he divested himself of his feathered cap and short cape. He truly was sorry if he had caused Cat any distress, but he did not feel up to any further confrontation. All he wanted to do was collapse into bed and bury his head in his pillow.

He winced at the ache in his sore shoulder as he tossed the garments down upon the stool in front of the hearth. "Whatever is amiss, can it not wait until morning?"

"It nearly is morning."

Martin vented a resigned sigh. "Very well. What have I done to vex you now?"

"I am sure you know full well what." Cat glared. "I might have been obliged to accept a few garments from you, but I made it abundantly plain I will not be beholden to you any more than is necessary."

Martin arched his brow in mild surprise. "You aren't . . . I didn't. All I bought you were some articles of clothing, a gown, a cap, an apron—"

"This is not a blasted apron."

For the first time, Martin noticed she clutched something in her other hand. Cat slapped it down upon the desk, the small silver flask he had hidden in her bed earlier that afternoon.

"Oh. That." He shrugged. "Damnation, woman, it is not as though I showered you with diamonds or ropes of pearls. It's just a trifle."

"It's not just a trifle. The cursed thing is made of silver."

Martin spread his hands in a helpless gesture as he sought to explain. "You were so upset by the loss of your father's flask. I knew I could not replace that, but I wanted to do something."

He frowned. "But I overdid it, didn't I? I have a tendency to do that. It was just that the silver one looked so fine. Should I have bought you a plain leathern one instead?"

"You shouldn't have bought me anything at all," Cat said with a furious stamp of her foot.

"I can see that. It was obviously a stupid gesture. I am sorry."

"N-no. It was a gesture of great kindness and—and I

have no way to repay you." Cat was swift to turn away, but not before Martin caught the glint of something in her eyes. Tears?

It was not often Cat displayed such womanly emotions. But if he had learned anything at all about the Irishwoman in these past few weeks, it was that Cat hated any display of weakness or vulnerability. Her ferocious pride and temper were often nothing more than a mask for the tender feelings she found it so hard to show. She had obviously been more moved by his gift than she cared to admit.

He approached her tentatively. Grasping her by the shoulders, he turned her to face him although he realized he risked getting his ears boxed.

But Cat merely stared at his boots, blinking fiercely. Martin crooked his fingers beneath her chin, obliging her to look up.

"The care that you have shown my daughter is more than payment enough. I am the one who is in your debt." He smiled. "Besides, why should there be any talk of repayment between friends?"

Cat sniffed, mopping her eyes with the back of her hand. "Ah, so is it friends we are now?"

"Well, you have not tried to skewer me or break my head for the past week. So I thought you must be starting to like me a little."

When her lips quivered, he tipped his head and peered coaxingly at her. "So am I forgiven for the flask? And for worrying you, or do you still want to kick my arse?"

Cat gave a reluctant laugh. "I suppose your arse is safe from me. At least for the moment."

She retrieved the flask from the desk, cradling it almost

reverently between her hands. "Usquebaugh . . . you even filled it with usquebaugh. However did you manage that?"

"I realize you have a poor opinion of London, but it is a port city. You can purchase most anything if you look hard enough. I have no familiarity with Irish whiskey so I can't vouch for the quality."

Cat uncorked the flask and took a swig, a blissful expression stealing over her features. "It's the finest I've ever had."

She offered the flask to him. But as he took it, his gaze was riveted on the drop that clung to her mouth, filling him with the overwhelming temptation to taste her lips instead.

It didn't help when Cat's tongue swirled sensuously over her bottom lip, capturing the drop, savoring it, turning her mouth a moist, luscious hue of red.

Wrenching his attention back to the flask, he took a huge gulp of Cat's whiskey and choked. He felt as though he had swallowed a mouthful of fire and it blazed down his throat, scorching everything in its path.

Eyes watering, he spluttered, "Sweet Jesu, woman. How—how do you drink this stuff?"

"It is a wee bit fiery with a sharp bite to it. It takes some getting accustomed to." She grinned. "Just like me."

When he continued to wheeze, she whacked him on the back, striking against his tender shoulder.

"Ow! Ow!" Hastily setting the flask down, he clutched at his throbbing muscle.

Cat studied him through narrowed eyes. "Aha! I told you so, Martin le Loup. I warned you you would regret it if you kept relying on only your arm muscles to draw the bow."

She clucked her tongue. "Ah, well, you'd best strip off your doublet and shirt. Let me have a go at you."

A go at him? Even in the midst of his pain, that conjured far too many heated images. "No, I thank you, Cat. Truly, I am fine. I—"

But Cat was already undoing the buttons of his doublet with a brisk efficiency. He made another weak effort to protest, but he had learned by now that arguing with Cat was like trying to resist the tide. Sometimes it was just easier to relax and let the current take you.

He flinched as she eased the doublet off his shoulder, and then drew his shirt over his head, the cool air striking his bare skin.

Sinking down onto the chair, he gritted his teeth and braced himself for the assault. But her hands were strong, gentle as she began to knead his shoulder, working her way down his arm.

After an initial throb of pain, the knots in his arm muscles began to give way before her warm, skilled fingers.

"Oh," he groaned. "Up a little higher. No, a little lower. Yes, right there."

He sighed as her fingers worked their magic on the sorest spot, thinking that if he had been a dog, his leg would have twitched with pure ecstasy. He leaned his head back and closed his eyes, giving himself over completely to her ministrations.

It was strange, he mused. He had never known the affection of a mother or a sister. Most of his relations with women had been of the fleeting kind. Those that had had any significance in his life, his daughter, Miri Cheney, and now Lady Danvers, consisted of him trying to be the protector and take care of them.

He had never before experienced a woman looking after him. The sensation was new and rather sweet. Martin found himself liking it, perhaps a shade too much.

He felt some of his tension ebb beneath Cat's healing touch, all his doubts and fears . . . Not vanishing precisely, but receding, no longer seeming quite so overwhelming.

At least not until Cat asked softly, "So what's wrong?"

He tensed all over again. "Wrong? Why—why nothing. What makes you think anything is wrong?"

"The fact that you are about as malleable as a fireplace poker." Cat dug in, massaging his shoulder joint. "I don't know where you went tonight or what you did, but I'll wager it was something more stressful and dangerous than totting up theater accounts."

"What have you been doing?" he attempted to jest. "Using the wise woman's trick of reading eyes?"

Martin froze. That was something that had never occurred to him before, although it certainly should have. "You can't do that, can you?" he asked anxiously, half starting to leap up from the chair.

Cat leaned on his shoulders, forcing him back down. "No, not very well. What I read is knots. And your muscles are pure plagued with them tonight."

As she resumed working upon his shoulder, she said, "You are as tense as some beleaguered beastie with a pack of hounds nipping at his heels."

She leaned forward to steal a glance at his face. "So what is troubling you, my edgy wolf?"

Martin stared deep into those wise Irish eyes and for a moment he was tempted to tell her everything about his dangerous service to Walsingham, the conspiracy plot, his tormenting doubts about Ned Lambert.

Cat was so strong and possessed of such a practical streak. She would not flinch, tremble with fear, or blanch with horror as another woman might. But Cat would certainly disapprove, think him more of an inept fool and poor father than she already did. Sinking knee-deep in such a quagmire when there was already enough danger to threaten Meg. Never mind that he had done so with the best of intentions, trying to secure a better future for his daughter.

Martin didn't know when Cat's opinion had begun to matter so much, but he was disconcerted to realize that it did. Besides, the woman had already taken enough risks on his daughter's behalf. Cat didn't deserve to be dragged into his troubles as well.

"Nothing is wrong," he insisted. "I am just exhausted. I spent a very tiresome evening in a smoke-filled crowded tavern in the company of some—some actors." He added with a grimace, "Some very bad actors as it happens. I would have far rather been at home with Meg and—"

And you, he nearly said. He broke off just in time. He closed his eyes again to avoid her probing gaze, trying to force himself to relax beneath her touch. He didn't know whether Cat believed his account of his evening. He could almost sense her frown as she went back to kneading his shoulder.

To divert her attention, he asked, "So how did you and Meg fare tonight?"

Cat's fingers dug in deep, relieving the pain in his

upper arm. "Well enough, but I am a bit concerned about Meg and her tutor. I am not sure young Master Naismith is a good choice as a music master."

"Why? The lad is very gifted with the lute."

"I don't deny that. But did you realize he was once a cutpurse? Apparently, he was not as gifted at thieving because it cost him an ear."

"Yes, I know all about that."

"And you still engaged him to teach Meg?"

"Sander no longer has any reason to steal. Besides his employment at the theater, he is frequently engaged to play for entertainments at many of the great houses in London. He has found a patron in Lord Oxbridge and has written several songs for his lordship."

Songs that Ned had had no qualms about passing off as his own, Martin thought wryly.

"Perhaps Sander was a pickpocket when he was young, but you forget, my dear, so was I."

"You must have been a deal more skilled at it than young Master Naismith." Cat paused in her massage to give a playful tug at one of his lobes. "You still have both your ears."

"I was luckier, that was all. I was never caught and it was not the penalty in France." His brow furrowed in a slight frown. "Actually, it's a rather odd sort of punishment. How does one deter a thief by removing his ear? It would make more sense to lop off the hand."

Cat snorted. "The English have their own brand of logic, incomprehensible to the sane world."

Martin smiled as Cat resumed kneading his arm. He realized he was starting to enjoy the warm feel of her hands on his bare flesh for a far different reason, but like some poor half-frozen beggar, he lacked the strength to draw away from the fire. But Cat's next words were like a splash of cold water.

"You do realize that Meg is smitten with Master Naismith?"

Martin's eyes popped open. "Don't be absurd. She is a mere babe."

"She is maturing faster than you realize. Give her a few more years and there is the promise of a lovely young woman budding there. The lads will be noticing and swarming round like bees after a honeypot."

Martin scowled, picturing young men sniffing about his little girl's skirts like a pack of randy hounds.

"They best keep their noticing to themselves or I'll lop off more than ears," he growled.

"I thought that was what you were grooming her for, to make a good match, to be some man's bride," Cat replied in an irritatingly reasonable tone.

"Yes, but not for years and years," he snapped. Shrugging off her hands, he shot to his feet, any pleasure he'd felt at Cat's touch replaced with annoyance and a strange feeling akin to panic.

He was ambitious for Meg to make a good marriage but the thought of anyone taking his daughter away from him caused a hollow ache to lodge in his chest. His little girl had been his for all too short a time.

"I know many girls wed at a tender age, but I don't believe in that. It is wiser for a woman to be more mature, older . . ."

"Like around thirty perhaps?" Cat asked.

"No!" He glared at her. "But nineteen or twenty at least."

When she had the impertinence to smirk at him, he bridled. "I have heard of many women who married later in life."

"Or not at all," Cat said with a rueful twist of her lips.

Martin regarded her curiously. He could only hazard a guess at Cat's age, somewhere in her mid-twenties perhaps. God knows she could be prickly and hot-tempered, stubborn and far too independent. But for a man who had the courage to tame her, there was also a womanly tenderness to be found, to say nothing of her physical charms, those vivid blue eyes, the silky red hair, and the firm, ripe breasts. So why had she remained unmarried?

Although he expected to be rebuffed, he asked, "What about you? Did you never consider being wed?"

Was that a flash of some remembered pain he saw in her eyes? If so, she was quick to shrug it off.

"Not really. My stepfather tried to arrange a match for me when I was fifteen, if for no other reason than to be rid of me. He sought to bundle me off to a chieftain in a clan far to the north. He even had my portrait done and sent."

Cat squared her shoulders defiantly. "Not that I would ever have submitted to such an arrangement, but happily nothing came of the scheme once O'Hare saw my portrait. It was a dreadful likeness. It made me look like a redheaded midget."

"Er, but, Cat, you *are* a red-haired midget."

"Varlet," Cat said with a mock growl. Doubling up her fist, she took a playful swipe at his ear.

Laughing, he caught her wrist, making amends for his teasing by kissing first one knuckle, then the next and the next. The tension in her hand relaxed, her fingers uncurling. Their eyes met and locked. She splayed her hand on his bare chest over the region of his heart.

His breath quickening, Martin bent closer to brush his mouth against hers. Just one kiss could do no harm. A light friendly one, or at least that was what he intended until his lips met hers and Cat responded. She returned the kiss eagerly, her lips parting, breathing whiskey and warmth, filling him with fire.

Pressing his hand atop hers, he held her palm captive to his racing heart. This . . . this was not wise, he told himself, but his head no longer seemed to be in charge.

He angled his mouth to deepen the kiss, her tongue engaging his in a fiery duel. She wrapped her arms about his neck and he hauled her hard against him, feeling the softness of her breasts through the thin chemise.

They traded kiss upon kiss with a desperate hunger. Martin fumbled with the ties of her chemise, nearly tearing the fabric as he shoved it off one shoulder. He emitted a low groan, his loins tightening as he cupped her breast. Warm and supple, the globe fit perfectly in his hand.

As he trailed kisses down her neck, Cat arched back, clinging to his shoulders. She gasped and caught her lower lip between her teeth as he bent lower, fastening his mouth over the rosy crest of her nipple.

Even as he tasted her, reason fought to reassert itself. Somehow he managed to draw back, wrench himself away from her. Cat let out a low cry of protest and he dragged his hands back through his hair, feeling as though he could have yanked out a handful in sheer frustration.

Panting, they stared at each other. A red flush stained Cat's cheeks, but the expression that stole across her features was not one of shame or modesty. Only pure consternation.

"Ah, Holy Brigid," she cried. "What the devil are we doing?"

"I—I don't know."

They sprang apart, moving away from each other. As Cat fumbled to draw up her chemise, Martin reached for his shirt and dragged it over his head. Any residual pain in his arm went unnoticed due to the far greater ache in his groin.

"I am sorry," he said, his fingers clumsy and wooden as he did up the lacings on his shirt.

"Bah to your apologies," Cat said. "You are not the only one to blame here."

"But I am the master of this household and for me to take such advantage of a lady beneath my roof—"

"I am not a lady and you most certainly are not my master. You are merely a man and I am a woman. What happened just now was . . . was perfectly natural."

"Natural, but wrong."

"Oh, yes, indeed. Very, very wrong. You—you have your ambitions, your Lady Danvers to consider."

"Yes, Jane," Martin replied, surprised by his lack of enthusiasm, appalled that he could not even conjure up an image of the lady's face at the moment.

"And—and all I want is to return to Faire Isle," Cat stammered. "I certainly don't need the entanglement of—of taking a lover."

"A lover!" Martin cried. "No, of course not. There is no question of anything like that between us."

"So no harm done." Cat attempted to smile. "It is not as though we are a stallion and mare in season. We both possess enough reason not to give way to such impulses again."

"No. Decidedly not," he agreed. But when he risked a glance in Cat's direction, the longing that still simmered in her blue eyes was near enough to draw him straight back to her arms.

He turned away and shrugged hastily into his doublet, not paying much heed to whether he buttoned it crooked or straight. When he dared look at Cat again, she had uncorked her flask and was taking several deep gulps of whiskey.

Fighting fire with fire, he was tempted to jest. Recollecting that it was his teasing that had sparked the mischief between them in the first place, he swallowed the remark.

Instead, he said in a tone of false heartiness, "It will be light soon. We'd best get to bed.

"Alone," he added hastily. "You to yours. Me to mine. . . ." He trailed off, realizing he was blithering like an idiot. He just needed to close his mouth now.

Cat nodded and corked the flask. For a woman who had not appeared the least embarrassed when he'd kissed her or nibbled on her breast, she suddenly looked adorably shy.

She said, "I fear I was terribly ungrateful before. I didn't even really thank you for *this*." She hugged the flask close to her.

"You're very welcome, but I told you. It was nothing, a mere trifle."

"No," she insisted. "Your gift means a great deal to me."

"Cat, if I gave you a thousand silver flasks, it wouldn't be a tenth of what you've given me. You have no idea how much it has eased my mind having you here to help me protect Meg. You make me feel as though I am not quite so much—"

Alone. He nearly said and was stunned. Until that moment, he had never realized that he was.

"Not quite so worried," he finished lamely. Summoning up a smile, he patted her awkwardly on the shoulder.

"Good night, petite chatte," he said softly.

But he doubted Cat heard him as she darted past him and out the study door.

※※※

CAT CURLED UP ON THE WINDOW SEAT IN MEG'S BEDCHAMBER, keeping as still as she could so as not to disturb the slumbering girl. Still unable to sleep, Cat clutched her precious flask and watched the first streaks of light break over the rooftops.

Good night, petite chatte. Martin's adieu lingered in her mind.

Little cat. Her mouth twisted in a reluctant smile. Cat would have gutted any other man who dared call her that. Why then had she allowed Martin to get away with it? Nay, even enjoyed hearing the absurd endearment fall from his lips? And why had she allowed him to give her such a costly gift?

She traced her fingertips over the silver flask and sighed. If she was going to torment herself with such unanswerable questions, she supposed she might as well ask the most difficult one.

Why had she stayed up all night waiting for Martin, frightened out of her wits that something dire had happened to the wretched man? She could tell herself her fear had been on Meg's account, but that was only partly true.

The child would have been devastated by the loss of her father, but Cat was disconcerted to realize Meg would not have been the only one.

When Cat had fretted and worried over his absence, the thought that Martin might never walk back through that door, that she might never again see his teasing smile, hear his hearty laugh, had brought a strange tightness to her throat.

Cat leaned her head wearily back against the wall. Oh, what folly was this? Martin le Loup was a charming rogue, but she had known such handsome rogues before, and she saw too clearly all the flaws in this one.

He was stubborn, reckless, and impractical, with far too great a penchant for drama and the grand gesture. But such failings seemed of little significance set next to his kindness, his courage, his humor, and his generosity.

And his steadfast heart. He would do anything for his daughter and that was what truly worried Cat. Exactly what was Martin doing to secure this dazzling future he envisioned for his child? She still had no idea what business kept drawing him abroad at night, but she was certain it had nothing to do with the Crown Theatre.

When he had finally crept home in the wee hours, he

had looked worn thin, almost haggard with whatever secret he was keeping. And this from a man who was usually so insouciant, so bounding with energy, being with him was like riding the tail of that fiery comet that still plagued the sky.

Whatever Martin was involved in, it had to be something dire and hazardous indeed to dampen the spirits of such a man. Perhaps the next time he set off at night, Cat might do well to follow him and—

What was she thinking? She had to sharply remind herself why she was here and that was not to protect Martin le Loup, but his daughter.

"The man is none of your concern. None of your concern," she repeated to herself several times as though it were some sort of protective chant. One that wasn't working, perhaps because her lips were still bruised and tender from the warmth of his kisses.

Christmas. It was still nearly five months away, she reminded herself fiercely. Five months in which to avoid becoming any further entangled with Martin. But Cat feared it might already be too late.

Fool that she was, she had gone and fallen in love with the man.

Chapter Fourteen

THE BELLS PEALED ALL OVER THE CITY IN WILD JUBILATION. One would have thought they signaled a great military victory or the birth of a royal heir. But it was merely the tribute that had to be paid whenever the queen embarked on her royal barge down the Thames. The sextons in each parish received extra compensation for performing this duty. It was a waste of good coin and an infernal racket all for nothing.

The *English,* Cat thought. But she curbed her disgust for the sake of her young companion. After weeks of keeping Meg confined to the house, it had finally seemed safe enough to allow the girl a brief outing to visit her father's theater. The fact that she might also at last catch a glimpse of her much-admired queen only added to Meg's excitement.

"Come on, Cat," Meg said, tugging at her hand, urging Cat toward the throng of spectators on Southwark's bank. Hats were doffed and handkerchiefs fluttered, as the crowd waved and cheered. A holiday mood reigned upon this warm summer's day, but Cat was wary, ever on the alert. She studied the assembled crowd, scanning faces, especially those of the women, to make certain no one appeared unduly interested in Meg. But all eyes were trained toward the river.

As Meg dragged Cat to the bankside, Cat glanced over her shoulder, looking for Martin, and discovered that he lagged behind.

They had been keeping a discreet distance from each other ever since that night they had given way to passion and nearly mated right there in his study. Cat had taken herself sternly to task, seeking to curb her desires and her foolish thoughts as well.

Fancying herself in love with the man! A notion born of too much usquebaugh and too little sleep. But she was honest enough to concede her attraction to Martin, especially when he was looking as fine as he did today.

He was clad in a velvet doublet and the hue matched the vivid green of his eyes. His short black cape dangled gallantly off one shoulder, his tight trunk hose emphasizing the muscular contour of his legs. The feathered toque he wore perched jauntily on his head, enhancing his handsome, dark raffish looks.

He was a sight to stir the pulse of any female with good red blood in her veins. But Cat doubted the woman that Martin escorted had anything but milk water coursing through hers.

Lady Jane Danvers strolled beside Martin, her eyes modestly cast downward. They were trailed by her ladyship's entourage, several male servants clad in livery and Mistress Porter, her maid, a sour-faced creature with gray-streaked hair.

The two women, their skirts stiffened with farthingales and their slow mincing steps, were the chief reason that Martin had fallen behind. Cat could have easily dispensed with their company.

But Lady Danvers had never seen the theater that she had invested in and Martin seemed eager to show it to her. Cat suspected that Martin was also anxious for his daughter to become better acquainted with the woman he hoped would become Meg's stepmother.

Cat herself had been curious to finally get a look at the lady. The woman was pretty enough, but quiet, prim, and dull. Garbed in her ecru silk gown, her fair hair bundled beneath a bon grace cap, her ladyship could have faded into the hazy afternoon and never been missed. At least not by Cat.

Martin was certainly attentive enough, speaking softly into Jane's ear. As though if he raised his voice a shade too loud, the poor thing might swoon, Cat thought contemptuously. But she could see where Lady Danvers's gentleness and air of vulnerability would appeal to a man like Martin with his romantic notions of chivalry and flair for drama. Her ladyship was the kind of woman he could kneel before and vow to slay all her dragons.

Very different from herself, Cat reflected. *I* am *the dragon.*

She was startled out of her glum reflections when she

realized Meg had slipped free of her grasp. Cat experienced a moment of panic until she spotted the girl a short distance away.

Watching her mother drown had given Meg a certain fear of water. But her desire to see the queen consumed all else, overcoming both her wariness of the Thames's flowing current and the strangers thronging the bank.

The girl attempted to push her way through the crowd to reach the edge of the shore. Darting over to her, Cat clamped her hand down on Meg's shoulder.

She bent low enough to growl in the girl's ear. "Meg, you promised. If we allowed you to leave the house, you swore to keep close to your da and me."

"But, Cat, I can't *see* the queen," Meg wailed.

And you are not missing much, Cat was tempted to retort. But she was not proof against Meg's beseeching green eyes.

Elbowing a stout merchant in the ribs, pressing past a skinny matron and her daughter, treading on the toes of a gangly sailor, Cat helped Meg move forward. Ignoring the curses and glares she received, she managed to work Meg to the front of the crowd.

The barge was nearly past the bend of the river, twelve burly men in scarlet straining at the oars, the queen barely visible beneath her golden canopy. Cat hunkered down and hoisted Meg up onto her shoulder, not an easy feat.

The girl didn't weigh much, but to make a good impression upon Lady Danvers, Meg was attired in voluminous skirts of her own. As Cat cautiously straightened, she could see little beyond the froth of pink silk. But she was rewarded by the sound of Meg's delighted gasp as the girl clutched at Cat's head and cheered along with the rest of the crowd.

Her shoulder muscle straining, Cat held Meg aloft as long as she could. As the cheering died and the crowd around them began to disperse, Cat figured the barge must have passed from view.

As she bent to lower Meg down from her shoulder, Cat lost her balance. Teetering backward, she twisted, using her body to break Meg's fall as they both hit the ground.

Cat bit back an oath at the jarring impact. Knocked breathless for a moment, she sprawled on her back, wincing at the jab of Meg's elbow as the girl scrambled off of her.

"Oh, Cat, are you all right?" she cried.

Cat could do no more than nod. She had taken far worse spills in her life riding the mean-tempered ponies in her stepfather's stables. But she had landed hard on her rump. As she sat up cautiously, she grimaced, knowing she was going to have a mightily bruised tailbone.

Regaining her feet, Meg peered anxiously down at her. "Are you certain you are not injured?"

"Only my dignity," Cat muttered.

"And fortunately, you don't have a great deal of that," a cheerful masculine voice asserted.

As Martin loomed in front of her, Cat felt a hot tide of color wash up in her cheeks. She realized that in her fall, her skirt had hiked up, revealing a fair amount of leg. Before she could react, Martin tugged her hem back down. Stealing his strong arm about her waist, he helped her to rise.

She might have been tempted to lean against him for a moment, but she was too aware of Lady Danvers and her maid approaching. Cat straightened stiffly, dusting off the back of her gown, feeling very much the fool.

But Martin looked more amused than vexed. His eyes dancing wickedly, he said, "I know how you feel about the queen, Mistress O'Hanlon, but you really must try to curb your enthusiasm."

Cat scowled at him. Before she could retort, Meg piped up, "Don't you be teasing Cat, Papa. You know it was me who wanted to see the queen."

"And did you finally get a good look at your great heroine?" Martin asked.

Meg heaved a deep sigh. "No. There were too many *daft* courtiers on the boat with her."

The girl spoke with such an unconscious imitation of Cat's own lilt that Cat was forced to laugh.

So did Martin. "*Daft* courtiers, is it now?" he chuckled, likewise copying Cat's brogue. "It appears Cat is after turning you into an Irishwoman."

"An improvement over becoming English," Cat retorted. "As for her speech, you've only yourself to blame. Your daughter has inherited your devilish talent for mimicry."

Martin grinned at her and the tension that had divided them this past week seemed to dissolve until Lady Danvers stepped forward.

Her lips curled in the tentative smile of someone who senses that something might be amusing but hasn't the least idea what it is. "I saw you tumble to the bank, Margaret. Were you playing some sort of a game?"

Recollecting that she was supposed to be here in the guise of lady's maid, Cat stepped back, trying to efface herself. But Meg caught at her hand, explaining to Lady Danvers, "I wanted to get a good look at the queen and Cat tried to help me. She lifted me up and we fell."

Mistress Porter bustled toward Meg, straightening the girl's ruff and plucking strands of grass from the sleeve of her gown. The maid pursed her lips at Cat in disapproval.

"A proper servant usually tries to protect her mistress from such a vulgar crowd," Porter said. "But perhaps being Irish, Mistress O'Hanlon doesn't know that."

Meg shied away from the woman, backing up against Cat. "Cat does protect me. Always. And she is not my servant. She is my *fianna*—"

Cat gave Meg's shoulder a warning squeeze.

"My friend," Meg concluded.

"Mistress O'Hanlon's services have proved invaluable to my daughter," Martin added with a warm glance at Cat.

Porter gave a haughty sniff and started to say something. But to Cat's surprise, Lady Danvers quelled her maid with a reproving frown.

"That will do, Porter." Her ladyship turned to Meg, tucking a stray wisp of hair behind the girl's ear. "I quite understand. I had someone who took great care of me for years and I regarded her as my dear friend. My old nurse, Sarah, was a very kind and good woman."

"When did she die?" Meg asked.

It might have been a good guess on Meg's part based on Lady Danvers's melancholy demeanor. But considering how earnestly Meg stared into the lady's eyes, Cat suspected otherwise. She gave Meg another warning nudge and the girl guiltily lowered her gaze.

Her ladyship looked mildly astonished by Meg's insight, but she answered, "I lost Sarah only recently. She died from a tumor."

Her voice dropped even lower as she added, "It—it was a most painful death."

"I'm sorry," Meg replied.

"At least now the poor woman is at peace," Martin said.

Her ladyship nodded, but Martin's attempt to comfort her only rendered Lady Danvers more melancholy. An awkward silence ensued.

The woman certainly knew how to leach the joy out of a pleasant afternoon outing, Cat thought. She was relieved when Martin suggested they continue on to the theater.

As they wound their way up the street to the Crown, Martin encouraged Meg to walk with Lady Danvers and her maid. The girl obeyed dutifully if not enthusiastically.

The theater was only a short way from the riverbank, but the narrow street was crowded with vendors, carts, and people streaming to the small arena opposite the Crown.

A group of men was playing at bowls on a patch of green outside a tavern. Normally Meg would have craned her neck to watch, her curiosity like an empty well, eager to drink in every new sight and sound.

But her disappointment at being so near Queen Elizabeth and not being able to see Her Majesty had cast a damper over Meg's spirits. That and striving to be agreeable to Jane Danvers, a lady so grand she could not venture abroad without her maid and an escort of serving men.

The men marched ahead of her ladyship, clearing a path for her and keeping back the crowd. Meg could not help reflecting that Cat would never required any man to pave the way for her, nor would have Meg's formidable mother—and Cassandra Lascelles had been blind.

But neither Maman nor Cat was a proper lady like Jane Danvers, all that Meg's father wanted her to be one day. Papa had never said as much, but Meg suspected he hoped to wed Lady Danvers and provide Meg with a new mother, the last thing she desired.

Unless it was Cat, Meg thought wistfully. But that was impossible, given the way Papa and Cat often quarreled and their very different views of the world, especially concerning the use of the ancient lore and the ways of wise women.

Considering the dark destiny that Maman had predicted for Meg, she supposed that her father was right to want her to be more like Lady Danvers.

But her ladyship seemed as restricted by the narrow confines of her life as she was by her corsets. As they picked their way up the street, Lady Danvers carried herself rigidly erect. Yet she managed to keep the hem of her costly gown out of the muck with an effortless grace Meg doubted she would ever be able to learn.

Meg knew that her papa was anxious for her to make a favorable impression, but she felt awkward and tongue-tied. She had not the slightest notion what to say to this woman with her perfect carriage and solemn demeanor.

At least her ladyship did not seem as cold and disapproving as her horrid maid. When Meg risked a glance at her, Lady Danvers fidgeted with her ruff, something Meg longed to do herself. The heavily starched frill made her neck itch.

Was it possible that this elegant lady was as ill at ease as Meg was? The notion struck Meg as ludicrous.

"It—it is very warm," the woman ventured.

"Yes, it is."

"And the street is so crowded."

Once again, Meg agreed politely.

"It rather surprises me, this crush of people. Where can they all be going? Your father told me there is no performance at the theater this afternoon."

"No, the actors are rehearsing a new play. I expect all these people plan to attend the baiting at the bear garden." Meg scrunched her face in a fierce scowl.

"You do not approve of such sport?" Lady Danvers asked.

"It is not sport at all. Setting a pack of dogs upon a poor chained beast! I wish the bear would escape and eat them all. Well, not the dogs. *They* don't know any better. But those wicked men placing their bets—"

Meg checked her angry tirade. Cat would have understood her need to vent her indignation, but Meg feared her ladyship would be shocked.

But Lady Danvers replied, "I quite agree with you. I have often wished the same thing myself, that the bear might enjoy a good meal of its tormentors."

Meg regarded the woman in astonishment. Perhaps her ladyship was not quite as prim and proper as she seemed. The woman's remark caused Meg to like her better in spite of herself.

"If I were the queen, I would outlaw all bear and bull baiting," Lady Danvers continued. "But I fear Her Majesty is rather fond of such blood sports herself."

"Oh." Meg pursed her lips. This was not information about her heroine that she cared to hear. But the thought that Lady Danvers knew the queen, had actually stood in Elizabeth's august presence, overcame Meg's qualms.

"So you have been to court? You know the queen? You have seen her? Spoken to her? How did she seem? What did she—" Meg tried to curb her eager questions. "I am sorry. I should not be badgering you."

"No, that is quite all right, my dear. Your papa told me you are a great admirer of Elizabeth. So was I."

Was? Meg homed in on the word and the shadow that seemed to pass over Lady Danvers's face.

"I cannot claim to know Her Majesty well. I have not been often in her presence, but when my father died, the queen was very kind to me and my brother. And this despite the fact that my father had greatly angered her."

Lady Danvers hesitated as though choosing her next words with great care. "No one can be more compassionate than Her Majesty toward widows or orphans or anyone who has suffered a grievous misfortune. But when it comes to doing what she believes necessary to keep her throne secure, Elizabeth can also be very . . . stern."

Meg read enough of Lady Danvers's thoughts to realize what the woman had meant to say.

Elizabeth can also be very hard, unjust, and cruel.

But Meg could hardly wax indignant over such criticism of her beloved queen, not when it hadn't been voiced aloud. Obliged to hold her tongue, Meg lapsed into a dour silence.

Her ladyship did likewise, appearing lost in her own thoughts. As though seized by a sudden impulse, she delved into a small purse she kept tied to her belt.

Inquisitive as always, Meg could not help trying to

steal a peek at the contents of the velvet sack. Lady Danvers yanked out something blue that she offered Meg.

"Here. You may have this."

Meg accepted a frayed, slightly soiled scrap of silk. Eyeing it dubiously, she said, "Er—thank you."

"That is a segment from the carpet that was unrolled for the queen on her coronation. After the ceremony, it was torn to bits by the crowd, eager for a remembrance of the great event. My old nurse was present and managed to secure a piece."

"Oh! Thank you," Meg repeated in a far different tone, regarding the soiled scrap of fabric in an entirely new light.

"That tiny bit of the queen's carpet was among my nurse's most valued possessions," Lady Danvers said in a constricted voice. "Sarey gave it to me upon her deathbed."

Meg cradled the fragment as reverently as though it was a holy relic. It took all of her willpower to surrender it back to Lady Danvers.

"Oh, n-no, your ladyship," she stammered. "You can't possibly wish to part with this. Such a treasure, a symbol of the day when Elizabeth became our beloved queen. I c-couldn't accept it."

"Yes, child. You can." Lady Danvers enfolded Meg's fingers around the cloth. "Keep it."

Her ladyship's smile was at once strangely bitter and hauntingly sad. "I am sure you will cherish that bit of silk far more than I ever could."

✥✥✥

CAT TRAILED BEHIND LADY DANVERS'S ENTOURAGE, IMPATIENT and testy at having to curtail her usual stride. But hanging to the rear gave her the best vantage point for watching over Meg.

It also allowed her to critically observe her ladyship's awkward efforts to befriend Meg. Lady Danvers had even resorted to offering Meg some sort of gift she removed from her purse. Cat couldn't see what it was. A coin perhaps.

Meg accepted it eagerly enough, but she still seemed stiff and reserved with her ladyship. Cat was ashamed of the satisfaction that gave her. If Lady Danvers was slated to become Meg's stepmother, Cat ought to wish for some affection and trust to build between them. For Meg's sake.

But Cat was finding it cursed hard to be that generous. Her irritable mood did not improve when Martin fell into step beside her and murmured in her ear, "So what do you think?"

Cat scowled as Porter stepped behind her mistress, fussing with a fold of her ladyship's gown and momentarily cutting off Cat's view of Meg.

"She's a bit broad in the beam for my taste."

"I'm not talking about the maid. You know perfectly well I meant Lady Danvers," Martin said.

Cat shrugged. "Is my opinion of any consequence?"

"Yes, it is." He surprised her by insisting, "What do you think of Jane?"

Cat's brows knit together in a frown. What did she think? That Jane Danvers was but a pale copy of Miri Aristide, the woman whom Martin had adored for so many years. That her ladyship possessed Miri's fair looks, but none of Miri's fey wisdom or quiet strength.

Jane was so sweet and gentle, Martin and Meg would

run completely roughshod over her. Her ladyship would never be able to manage such a rogue stallion and his head-strong filly, never be able to scold and comfort, love and protect them.

Not the way I could, Cat reflected and then started, wondering where such a wayward thought had come from. Heat stung her cheeks as she realized Martin was regarding her, waiting for her answer.

She swallowed, for once trying to be tactful. "Lady Danvers seems like a—a most respectable woman. She—she's blond like Ariane's younger sister, although not as lovely as Miri."

"There will only ever be one Miri," Martin said, his voice so soft with remembered affection, Cat felt as though someone had raked claws across her heart. A strange sensation, uncomfortably akin to jealousy, and Cat did her best to shake clear of it.

Martin hastened to add, "But Jane does have her own quiet kind of beauty. A fair English rose."

"I am not the best one to judge," Cat replied tartly, "being but a weed myself."

"No, you are more like the heather growing free and wild in your Irish hills." His gaze was warm and admiring, touching Cat in all her most vulnerable places and angering her at the same time.

She was struggling so hard to keep her shield in place and he wasn't making it easy for her.

Cat forced her lips into a sneer. "How clever of you to compare me to something you have never seen before."

"But I have. Through your eyes."

Damn the man. Why did he have to say things like that or smile at her that way, forcing her to acknowledge what she didn't want to face?

She wasn't exhausted, her head befuddled with whiskey. She was stone-cold sober and she still thought she was in love with him.

Thought she was? No, she knew it, felt it, to the very marrow of her bones. Cat came to an abrupt halt in the middle of the street, using the only weapon she had to hold him at bay, the sharp blade of her tongue.

"How charming, Master Wolfe," she said, infusing her voice with contempt. "But you'd best save your flattery for a woman who sets some value on it. If you aspire to be a gentleman, they don't waste such compliments upon their servants."

Martin blinked at her sudden assault. "Sweet Jesu, Cat. You know I don't regard you in that light."

"You've no business regarding me in any light at all."

Cat lengthened her stride, leaving him looking angry and hurt. But far better that than his guessing the truth.

She loved the man. But if she spent one more moment in his company, she was going to break something over his thick, obtuse head.

※※※

CAT PACED ALONG THE OUTER RIM OF THE PIT, STARING GLUMLY up at all the vacant galleries. The Crown had lost much of the magic of her first visit, when she had been so spellbound by Martin's performance. Perhaps it was because she didn't care much for the present role he was playing, escorting Lady Danvers about the theater, introducing her to the members of the acting company.

Cat could tell from Martin's exaggerated gestures he was doing his best to entertain her ladyship, coax the melancholy woman into smiling. He might as well have been performing on the stage.

Perhaps he would succeed better with Lady Danvers if he devastated her with one of his intent, sincere looks the way he often did Cat.

Cat sighed, doing her best to dispel the resentful thoughts. Wit and charm came as naturally to Martin le Loup as breathing. He could hardly be blamed if Cat had fallen in love with him. It was purely her own folly and she needed to conquer it, remember that she was here to look after Meg.

Cat would never have wished for Meg to be in any danger, but it would have helped greatly if Cat had had something of importance to do. Draw forth her hidden dagger and fight off one of the Silver Rose witches or the Dark Queen's soldiers.

But according to the last missive Cat had received from Ariane, the dangers threatening Meg had greatly diminished.

Ma chère Catriona, the Lady of Faire Isle had written.

> *At my behest, my brother-in-law journeyed to Paris to see if he could discover anything more. After much discreet investigation, Simon found out that many of the coven were killed or arrested that night on the cliffs. The witches brought to Paris were executed.*

Whether Catherine learned anything about Megaera,
I cannot be certain. The members of the coven were
so fanatically devoted to Meg, I doubt they would be
induced to talk, even under torture. Perhaps that is
wishful thinking on my part.

　　But if the Dark Queen had discovered she was
tricked regarding the identity of the Silver Rose, Simon
discerned no sign of it. Surely by now Catherine would
have descended upon Faire Isle like an avenging fury,
but all remains quiet here . . .

The rest of the letter contained cheerful assurances of
Ariane's good health and that all was well with both her
and the babe, something that Cat wished she could entirely
believe.

Ariane had concluded by cautioning Cat to maintain
her vigilance over Meg, not that Cat needed to be reminded. But the only danger Meg suffered at the moment
was a surfeit of sweets.

The girl strolled about on stage with one of the actors,
old Arthur Lehay. The portly man plied Meg with crystal-
lized ginger.

"Your young mistress has torn the hem of her gown," a
cold voice announced. To Cat's annoyance, she found Mistress Porter at her elbow.

"Has she?" Cat asked. "I daresay there is plenty of
frock left, enough to garb two wee lasses."

When Porter scowled in disapproval of her attitude,
Cat shrugged and added, "I'll be after mending it when we
return home."

"*I* am always prepared to serve milady should any such

disaster occur," Porter informed her smugly. "I never travel anywhere unless I am well armed with needle and thread."

"I prefer a sharp dagger myself," Cat drawled. "Your needles wouldn't be of much use in a good scrap. Although I guess you could jab one in your enemy's eye if you had to."

Porter gasped, regarding Cat with huge eyes, and backed warily away from her. But Cat's satisfaction in the woman's retreat was marred as she saw Meg disappearing backstage. The girl glanced about her as though searching for someone and Cat had no doubt who it was.

All of the players had taken their bows and paid their respects to Lady Danvers. All save one . . . Alexander Naismith.

Chapter Fifteen

"SANDER?" MEG CALLED SOFTLY.

She crept behind the painted cloth hanging at the back of the tiring-house. There was no one backstage except for one of the hands sorting through some rusted armor that had been donated to the theater. The man respectfully doffed his cap and nodded to Meg in greeting.

Meg gave him a shy smile. She thought of asking him where she might find Sander, but was too embarrassed, fearing her blushes would betray her.

She wandered toward the stairs that led to the balcony above the tiring-house. Sander said he often crept up there to work on his music, the inn where he lodged being far too crowded and noisy.

Little light reached the spiral stairs that wound through

the upper reaches of the theater. Gathering up the hem of her skirts, Meg picked her way carefully. As she rounded the curve, she blundered into a couple engaged in a tryst. A blond-haired woman held her fan coyly in front of her lips. A tall gentleman garbed in a fine silk doublet leaned close, appearing on the verge of trying to steal a kiss.

Their flirtation interrupted, both turned to stare at Meg in surprise.

"Oh! I beg your pardon," Meg stammered, her cheeks firing. Whirling about, she rushed down the stairs. She fled toward the prompter's door that led back to the stage.

"Mistress Margaret, wait!" A familiar voice called after her.

Sander? Meg turned back hopefully, but the only one approaching her was the woman from the stairs.

"You appear to be lost, young mistress. Might I be of some assistance?" the blonde cooed in falsetto accents, peering down at Meg over the rim of her fan, a teasing glint in the blue eyes.

Sander's eyes. But this garish creature, corseted in a faded blue gown, her cheeks painted with rouge, bore little resemblance to Meg's friend and handsome young music master. Numb with shock, Meg gripped her hands tightly together.

"It is me, milady. Your humble servant and tutor," Sander said in a more normal tone. His usually elegant bow was made clumsy by his skirts. "What! Don't you recognize me?"

Meg nodded unhappily.

"I was trying on my costume for our new play. What do you think?" Sander twirled about in a circle.

Meg had never seen him garbed for one of his performances. She hated it. It did not fit at all with her heroic image of Sander. And that scene she had interrupted on the stairs. . . . Had Sander been rehearsing with another actor? It seemed an odd, dark sort of place to practice one's lines.

"It—it is a very nice gown," Meg muttered, staring down at the floorboards.

Sander must have sensed her discomfort because he stopped preening and stripped off his wig. Bending down, he whispered in a conspiratorial tone. "How have you been? How are you faring with your scrying ball?"

"Not well. I have stared into it for hours until my eyes are crossed. But I see nothing."

"You keep at it. I am sure you will master it in time. You are such a clever girl, Meg."

Meg? It was the first time Sander had ever spoken to her so intimately, called her by name.

"Are there any other mysterious objects you require me to purchase for you?" he asked. "I will do my best even if your father should have my hide for it."

"No, I need nothing." Meg risked a glance into his eyes. She did not mean to invade the privacy of his mind, but his thoughts were so close to the surface, shining there for her to read.

"What an angel she is. I'd do anything in the world for her. Anything."

A tingle of warmth spread through Meg. Despite his woman's garb and rouged cheeks, he seemed more like her Sander again. Meg smiled at him, but the expression froze on her lips as a shadow fell over them, Sander's companion from the stairs.

"Ah, Sander. This is where you disappeared."

"Milord." Sander straightened away from her.

Meg's brow puckered in a slight frown. The stranger seemed vaguely familiar to her, but he was not one of the players. Meg did not need Sander's deferential greeting to tell her that. The stranger's doublet and trunk hose appeared costly and new, not like the castoff clothing the players bought for their costumes.

His slender fingers glittered with rings. His patrician features were lean and arrogant, his dark blond hair slicked back from his brow.

"You have clearly been holding out on me," the man complained, draping one arm about Sander's shoulders in negligent fashion. "Who is this young beauty you have stolen off to meet?"

Meg did not care for his flattery. She knew she was no beauty. Nor did she like the possessive way he touched Sander. It made her skin prickle with uneasiness and made her hot with jealousy all at the same time.

"This is Master Wolfe's daughter. Mistress Wolfe, may I present to you his lordship, Edward Lambert, the baron of Oxbridge."

Meg dipped into a stiff curtsy. Lord Oxbridge, her papa's patron and Lady Danvers's brother. Now Meg remembered him from that terrible day when her papa had saved Lady Danvers from drowning. Meg had been so afraid of seeing her father swept away by the river's current that she had taken little note of his lordship.

Lord Oxbridge smiled, his gaze raking over her with such keen interest it rendered Meg uncomfortable.

"So this is Margaret Wolfe, the remarkable girl I have heard so much about."

"I am Margaret Wolfe," Meg replied primly, "but I am not all that remarkable."

"Oh, I believe that you are. Your father has been most remiss about allowing me to further our acquaintance. But happily Master Naismith here has been telling me much of your accomplishments." His lordship exchanged a warm, intimate look with Sander.

Meg could not imagine why such a powerful nobleman as Lord Oxbridge would be interested in becoming better acquainted with an insignificant eleven-year-old girl. She should have been flattered that Sander spoke of her so highly. Why then did it feel more like a betrayal?

His lordship removed his arm from Sander's shoulders. He tried to cup Meg's chin, tilt her face upward to inspect her further as though she were some strange curiosity.

Meg shied away from him. She was tempted to try to read his lordship's eyes, but they seemed so restive, half-veiled by his light blond lashes. Even if she succeeded in prying her way into his head, she had a queasy feeling she would not like what she found there.

"Meg?"

Much to her relief, Meg heard Cat shouting for her. She saw the woman emerge backstage from the door at the opposite side of the theater. Mumbling some excuse to Sander and his lordship, Meg all but fled toward her protector.

Cat greeted her, hands splayed on her hips, looking far from pleased that Meg had wandered out of her sight.

"Margaret Wolfe. How many times must I tell you—" Cat broke off with a grunt as Meg hurled herself at her, wrapping her arms about Cat's waist.

Cat's vexed tone immediately softened to one of concern. "Sweetling, what is it? What's amiss?"

Meg burrowed her face against Cat. She hardly knew how to answer her, not fully understanding herself the turmoil that roiled through her. Even without reading eyes, Meg sensed something. The air in the theater was oppressive, thick with secrets swirling about her. The feeling emanated not just from Sander and his lordship, but Lady Danvers as well and even Meg's own beloved papa.

The only one at the moment who felt completely forthright and true was her Cat, and Meg clung to her tightly.

"Nothing's wrong," Meg whispered. "I am just tired and I want to go home."

✸✸✸✸

MARTIN FROWNED SLIGHTLY WHEN HE NOTICED HIS DAUGHTER disappear backstage. Meg was familiar with most of the acting company and the stagehands. She ought to be safe enough within the confines of the theater, but Martin was relieved all the same when he saw Cat heading after Meg.

He tried to keep his attention focused on Jane, but Martin could not keep his gaze from following wistfully after Cat.

Cat had been so sharp with him during the course of this outing. No doubt part of it was because of her disapproval of his interest in Lady Danvers, his plan to secure a proper English mother for Meg instead of surrendering his daughter to Ariane's teaching on Faire Isle.

But he feared Cat's prickly attitude owed more to that incident in his study. Never had the remembrance of stolen moments of passion been so sweet to Martin and never had he regretted anything more.

He had paid a heavy price for letting his desire get the better of him, measured in the distance that stretched between him and Cat. Mon Dieu, how he hated it, the tension, the awkward silences that had sprung up between them this past week.

He keenly missed her companionship, their easy banter, even the fierceness of their quarrels. Cat's friendship had become a refuge for him, and the Lord knew he needed one, with all his worries pressing down upon him, all this intrigue nipping at his heels.

When he saw Robert Poley come strolling into the Crown, Martin bit back an oath, realizing that he could have no peace from all the infernal conspiracy and plotting, not even here in his own theater.

Murmuring his excuses to Lady Danvers, Martin leapt from the stage and hastened forward to intercept Poley.

"I am sorry, sir. But the theater is closed. There is no performance scheduled today," Martin announced in hearty tones for the benefit of anyone who might be heeding the conversation. Leaning a little closer to Poley, he hissed, "What the devil are you doing here?"

Poley bowed and smiled with his usual amiability. "No performance? That is certainly a great disappointment."

He added under his breath, "There are developments, Master Wolfe. Our mutual employer waxes impatient."

Martin tensed at the reference to Walsingham. After learning who Poley was, Martin had abandoned all pretense with the man. Walsingham might like to play his deep games, keeping his agents unaware of one another.

Martin felt it might be more to their mutual benefit if Poley knew that he and Martin were working for the same cause.

Not that Martin harbored any illusions about his fellow spy or entirely trusted the man. If this dangerous affair went awry and blew up in their faces, Poley would look to his own skin and Martin would do the same.

While pretending to admire the theater, Poley continued, "Babington has yet to rise to the bait and reply to the Scottish queen's letter. We still have no idea who all six of the assassins are. Sir Francis feels we cannot risk waiting any longer. He means to issue arrest warrants soon for all of those under suspicion."

"Including Lord Oxbridge?" Martin asked anxiously.

"I don't know. But certainly for Father Ballard, John Savage, and Sir Anthony Babington. Have you remarked how edgy Babington has been of late? I think he is losing his nerve, preparing to bolt. He has been avoiding his own lodging and staying with me. I haven't had a chance to go through his things yet, but I notice there is one canvas bag he guards rather jealously."

"What do you think is in it? Letters from the Queen of Scots or some of his fellow conspirators? Surely even Babington would not be fool enough to keep such damning evidence."

Poley shrugged. "I think the young ass is fool enough for anything. Anyway, arrests are imminent. I just thought you should be on the alert."

"Thank you."

Poley nodded and announced in a louder tone, "Please do keep me informed, Master Wolfe, of when the new play is to be performed."

"I will indeed, sir."

Biding a cheery farewell, Poley took his leave, allowing Martin to return to Lady Danvers. She was still on stage with Arthur Lehay. The old actor and one of the other players were demonstrating to her ladyship how the trapdoor worked.

Martin struggled to mask his inner turmoil as he joined her upon the stage. Jane turned to him with a shy smile and mock shudder.

"Master Lehay has been showing me your secrets, sir. How the devil might be summoned from the depths of hell to terrify the audience."

Or angels dragged under, Martin thought with a sharp pang as he gazed down at Jane's innocent face. He forced a smile to his lips.

"I hope you feel that your investment has been well spent. The design of the Crown is far superior to the theater in Shoreditch."

"I would have no way of judging. I have never attended any performance there. Ned is the one who is so fond of such public diversions."

"What pastimes do amuse you, my lady?"

"I prefer a quiet afternoon spent alone with a good book or my stitching." Jane gave a self-deprecating laugh. "I am sure you must find me rather a dull creature."

"Not at all. I have been craving a little quiet myself," Martin said, although he did not share Jane's love of solitude. His gaze shifted involuntarily toward the door where Cat had vanished backstage.

"Is something wrong, Marcus?" Jane asked. "You seem rather . . . tense."

Martin wrenched his attention back to her. "No, I am fine," he lied.

Nothing was wrong. Nothing except that Jane's worst dread might be about to come true. Her brother could well be lodged in the Tower by this time tomorrow. Would it be a kindness or pure folly to attempt to warn Jane? What if Ned truly was guilty?

Although Martin felt wracked with guilt himself, he said, "What were we speaking of before? Oh, yes, your brother's diversions. I understand he is a planning an excursion to France."

"You sound as though you disapprove." Jane cast him a wry look. "I hope you are not one of those insular Englishmen who despise the French."

Martin was hard-pressed to keep a straight face. "No, the French have their uses. They are at least tolerable winemakers. Er—has Ned many acquaintances in France?"

"Ned makes fast friends wherever he travels." Jane lowered her gaze, her expression downcast. "I think it would be a good thing if he went. He'd be safer there."

"Safer?"

"France is a far healthier climate for those of our faith. There are many exiled English Catholics living in Paris. These are such perilous and uncertain times. One never knows what might happen."

From the tense expression on her face, Martin feared that Jane did know. Or at least she suspected that Ned might be involved in something dangerous.

Martin pressed her hand. "I would never wish harm to befall either Ned or you. If there is anything I can do, if you could bring yourself to—"

He almost asked her to trust him, but he had no right to do that. Walsingham had engaged Martin to help expose the conspiracy and in particular find evidence against Ned Lambert. Martin knew the rewards if he succeeded, the risks he ran if he failed, especially if he sought to deceive Walsingham.

But it didn't matter. He could not secure his future or Meg's at the expense of this lady's gentle heart. Carrying Jane's hand lightly to his lips, Martin formed his resolve.

If any damning proof of treason existed against Ned Lambert, it must be tucked away in Babington's mysterious canvas sack. Poley was bound to discover it and the other agent would have no qualms about handing it over to Walsingham. Ned Lambert and his sister had only one chance. If Martin got to that evidence first. . . .

THE LATE AFTERNOON SUN SPREAD A GOLDEN GLOW OVER THE dark waters of the Thames as the boatman conveyed Cat, Martin, and Meg across to the city.

Meg was wedged in close to her father, his arm draped protectively around the girl's shoulders. Meg snuggled against Martin, her forlorn expression a marked contrast to the excitement with which she had begun the day.

The girl had been so hopeful of obtaining a glimpse of the queen. But Cat believed that Meg's low spirits had less to do with what she hadn't seen and more to do with what she *had*—her young hero cavorting about in his gown with Lord Oxbridge.

Cat had observed enough of the two men to form suspicions about the relationship between his lordship and the young actor. It was not an unusual practice amongst the nobility to enjoy the favors of a comely lad and Sander Naismith seemed like an ambitious boy with few scruples about what he'd do to advance himself.

Cat was unsure how much of the interplay between the two men Meg had understood. Certainly enough to trouble the girl. Her dark expression was a cloudy mirror of her father's.

There was something greatly amiss with Martin as well. From the shadows backstage, Cat had observed his brief conversation with the amiable-looking stranger who had wandered into the theater. For all the apparent congeniality of the encounter, Martin had returned to the stage looking like he had swallowed a pistol ball.

As he cradled Meg close to him, Martin's thoughts were clearly far away. He drummed his fingers against his knee with a restiveness Cat recognized all too well. The man would be stealing off tonight on one of his mysterious errands. Cat was dead certain of it.

As the shore receded in the distance, Cat thought back to the day she'd first come to Southwark, shadowing Martin in her search for Meg. It felt like a lifetime ago, her only loyalty then to the Lady of Faire Isle, Cat's sole purpose to carry out Ariane's commands to retrieve the girl.

When had that all begun to shift and change? Perhaps from that very first night when she had watched Martin bend so tenderly over his daughter while Meg slept, tucking her in. Cat only knew that it no longer required any orders from her chieftain.

Cat would willingly sacrifice her life for either Martin or Meg. She loved both of them so much her heart ached with it.

There could never be any permanent place for her in their lives. Cat knew that, but she refused to let herself sink into a melancholy over the fact. There would be time enough to wallow in usquebaugh and misery when she returned to Faire Isle.

Right now she had a new mission. To make certain Martin and Meg would always have each other. Cat had been sent here to protect Meg. That included the child's heart as well, making sure Meg did not lose her father to any reckless venture. Cat clasped her hands together, forming a steely resolve.

Whenever the wolf left the house tonight, the huntress would be hard on his heels.

Chapter Sixteen

Perhaps the luck was with him for once, Martin thought as he crept through the garden toward Robert Poley's house on the fringe of London. The night sky was overcast, shadows chasing across the face of the moon, making visibility poor for honest citizens, but perfect for anyone bent on more unlawful pursuits.

Martin crouched in the bushes, peering up at the two-story timber-frame house, which appeared dark and silent at this hour. He knew that Babington and Poley had gone out for another rendezvous at the Plough Inn with Father Ballard and John Savage. Savage's suspicions of Martin would likely be exacerbated by his absence but that was the least of Martin's worries at the moment.

His chief concern was how to climb up to Babington's room on the second floor without rousing the household or slipping and breaking his neck.

Stealing a furtive glance about him, Martin stole across the expanse of lawn, heading for a large oak tree. It had been a long time since he had climbed a tree and he found it a difficult prospect in the dark. The rough bark abraded his palms, his boots slipping as he scrabbled for toeholds.

He hoisted himself up to a divide in the trunk where he was able to pause and contemplate the stout branch that angled off to his left. The limb extended conveniently close to Babington's window ledge. But was it strong enough to hold Martin's weight or would it snap and send him plummeting to the ground?

The wind whipped a lock of hair into his eyes, an ominous rumble of thunder sounding in the distance. Martin realized he had no time to sit and ponder his options. He was tempted to offer up a silent prayer, but it hardly seemed wise to call the Almighty's attention to oneself when engaged in such nefarious enterprise.

Steeling his courage, he inched out onto the branch. When it swayed beneath his weight, his breath caught in his throat. But the limb held. Working his way to the end, Martin swung himself up onto the window ledge.

His skills as a thief in Paris had been restricted to picking pockets and cutting purses. He'd had a few friends who were more venturesome than he, breaking into shops and houses.

Of course, most of them were dead, having wound up doing the hempen jig at the end of a hangman's rope. Not the most comforting recollection to be having at the moment, Martin thought. Instead he sought to recall all he had ever been told about breaking locks and jimmying windows.

Neither skill proved necessary. Not only had Babington been imprudent enough to leave his window unlocked, he had left it cracked open as well to air the room.

"My *bon chance* continues," Martin murmured as he cautiously forced the casement open farther and eased himself inside.

The room was so dark he could barely make out more than the shadows of the tester bed and wardrobe trunk. Martin swallowed an oath when he almost tripped over a low stool. He could scarce see his hand in front of his face. He was going to have to risk lighting a candle.

Fumbling in the pouch attached to his belt, he drew forth the flint, tinder, and small wax taper he had brought. The seconds that passed felt more like hours to his tautly stretched nerves. But he succeeded in coaxing the wick to light at last.

Shielding the flame from the draft, he subjected the room to a swift inspection. Babington clearly intended his sojourn at Poley's house to be brief. Sir Anthony had brought few of his belongings with him.

Martin found a brass candle holder and propped his taper on a small writing desk. A quill pen lay across a letter that Babington had begun and not yet finished. Martin snatched it up hoping it might be Babington's reply to the Queen of Scots, naming his fellow conspirators.

But if it was in code, Martin would never be able to read it and discover whether Ned's name was on the list. As he scanned the page, Martin was relieved to see the letter was not in cipher. To his disappointment, the missive was not addressed to the Scottish queen but Robert Poley.

> *Robyn,*
>   *I am ready to endure whatever fate shall befall me. I am the same as I always pretended. I pray God you be as true and ever so remain toward me . . .*

Martin frowned at the place where the words trailed off as though the writer had run out of time or simply lost the heart to continue. Poley had been right about Babington having doubts about the enterprise he had embarked upon. Misgivings that came far too late.

The tragic romantic young idiot, Martin thought. Suppressing the compassion he could not afford, he replaced the letter and quill carefully so they looked undisturbed.

What he needed to find was that mysterious canvas bag Poley had mentioned. And find it swiftly unless he wanted to be caught in a storm. It would be a long trudge from here back to Cheapside in the pouring rain.

Martin moved quietly but efficiently about the room, rummaging through an ambry and a wardrobe chest, looking behind furnishings. He was rewarded when he discovered the canvas sack tucked under the bed.

With a grunt of satisfaction, he drew the bag out into the light. Good fortune? His luck tonight was nothing short of miraculous. He was not a gamester but it was a pity he had not had time to hazard a few hands of cards before returning home.

Martin delved inside the sack, hoping to find a thick packet of letters. His fingers struck up against a heavy rolled canvas. Martin drew it out and unfurled it, examining it close to the candlelight.

It was a painting of six gentlemen attired in their finest garb, Babington positioned proudly in the center, the painting etched with some sort of Latin inscription.

What the devil? Martin frowned, incredulous. This is what Babington had been guarding so protectively? A portrait of him and five of his . . .

Martin sucked in his breath as the realization struck him. So sure of their success, Babington and his band of conspirators had posed for a portrait, recording their images for posterity. The fools, the bloody damned fools!

Martin studied the faces of the other men, most of them unknown to him, but that was of little importance. He would leave it to Walsingham to sort out their identities. Martin cared about only one thing. Ned Lambert was not among them.

With a taut smile of satisfaction, Martin rolled up the portrait. As he thrust it back into the bag a flare of lightning lit up the room. In the mirror opposite he caught the shadowy image of a cloaked figure hovering behind him.

He didn't know when or how, but he was no longer alone. Someone had followed him through the window. It took all of Martin's will not to flinch, not to betray his awareness of the other intruder. He proceeded with securing the portrait in the canvas bag, drawing the strings closed. Every muscle tensed, every nerve on the alert.

When he heard the floor creak behind him, Martin dropped the bag and whirled. In one swift lunge, he pounced. Seizing his opponent by the throat, he drove him back against the wall.

The hooded figure gasped, clutching at Martin's wrists in an effort to break his hold. Martin mercilessly tightened his grip.

"Martin," the intruder wheezed. In the struggle, his hood fell back. Or rather *hers* did. Martin stared down in disbelief into widened blue eyes, familiar strands of fiery hair tumbling loose from a chignon to straggle about a face that was turning an alarming shade of red.

"Cat!" Horrified, Martin released her, his hands falling back to his sides.

Cat staggered away from the wall, rubbing her neck and inhaling gulps of air.

"Mon Dieu. How badly did I hurt you? Are you all right?" he demanded anxiously.

Any other woman would have swooned at such a rough assault or even trembled. But Cat looked up at him and actually managed to grin.

"That—that was amazing," she rasped. "I had no idea you could strike so swiftly. Perhaps you are somewhat capable of looking out for yourself."

"Somewhat?"

"I knew it was you so I wasn't fighting after my usual fashion. Lucky for you. Otherwise, I'd have rammed your bollocks so hard you'd be wearing them for a cap."

The image was evocative enough to make Martin's privates shrivel closer to his body. His concern rapidly dissolved into anger.

"Damnation, woman." It was all he could do to remember to keep his voice down. "What the devil are you doing here?"

"I might ask you the same thing."

"I asked you first. How did you even get in here?"

"I just waited and followed you, up the tree and in the window." Cat scowled. "Although I'm a damned sight better at climbing than you are. I thought you were going to break your fool arse."

"Never mind my arse." Martin bent closer to her until they were practically nose to nose, hissing in each other's faces. "Why aren't you back at the house? Who is guarding my daughter?"

"I left Jem and Samuel sitting up, armed with pistols, the doors and windows all barred. Things have been quiet enough I am confident Meg will be fine. I am more concerned that nothing should happen to her idiot of a da."

"Her da is just fine. At least he was until you sneaked up behind him and gave him an apoplexy." Martin stormed away from her to retrieve the canvas bag he had dropped.

Cat followed hard on his heels. "Doing fine, is it now? I knew you were up to something dangerous, but I never expected even you would be reckless enough to resume your old ways as a thief."

"A thief! What are you talking about? I am not stealing anything."

When Cat stared pointedly at the bag in his hand, Martin grimaced. "Oh, well, yes, I am stealing this."

"That painting you were so occupied in studying when I clambered in the window?" Cat sniffed. "That's daft. I doubt it will fetch enough to make it worth risking your neck."

Martin glared at her. "I survived on the streets of Paris for years on my wits and nimble fingers. I hardly need you to lecture me on how to be a successful thief—"

He broke off, tensing and listening. Sounds carried

from beyond the door, footsteps and muffled voices. Martin could not catch what was being said, but the fearful tone was clear enough.

"Now look what you've done," he growled at Cat. "Awakened the entire household."

"Me? It was you stomping about and slamming me against the wall—"

Martin clamped his hand over her mouth. "We have to get out of here now. I have no time to explain, but I must secure this painting. Will you trust me, help me?"

Cat stared at him over the mask of his fingers, her blue eyes seeming to pierce deep into his. He feared she'd put up one of her usual arguments, but she nodded almost without hesitation.

Martin blew out the candle and they both headed for the window. Cat swung out onto the branch and scrambled down the tree first. The woman was so cursed nimble she might well have truly been a feline. Martin tossed the canvas sack down to her and followed suit. His progress down the tree was far more awkward and noisy, shaking branches and rustling leaves.

By the time his boots struck the ground, a servant had appeared at the window above him. A gray-haired old man in a nightcap held a candle in his wavering hand. He squinted down at Martin and cried, "Ho! You there! Stop, thief."

Martin relieved Cat of the canvas sack and the pair of them tore out of the garden and down the street. Martin risked a look back over his shoulder.

The elderly servant had succeeded in rousing the rest of Poley's household or perhaps Martin himself had done that. He could hear other voices and picked out the gleam of a lantern.

"Come on. This way," Martin said, although he had not the least notion where he was going himself. He was completely unfamiliar with this part of the city. He seized Cat by the hand, desperately tugging her down a narrow alley. Not the safest maneuver perhaps, given the dangers of London at night.

But even the footpads and cutthroats seemed to have retreated within doors in the face of the oncoming storm. Successive bursts of lightning illuminated the way as Cat and Martin emerged onto a square of closed-up shops.

Martin dragged Cat down behind a conduit, using the massive public fountain for cover while he fought for his second wind and strove to get his bearings.

"Where—where the blazes are we?" she panted.

"No idea. Too damned far from home, that's certain."

"Why didn't you have the wit to hire a horse?" Cat grumbled.

"Horses are of little use in a robbery unless you're a highwayman."

"I think one would come in mighty useful right about—" Cat began. But Martin shushed her, listening intently for any sound of pursuit.

He heard nothing beyond Cat's quickened breathing and the gurgle of the fountain. When the first splash of water struck his hand, he thought it came from the conduit.

But the first fat wet drop was swiftly followed by a second and third. Dismayed, Martin glanced upward as the sky gave another angry rumble. The heavens opened up and began to pour.

"Merde!" He groaned, tugging frantically at the fastenings of his doublet in an effort to thrust the canvas bag beneath his shirt.

His luck had finally run out.

※※

THE JOVIALITY IN THE PIGEON'S TAPROOM CONTINUED UNabated despite the storm or perhaps because of it. The Southwark tavern was thronged with patrons laughing, singing, swilling ale, and rejoicing to have escaped the deluge drumming against the building's slate roof.

The only one not sharing in the merriment was the quiet gentleman who occupied a table alone in the farthest corner. Few remarked on his presence. Those who did snorted in scorn of the man's fair looks, his long softly curling hair, trim sandy-colored beard and mustache.

He bore the look of a foreigner, no doubt one of those simpering Frenchmen was the contemptuous verdict passed upon him. A contempt that Ambroise Gautier returned in full measure. He pressed a scented handkerchief to his nose. Faugh! It reeked worse than a kennel of wet dogs in here. No, he decided. The dogs would smell better than this horde of Englishmen sweating into their damp woolen garb.

The Pigeon catered to the lowest sort of clientele, watermen, dock laborers, itinerant musicians, actors . . . The Dark Queen's agent shuddered and tried to take a sip of the piss that the tavern keeper had assured him was the finest wine to be had in all of London.

The tragedy of it was that the landlord was probably right. His lips twisting into a disgusted moue, Gautier pushed his cup away from him. He was sure he must have borne far worse trials in the service of his royal mistress, but Gautier was having trouble recalling them.

He would have sold the silver buckles off his shoes for a good Bordeaux right now, if for no other reason than to celebrate the success he had achieved.

Against all odds, he had located Martin le Loup and his wretched daughter in this teeming city of crude, stinking Englishmen. But perhaps a toast would be premature.

He had found the little witch, but getting his hands on the Silver Rose was proving a greater challenge than he had anticipated. Between her father and that redheaded Irishwoman who worked for the Lady of Faire Isle, the girl was closely guarded.

Gautier had brought two of his most trusted men with him from France. Enforced by such seasoned mercenaries as Jacques and Alain, Gautier might have been able to mount a successful assault on le Loup's house. But Queen Catherine would expect him to handle this affair as discreetly as possible without drawing any attention from the English justices.

Gautier's task would have been so much easier if all he needed to do was kill the child. But above all else the Dark Queen wanted that damnable *Book of Shadows*. If Gautier dared return to Paris without it, he might as well slit his own throat.

He had formulated a plan, but he needed assistance. Fortunately, he had a fair idea where he might find the help he required.

Gautier's eyes narrowed as the person he had been waiting for entered the tavern. The young man darted inside, rain water streaming off his cloak and doublet, turning his feathered cap into a soggy mass.

The young man's friends called out greetings, teasing him about his sodden state.

"Damnation, Sander. About time you arrived."

"We thought you'd been washed away."

"You look like a drowned rat."

"You'd have been better off in one of your gowns, lad. You could have tossed your skirts over your head."

Alexander Naismith merely laughed and flicked his finger in a rude gesture. He stripped off his cap and shook out his wet hair, revealing a brief glimpse of the ugly stump where his left ear should have been.

Naismith's friends tried to beckon him over to the table to join them, but the boy declined, insisting he needed to change into dry clothing first. He headed for the stairs that led up to his lodging above the tavern.

Gautier tossed a few coins down on the table and swiftly rose to his feet. A drunken actor leaped up onto his chair and began to declaim some melodramatic speech in slurred accents.

Amidst all the hoots and catcalls from the other patrons, Gautier reached the stairs and followed Sander unnoticed. The boy's boots left a trail of water down the hallway, but his soaked state seemed to have done little to dampen his spirits.

Naismith whistled a jaunty tune as he unlocked the door to his room. He started a little when Gautier accosted him, hanging back in the shadows of the landing.

"Alexander Naismith?"

Naismith craned his neck, squinting in Gautier's direction. "Who is there?"

"One who has witnessed your performance," Gautier purred. "I am a great admirer."

The boy laughed. "I have many of those, sir, or should I say monsieur. Unfortunately, I am not in the market for any more admiration. My current patron is a most jealous—"

He broke off as Gautier stepped out of the shadows. Naismith went white with recognition. He made a frantic effort to bolt inside his room and close the door. Gautier was too fast, too strong for him.

Ramming his shoulder against the door, he forced his way inside. Before Naismith could draw out his dirk, Gautier had him pinned to the wall, his blade at the boy's throat.

A flare of lightning illuminated the young actor's wide, terrified eyes. "W-who are you? What do you want? If you are after my purse, y-you will find little in it besides a few pennies—"

"I am sure you know quite well who I am and what I am after," Gautier interrupted silkily. "And it is not your money. I am seeking the Silver Rose."

"I—I don't know what you are talking about."

Gautier lovingly stroked the blade of his knife along that slender white throat. "Our acquaintance would proceed much more amicably if you did not lie to me."

"I am not. I—" Naismith gasped as Gautier pressed the blade just hard enough to draw a thin trickle of blood.

"When I said I admired your performance, I was not talking about the one I saw the other day at the Crown

Theatre. I was far more impressed by the role you played that other night. Atop the cliffs."

Naismith's trembling lips moved in a feeble attempt at more denial, but all that escaped him was a frightened moan.

Gautier shoved up Naismith's wet sleeve. Even in the semidarkness, the brand of the rose blazed an angry red against his pale skin.

"That is the danger of dancing in the moonlight with witches, little man." Gautier's teeth flashed in a feral smile. "Even a clever boy like you is apt to get burned."

Chapter Seventeen

THE RAINSTORM CONTINUED UNABATED, BUT THE RED HART where Cat and Martin had found refuge was warm and dry. Martin had secured them a room at the back of the inn. It was a modest bedchamber, but far cleaner and more comfortable than the one Cat had occupied when she had first arrived in London. As she peeled off her sodden cloak, her red hair streamed about her face in damp rivulets.

She slicked her hair back and hung her cloak over the back of a chair near Martin's discarded doublet. He had already stripped down to his shirt and breeches. After tossing another log on the fire, he padded over to the window in his bare feet.

He cupped his hands about his eyes and strained to peer into the darkness. "I believe we have eluded any pursuit, but it will be as well to lie low for a while, at least until the storm passes."

The deluge had dispelled the usual warmth of August, bringing a chill to the air. Cat rubbed her arms, a shiver coursing through her.

"We are likely to be trapped here for a few more hours at least. You ought to take off your wet shoes and hose, try to get as dry and comfortable as you can." Martin pulled a face as his eyes skimmed over her attire. "I notice you are back in my breeches again."

"I do seem to have trouble keeping out of them," Cat replied with a mischievous smile. "Although they are miserably damp at the moment."

"Why don't you take them off?" Martin suggested, his teeth flashing in a wicked grin. "I would not want you to catch your death, *petite chatte.*"

Cat shook her head and gave a wry laugh. Their recent adventure had shattered the reserve between her and Martin, restoring their familiar pattern of teasing and bickering. The narrow escape had filled them both with a sense of exhilaration, perhaps dangerously so, Cat thought.

Folding her arms demurely across her bosom, Cat said, "Much as I appreciate you engaging this room, building up that fine blazing fire, I suspect all this solicitude has more to do with preserving that blasted painting than ensuring my good health."

Although Martin made an indignant disclaimer, he strode to the small pine table where he had unrolled the canvas and laid it out carefully.

"Do you think it sustained any damage?" he asked anxiously.

Joining him, Cat shook her head. She was still unable to understand why Martin had been so desperate to acquire the painting. It was merely a depiction of six English gentlemen decked out in all their finery. The man positioned at the center of the group was young and handsome enough, but Cat thought his expression made him look rather like a dream-ridden sheep. There was nothing in the least remarkable about the portrait except perhaps for the Latin inscription.

"*Hi mihi sunt Comites, quos ipsa Pericula ducunt,*" Cat intoned.

"You read Latin?" Martin asked eagerly. "What does it mean?"

Cat thought a moment and then translated roughly, "These men are my companions, whom very dangers draw."

The motto meant nothing to her, but it appeared to have significance to Martin because he muttered under his breath. "Could Babington possibly be any more of a fool?"

"Who is Babington? What dangers? What is so valuable about this painting?" Cat demanded. "Who are these six peacocks?"

"Dead men. Or they soon will be." Martin's satisfaction in having successfully stolen the portrait appeared to fade. He gave Cat a grim look. "Mon Dieu, you have no idea how much I wish you hadn't followed me tonight. The last thing I wanted was to drag you into this wretched affair. I am sorry."

But Cat waved his apology aside with an impatient gesture. "It was my own choice to track you down. But I would like to know exactly what I am now involved in."

"You aren't going to like it."

"Tell me anyway."

He was prevented from answering when one of the logs shifted on the fire, threatening to roll off the hearth in a shower of sparks. Cat suspected Martin's assiduity in attending to it stemmed as much from a wish to evade her questions as from preventing the room from catching fire.

Jabbing the log back into place with the poker, Martin kept his back to her. Cat followed him to the hearth, her wet shoes squelching. She sank down on a low stool to remove them and her hose. Her cloak had done a fair job of protecting her shirt, but the breeches bagged about her knees and clung to her calves in a fashion that was wet and miserable.

After a moment's hesitation, she stood and loosened the belt that held her dagger. Bracing against the wall, she started to shuck off the breeches. That at least gained Martin's full attention.

His eyes widening, he exclaimed, "Cat, what are you doing?"

"Taking your advice."

"I was only jesting." He beat a hasty retreat and made a great show of staring fixedly out the window.

Cat paused in her struggles with the damp fabric long enough to reach out and poke him between the shoulder blades. "There is no need for you to play the gentleman. We both know I am not afflicted with maidenly modesty. Besides, you'll only strain your eyes trying to catch my reflection in the windowpane."

"I'd never," Martin protested, but he came about with a sheepish look. He made no further pretense of averting his gaze as she worked off the breeches.

Martin's shirt came well below her knees, but she must have afforded him a generous glimpse for he said admiringly, "You have a lovely pair of legs."

"Thank you. They are a trifle on the short side, but they get me where I need to go." She glanced up at him. Although she smiled, her gaze was piercing and direct. "Enough stalling, le Loup. You are involved in some manner of trouble. You have been ever since I arrived in London. What is going on? I want the truth. I believe I have earned it."

"You have and so much more I can never repay." But Martin still felt reluctant to commence a tale that he knew could only earn her contempt for his recklessness, folly, and duplicity. It had been so sweet tonight having Cat laugh and spar with him in the old familiar way. He was reluctant to see it end. She had seemed so much like his Cat again.

His Cat? Martin brought himself up short. It was a jarring thought for someone who had been attempting to court another lady and a false notion as well. Catriona O'Hanlon was not the sort of woman who would ever belong to any man.

Leaning against the wall, he launched into his explanation. "I suppose it all began about nine months ago, the afternoon our acting company performed in the courtyard of an inn outside of Norwich. By pure chance Sir Francis Walsingham had stopped there during his travels to rest his horses. Walsingham is a member of the privy council and the principal sec—"

"I know who Sir Francis is and what he does," Cat interrupted. "The queen's spymaster is well-known even in the farthest reaches of Ireland. What has that devil to do with you?"

"I work for him."

Doing his best to ignore her stunned expression, Martin went on. "Despite the fact that I was attired in the motley of jester for that afternoon's performance, my English flawless, Walsingham recognized me. He remembered me as the Martin le Loup who once traveled with the deputation from the king of Navarre. We were sent to secure badly needed funds for the kingdom's defense against the duc de Guise's Catholic forces.

"I played little part in those negotiations. I was here more as Navarre's eyes and ears, to gauge the mood of the queen's council members, to judge if there might be a possibility of English military support. A small role, but Sir Francis took note of me. That's what he does and he never forgets."

"The man does have a sinister reputation." Cat hung the breeches to dry on a nail that protruded from the mantel. "Is Walsingham truly as black-hearted as I have heard?"

"No, he is a man of deep faith and conviction. But he also possesses an astonishingly subtle and devious mind. I suppose one could best describe him as a religious Machiavelli."

"Sweet Mother Earth! I can scarce imagine a more dangerous combination. So what happened when he recognized you?" Cat demanded. "I suppose the man wanted to know what the devil you were doing, wandering through the countryside, passing yourself off as an English actor."

"He did, indeed. I tried to fob him off with some tale of having fled France to escape creditors. I don't know if he believed me. One never does with Walsingham.

"He could have had me arrested merely for entering

the country without the proper papers, let alone on the suspicion I might be a French spy. Instead he offered me employment."

"You mean forced you into his service."

Martin wished he could allow her to believe that, but he shook his head. "There was little force involved. Walsingham did apply some pressure, hinting that Meg and I could be deported back to France. But I could have snatched Meg up and fled, tried starting over again in some other country, perhaps even your Ireland. But Walsingham dangled before me the chance of advancement, the prospect of obtaining a future for my daughter beyond my wildest dreams. And I took it, never pausing to weigh the risks or count the costs."

Cat said nothing, but her expression was grave as she listened. She sank down upon the stool in one of those unladylike postures that was so typical of Cat. Her legs sprawled slightly apart, her elbows resting upon her knees. His shirt dangled between her thighs in a provocative fashion that roused Martin in spite of himself.

He focused his attention on the bricks of the fireplace as he told her everything, holding nothing back this time. He spoke in a flat tone with none of his usual flourishes, relating the details of the Babington conspiracy, all the subterfuge Martin had resorted to in order to gain evidence for Walsingham, including being obliged to spy upon Ned Lambert. He concluded with his raid upon Poley's house and his reason for confiscating the portrait.

". . . and there they are, Babington and his fellow conspirators depicted in all their fools' glory." Martin gestured to the portrait. "Their death warrant signed in a rainbow of oil colors. But when I hand the painting over to Walsing-ham, at least one neck will be saved. This surely must ex-onerate Jane's brother."

Cat gave a faint nod of agreement. She stretched out her legs, her eyes downcast as she regarded her bare toes. Between her continued silence and the relentless drum of the rain against the window, Martin's nerves felt strained to the snapping point.

"You might as well say what you are thinking. You have never spared me before. Go ahead. Tell me what an irresponsible knave and idiot I am."

"Very well. You're an idiot."

Martin winced. He'd expected her to agree. But did she have to oblige him quite so cheerfully?

"I have always known exactly who you are, Martin le Loup," she said with a small quirk of her lips. "A bit of a rogue, a bit of a scoundrel, *and* an idiot. A brave, reckless, noble idiot."

Instead of the scorn he'd anticipated, Cat regarded him with a strange softness in her eyes.

"*Noble?*" he echoed. "Woman, have you even been lis-tening to me for the past fifteen minutes? The things that I have done—"

"Were extremely dangerous," she interrupted. "And while I cannot approve of you taking such risks, you are about to bring a parcel of scheming rascals to justice."

"To torture and death, you mean. And one of those ras-cals, Ballard, is a priest." Martin turned away from her, staring out the window where the sky continued to bleed dark rivers of rain down the glass. "The Lord knows I am not a religious man, but the years of my youth that I spent among the prelates of Notre Dame gave even me a certain respect for those who take holy orders."

He added bleakly, "I am not sure what transgressions are enough to send a man to hell, but betraying a priest must surely be a black enough sin."

Cat crept up behind him and rested her hand on his shoulder. "In my opinion, this John Ballard relinquished any claims to holiness when he planned to become an assassin. I don't claim to understand the ways of the Catholics or the Protestants. But from what I know of your Christ, he advocated love, peace, and forgiveness, not murder."

Cat tugged at his arm, coaxing him to face her. "None of the motives of these conspirators strike me as being all that noble or pure."

"Have my own been any better?" Martin asked. "When I worked as an agent for Navarre, most of my work involved scouting the duc de Guise's army or trying to raise support for a small beleaguered kingdom. At least there was some fairness, some honor in that. But this sordid affair—engaging to spy and deceive, encouraging other men in their treason in order to trap them." Martin dragged his hand wearily over the ends of his beard. "And all for what? To obtain a fake coat of arms and a parcel of land."

"You sought a safe haven for your daughter. *You* weren't planning to assassinate a queen."

"No, I'm only helping Walsingham bring another to her ruin and death."

"Mary Stuart did a fair job of accomplishing that by herself." Cat stroked her hand down his cheek in one of those gentle gestures that was rare from her and all the more sweet for that. "I have no love for Elizabeth, but there is no courage in the strike of an assassin's knife. The only way I would ever agree to fight the Tudor woman is if I could look her straight in the eye, my sword against hers."

"That is because there are very few women like you. Or men either for that matter."

"Like me?" She gave a self-deprecating laugh. "And just what kind of person would that be?"

"One of honor, wisdom, and courage. Like your Red Branch knights, your Grania and Brian Boru, all those generations of Irish heroes you celebrate in your stories. It is their blood that courses through your veins."

Cat smiled sadly and shook her head. "I think that blood has become a bit thinned during my wanderings."

"No." Martin traced his fingertip over the arch of her brows, her eyes such clear, pure lakes of blue. "Even exiled from your country, you carry Ireland in your eyes, all its strength and wild beauty."

"Ah, don't be daft," she said, but she blushed in a way she would never have done if he had heaped upon her the sort of flowery compliments he usually reserved for women.

Cat was such a practical woman, gifted with a direct wisdom. She saw things much more clearly than he. He felt as though with a clean stroke of her knife, she had cut through all the guilt, all the conflicts of conscience that had been tormenting him.

He didn't deserve the comfort she offered, but he could not stop himself from reaching for it all the same. He stole his arms about her waist, drawing her closer.

Cat came to him without hesitation, burrowing her face against the hard warmth of his chest. Martin rested his chin atop her head, her hair still damp. He breathed in the aroma that was Cat's alone. No cloying perfume, but something that was earthier, more elemental, sweet rain and fresh summer wind.

He held her thus for what seemed a long time, no sounds except the drumming of the rain, the crackle of the fire, and the steady thud of their hearts.

There was something tender about Martin's embrace and Cat tried to not hunger for more. She was grateful to be able to hide her face against him, lest he read her folly in her eyes. How deeply she had fallen in love with him, how shaken she was to realize the dangerous risks he had been taking. The thought of Martin being killed, of losing him, sent a small tremor through her.

He could never be her man. They would part ways in a few months' time, likely to never see each other again. Hard and painful as that was, Cat was certain she would be able to endure. Just as long as she knew he remained alive, somewhere out there striding his way through the world after Martin's own inimitable fashion.

Cat tipped her head to gaze up at him. "When you give Walsingham that painting, you'll be shed of him. Your part in all this will be ended, won't it?"

"I believe so. But if anything should still go awry, if something were to happen to me, you'd look out for Meg." It was not a question on Martin's part, merely a statement from which he appeared to derive great comfort.

"You know I would," Cat assured him. "But nothing is going to happen to you."

"But if it did—" he began, but she silenced him before

he could tempt fate any further. Straining on tiptoe, she pressed her lips to his.

Martin hesitated only a heartbeat before burrowing his fingers beneath her hair. He cradled the nape of her neck, his lips moving over hers in a kiss that was warm and lingering.

He drew back and gazed at her, her hunger mirrored in the green depths of his eyes.

"Cat," he said hoarsely. He moistened his lips and she could tell what he was trying to do. Muster the strength to resist temptation, summon up all the good reasons they should back away from each other.

Reasons that she understood far better than he. Of the two of them, she would be the one most likely to limp away from any casual coupling with a bruised heart.

And she didn't give a damn. She had walked through this world with her heart untouched and detached for far too long. Even the pain of knowing what it was to love Martin and then losing him would be nothing compared to the emptiness of never loving him at all.

Reaching up, she traced her fingers, lightly, tantalizingly against the barrier of his lips. Martin stared down at her, an agony of longing in his eyes.

"Cat, we—we should not—"

Cat expelled a breath rife with the frustration of desire too long denied. "Yes, damn it. We should."

Curling her fingers in the folds of his shirt, she yanked his mouth back down to hers. Martin gripped her shoulders as though to thrust her away.

Cat's tongue darted out, caressing the seal of his lips,

seeking entry. A tremor coursed through Martin, and it was as though she could feel something break inside the man like a storm erupting in the sky.

With a low growl, he wrapped his arms around her. His hands roved boldly over her body as he deluged her with kisses, raining them down upon her cheeks, her eyes, her chin, finally settling upon her mouth. His tongue claimed hers in a white-hot collision that robbed her of breath.

Locking her hard against him, he hiked up her shirt. Cat gasped as he cupped the bare skin of her buttocks, the heat of his hands sent a rush of molten warmth straight to her feminine core. Kissing her ferociously, Martin drew her hips so tight against him, she thrilled at the feel of his erection straining against his breeches.

She shivered with need, straining frantically to get closer. Martin dragged his mouth from hers, his breathing coming hard and quick.

"Ah, God," he groaned. "I am a worthless rogue. A complete scoundrel. A very wicked man."

"I know," Cat breathed, rubbing against him, fairly shimmying up the man the way she had done the tree. "It is one of the things I—"

She nearly said love best about you. Despite her passion-drugged senses, she retained enough wit to amend. "One—one of your better qualities."

Martin gave a ragged laugh. Although his body throbbed with need for her, he removed his hand from her bottom. Smoothing her shirt back down, he made a noble effort to put her away from him.

But his heroics were all in vain because Cat caught the

ends of the shirt and wrenched it over her head. His mouth went dry as his gaze raked over her small firm breasts, the red-gold dusting of hair at the delta of her legs.

Martin groaned, his erection tightening to a painful degree. "Cat, have mercy."

"No." She tossed the shirt at his feet like someone flinging down a gauntlet. "It's a damn dark wet night out there and we've just had a narrow escape. The world won't end and the sky won't fall if we find a wee bit of pleasure in each other. But then I am not troubled by your church's notions of sin. I am after all only a pagan."

That was exactly what she was, Martin thought. A pagan goddess, brazen and proud in all her naked glory, hands planted defiantly on her slim hips, her legs braced slightly apart.

She shook back her hair, the fire-colored strands spilling about her white shoulders, her eyes blazing like bright jewels. Martin moved toward her like a man all too willing to fling himself on her sacrificial fire.

He had always taken the initiative in any lovemaking. He was after all a Frenchman. But he allowed her to undress him, Cat's fingers deftly unlacing his shirt. She ripped it off over his head, her gaze roving appreciatively over him.

Tossing his shirt aside, she lightly scored her nails over his bare chest as she prowled around him in a way calculated to drive him mad.

He felt dazed with heat and desire as she wrapped her arms about him from behind, flattening the warm globes of her breasts against his back. She swirled her fingers through the hair dusting his chest, inching lower with each stroke toward his breeches.

Unfastening them, she released his erection. He almost moaned with relief until her hand closed over him, the mere heat of her touch enough to make him lose control.

"Sweet Jesu, woman, what are you trying to do to me?"

"Make you come apart in my hands," she purred, nipping playfully at his arm. He could tell she was delighting in her power over him, perhaps a shade too much. It was damned time he regained some control over this situation.

Catching hold of her wrist, he brought a halt to her bold exploration. Whipping about to face her, he murmured, "No, what you are doing is bringing me to my knees."

He knelt down before her, slanting a wicked glance up at her. Before Cat guessed what he meant to do, he cupped her buttocks and yanked her close, burying his face in the nest of curls between her legs.

Cat cried out at the delicious shock of an audacious kiss unlike any she'd ever experienced. The heady sense of power she had been feeling ebbed from her as Martin forced her legs farther apart, teasing her with his tongue.

She shook, clutching at his shoulders as her body reacted with surprising swiftness, shattering her with mind-numbing sensations of pleasure that left her too weak to stand. Quivering, she sank to her knees beside him. Martin's smile was far too smug.

"You—you French devil," she panted.

"Irish witch," he laughed.

Cat pounced on him, dragging him to the floor, where they kissed, wrestled, and caressed. After what she had just experienced, Cat didn't think it possible her desire could rage again so soon. But it flooded through her all over again with his every skillful touch. As she had always suspected, the man was infernally clever with his hands.

Cat scarce knew how Martin freed himself from the rest of his garments. She would have liked a moment to catch her breath, savor the sight of his naked body, all hard muscle and sinew and sweat. But he rolled her onto her back.

Bracing himself over her, he kissed his way down her throat to her breast, capturing first one nipple and then the other. As he laved her with the wet heat of his tongue, Cat closed her eyes and bit down upon her lip to keep from crying out at the sheer pleasurable torment of it.

It was as though he sought to brand her with his touch, his scent, his kiss, over every inch of her body. Cat knew she would carry the taste and feel of Martin le Loup to the end of her days.

It was only going to make it harder when the time came to leave, surrendering him to his English life, his Lady Danvers. Cat didn't care. She desperately wanted this, needed these few stolen hours.

When Martin finally plunged inside of her, she gasped at the shock of their joining. As her body stretched to accommodate him, it was as though he filled her completely.

Her eyes fluttered open to find him staring down at her with wonder in his gaze.

"Mon Dieu, Cat!" he said hoarsely. "You are so warm and tight. You fit me like—like—"

"A glove?"

"No, as though our bodies were fashioned for this, to belong together."

Cat's throat constricted. She wished he meant that, but she was certain that it was no more than the tender words Martin would feel obliged to whisper to any woman he bedded.

She buried her fingers in his hair and yanked his mouth down to hers. Bracing her feet against the rough wooden floor, she lifted her hips, urging him into action. His first thrusts and her response were a little awkward, more of a collision until she caught his rhythm.

Rocking against him, her body moved in time with his in a fluid motion as smooth and tempestuous as waves foaming over the shore. All trace of Martin's feigned English accent vanished as he breathed endearments and wicked profanities in a stream of fluent French.

As he plunged harder and deeper, Cat's tension coiled tighter and tighter. She raked her nails across his back and cried out his name as she experienced another ecstatic release, intense ripples of pleasure spiraling through her.

Martin gave a final thrust and shuddered as he spilled his seed deep inside her. He collapsed against her. Cat felt the thunder of his racing heart, echoing hers.

She wrapped her arms fiercely about him, holding him close as their labored breathing slowed. To her dismay, Cat's eyes prickled, threatening to fill with tears.

Their lovemaking had been nothing short of miraculous, a physical joy like nothing she had ever known. But she realized she had offered Martin more than her body this night. She had opened up her heart and soul to him as well, making herself more vulnerable than she ever had to any man.

As Martin drew back, she blinked hard lest he catch

her out in her lies, realize that what had just happened meant far more to her than a fleeting pleasure.

The depth of her emotion was difficult to conceal when he gazed down at her with such warmth. He tenderly stroked back damp strands of hair from her brow.

"Catriona."

He hardly ever called her that. Cat swallowed hard, feigning a languid smile.

"Whew. That was—was—"

He grinned. "Yes, it was. Wasn't it?"

She winced, her back and bottom beginning to feel the effects of their vigorous lovemaking, pounding against the hard floor.

Martin eased off her, eyeing her with concern. "Was I too rough? Have I hurt you?"

More than you'll ever know.

Cat forced a laugh. "I don't bruise that easy. But I might have a splinter in my arse."

Martin chuckled. Before she knew what he was about to do, he had her scooped up high in his arms. Carrying her over to the bed, he murmured, "We'll have to see what we can do about that."

Chapter Eighteen

THE FIRE BURNED LOWER, THE LOGS REDUCED TO GLOWING embers. At some point during the last hour, the downpour had slackened to a dull patter of rain against the window. Martin had no idea when. During the second time he and Cat had shattered in each other's embrace? Or had it been the third?

A hazy smile played on his lips, his eyes narrowed to half-slits. He felt more relaxed, replete, and content than he could remember being in a long time. He shifted, seeking a more comfortable position on a mattress so hard-worn; it had a tendency to roll the bed's occupants toward the sagging middle.

Not that he had any right to complain. He and Cat had wreaked their own share of damage upon the bedstead. He feared that some of the rope springs might have snapped during one of their vigorous bouts of lovemaking, and he was certain they had ripped one of the ancient sheets.

Most of the bedclothes were tangled in a heap on the floor. Martin leaned over the side of the bed and snagged the coverlet. He dragged it to the woman curled up on the opposite side of the bed, her back toward him.

Much to his disappointment, he feared that Cat had fallen asleep after their last tempestuous climax. He would have preferred that she do so cradled in his arms, her head nestled against his shoulder. But he saw that she was wakeful, watching the rain trickle down the windowpane.

He tucked the coverlet about them and snuggled close to her. His heart felt so extraordinarily full. He was bursting to pour a wellspring of romantic words and foolish endearments in her ear. But he doubted Cat would welcome them.

He contented himself with caressing his fingers over the place on her bottom where he had removed the splinter.

"How is your arse?" he inquired tenderly.

"Tired," she said with a weary laugh. "I am summoning the ambition to rouse myself and get dressed. We ought to get back before morning. Meg will be very alarmed if she wakes to find us both gone."

"Morning is a long way off. It cannot be much past midnight and it is still raining," he protested. "We have plenty of time."

"But you must be eager to get that portrait to Walsingham. If Babington discovers it has gone missing, the man will likely panic and bolt. I doubt your employer would be pleased about that. After all, there is your reward to consider. Do you think Walsingham will keep his promises to you?"

"I suppose so. He tends to be a man of his word." Martin ought to be rejoicing at the thought of achieving his long-sought-after goal. He was surprised by his own lack of enthusiasm.

He tried to kiss Cat's shoulder, but she dragged the coverlet higher.

"You will finally be able to go to Lady Danvers and lay your heart at her feet."

Martin flinched with guilt at the mention of Jane. In truth he had given little thought to her of late and none at all during these past few hours. He would be obliged to go to her, if for no other reason than to assure her she could stop worrying about her brother. And he would have to be honest enough to tell her why he was so certain of this, confess how he had spied for Walsingham.

Martin hoped Jane would be able to forgive him. But as for wanting anything more from the woman, he was stunned to realize that he didn't.

Cat shrank away from him to the very edge of the mattress. It was as though now that the lovemaking was done, she had already grown weary of his touch. Or perhaps it was his faux pas in allowing his thoughts to stray to another woman while the bed was still warm from their passion. But damnation. He hadn't mentioned Jane's name. Cat was the one who had reminded him of her ladyship.

The candles had long ago guttered out. Only the red glow of the fire provided what flickering light there was to be had. Martin rose up on one elbow, squinting down at Cat, wishing he could better see her face.

He brushed back the tangle of strands from her cheek. He confessed tentatively, "I can't even think of Jane. After all that we just shared—"

"Don't," Cat said sharply.

Martin's hand stilled. "Don't what? Touch you or—"

"Don't feel obliged to make pretty speeches or vows of devotion just because we bedded." She rolled over enough to frown at him. "We both know this was naught but a pleasant interlude. Two warm bodies relieving pent-up desire on a wet rainy night. The earth didn't move and the sky didn't suddenly rain stars."

Maybe not for her. Martin expelled a deep breath feeling like a barque that had been coursing the waves only to suddenly have the wind taken out of its sails.

"Pardon me for trying to be gallant," he muttered. Flinging himself to the other side of the bed, he punched his thin pillow in a vain effort to plump it.

"I am sorry if I wounded your masculine pride—" Cat began.

"*Non, pas de tout.* I am not that arrogant about my skill in bed." Martin grimaced. "Well, yes, I guess I am. When I finish making love to a woman, I am not accustomed to having her yawn, roll over, and start to snore."

Cat jerked upright, clutching the coverlet to her breasts. "I did nothing of the kind. That is the sort of behavior that is considered the prerogative of you men."

"I have never been that insensitive." Martin jammed the pillow behind his head. "Even when I paid—"

Martin checked himself, but not in time. Cat smirked at him.

"You *paid* to bed a woman? Never would I have imagined the dashing and lusty le Loup would have to resort to that."

"I was very young," Martin snapped. "It was how I parted company with the burden of my virginity. I was only eleven."

"*Eleven!*"

"Twelve, perhaps."

When Cat eyed him skeptically, he conceded. "All right. I may have been closer to thirteen when I surrendered to the charms of Daphne la Bouche, one of the most skilled prostitutes to ever walk the streets of Paris."

"Daphne the mouth? Why did they call her that? Oh!" Understanding lit Cat's eyes. Some of his irritation fading, Martin grinned in spite of himself.

"From that wolfish look of yours, I am assuming the sobriquet was not bestowed because of the wench's fondness for gossip."

"No, Daphne was incredibly tight-lipped, especially when she—ooof." Martin grunted when Cat poked him sharply in the ribs.

"I comprehend without you painting me any vivid pictures."

Martin subsided, suppressing his smile. At least his bawdy reminiscences had had the effect of luring Cat back to his side. He draped his arm about her. "I had to pick a great many pockets to afford Daphne's services. She might not have been some beautiful courtesan, but she didn't come cheap."

"Was she worth it?"

"*Oui.* She was very good. She provided such a dizzying introduction into the rites of Venus, I was completely taken with her. I returned to the brothel the next day with a wilted nosegay, vowing to make her my mistress and rescue her from her tragic profession even if I had to steal the purse of the king himself."

"And how did Mademoiselle la Bouche respond to this generous offer?"

"When she got done laughing at me, she boxed my ears, threw me out, and prepared to entertain her next client."

Cat chuckled, but her voice was not without sympathy as she stroked his chest. "Poor daunted wolf cub. But what a remarkable lad you must have been."

"Remarkable?" Martin snorted.

"Yes, I find it amazing that you were still able to retain such passion for life, such a romantic view of the world considering your circumstances. Abandoned by your mother, no family, no home, only yourself to rely upon. There had to have been times when you were cold, hungry, and desperate."

"There may have been." Martin shrugged. He had always been good at suppressing the darker moments of his life. He wrapped both arms about Cat, depositing a kiss atop her head.

"Sometimes the only way to survive the grit of the streets is to learn to walk with your head in the clouds. Besides, I was not entirely friendless. There was an old woman, a flower vendor who was kind to me. She was sort of the patron saint of street urchins although there was nothing particularly saintly about her. Tante Pauline could outcurse and outdrink any of the draymen who drove wagons through Paris."

"Tante Pauline?"

"That's what everyone called her. I never knew her real name." Martin smiled at the memory of the scrawny old woman with her gap-toothed grin. "She saved me from an empty belly many a time, sharing her bread and cheese with me. Besides selling her flowers, Tante Pauline claimed to be a bit of a gypsy, able to read palms. She even taught me how to fashion a charm to ward off witches."

To her credit, Cat tried to keep a solemn face, but her lips quivered as she demanded, "What sort of charm?"

"A sack containing an extremely odiferous mixture of herbs and garlic."

Cat shouted with laughter as he had feared she would.

"All right, it was pure superstitious nonsense. I know that now. During my youth, I might have been bold enough to risk my neck in the hangman's noose, but I was petrified of anything to do with sorcery. There was nothing I feared so much as a witch."

Cat's brow furrowed. "Then why did you ever—"

"Ever what?" Martin stroked her back, enjoying the smooth warm feel of her skin.

Cat hesitated a moment before finishing. "Share a bed with Cassandra Lascelles."

Martin's hand stilled, the mention of the woman's name like the swift thrust of a knife between his ribs.

"I believe that is a subject best left alone," he said tersely.

He resumed his caress, but Cat squirmed away from him. She raised herself up enough to regard him gravely.

"You have left it alone far too long. I realize you find it uncomfortable to talk about Cassandra—"

"*Uncomfortable?*" Martin choked. "The memory of that woman sickens me."

"She was not your lover then?"

"My lover? Christ, no. I only ever lay with her that one time. But that was enough to—to—"

"To father Meg."

"Meg is the only good thing to come out of that night." Martin ground his fingertips against his eyes in an effort to stem the nightmarish images trying to storm his mind. "The rest is all . . . poison."

"The only way to get rid of poison is to purge it." Cat brushed the hair back from his brow. "Tell me what happened."

But Martin thrust her hand away and sat up. He kicked the coverlet off and swung his legs over the side of the bed.

Cat regretted she had ever spoken. But Cassandra Lascelles was a shadow darkening the lives of Martin and his daughter. She would continue to haunt both of them as long as Martin refused to acknowledge her presence.

Cat bit down upon her lip. Her time with both Martin and Meg was so short. She could not love and protect them to the end of her days as she longed to do. But if she could at least banish the specter of Cassandra—

Cat studied the rigid line of Martin's back, reaching out to touch him, only to draw her hand back. She feared she had pushed him too far. She so little expected him to speak; she was startled when he did.

"I was only eighteen when I crossed paths with the Lascelles witch," he began haltingly. "It was the same summer I met Miri Cheney. She was like something out of a dream with her pale gold hair, her fey eyes, and that strange mystical way about her. I was dazzled, completely in love with her."

"Yes, why wouldn't you be?" Cat asked wistfully.

"At that time, I shared a lodging in Paris with my good friend Captain Nicholas Remy. As close as you are to Ariane, you must be acquainted with him."

"I know that he is considered a great hero," Cat replied. "A champion of the Huguenot cause. He married Ariane's sister, Gabrielle. But I have never actually met the man."

"Remy is a genuine hero, brave and skilled in battle, honorable to the core. He was also the truest friend I'd ever had, like a brother to me." Martin paused expelling a gusty breath before he was able to continue.

"Cassandra Lascelles was as mad as she was evil. She had this damnable notion that she was destined to give birth to a dark sorceress who would topple the thrones of men and restore the daughters of the earth to power."

"Being a true wise woman has nothing to do with power," Cat interrupted. "It is about acquiring wisdom and healing, learning to live in harmony with the earth, not spreading darkness and destruction."

"Obviously, no one ever explained that to Cassandra."

"From what I've heard about Cassandra, there was no explaining anything to the woman. She was obsessed with her insane dreams of glory."

Martin sighed. "Unfortunately, her obsession included Remy. She wanted him to be the father of her child. She threatened to destroy the captain with her black arts if she could not have him in her bed. Incredible as it sounds, she had actually fashioned this cursed medallion to gain power over him.

"The night she had determined to seduce him, I went in his stead. Frightened as I was of witches, I thought I could deal with Cassandra far better than my honorable friend, Remy. I was very full of myself, even more than I am now." Martin gave a mirthless laugh.

"That night was cursed with a storm far worse than this one. The sky roiled with black clouds, the heavens rent with such thunder and lightning as though the world stood poised on the brink of destruction."

He paused, his arms braced rigidly on either side of him. "I crept into the inn room where Cassandra waited for Remy. I knew the witch had a fondness for strong drink. My plan was to get her so drunk she would forget about Remy and surrender the dark charm she threatened to use against him. But there was one thing I had not counted upon and that was the charms of Cassandra herself."

He shuddered. "She was stunningly beautiful after her own cold fashion. Long black hair, dead white skin, and those unseeing dark eyes. I managed to get her drunk, but she wreaked havoc with my senses as well. She wore such a strange seductive perfume. It seemed to seep through my very pores, getting into my head, stealing away my reason, robbing me of my will. When the witch realized that Remy was not coming, she decided to—to have me instead.

"Before I knew what was happening, I had tumbled into bed with her, forgetting my love for Miri, my purpose for being there, forgetting everything except for the lust Cassandra aroused."

Martin hung his head and concluded hoarsely, "After I left the inn that night, I remember falling to my knees, heaving my guts. I felt so—so tainted. It was a long time after before I could even look Miri in the eyes, let alone touch her."

It was a humiliating confession for any man to make. Martin had never spoken about what had happened that night, even to Miri. He could not imagine how Cat had induced him to open up to her.

She should have had nothing but scorn for his weakness, but she wrapped her arms about him from behind, her voice as warm as her touch.

"Martin, I have known a great many daughters of the earth capable of brewing up a potion or perfume capable of seducing a man. I admit I used to think nothing of it. I was so bitter after Rory O'Meara broke faith with me; I used to say, 'Bah! Let men look to themselves.' But it is as wrong for a woman to take advantage of a man as it is the other way round."

Martin shifted to face her and found her fierce blue eyes soft with understanding and compassion. The kiss that he brushed against her lips was as filled with gratitude as it was tenderness.

Much as he hated to admit it, Cat was right. It had helped to let go of some of those poisonous memories even if he had not been able to be completely honest with Cat. There was still one fear regarding Cassandra and his daughter that lingered to haunt him, a fear so great he could scarce acknowledge it to himself.

He pulled Cat into his arms and tumbled her back down onto the mattress. Their lips met in a kiss rife with warmth and passion until Martin was suddenly struck by something she had said.

Poised over her, he drew back to demand, "Who the devil is Rory O'Meara?"

"No one. A lad I once knew."

She sought to distract him with another kiss, but Martin reared back. "That is hardly fair. I have shared all my darkest secrets with you."

"Life *is* unfair," she replied saucily, curling her fingers in his chest hair. "Has no one taught you that by now?"

"I learned enough to get what I want. By fair means or foul."

Pinning her to the mattress, he dug his fingers in her ribs, subjecting her to a merciless tickling. Cat writhed, pummeling his arms and choking with laughter.

"All right, stop it, you French fiend," she gasped. "I'll tell you."

When he ceased, she glared up at him. Ignoring her ferocious scowl, he kissed the bridge of her nose.

"Rory was my stepfather's nephew," she said reluctantly. "The tanist of the O'Meara clan."

"Tanist?"

"It is a title bestowed on the heir apparent, the man who will eventually become the next chieftain, like the prince of his clan, and Rory seemed every bit the prince to me. He was sinfully handsome with his burnished red hair, blue eyes, and broad shoulders. All the lasses were mad about him."

When Cat actually sighed at the memory, Martin frowned. "How strange. I've already taken a decided dislike to the man."

Cat laughed, but her smile took on a rueful quality. "I never thought Rory would look twice at the likes of me with so many beautiful lasses swarming over him, much more feminine and graceful.

"And *taller*," she added. "And yet the spring I turned fifteen he did notice me. It—it was like a miracle the first time he smiled at me. As though all the rest of the world fell away, all the misery, the slights and scorn I experienced in my stepfather's household faded to nothing."

Martin's frown deepened, his dislike for this *prince* of Cat's memory escalating to loathing. Maybe he didn't want to hear anything more about Rory O'Meara.

But when Cat paused, he said, "Go on."

"I was completely smitten with him. And he was charming enough to make me believe he loved me. I surrendered my virginity to him on a warm spring night in a field of heather."

Her blue eyes clouded, and she shifted her head upon the mattress in an effort to avert her face. "After Rory got what he wanted from me, he scarce looked back. It is not a new tale, the same pathetic story that has befallen many a foolish maiden."

Her lips tightened with self-disgust. "I thought I would have been far wiser than that. Within a week of bedding me, Rory plighted his troth to the daughter of the chieftain of a neighboring clan, a pretty plump creature far softer than my bony self and possessed of more wealth and importance."

Cat hunched her shoulder in a slight shrug as though the matter were of no consequence. But when Martin caught her chin, obliging her to look at him, he could see the hurt girl in the woman's eyes.

Martin brought one of her hands to his lips, kissing her

fingertips. "So the villain broke your heart. I'd like to set sail for Ireland tomorrow and break his head."

"That would be ill-advised. The last I heard of Rory he had become the chieftain of the clan when my stepfather died. Like most of the Irish, the O'Mearas can be a vengeful lot when their chief is threatened."

She tipped up her chin proudly. "Besides, I don't need you to break his head. What fun would that be? I'd prefer to do it myself."

Cat's lips tilted in a feline smile. "In fact, that is exactly what I did."

Martin chuckled. "Ah, *ma petite chatte.* I should have guessed as much."

"It was my gift to Rory on his wedding day, a good hard punch that broke his nose. My mother swooned from shame at my behavior and my stepfather soundly beat me for it. I didn't care. It was worth it. By the time my aching back had healed, I never spared Rory another thought."

"Truly?" Martin asked skeptically.

She regarded him with a sad smile. "Hearts don't break, Martin. They just bruise a little. I learned to be more cautious."

"So cautious you closed yourself off to other men ever since."

"I have had other lovers."

"But you never allowed yourself to take any risks again, indulge in that kind of love that transports you above the earth, consumes your entire being."

Cat gave a scornful sniff. "You mean the way that you were with Miri Cheney."

"After what happened with Cassandra, I hardly felt fit

to touch Miri's boots. But yes, I did spend years striving to be worthy of Miri."

"Are you saying that during all that time you remained celibate?"

"Well . . . no. My travels and duties to the king of Navarre often took me far from Miri's side. Occasionally, I had to indulge the lustier side of my nature, but that had nothing to do with my adoration of Miri."

Cat's sudden lunge caught him off guard. She shoved him onto his back and loomed over him with a look of fierce reproof.

"Do you know the trouble with you, Martin le Loup?"

"No." Martin sighed. "But I feel certain you are about to tell me."

"You view love as this exalted thing, worshipping the woman of your affections as though she were some distant star." Cat punched her fist in the air in a frustrated gesture. "You need a woman who knows how to get right down there, thick in the muck of life, sweating and fighting alongside you, the two of you looking out for each other, nurturing and—and protecting."

"And I suppose this romantic vision of yours includes two warm bodies rubbing together for their mutual bene-fit?" Martin asked with a sardonic lift of one brow.

"Yes, that is most certainly a part of it."

"What about two hearts and souls touching as well? *La grande passion?* You don't believe in that?" he demanded.

Cat rolled off of him. "I suppose it happens, but it is as rare as that comet streaking across the sky. All I am saying is, the next time you see Lady Danvers, instead of assault-ing her with elegant speeches, you—you should grab her and kiss her like there is no tomorrow. Or you may well spend the next ten years courting her."

Cat flung herself out of bed and strode over to the fire. She yanked on her breeches and started to get dressed.

Martin remained flat on his back for a moment, feeling stunned. Never in all of the times he had pleasured a woman had he ever had one leave his bed and bluntly order him to go make love to someone else.

He jerked upright, seething to tell Cat what she could do with her advice. There was only one woman in the world he wanted to kiss and that was the stubborn, infuriating redheaded sprite jamming herself back into his breeches.

Because he loved her.

Mon Dieu. Martin's breath stilled, his anger fading before the staggering realization.

He . . . he loved Cat. What an idiot he was not to have figured it out sooner. She was the last sort of woman in the world he would have ever expected to seize hold of his heart this way. Strong, tough, too infernally independent and proud for her own good.

But when Cat revealed the gentler, more tender side of her nature, she left a man feeling as though he had been entrusted with a most precious gift.

Never had Martin known any woman so capable of infuriating him one moment, then arousing him the next. Watching her dress, the supple curves of her body bathed in firelight, was enough to get him hard all over again.

But what he felt for her was far more than mere desire. He could be himself with Cat, tell her anything, bare all his own weaknesses, with no need to pretend, no fear she would find him less of a man.

He loved Catriona O'Hanlon and Martin's first impulse was to leap out of bed, seize her in his arms, and tell her so. He was checked by one thought.

She would never believe him. Why should she, after watching him court Jane Danvers all this while, after listening to him spout his adoration of Miri? She would think him a romantic fool who bandied about the word *love* with little restraint and she'd be right.

How could he convince her that what he felt for her was more real than anything he had ever known in his life? He couldn't and he didn't have the right to try.

He still had his daughter to consider. All Cat wanted to do was return to Faire Isle, a place of all those strange mystical associations he had to banish from Meg's life. If Martin had any doubt of that, his recollections of Cassandra tonight were a bitter reminder.

Cat paused in lacing up her shirt long enough to cast him an impatient look. "The rain has stopped. We have to go."

Martin nodded and levered himself out of bed. After his nightmarish interlude with Cassandra, he had come to loathe storms. Never had he thought to feel so bleak to see one come to an end.

⧓⧓⧓

THE GENTLEMAN USHER ALLOWED WALSINGHAM TO PASS INTO the queen's inner sanctum, a privilege few were accorded, especially at such a late hour.

Like Walsingham himself, the queen was noted for laboring over reports and matters of state far into the night, the only person in the kingdom whose stamina rivaled his own.

But the queen was not at her desk as usual. Only a few candles were burning, the maids of honor huddled together, speaking in nervous whispers.

Walsingham could well imagine the state of the queen's temper ever since she had read the translation of Mary Stuart's infamous letter.

But it was difficult to gauge Her Majesty's present mood. She had her back to him, her tall slender form swallowed up by the shadows near the window. Walsingham could make out little beyond the red gleam of her hair, the sharp outline of her profile as she stared outward, studying the night sky.

The storm had passed over; the clouds had dispersed enough to reveal a pale sliver of moon, the ominous streak of the comet.

Although her courtiers repeatedly begged her not to tempt fate by looking at the strange phenomenon, it was typical of Elizabeth's defiance and courage that she persisted in gazing at the comet so boldly.

The stiffening of her shoulders told Walsingham she was well aware of his presence, but she refused to acknowledge him.

"Your Majesty," he murmured, kneeling stiffly before her.

Still she avoided receiving him and Walsingham knew full well why. Elizabeth was mistress of the arts of procrastination and delay, a policy that served her well in many instances, but it would no longer do so in the matter of the Queen of Scots.

For her good, for the good of the realm, he had to make her see that and face the grim task ahead of her.

The queen's voice came softly at last, "Have you heard the latest from Rome?"

Sir Francis shifted uncomfortably on his aching knees. "No, Your Grace."

"The Pope is thinking of issuing another bull of excommunication."

"Against whom?"

"Not *whom*. Against what. His holiness plans to excommunicate the comet. Do you not find that both amusing and astonishing?"

"Nothing could astonish me regarding the superstitious folly of the papists."

"It might be a good thing. If it focuses the attention of my enemies on finding a way to destroy the comet, perhaps they might for a while forget about destroying me."

She flicked an impatient glance his way before turning back to the window. "Get up, before you wear out your knees, old Moor."

Walsingham rose stiffly to his feet, wincing at the crack of his knees. "Your Grace has—had time to thoroughly peruse the Scottish queen's letter?"

"Yes, I have *perused it*. How you must be rejoicing. At long last, that foolish woman has played right into your hands."

"I assure you I take no pleasure—"

"God's death!"

Walsingham leaped back at the sudden flare of her

anger. The queen was known to cuff and spit upon her courtiers when gripped by the formidable Tudor temper. Once she had even flung her slipper in Walsingham's face.

He watched warily as Elizabeth's hand clenched upon the window ledge. But after a tense moment, she appeared to master her rage, going on in a wearied tone.

"Spare me your assurances. Like a most diligent spider, you have woven your webs these past ten years and more, hoping to destroy Mary Stuart."

"Only because I can see no other way to secure your safety and that of your realm."

"But I am the one who will have the blood of a kinswoman on my hands. It is an evil precedent to set, taking off the head of a lawful queen."

Walsingham forbore to remind her that it was one that had already been set by her father. None dared speak the name of Anne Boleyn to the queen. Elizabeth herself never mentioned her mother.

The queen's hand came up to massage her temples. "I suppose Mary must now be tried."

"She should be fetched to the Tower—"

"No," Elizabeth snapped. "I will not have the trial in London, where I shall be obliged—

"No," she repeated in a lower, equally forceful tone. "You will prepare me a list of other suitable sites for the trial. I will study them at length, give it my due consideration."

Walsingham grimaced, recognizing another delaying tactic when he heard it. "Your Grace—"

"A list, Sir Francis. Present it to me tomorrow," the queen said in a tone that brooked no further argument.

Walsingham sighed. "Yes, Your Grace."

"Now what of the others? The six *gentlemen*." The queen laid scornful emphasis upon the word. "Have you uncovered the identity of these bold gallants who have vowed to take my life?"

"That is what I came to tell you," Walsingham said. "One of my agents waited upon me but an hour ago with new evidence. I now have the means of identifying all the conspirators. I have issued warrants for all of them, including this witch who appears to have been involved in the affair."

"The Silver Rose creature that you spoke to me of." Elizabeth gave a disgusted shake of her head. "Plots to attack me with witchcraft. Whatever next?

"Very well, Walsingham. Make your arrests and your damned list. Just leave me in peace. At least for the rest of this night." Without looking around, the queen dismissed him with a tired wave of her hand.

Walsingham bowed and retreated, hastening to carry out her orders before she changed her mind and found some reason to forbid the Queen of Scots's trial.

Walsingham knew his diligence was going to cost him dearly. Someone would have to be blamed when the ax separated the Stuart woman's head from her shoulders. He fully expected most of the royal displeasure to fall on him, and he was prepared to endure it.

As to the arrest of the Silver Rose . . . Walsingham experienced a prick of conscience. Martin le Loup had done the secretary a great service by uncovering that portrait and bringing it so promptly to Walsingham's attention.

The death of the witch would be poor repayment for

Martin's bold actions. Walsingham feared that Martin would take it very hard and he was sorry for that.

But Walsingham could not allow any partiality for Martin to sway him. As always, Sir Francis saw his duty clearly, and was prepared to do it. No matter the cost.

Chapter Nineteen

THE LATE AFTERNOON SUN SLANTED WARM RAYS OVER THE rough-hewn kitchen table where Maude peeled apples, the fruit red and glossy in the wicker basket. A haunch of venison roasted on a spit over the fire, the mouthwatering aroma mingling with the fragrance of stalks of dried herbs suspended from the ceiling.

Sights and scents that were familiar to Cat, but they seemed almost disconcertingly normal after last night's adventure. The theft of the painting, the narrow escape, the storm, and those stolen hours in Martin's embrace all felt like a dream.

But one had to sleep in order to dream and Cat had done very little of that upon her return to the Angel. She had been relieved to discover Meg sound asleep despite the storm. The girl was far too good at reading eyes, and it would have been both embarrassing and awkward for Cat to explain her absence.

But Meg had not even roused when Cat crept into their bedchamber. The girl had slumbered on while Cat spent the remaining hours of the night upon the window seat marveling at her own folly in giving way to her love for a man who would never return the emotion. She could not bring herself to regret it though, and such conflict of thought and feeling had not been conducive to sleep.

Knuckling her tired eyes, Cat hunkered down near the lanky young man writhing on a pallet in the corner. If Cat had spent a restless night, she was obliged to concede that Jem had endured a worse one. Lank strands of dirty blond hair straggled across the manservant's angular face as he gazed at Cat with misery-rimmed eyes, his hand clasped to his swollen jaw.

"Open up, lad, and let me have a look," Cat coaxed for the third time.

When Jem persisted in shaking his head and shrinking away from her, Cat gave a vexed sigh. Lack of sleep and fighting to subdue heartache did little for one's patience.

Although Jem was more than twice her size, all gangly legs and sinewy arms, Cat seized him by his shirt strings and growled, "Open your mouth unless you want me to kneel on your chest and pry your jaws apart."

Jem moaned but parted his lips a fraction. Cat cupped his chin, obliging him to open wider. She examined the reddened gum swelling around the tooth browned with decay.

Mistress Butterydoor loomed behind Cat, squinting at

the boy. The old woman nodded her head and pronounced sagely, "Hare's brains. You need to rub them over the sore gum. Works wonders to soothe teething babes."

Cat bit her tongue to avoid saying exactly what she thought of such an idiotic and disgusting practice. She and Agatha had reached a truce of sorts recently and Cat strove to keep it, at least for Meg's sake.

"I believe Jem is well past such remedies, Mistress Butterydoor. That tooth is going to have to come out."

"No," Jem shrieked.

To Cat's surprise, Agatha grudgingly agreed with her. "You best have master send for Turner, the barber over on Gunning Street."

"Mmmph!" Jem shook his head, clamping his hands over his mouth.

"There, there, m'dear." Agatha elbowed Cat out of the way as she bent down to brush Jem's hair from his eyes. "Master Turner's good at drawing teeth. He does it right quick and he'll trim that mop of yours as well. I daresay you could use it."

Jem's only response was another pathetic moan. Cat left Agatha to comfort the boy as best she could while Cat went to find Martin. He had gone out on an errand earlier and upon his return closeted himself in the study.

Cat encountered Meg hovering on the kitchen threshold. The girl regarded Cat anxiously. "How is Jem? Samuel said he—he was like to die."

"Samuel is a great gossiping idiot who spreads rumors faster than a tinker." Cat gave Meg's shoulder a comforting squeeze. "Jem will be fine as long as that rotten tooth is pulled."

Meg flinched, rubbing her own jaw in a sympathetic gesture. Stealing a furtive look about her, she beckoned Cat to come closer so that she might whisper.

"There might be something I could do to help Jem. I remember a remedy that I read about in—in a book somewhere."

Cat tensed. From the way Meg avoided her eyes, Cat had little doubt which book the girl meant.

"There is a potion that you apply to a handkerchief and hold over a person's nose and they lose consciousness. If I did that for Jem, everyone would merely think he fainted and he would not have to endure the pain. I'd have to be careful because if you use too much of the potion, a person could—"

"No!" Cat whispered back. "That would not be wise, Meggie."

Meg frowned. "Is it wiser to let Jem suffer?"

"He won't."

Another dramatic groan emanated from the kitchen to defy her assurances. Cat grimaced.

"The lad just needs to pluck up his courage. A few good yanks and it will be all over."

Meg did not look convinced, but when Cat encouraged her to go out in the garden and well out of earshot of Jem's misery, the girl complied.

Only after Meg had gone did Cat frown, troubled by the girl's suggestion. It had been a long time since Meg had even hinted at any of the extraordinary knowledge she had gleaned from the *Book of Shadows.*

Meg seemed so absorbed by her struggles to learn the lute, perfect her stitching, and transform herself into a proper English lady; it was as though she, too, had determined to bury her past. She no longer kept her witch-blade hidden in the pocket of her gown or consulted the unusual spyglass she had fashioned to study the comet.

Cat had almost allowed herself to forget all the girl was capable of. She should have known better. Abilities and knowledge like Meg possessed were not so easily denied, the temptations presented by such power always there.

Whether Meg went to Faire Isle or not, the girl needed to learn to cope with her rare gifts. Somehow Cat would have to find a way to persuade Martin of this.

But when she entered his study, she realized it would not be a propitious moment to broach the subject. His desk was abandoned, quill, ink, tally markers, and ledger books littered across the surface. Martin stared out the window, the cast of his face grim.

His expression lightened as Cat entered the study. Their eyes met and for a moment Cat felt as though the very air between them grew heavy with memories of last night. Accustomed to meet any man's gaze boldly, she did something she had never done before. She was the first to look away.

"So how is our long-suffering Jem?" he asked.

Cat's lip curled with scorn. "Carrying on like a wee babe. Mistress Butterydoor says we'd best send for Master Turner and I agree. Before Jem provokes me into solving his problem after my own fashion."

When Cat struck her fist into the palm of her hand, Martin smiled. "Poor Jem. Very well. Send Samuel to fetch the barber."

Cat nodded. It cost her great effort to be at ease with Martin, to pretend that last night had been nothing more than a casual encounter, a passionate ache that had been cured by a heated tumble between the sheets.

Never mind that their embrace had only deepened her longing for him, strengthened the love she felt. She comforted herself that at least she still had her pride. Martin would never know of her folly.

When he turned back to the window, Cat studied the rigid line of his back. Martin's ready smile and light tone might fool the rest of the world, but Cat knew the man too well to be deceived.

Joining him at the window, she had to resist the urge to massage the tension from his neck. Given how easily her desire for him could ignite, she had best start learning to keep her hands to herself.

Folding her hands in her apron instead, she asked, "What's amiss? I expected a little more swagger after your meeting with Walsingham. You assured me that all had gone well."

Martin shrugged. "Well enough. Sir Francis seemed very pleased with me. He promised me I shall be amply rewarded for finding that portrait and that I may consider my part in this affair at an end. I need involve myself no further."

He admitted reluctantly, "But this morning, I risked going back to Poley's house."

"Martin!" Cat vented her alarm and frustration by punching his arm.

"I know." He winced, rubbing the place where she had jabbed him. "I know it was a damned fool thing to do. But after all the risks and dangers of the past week, I had to know the outcome.

"I watched from a distance when they arrested Ballard. He had come looking for Babington and they seized the priest in Poley's garden. Babington managed to escape in the nick of time."

"Ah, so that is what has you so tense."

"No, I confess part of me actually hopes the young fool might avoid the horrors of a traitor's death." Martin sighed. "But when the queen's soldiers raided the house, they arrested Robert Poley."

"Poley? But he is one of Walsingham's men, the same as you."

"The dangers of being a spy, my dear. It is all too easy to be mistaken for one of the conspirators. Walsingham warned me to stand clear when the arrests were made."

"And you should have listened to him!" Cat said fiercely.

"I realized that as I watched that poor devil Poley being dragged away. There but for the grace of God . . ." Martin trailed off, leaving the sobering thought unfinished.

"It felt so strange as I made my way back home, unscathed. The rumors had already begun to spread through the streets of a plot to assassinate the queen, a Catholic conspiracy to overthrow the kingdom. Everywhere I went I heard exclamations of horror and prayers for the safety of the queen and all her loyal subjects.

"*God deliver us from the devil, the Pope, and the comet,*" Martin quoted wryly. "And then everyone simply went on about their everyday affairs."

"It is how people survive, Martin," Cat said. "Life is made up more of smaller things and ordinary moments than great events or cataclysmic happenstances and we should all thank the good Mother Earth for that."

"I suppose so. Although last night was far from ordinary." Martin startled her by entwining his fingers with hers. Her heartbeat quickened. She had to remind herself it was but a casual gesture on his part. After all, they had been friends before they had become lovers.

"Cat . . ." Martin began.

"Yes?"

When Cat regarded him with that cool, clear gaze of hers, he was unable to continue. Martin had never been a silent man or a stoic one. It seemed damned unnatural to him to hold his peace, to feel the depth of love that he did for this woman and not tell her so.

He suddenly realized it was not the rest of London going calmly about its business today that disturbed him. It was Cat. After the kind of passion they had shared last night, how could the woman look so—so blasé and completely untouched? It irritated him to the point of wanting to haul her into his arms and kiss her until she pleaded for mercy. The devil take whoever might walk in upon them.

He was spared the folly of such an action by the sound of someone hammering at the front door, clamoring for admittance.

"I had better attend to that," Cat said. "Answering the door is usually Jem's task, but he is hardly in a fit state to do so."

Cat hastened from the study, only lowering her guard as she headed to the front door. It was one of the most damned disconcerting things about Martin le Loup, how

the man could make a woman feel ravaged just with one
sweep of his wolfish green eyes.

Flushed with warmth, Cat had to resist the urge to fan
herself with her apron. She took a moment to compose herself into the guise of a proper maidservant. She swung open
the door, catching the person on the threshold in mid-knock.

Alexander Naismith lowered his fist. The boy appeared
to be in quite a state, his blond hair disheveled, his face
streaked with sweat as though he had run all the way from
Southwark to Cheapside.

He swept off his cap, panting. "M-master Wolfe. N-need
to see him at once."

Before Cat could reply, Naismith shoved past her. Martin must have heard the commotion because he emerged
from his study, his brow furrowed with concern.

"Sander? What's wrong, lad? Is something amiss at the
theater?"

The boy doubled over, clutching his side as he sought
to catch his breath. "N-not the theater. Strand House. The
queen's soldiers s-stormed the Lambert place. They had an
arrest warrant, Master Wolfe. You must go, t-try to help."

Martin and Cat exchanged a stunned look.

"But surely that is impossible," Cat said. "Didn't Walsingham assure you—"

But Martin silenced her with a slight shake of his head,
warning her to take care what she revealed in front of
Sander.

Martin rested one hand bracingly on the boy's shoulder. "Are you telling me his lordship has been arrested?"

"N-no. I have no idea where Ned is. It's his sister
who—who has been accused of treason."

Sander straightened, announcing in dismayed tones, "Lady Danvers has been taken to the Tower."

Martin's face drained with shock and consternation. He paced the hall, dragging his hand down his face, his inner turmoil all too apparent.

He came to an abrupt halt as though he'd reached some decision and Cat was very much afraid she knew what it was. Turning to Sander, he thanked the boy for bringing him the tidings.

"Now hie off to the kitchen and recover yourself. Agatha will give you some ale."

"But poor Lady Danvers! You will rush to her aid?"

Martin nodded. Clapping the boy on the shoulder, he sent Sander off. Cat waited until the boy was out of earshot before she rounded on Martin.

"Go to her aid?" she exclaimed as she trailed Martin back into the study. "Whatever do you imagine you are going to do? Not even you can storm the Tower of London."

"No, but I can start by storming Walsingham's office." Martin struck his fist against the mantel and cursed.

"Damn the man and his evasive tongue. Last night Walsingham swore to me he had no intention of arresting Ned Lambert. But the old devil had to have been plotting this all along, to seize Jane instead."

"Walsingham must have had some reason—"

"Reason! What reason could he possibly have for arresting one of the kindest, most gentle ladies in all of London?"

"None, I suppose. The woman is an angel." Cat was unable to keep the bitter edge from her remark, but Martin appeared to take no heed of it.

As he snatched up his cloak, she blocked his path, making one last desperate effort to reason with him. "Martin, Walsingham told you your part in all of this is at an end. He all but warned you to involve yourself no further. I understand your . . . your feelings for Jane Danvers, but all you will succeed in doing is endangering yourself. I don't see how you can help her."

"I don't know either, but I have to try." Martin's gaze met hers, his green eyes seeming to beg for her understanding.

Cat understood all too well. Asking Martin le Loup to ignore a damsel in distress was like expecting the fire not to burn. Especially the woman he wanted to make his wife and Meg's mother.

Cat experienced a surge of jealousy, but she managed to swallow it. She even managed a thin smile as she said, "Oh, very well. Go see what can be done to rescue your lady love. I would ask you to be careful, but one might as well expect the Pope to become a Puritan."

Martin returned her smile. "I will take care. I swear I will return to you . . . and Meg before you know I have gone."

"We'll be here."

Martin reached for her hand, but Cat evaded his grasp, striding out of the study swiftly. Martin watched her go with regret, wishing he could have told her.

It was not love drawing him to Jane's rescue. It was guilt.

※※※

THE TOWER OF LONDON HAD STOOD SENTINEL OVER THE port of London since the twelfth century. Fortress, palace, prison, the white tower surrounded by its strong curtain wall was a source of both pride and terror to Londoners.

Martin recalled how on his first visit to the City, he had taken great glee in reminding one arrogant Englishman that the stout keep the man boasted of had actually been built by William of Normandy and was constructed of imported *French* stone.

That barb felt like a lifetime ago. As Martin followed the yeoman warder deeper inside the fortress, it was as though he could feel the full power of the English realm bearing down upon him.

The chill that settled in his bones came from more than the dank stone walls. Martin could hear the groans of despair emanating from the cells, the clank of chains. The prison reeked of fear and hopelessness. It horrified Martin to think of the gentle Lady Danvers walled up in such a place.

How such a thing had come to pass, Martin still had no idea. He had been unable to track Walsingham down and demand an explanation. Either the secretary was avoiding Martin or Walsingham had difficulties of his own. At Whitehall, Martin had heard more rumors. The Queen of Scots was going to be arrested, and it was said Elizabeth was not pleased.

Unable to confront Walsingham, Martin had turned to the only other course he could think of. He had bribed one of the Tower guards to allow him to visit Jane. At least he would be able to see how she fared and discover from her the nature of the charges against her.

As Martin trailed the guard over the rough uneven

floor, he felt he might as well have been shackled himself, his every footstep weighted with guilt.

If he had been honest with Jane, if he had at least warned her that Walsingham had targeted the Lambert family for investigation, could Martin have somehow prevented Jane from coming to this? To what degree was he inadvertently responsible for her arrest?

That was something Martin could only know after he had spoken to Jane. He dreaded facing the lady and confessing his own treachery in acting as Walsingham's spy.

Martin sought to steel himself as the warder unlocked the door to Jane's cell.

"I can give you ten minutes," the guard reminded him tersely. "No more."

Martin nodded as he entered the cell and the door was locked behind him. He was a little relieved to discover the room was not the rat-infested dungeon he had been imagining, with Jane in chains, huddled on a bed of straw.

Her ladyship was imprisoned as befitted her station, in a chamber with a high arched roof and three crosslet windows. It was furnished with a tester bed and a small table spread with a modest repast of bread, wine, and cheese. A pallet had been provided for Lady Danvers's maid, but Jane was alone.

She was seated upon a low stool beneath one of the crosslets, struggling to use the meager light for her stitching. She glanced up as Martin entered, her face working with some strong emotion, her lips trembling.

Martin understood he'd been her only visitor since her arrest. He half expected her to leap up and hurl herself sobbing into his arms. Most other women certainly would have done so.

But Jane made a swift recovery. She rose with dignity and extended her hand as graciously as though she were receiving him in her sitting room.

"Master Wolfe."

Martin would have found it easier to deal with tears. At least he could have held her, tried to comfort her. Her quiet courage was enough to unman him, driving the spikes of his guilt deeper.

"Your ladyship." Martin swept an elegant bow, trying to match her pretense. But something about the tilt of Jane's chin reminded him of Meg when she was trying too hard to be brave.

Unable to keep up the charade, Martin seized her hands between his own. "Jane, I came as soon as I heard."

"How very good of you."

"There is nothing the least good about me." Awareness of his duplicity made it hard for him to look her in the eye. "I am the most accursed villain, the vilest wretch."

His outburst clearly surprised her. She attempted to laugh. "No, according to the Crown, that would be me."

"I don't know how you came to be arrested, but I swear I'll have you freed before the sun sets." A reckless promise and Martin sought to curb himself. The last thing Jane needed from him was some of his usual bombast.

"As soon as I find Walsingham, I am sure I can amend this matter. I—I have some acquaintance with the secretary—"

She cut him off with a sad shake of her head. "That is a very kind offer, Marcus, but this is a little different from a tumble into the Thames. I fear you will not be rescuing me this time."

Martin squeezed her hands. "This is all some sort of nightmarish misunderstanding. It has to be. What do you stand accused of?"

"Conducting secret meetings with an enemy of the crown, a Catholic priest."

"That is utter nonsense."

"No, it isn't." Jane withdrew her hands from his grasp. "I am guilty as charged."

Martin stared at her, too astonished to reply.

She continued, "That is why when the warder offered to allow my maid to stay with me, I refused. I saw no reason poor Mistress Porter should be forced to share my imprisonment. I alone brought myself to this pass."

Martin found his voice at last. "You are telling me that *you* participated in the plot to assassinate Queen Elizabeth?"

"No!" Jane looked appalled by the very suggestion of such a thing. "Upon my honor, I had no idea Father Ballard was involved in any such conspiracy. In my more bitter moments, I have felt angry and disappointed in Elizabeth, even betrayed, but I still regard her as my sovereign queen. Never would I seek to harm Her Majesty."

She sighed as she admitted, "But I have been meeting with Father Ballard ever since he arrived in London, smuggling him into Strand House late at night to say mass, to administer the sacraments of confession and communion. Acts of faith that in these regrettable times are now considered acts of treason."

After all the dangerous risks he had taken himself,

Martin was the last person with the right to reprove Jane. But he could not help remonstrating gently, "Good Lord, Jane. I understand your feelings, or at least I am trying to. But you knew harboring a Catholic priest is illegal. Is your life really worth a mass?"

"No, my *soul* is. We have never discussed religious beliefs. I have no idea what yours are, nor do I need to know. I have never sought to pass judgment on the faith of others."

Jane turned to the window, the light passing through the narrow crosslet playing over her pale features, her face steely in its resolve.

"I and those whom I am responsible for, the servants of my household, we have been raised to believe in the truth of the Catholic religion. From the time we were born, it has been our source of strength, making the suffering in life and even the prospect of death bearable. To have that all taken away with the stroke of a pen, a royal seal upon a parliamentary decree—"

Jane's lips thinned into a taut line. "It is hard, cruel, and unendurable. Yes, I would risk my life for a mass, to bring such comfort to my people, even if I must defy both my queen and country. Because it is the right thing to do."

She turned back to Martin with a wan smile. "It seems I have inherited my share of the rebellious Lambert blood after all. It is rather ironic to think that I was always so afraid Ned would be the one to end up on Tower Hill."

"Where is your brother?" Martin asked.

"I don't know. Happily he was not at home when the soldiers came to arrest me. I pray that he has gone into hiding and has the sense to stay there." For the first time, a crack appeared in her composure. She clutched at Martin's arm.

"I am terrified that Ned may do something foolish in an effort to rescue me. You must prevent him. Persuade him to escape to France until this matter is settled."

Martin covered her hand with his. "I will do my best. But if you were my sister, I know full well I could never be persuaded to slink away and abandon you."

"Your sister?" Jane regarded him with a quizzical lift of her brows. "There was a time when I believed you regarded me in a different light."

"Jane, I—" he began regretfully, but she silenced him by pressing her fingers to his lips.

"It is all right. It has been a long time since I inspired anything but brotherly devotion in a man. Most courtships are based on matters of rank, property, and convenience. Unfortunately, I have turned out to be a most *inconvenient* woman."

"Oh, Jane," Martin groaned and carried her hand reverently to his lips. "Although I do hold you in the highest regard, I am ashamed to admit I wooed you because of your position, because I thought you would make an excellent mother for my daughter."

"What a great compliment that is. I thank you for it." Jane pressed his hand and drew away from him. "There is no need for you to be ashamed, Marcus. You have been a good friend to both Ned and me."

"No, damn my eyes. I haven't."

When her eyes widened in surprise at his vehement words, Martin fortified himself with a deep breath and told her everything about all the months he had acted as Walsingham's spy.

Jane received his confession quietly, her face more

drawn with sorrow than anger. When he at last fell silent, she said, "If I had been fortunate enough to have a daughter like Meg, I should have done the same as you. Undertaken any employment, endured any risk to secure her future."

Martin could only gape at her, both astounded and humbled by her understanding and forgiveness. "You truly are an angel."

Jane gave a dry laugh. "If you believe that, you and I would have been indeed ill-suited for one another. I am far from angelic. I can pardon you so readily because there is nothing to forgive you for. You did your best to exonerate Ned. You had no notion I was the one who needed your protection."

"It never even occurred to me you might have been meeting with Ballard. So where the devil did Walsingham gather his evidence against you?"

"From Master Timon."

"Your brother's valet?" Martin asked. "He was the one who betrayed you?"

"Both Ned and I mistook Timon for a devout Catholic, but it appears he has been studying the New Learning for some time. He was afraid to reveal his Protestant leanings for fear of losing his post. Trapped between his loyalty to my family and his new faith, poor Timon's conscience was torn in half."

"A fact that Walsingham was no doubt swift to exploit," Martin said acidly.

Jane gave a sorrowful nod. "My poor Sarah felt her soul was in jeopardy for want of a Catholic priest. Master

Timon feared for his because he tried to help me smuggle one into the house."

"This religious conflict is damnable."

"You are right and sometimes I fear we will all end up damned because of it. So much shedding of innocent blood on both sides," Jane murmured.

"They shall not have a single drop of yours," Martin insisted. "It is illegal to consult a Catholic priest, but I have heard that the queen can be tolerant and pardon such an offense. It is the assassination plot that puts you in such jeopardy. If we can convince the queen you had no part in that—"

"That may prove difficult," Jane interrupted. "Treason is not the only charge against me. I am also accused of practicing witchcraft."

"What!"

"Timon told Walsingham about Ned's hidden room. The secretary believes I am the one who has been using it for some sinister purpose."

"Bah! Sir Francis is a sensible man. Why the deuce would he believe that?"

"I don't know. I don't fully understand it myself." Jane lifted her hand in a wearied gesture. "There was some reference made in a letter from France advising the conspirators to seek the aid of a sorceress. Since I was involved with Ballard and because of Ned's secret room, Walsingham somehow leapt to the conclusion that I might be this—this Silver Rose."

Martin's breath caught in his throat. At the sound of that dread name, he felt as though his heart stopped.

"Who?" he rasped.

"The Silver Rose. Apparently some strange stories have circulated abroad about a legendary sorceress who once threatened the life of Queen Catherine. This witch is now believed to reside in England."

Martin felt his face drain of blood. He had to turn away from Jane to avoid revealing how badly shaken he was. He knew that tales about Meg were rampant in France among the daughters of the earth. But the thought that the legend of the Silver Rose had spread far enough to gain Walsingham's attention filled Martin with alarm. He could scarce concentrate on the rest of what Jane was saying.

"Of course, I have often traveled through France with my brother, but to suspect me of being this powerful French witch . . . It seems so ridiculous I could laugh." Jane made a half-hearted attempt to do so. "I suppose now I must fear for my ear as well as my neck."

Jane's last remark started Martin into swiveling around to face her. "Your pardon?"

"My ear," she repeated, her hand going up to tug at hers. "That is how the law often punishes those convicted of practicing necromancy. They lop off your ear."

Martin frowned. "I thought that was the punishment for theft."

"It can be. It can also be the sentence for spying." Jane cast him a wry look. "But more often the taking of an ear is the punishment for those accused of sorcery, like young Master Naismith."

"Naismith?" Martin echoed hoarsely.

Jane pursed her lips. "One would have thought losing his ear would have taught the wretched boy a lesson. But I have recently come to believe that it is Sander Naismith's deplorable influence that has kept Ned so interested in the forbidden arts."

Martin's mind reeled. Sander had told Martin he lost his ear for stealing. Why would the boy lie about that? Martin could think of no good reason.

He was made more uneasy as he recollected he had not been the one who had sought Sander out to teach Meg to play the lute. It had been the other way around, Sander eagerly offering his services.

Too eagerly perhaps? Was it a mere happenstance that a boy who had dabbled in the occult should have evinced such interest in tutoring Martin's daughter? A further coincidence still that Sander had been the one to bring Martin the tidings about Jane and beg Martin to rush to her aid? Sander had never demonstrated any degree of regard for her ladyship's welfare before.

Martin sought to quiet his fears, tell himself he was becoming alarmed over nothing. Meg was safe at home and she had Cat with her. But it chilled Martin to think that he had left that duplicitous Naismith roaming tamely about his house.

Assaulted by such thoughts, Martin scarce noted the warder's return to inform him his time was up. Martin bid a swift farewell to Jane, urging her to keep her spirits up. He pledged to return soon, promising . . . He hardly knew what else he promised her.

Jane's plight momentarily paled beside the urgent, instinctive need he felt to get home to his daughter.

MEG DANGLED HER LEGS OFF THE STONE BENCH IN THE GARDEN, resisting the urge to clap her hands over her ears. She could still hear poor Jem's pathetic cries carrying from the kitchen.

She gripped her hands tightly together in her lap instead, trying not to think about that spell she had conned from the *Book of Shadows,* the one that could so easily have rendered Jem unconscious. No doubt Cat had been wise, admonishing Meg to forget about it.

The trouble was that Meg could not seem to do so. Her memory was far too good. She had learned of that particular potion when Maman had ordered Meg to study the *Book* to find a cure for Maman's blindness.

Although she had succeeded in doing so, Meg had lied to her mother. The cure had involved using the potion to render a person unconscious and then described a delicate magic for stealing their sight and gifting it to another. The donor would end up blind, perhaps even dead if given too much of the sleeping potion. But that would never have troubled Cassandra Lascelles.

Perhaps Meg was as evil as her mother to consider using that sleeping potion, even in an attempt to do good. She ought to find the courage to destroy the *Book of Shadows,* but Meg feared it was already too late.

So much of the book was stored in her head and she was increasingly tempted to use her knowledge. If only she had been able to learn how to master the scrying ball. But she hadn't.

Now there seemed only one way to ever learn the truth about herself and her destiny. Necromancy. She would have to attempt the spell to raise the seer Nostradamus from the dead. Just the way Maman had done.

Meg's thoughts were disrupted as she heard someone emerge from the house. She glanced up eagerly, hoping it would be Cat, come to tell her poor Jem's ordeal was over.

To her astonishment, it was Sander hastening toward her down the garden path. The sunlight glinted off the damp strands of his blond hair, his handsome face sporting a fresh-scrubbed look as though he had just washed up in the kitchen.

Somehow it only added to his charm. Meg's heart lifted at the sight of him until she recalled the details of their last meeting at the theater.

Her joy at seeing him subdued, Meg ducked her head. Her lack of warmth must have conveyed itself to Sander. He halted a foot away and asked hesitantly, "Do you mind if I bear you company awhile, Mistress Margaret?"

Meg shrugged.

"It is just that the barber has arrived. He is fixing to cut out poor Jem's tooth with a most wicked-looking knife and I confess to being a bit squeamish."

Meg kept her gaze fixed on the buckles of her shoes. "Why are you even here? It is not the day for my lesson."

"I came to see your papa. I had a message for him."

"Oh." Meg sniffed. "I suppose it was from your friend, Lord Lambert."

"Lord Lambert is my patron, Meg. I do my best to please him. When you are poor, it is the only way to get ahead in the world."

Sander hunkered down in front of her and reached for her hand. "But I have only one true friend and that is you."

Meg could scarce believe him. But when she risked a

glance into his eyes, they were so open, so sincere, his smile so warm, she melted in spite of herself.

Scooting over on the bench, she said, "You may sit with me for a bit if you wish."

But Sander only laughed and shook his head at her. "You astonish me, Mistress Margaret. I am surprised to see you so willing to idle here when there is such great excitement to be had."

"What excitement?"

"The queen. She is going to honor the Lord Mayor and his council by attending a feast. There should be a grand procession through the streets at any moment. The whifflers are already clearing a path. Do you not want to finally catch a glimpse of Her Majesty? She will be on horseback. You shall not be able to miss her this time."

"Oh!" Meg leapt up from the bench in her excitement. But she sobered as she remembered. "Papa is not here to take me. And Cat is occupied with helping Jem."

"Poor devil. It is sure to be a gruesome business." Sander gave an exaggerated shudder. "I should not care to be here to hear his shrieks. If you and I were to nip down to the end of the street, we should have a grand view of the procession and avoid all the unpleasantness."

Meg fretted her lip, the temptation overwhelming. She ruefully shook her head. "I can't. Cat would not like it. She would be vexed with both of us."

"She'll never know. It is only to the end of the street, Meg. We'll be back in a trice."

As Meg continued to hesitate, Sander fetched a deep sigh. "It will be a wonderful opportunity to see the queen. I doubt you'll soon have another as good as this."

Meg shifted from one foot to the other in an agony of indecision. A bloodcurdling scream from the kitchen tipped the scale. She glanced up at the handsome boy coaxing her with his smile and shyly slipped her hand into his.

†††

CAT STRODE OUT INTO THE GARDEN, TAKING A FORTIFYING GULP of fresh air. Her face streamed with sweat and her apron was spattered with Jem's blood. She stripped off the apron, still feeling half-deafened by the young man's roars of pain.

The tooth had been rooted far deeper than expected. While Master Turner had performed the extraction, it had taken the combined efforts of Cat, Agatha, and Samuel to hold Jem down. Cat felt like she had been wrestling a bear until mercifully Jem had fainted.

As stressful as the tooth drawing had been, at least it had provided a distraction from worrying herself to death about Martin.

The extraction might have gone more smoothly if Master Naismith had made himself useful and remained to lend a hand, Cat thought caustically. But it had scarce surprised Cat when Sander had proved too fainthearted for the task and had slunk out of the kitchen to join Meg.

Mopping the sweat from her brow, Cat headed into the garden to inform Meg that Jem's misery was over. She drew up short when she realized the stone bench was empty. There was no sign of Meg or Naismith either.

Cat tensed when she saw the garden gate ajar. But she sought to reassure herself. Meg must have wanted to return to the house, but to avoid the distressing scene in the kitchen, she had gone round to the front door.

Cat hurried through the gate, emerging into the street. The narrow thoroughfare bustled with its usual afternoon activity. Vendors crying their wares, beggars pleading for alms, goodwives haggling for bargains, a burly drayman cursing and trying to clear a path for his cart laden down with ale barrels.

Cat blinked when she caught sight of a familiar figure halfway down the street, Meg on the verge of disappearing from view, her hand linked with Sander Naismith's.

What the devil did the girl think she was doing? Cat bit back a vexed oath. When she caught up to Meg, she would give the girl a thunderous scold. As for Naismith, the lad would regret he still had an ear after Cat was done boxing it.

Cat thrust her way through the crowd, ignoring the indignant protests and curses directed at her.

"Meg," she called, but she could scarce make herself heard above the din of voices and the heavy clatter of the cart horse's iron shoes.

Struggling forward, Cat collided with a tall, elegantly dressed man. Impatiently, she tried to shove past him, but the man deliberately blocked the path.

"Get the blazes out of my—" Cat's words choked to a halt as she stared up at familiar smooth features, the curling sandy beard and hair, the genial smile that did not match those cold eyes.

"Gautier!" Cat reeled back in shock.

"You know my name, mademoiselle," he purred. "You have the advantage of me. But not for long."

As he reached for the hilt of his sword, Cat scrambled

for her own knife. To her surprise, he only smiled and nodded.

It never occurred to her that it was a signal until it was too late. She caught a blur of movement from the corner of her eye as the cudgel whipped down, colliding with her temple.

She gasped, the street before her exploding in a blur of pain and white-hot stars. Staggering, Cat sought to remain upright even as blood streamed down her face, obscuring the vision of her right eye.

She clutched at Gautier, tried to raise her knife only to have it easily knocked from her grasp. She attempted to shout but her voice was drowned out by his.

"Help. This poor woman has been assaulted, her purse snatched. Someone look to her while I pursue the thief."

"No, he—he is lying. He's the one . . ." Cat's voice trailed off to a whisper, as her legs buckled beneath her. She tried to hang on to Gautier, but he wrenched away. Cat tumbled to the street, clutching at air as webs of darkness danced before her eyes.

"Meg." Cat made a frantic effort to crawl forward, regain her footing. She gained no more than a few inches. As darkness overtook her, she was dimly aware of the crowd gathering around her, the hubbub of voices growing ever fainter.

Meg and Sander were nearly at the turn onto the next street when she glanced back in time to see Cat fall.

"What?" The girl craned her neck. She tugged urgently at Sander's hand. "Sander, I think something has happened to Cat. We've got to go back."

But to her surprise, Sander's grip tightened on hers, a strangely exultant look on his face.

"No, what Cat has done is delayed him, given us our chance."

"Delayed who? Our chance to do what?"

"Escape."

Before Meg could protest, Sander wrenched her arm, all but yanking her off her feet. She tried to hold back, but he dragged her ruthlessly along, growling one urgent word in her ear.

"Run!"

Chapter Twenty

THE THEATER WAS EERILY SILENT IN THE FADING LIGHT, THE actors and the servants who cleaned the Crown long ago gone home. Meg cowered against the tiring-room wall, her arms bruised and sore from Sander's rough grip.

They would be safe hiding at the theater, he had insisted when he had half-forced, half-coaxed Meg into fleeing to the Crown. But Meg had begun to fear that the one she needed saving from was the boy prowling the tiring-room like a caged tiger. The boy she had once trusted with all her heart, believing he was her friend, had abruptly transformed into this alarming stranger.

Meg felt confused, frightened, and angry in a way that she had not since the days she had lived with her mother in Paris. Sander appeared as tense as she. He dragged his hands through his hair, starting at every sound like some harried beast.

Meg eyed him reproachfully. "You have to let me go home," she insisted for the tenth time. "I think Cat was hurt. I have to help—"

Meg broke off, shrinking back when Sander rounded on her. He raised his hand. But when she braced herself for the blow, Sander lowered his arm with a frustrated sigh.

"Damnation, Meg. Don't you understand?" he pleaded. "I am trying to rescue you."

"Then why don't I feel rescued?" she retorted. "I feel more like—like I am your prisoner."

And she well knew what that felt like, Meg thought bitterly. She had learned long ago from her own mother what it was to be held hostage to someone else's schemes. But she had never imagined Sander to be scheming anything . . . until now.

"You saw that man coming after us?" Sander demanded. "His name is Ambroise Gautier. He works for the Dark Queen. He forced me to lure you out of the house. I didn't want to, but if I had not complied, he would have killed me and just found another way to get at you. I hoped to find some way for the two of us to escape and I did, thanks to Mistress O'Hanlon. If she had not provided a diversion, you would be in Gautier's clutches by now."

"My *fianna* is not a diversion. What if Cat was—" Meg trembled. No, she refused to believe that Cat had been killed. Her friend was too fierce, too strong to be so easily bested. Even now Cat was likely searching for Meg. And no doubt her papa was, too.

The thought heartened Meg enough to arch her head

and challenge Sander. "You claim to be saving me. Why should I believe you?"

"Because I was honest with you about Gautier. I explained everything." Sander braced one hand on the wall above her head and leaned down closer to her. "And I know you can read eyes. What do mine tell you?"

Meg stared at him fiercely, attempting to pierce those blue depths. She could see that he was partly telling her the truth, at least about not wanting to surrender her to Gautier. But the rest of his thoughts were so murky and—

Meg caught her breath as she was struck by the realization that Sander had not explained everything.

"How—how do you know of the Dark Queen? Or anything about reading eyes?" she faltered.

"I know a good many things. Like who you really are."

Meg's heart missed a beat, but she tipped up her chin. "What do you mean? I am Margaret Elizabeth Wolfe."

"No, you are not, *Megaera*." He smiled and patted her cheek. "My Silver Rose. I am a member of your coven, one of your devoted followers."

"My followers were all women. I—I mean I don't have a coven. I—I don't have the least idea what you are talking about."

Sander laughed. "You require proof, my young queen?" He shrugged out of his doublet and shoved up the sleeve of his shirt, displaying his forearm. Meg stared at the scarred brand of the rose carved into his white flesh. She blinked, scarce able to believe her eyes.

"No, it's not possible."

"You give me little credit, Meg. I am a brilliant actor. I can play the role of a woman to perfection." Sander coyly fluttered his lashes. "A pity you never had the chance to see me perform. There are some shrewd—or perhaps I should say *were* some—clever women in the coven, but none of them ever guessed I was born crested, not cloven."

Meg cast a dazed look up at him. "But why ever would you do such a thing?"

"Why? Because I have been fascinated with the forbidden arts ever since I was a young lad. My parents apprenticed me to a blacksmith, but I had no liking for the trade. I saw quickly that it would be nothing but a lifetime of hard, backbreaking, sweaty labor. I realized I was meant for better things when a strange man passed through our village.

"Master Gervais was a Frenchman by birth, what you would call a *gitan*. But certainly no ordinary gypsy. He was a man of many accomplishments, actor, musician, conjurer, and fortune-teller. He took a liking to me and I ran off with him to London. He taught me all that he knew of magic and performing, even how to speak his language. When we could not find work among any of the acting companies, we made a fair living with Gervais's scrying ball, conjuring up the voices of angels to console poor grieving folk."

"You mean you cheated people," Meg said indignantly.

"Belike we did. But we were convincing enough to get accused of necromancy. Gervais was convicted of sorcery and hung. I was *fortunate* enough to receive a lighter punishment." Sander laid sarcastic emphasis upon the word. "All they did was hack off my ear. That was when I realized something about justice. It is dispensed according to the size of one's purse and one's rank.

"What is considered a crime in a poor man is often a mere eccentricity among the great. So I set about finding myself a more powerful patron."

"Lord Oxbridge."

"Yes, Ned. His lordship has a, er, penchant for handsome and clever young lads. When he realized I shared his interest in the occult, he became quite taken with me. Enough to let me accompany him on one of his journeys to France and that was where we first heard of your legend, Megaera."

"My name is Meg," she insisted stubbornly, but Sander ignored her.

"We stumbled upon the coven by pure chance when we were traveling through Brittany. Ned and I thought it might be amusing to pass me off as a woman and see if I could insinuate myself into the group."

"You would not have been so amused if those witches had discovered your secret. They would have torn you apart."

"No doubt. Most of your devoted followers are a trifle demented. Rabid man-haters, every last one of them."

"I begin to understand why."

"Nay, do not hate me, Meg."

When Sander tried to stroke her hair back from her brow, Meg shied away, glaring up at him.

"My eyes never lied to you when you read my thoughts and I conveyed how much I admire you, how astonishing a woman you will be when you are grown. I joined your coven as a jest at first, out of mere curiosity. But I became more and more intrigued with what I heard about your powers and the *Book of Shadows*. When we learned that you had been brought to England, Ned and I resolved to find you.

"You can't imagine how astounded Ned was when you turned up here in London under our very noses. If your papa had wanted to keep you hidden, he should have been more discreet."

Sander chuckled. "But no one likes to perform at center stage more than Master Wolfe."

"Don't you dare speak of my papa in that sneering tone," Meg cried. "He—he has never been anything but generous and kind to you."

Sander shrugged. "He's a fool for all that. He has no idea of the kind of power you possess, does he? I was not sure how much I believed myself. So I set about slowly to win your trust."

"Which I never should have given."

"The more time I have spent in your company, the more amazed I am. You are so quick and clever. Your followers claim that only you could translate the *Book of Shadows* and I believe it."

"It hardly matters because I no longer have the book."

"Now *that* I don't believe. You have had me procure some mighty strange things from the apothecaries, to say nothing of those precise instructions you gave me for acquiring those intriguing lenses. What did you do with those, I wonder? And what potions have you been brewing?"

Meg compressed her lips and turned her head away, but Sander caught her chin, forcing her to look at him.

"You also have the most extraordinary memory of anyone I ever met. I'd be prepared to wager you have most of the spells of that book stored in your head, hmmm?"

Sander stroked his fingertips lightly over her brow. "And your father would have you waste your life embroidering samplers and playing the lute very badly."

Meg thrust his hands away. "What do you want from me?"

"Why, only to help you become the powerful sorceress you are destined to be."

No, what he wanted was to use her, to acquire her power and knowledge for himself. Meg could read that much in his eyes. She wondered why she had not seen it sooner.

A memory stirred, Cassandra Lascelles's cold voice echoing in her head.

"You have learned to read eyes well, Megaera. I sense that you have begun to fancy yourself very clever, my daughter. But there is a danger in waxing too smug, especially with a man. You can be tricked into seeing what you want to see in his eyes. What he wants you to see."

Her mother was right. Which left Meg tormented with the question: what else had Maman been right about?

"I have no interest in becoming any kind of sorceress. I demand that you take me home. Right now," Meg cried shrilly.

But she was stilled when Sander clapped his hand over her mouth. He cocked his head to one side, listening intently. The sound of footsteps. Someone was crossing the stage, approaching the back of the theater.

Cat? Papa? Meg quickened with hope. But when she sought to thrust Sander's hand away and cry out, he seized her about the waist. Crushing her to him, he muffled her more ruthlessly.

Meg struggled, kicked, and tried to sink her teeth into his palm. Sander cursed when she stamped down on his foot.

"Don't be a fool, Meg," he whispered harshly in her ear. "What if it's Gautier? Do you really want to end up at the mercy of the Dark Queen?"

Sander's words caused her to freeze. She ceased her struggles with a tiny whimper.

"Now be quiet."

When he was satisfied with her compliance, he released her. Thrusting Meg behind him, Sander drew out his dirk and stood poised, tense, waiting.

Meg scarce dared breathe as the footsteps hesitated, then came closer, heading straight for the tiring-room. Her hand moved instinctively toward the hidden pocket in her gown, but it had been a long time since she had armed herself with her syringe. Not since the day Cat had become her *fianna*.

A floorboard creaked beneath the weight of a heavy foot. Whoever approached was making little effort to conceal their presence.

"Sander?" a man called softly.

Sander expelled a long breath and sheathed his knife. Parting the tiring-room curtain, he replied. "Ned, over here."

Lord Oxbridge ducked behind the curtain, what little daylight remained outlining his sharp aristocratic profile. Sander might have been relieved to see him, but Meg regarded Ned Lambert warily.

"Sander, where the devil have you been? I have been looking everywhere for you." His lordship's gaze flicked in Meg's direction. "And what is she doing here?"

"It is a long story. Suffice it to say there is another contender here in London striving for the prize. We can't afford to wait any longer, Ned. We have to take the girl and leave England tonight. As soon as it gets dark we—"

"None of us are going anywhere. Especially not *her.*" The look his lordship directed at Meg was so hard and angry, she shrank away from him.

Sander appeared startled by Lord Oxbridge's vehement words, but he recovered, waving his hand in a dismissive gesture. "I know you hoped I would coax her into telling what became of the *Book of Shadows,* but we've no time to worry about that now. It doesn't matter anyway. I believe the girl knows most of the spells. Megaera *is* the book."

"Damn the book," Lord Oxbridge interrupted impatiently. "Do you think I care about any of that—that sorcery now? Don't you know what has happened to my sister?"

Sander blinked. "Oh, *that.* Yes, I had heard Lady Danvers was taken to the Tower. It proved most convenient actually. I was able to use the tidings to get rid of Master Wolfe so I could—"

"*Convenient?*"

Sander made haste to amend his tone. "I did not mean that precisely. It is most unfortunate about your sister, but she appears to have brought it all upon herself, smuggling in a priest to say mass in your home. You are fortunate it is not you in the Tower."

"Jane only did what I should have had the courage to do myself." A red tide of color flooded Lord Oxbridge's cheeks. "I should have been the one arrested. I was the one who furbished that secret room with all the occult symbols in my stupid quest for the philosopher's stone."

"What has that got to do with anything?"

"You haven't heard the worst of the accusations against my sister? Jane is accused of plotting to use witchcraft against the queen. I have no notion how it is possible, but somehow they have come to believe that Jane is the Silver Rose."

Silent and forgotten, Meg followed the exchange between the two men with growing consternation. She thought of Lady Danvers with her sad, haunted eyes, but still so kind, gifting Meg with what was now her greatest treasure, that scrap of the coronation carpet. And now that same gentle lady was imprisoned in the Tower, accused of being the Silver Rose in Meg's stead?

Meg was horrified when Sander started to laugh. Lord Oxbridge looked as though he wanted to strangle Sander and Meg could not have blamed him as she had another daunting realization about her once-beloved friend.

Sander Naismith was completely selfish, had no true empathy for anyone save himself.

But faced with his lordship's glare, Sander struggled to contain his mirth. "S-sorry. But you must see the absurdity of it yourself. The saintly Jane suspected of being an evil sorceress? You have often complained yourself of how tiresomely virtuous your sister is."

"Yes, I have, to my shame," Lord Oxbridge said. "Jane has looked after me since we were children. She has sacrificed much for my sake, and I have heedlessly taken all that she had to give."

"And I am sure she would willingly give her life to keep you safe."

"No doubt she would, but that is one sacrifice too

many to accept, even for a worthless wretch like me." Lord Oxbridge squared his shoulders. "I have only one hope to save Jane and that is to claim that I was the one meeting with Father Ballard. I will admit that any attempt to deal in the dark arts was mine."

He turned to Meg and she was surprised to see a trace of gentleness, even nobility in his lean, dissipated features. For the first time, she perceived a faint resemblance to his sister.

"I am sorry, Margaret," he said. "But I am also going to have to take you before the queen's council. You have to confess that you are really the Silver Rose."

Meg's heart thudded. She could see the justice of that, but her mouth went dry with fear at the prospect. Before she could frame any sort of reply, Sander thrust himself between her and Lord Oxbridge.

"Have you completely lost your wits?"

"No, I believe I am thinking clearly for the first time in my life."

"Fine. Go play the hero if you've the stomach for it." Sander sneered. "But I am damned if I'll stand aside while you throw away everything I've worked and risked my neck for all these months. All the power and knowledge that girl represents."

"Get out of my way, Sander." When Sander refused, Ned gave him a violent shove. Sander staggered back, falling over a wardrobe trunk.

Struggling to regain his feet, he shouted, "You are not taking Meg anywhere."

"I quite agree," a silken voice hissed. The curtain behind Lord Oxbridge stirred and it was as though one of the shadows had sprung to life.

It seemed to envelop Lord Oxbridge. Meg caught the flash of a knife and then his lordship's throat blossomed bright red. He did not even have a chance to cry out, merely looked stunned as he crashed to his knees, collapsing onto his side.

Meg blinked, unable to fathom what had just happened. It was all over so swiftly. She stared down at the crimson droplets that had spattered her sleeve, caught the sticky sweet scent. Blood.

She struggled to accept that she had just watched a man being killed. Her mother and the members of her coven had performed many acts of violence, but Meg had never borne witness to any of them. She had been haunted by them anyway, always believing she could clearly envision the horrible deeds.

But the reality of murder was so much worse than anything she could have ever imagined that her breath escaped in a ragged sob and she started to shake.

The shadowy figure assumed the solid shape of a man. Still clutching his knife, he regarded the fallen Lord Oxbridge dispassionately.

"Your pardon, monsieur," he said. "But you should not have intruded. You have no part in this little farce and it is I who shall direct the final act."

The man's French accent penetrated through the haze of Meg's shock. This had to be Gautier, the Dark Queen's agent that Sander had warned her about. But Meg still felt too numb to move. She stared down into his lordship's sightless eyes and trembled.

Sander was as immobilized with shock as she. By the time he was galvanized into action, it was too late. As he drew his dirk to defend himself, two other men stormed into the room. Seizing Sander, they pinned his arms behind his back.

Gautier ambled toward him and laid the edge of his bloodied knife against Sander's throat. Meg whimpered, certain she was about to see Sander murdered as well.

Sander struggled frantically, his eyes rolled back in terror. "P-please, m'sieur."

Gautier clucked his tongue. "You disappointed me, Monsieur Naismith. A clever player such as you. I thought you understood your part, but you have deviated from the script. I should slit your worthless throat as well, but I still may have need of you."

Sander moaned with relief as Gautier removed the blade from his throat. The Frenchman wiped the knife clean on the front of Sander's shirt. He sheathed it before turning to Meg with a most civil nod.

"Ah, la petite Mademoiselle la Rose. We meet at last."

Meg could only gape up at him. Peering into his eyes, she swiftly saw all she needed to know. This man's heart was encased in ice; the blood that ran through his veins was cold. Exactly like Maman.

If she had been afraid before, her pulse now thundered with pure terror, although she strove not to show it.

As he stalked toward her, Meg found her voice at last. "You stay away from me. If you harm me, my papa will come and—"

"I trust your papa will come. Shall we dispatch a note inviting him and request that he also bring the *Book of Shadows*? Don't trouble denying you have it. I overheard your conversation with these two gentlemen."

"Even if I do have the book, my papa knows nothing of it. He—he wouldn't know where I have it hidden."

"Then I suggest we tell him or—" Gautier's teeth flashed in a feral smile. "Do you know what I do to witches, child?"

"B-burn them?" Meg faltered.

"That requires entirely too much effort, gathering wood, hauling it, building a fire. There is a much simpler way."

Gautier snapped his fingers and one of his men fetched him a length of stout rope. Meg stared at it in horror. But still she could not seem to move, even when Gautier fitted the end of the noose about her neck.

Chapter Twenty-One

CAT LIMPED UP THE STAIRS, UNSTEADY ON HER FEET. THE hours since she had been carried back to the Angel were a blur, a nightmare from which there was no waking. Her head throbbed from the blow she had taken, a thick linen bandage wrapped round her brow, protecting the place where Master Turner had stitched up the gash in her temple.

Each step that she took jarred all the way through to her skull. Only a supreme effort of will kept her on her feet. Her stomach roiled but perhaps that was due as much to the emotions that had consumed her ever since Meg's abduction—fear, despair, and self-blame.

She kept rehearsing the event over and over in her mind, berating herself, trying to think what she might have done differently. If only she had not been so distracted helping Jem or if she had obliged Meg to remain in the kitchen. If only she had sent Naismith on his way or if she had been more wary or a little quicker.

If only . . . if only. All such thoughts did was make her head ache worse. Cat did her best to cease the futile exercise.

Her head reeled as she reached the top of the stairs. Gripping the railing, she paused a moment until the house stopped spinning and she was able to gather her strength. In the hall below, the entire household waited, their faces anxious and distressed. Both Maude and the kitchen boy were in tears, old Agatha's eyes red-rimmed.

They all stared up at Cat with such desperate hope, it astonished her. It was as though somehow they expected she would be able to set everything right. When in the blazes had she begun to inspire such confidence in these people, even the crotchety Mistress Butterydoor? It weighed heavily upon Cat, for she felt it was a confidence she little deserved.

Stumbling away from the steps, she approached the door to Meg's bedchamber where Martin had shut himself away, forbidding anyone to come near him. Ever since his return from the Tower, he had seemed distraught to the verge of madness and Cat had been terrified of what he might do.

Rescuing Meg would require a cool and collected head. Martin could be impulsive and reckless even at the best of times.

But as Cat peered into the chamber, she found Martin on the edge of the bed, the ransom note he had received clutched in his hand. Shoulders slumped, he looked completely drained of the brash manner with which he usually took on the world.

His gaze roved bleakly about the room scattered with Meg's books, her writing desk, her lute, the wardrobe overflowing with all of her costly gowns. Cat could only imagine how it all must mock him, the trappings of the safe refuge he believed he had created for his daughter. It taunted Cat as well.

"Martin?" Cat stole into the chamber and closed the door.

At the sound of her voice, Martin roused himself to scowl up at her. "Cat, what are you doing up here? Go back down to my bed."

"I am fine." Her assertion was belied as she swayed on her feet. Martin leapt up to brace her.

"Fine? Damn it, woman, you are ready to keel over. You will be of no use to Meg if you fall and crack your head open again."

"I was already of no use to Meg." Cat thrust his hands away, and then eased down onto the edge of the bed.

Something gentled in the harsh lines of Martin's face. He stroked his knuckles alongside her cheek.

"You did all that you could, my valiant Cat. Fighting those villains alone. You were not the one who failed Meg. I did. You tried to warn me there might be something amiss with Alexander Naismith. I didn't listen."

"All the more reason I should have been vigilant when I knew that varlet was about the house."

"No, I am the one who should have been here instead of rushing off to Lady Danvers's aid. Little good that I did there. Little damned good that I am to anyone—"

"Peace, Martin." Cat stayed him, squeezing his hand. "We'll have time enough for sorting out blame when we have Meg home safe. We can take turns kicking each other in the arse then. Agatha told me you received a ransom note?"

"Yes, one of those cowards tied it to a rock and chucked it through the window." Martin handed Cat the crumpled note.

Pressing one hand to her brow, Cat squinted at the parchment. Despite the pain splitting her head, it took little effort to read it. The note was written in French, glaring its message in bold, flowing script.

> *Greetings, Monsieur le Loup,*
>
> *Your enchanting young daughter graces me with her presence. Have no fear. The child is safe with me and will remain so as long as you oblige me in a certain matter. Please be so kind as to bring me the* Book of Shadows.
>
> *Your daughter informs me that you might be astonished to learn you have it in your possession. I fear Megaera has been rather a naughty girl. She instructs you to look for the grimoire behind the unicorn.*
>
> *I am willing to take this dangerous book off your hands in exchange for your daughter's life. I will meet with you at your theater at midnight. Come not a stroke later or I regret that your child will meet with a most unhappy accident.*
>
> > *Your obedient servant,*
> > *A.G.*

For a threatening note, it was couched in the most courteous of tones, after Gautier's silken fashion. Cat could well imagine how the captain must have smirked while he wrote it.

"Gautier. The bastard." She crushed the note in her fist.

"So this was written by the same man who attacked you on the street?" Martin asked.

"Yes, Captain Ambroise Gautier. He works for the Dark Queen."

"And how did Sander become enmeshed with him?"

"I have no idea. Perhaps I can induce the boy to tell me before I throttle him," Cat replied. "But the important thing right now is to recover Meg."

"And how are we to do that? This Gautier demands the impossible. The *Book of Shadows*. What the devil is it going to take to convince these fools that we don't have that accursed book?" Martin paced, flinging up his hands in frustration and anger. "If I did, I vow I'd hand it over to the devil himself, just to buy Meg and me some peace."

Cat hesitated before venturing, "Meg says the book is to be found behind the unicorn."

"Gautier likely has her so frightened she would say anything. If that villain has hurt so much as one hair of my babe's head, I'll cut off his bollocks and feed them to him."

"And I will help you roast them. But for now, you had better check behind the tapestry. I—I have always suspected Meg has a hiding place somewhere."

"So what if she does? For some girlish trinkets perhaps. But my daughter does not have that cursed book of black magic. If she had ever stumbled across it, she would have told me and we would have gotten rid of it. Meg wouldn't want to keep the damn thing any more than I would."

Martin's denial was so fierce, it held an edge of desperation. Cat's heart ached for him, knowing what a blow he was about to receive, wishing she could spare him.

"Go look, Martin," she said quietly.

He stared at her so hard, she could not meet his eyes. Striding over to the tapestry, he wrenched it aside, exposing the plain boards of the wall.

"There is nothing here—," he began, only to check himself. Snatching up one of the candles, he examined the wainscoting.

As he pried away a loose board, Cat heard his breath hitch. How sharply did she regret that she had never prepared him for this moment, never said a word about Meg's continued fascination with the ancient knowledge. Cat knew Martin would not have wanted to hear it, but she should have forced him to listen. Anything would have been better than him discovering the truth this way.

He reached into the opening behind the board and drew forth a small canvas sack. He upended it, dumping the contents beside Cat. All of Meg's secrets spilled across the bed, her spyglass, a scrying ball, packets of dried herbs she used in brewing her potions. The final thing to emerge was a carefully wrapped object. Martin stripped away the linen to expose the witch blade.

He touched the hilt, his voice rife with disbelief. "No. I—I got rid of this infernal thing. I threw it into the pond."

"Not deep enough. Meg fetched it later. She used to carry the weapon with her everywhere. Not filled with poison," Cat added hastily. "Only a sleeping draught. She used it on me that first day when you and I dueled at the theater. That was what felled me. Not the blow from Agatha's cane, but Meg's potion. She only stopped carrying the weapon after—"

"After what?" Martin snapped.

"I—I threatened to tell you that she had it," Cat replied in a low voice. "But I don't think that was what stopped her. I think it was because after I came with all my vows to protect her, to—to protect both of you, Meg felt safe. She felt like she no longer needed the weapon."

Cat winked back fierce tears. "I wish I had never interfered. I wish Meg had her witch blade with her right now."

"For the love of God, Cat. She's only a child."

"No, she's a daughter of the earth and an astonishing one at that. She—"

Cat only stopped when she realized the way Martin was looking at her, his eyes glinting with hurt, accusation, and betrayal. And no doubt she deserved it. But this time she forced herself to meet his gaze.

"Was that all that was tucked away in her hiding place?"

"Isn't this enough?" Martin demanded. But he returned to the loose board. Bracing himself as though he was about to thrust his hand into a nest of vipers, once more he groped inside.

He drew out a small worn book no larger than the size of the bible. He simply stared at it for a moment like a man who has received the final blow.

Cat's heartbeat quickened as Martin strode back to her. She flinched as he hurled the book in her lap.

"Is that it? The *Book of Shadows*?"

"I—I believe so." Cat had never set eyes on the book

herself, although years ago she had joined the Lady of
Faire Isle in a desperate search for the dangerous text. The
book certainly matched the description she had been
given, ancient, bound in worn black leather, no title embla-
zoned on the cover.

It was so harmless looking, but as Cat stroked her fingertips down the spine, she shuddered, able to sense the
book's dark power. When she opened it, the pages were
brittle with age, the parchment covered with strange symbols that whispered of ancient knowledge long lost to the
world, secrets that had better remained so.

"Is that the *Book of Shadows*?" Martin demanded
again. "Can you read it?"

"Only a little. The book is written in a language dating
back to the earliest days of the daughters of the earth and
it is encrypted as well. Only a few wise women could translate this, Ariane and the Dark Queen perhaps."

"And my daughter," Martin added flatly.

"Yes, most certainly Meg. As I told you, she is very
gifted."

"But you didn't see fit to tell me about much else. You
knew she had that damned book. All this time, you *knew*."

"No, I only suspected that she might. As for the rest,
Meg told me in confidence. I could hardly win the girl's
trust if I betrayed her secrets. Even to you."

"Her trust? What about mine? You knew how I felt
about her meddling with this damnable magic, these infernal instruments. Do you know what Cassandra did with
this blasted witch blade, the hideous death she inflicted
upon innocent people?"

"Meg only used it for protection."

"Maybe what my daughter most needed protection from was you."

"What do you mean by that?" Cat cried.

"That no matter what agreement we made between us, you hoped to carry Meg off to Faire Isle, to draw her back into your world of witchery and magic. That is why you allowed her to keep these things." Martin gestured furiously to the objects strewn across the counterpane.

Cat flushed and retorted, "I admit that I felt Meg's talents would be wasted in this snug English life you had planned for her. There is a difference between good magic and bad. Meg needs to learn the difference and you are far too blind to teach her."

"I have been blind about a lot of things. But at least now I have the means to ransom my daughter." Martin wrenched the book from Cat's grasp.

Cat regarded him in dismay. "You can't think of surrendering that dangerous book to Gautier."

"I don't give a damn about the book or what becomes of it. All I want is my daughter back."

"That is all that I want too, and that book is the only leverage we have. If you think that by handing that book over to Gautier, he will politely return Meg to you, then you know nothing of the man or the woman he serves. We have to use our heads, think—"

"There is no *we* involved here, Mistress O'Hanlon. Meg is my daughter and I will be the only one to protect her, just as I always should have done."

"It is my province as well. If you think I intend to remain tamely here while—"

"That is exactly what you will do."

As Cat struggled to rise, Martin thrust her back down. "You are in no condition to go anywhere." He added in clipped tones. "Even if you were, neither I nor my daughter has any further need of your services."

As Martin stormed out the door, Cat tried to go after him, but her head reeled again. She sagged back down on the bed, cursing both Martin and her own weakness.

Angry and hurt, Martin was about to do exactly what she had feared, rush headlong into disaster, and Cat was powerless to stop him. Even if she went after him, he'd never listen to a word she had to say. He no longer trusted her. He likely never would again, Cat thought bleakly.

She buried her face in her hands, weighted down with a sense of failure and despair.

"Mistress Cat! Mistress Cat!"

The urgency in Agatha Butterydoor's voice forced Cat to look up. The old woman rushed panting into the room, wringing her hands in her apron.

"Oh, Mistress Cat. I believe the master has finally been driven out of his wits with grief. He is charging off all alone to fight those varlets who took Mistress Meg."

"I know," Cat said dully.

"Then why are you just sitting there? Why are you not going with him to save our precious girl?"

"Because I am not wanted. Master Wolfe has ordered me to remain behind."

Agatha glared at her, the woman's double chin aquiver. "When have you ever heeded his commands before? And what about your oath to Mistress Meg? Are you that girl's feedaddle or aren't you?"

"Her *fianna*," Cat corrected. The word spoke to her of

generations of proud Irish warriors, all the notions of duty and honor instilled in her by her father, reminding her of Tiernan of the Laughing Eyes . . . reminding her who she was.

Cat squared her shoulders. "Yes, that is exactly who I am, Mistress Butterydoor. But I am going to need your help to get ready. I have to change out of these useless petticoats and I'll require a weapon."

The woman braced Cat with her stout arm, helping her to rise. "Of a certainty. Shall I fetch your sword?"

"No, Mistress Butterydoor, I'll need a weapon of a different sort. This Gautier is a treacherous bastard."

"You've encountered the man before?"

"Oh, yes," Cat replied. "But this time I won't be the one running away."

※※※

MARTIN HOPED HE WOULD POSSESS THE ADVANTAGE OF SURprise by arriving early. He knew his theater well, but then, he reminded himself, so did Naismith.

But even the Crown seemed an alien place to Martin tonight, the silent tiers of galleries bathed in moonlight. He felt estranged from his entire world, nothing or no one who they had seemed.

Jane Danvers, Sander, his own daughter. But the one whose duplicity cut him the worst was the woman he had most come to trust and rely upon.

Cat.

But Martin could not bear to think of her now. He was going to need all his wits about him to see Meg safely through this.

By arriving early, he hoped to set a trap of his own. But as he crept along the lower tier of galleries, the sight that greeted him drove all thoughts of caution out of his head.

Meg was positioned center stage, pooled in a circle of light provided by several lanterns. Her hands bound behind her back, she was perched precariously upon a stool. A thick rope was knotted about her neck, the noose suspended from the gallery that overhung the stage.

Martin drew in a sharp breath, his heart missing a beat. Not only had Gautier anticipated his early arrival, the bastard had arranged this cruel scene in preparation. Even realizing that, Martin could not contain the strong surge of emotion that coursed through him.

"Meg," he rasped. Scrambling over the railing, he leapt down into the pit.

His daughter was so still, Martin feared the worst. But Meg stirred at the sound of his voice, squinting into the darkness.

"Papa?" she quavered. Her face was pale with fear, but unstained by tears. Obviously she had made a valiant effort to be brave, denying her captor the satisfaction of seeing her weep.

The realization only wrenched at Martin's heart the more. He charged forward, drawing his sword. Before he could vault up onto the stage, a cool voice warned him.

"That is close enough, Monsieur le Loup."

A tall raw-boned man emerged from the shadows, a shock of raven hair framing his hawk-like features. Grinning, he placed one thick boot against the stool. Meg gave a terrified whimper.

"No!" Every instinct Martin possessed urged him to

rush the villain, run him through. But he knew he'd never get there in time before the bastard kicked the stool away.

Martin came to a halt. "Damn you, Gautier, if you hurt her—"

"I assure you, monsieur, the child shall not be harmed if you do exactly as I say."

Martin's gaze narrowed as he realized the silken voice did not emanate from the man threatening Meg. Gautier had concealed himself somewhere offstage.

"Cast your sword aside and remain down in the pit or I will be obliged to command Jacques to kick away the stool. Your daughter has a most delicate neck, monsieur. So easily snapped."

Martin ground his teeth in rage and frustration. He had little choice but to obey. Flinging his sword away from him, he held up his hand to show that he was disarmed. With the other, he displayed the *Book of Shadows*.

"Let my daughter go, Gautier. I have brought you the God-cursed book."

"Oh, Papa, I—I am so sorry," Meg said. That in the midst of all this horror his daughter should look so guilty and apologize to him was almost more than Martin could bear.

He did his best to cast her a reassuring smile. "Everything will be all right, petite."

"Indeed it will, mademoiselle," Gautier called out. "Just as long as you remain still until your Papa and I have concluded our transaction."

Martin attempted to home in on Gautier's place of concealment. The man had to be backstage, speaking and watching through the prompter's wicket.

"You will pardon me if I am a bit skeptical, Master Wolfe," Gautier said. "Before I can release your daughter, I must determine the book's authenticity. My royal mistress, Queen Catherine, has been tricked twice before in her efforts to gain possession of the book."

Martin waved the volume tantalizingly aloft. "Come examine the text for yourself," he challenged, thinking that if he could overcome Gautier, get a blade to the man's throat, he could force him to order Meg's release.

As though the man was able to guess Martin's thoughts, he chuckled. "I think I prefer to remain where I am. Master Naismith, you claim to have some knowledge in these matters of the occult. Go down and inspect the book."

Martin had all but forgotten Sander's part in all this. The boy emerged from backstage, his usual swagger markedly absent. He descended into the pit, flinching before Martin's glower. Approaching Martin warily, Sander had enough grace to look abashed.

"I am s-sorry, Master Wolfe," he stammered. "I meant Meg no harm. I didn't want to help Monsieur Gautier, but he forced me to—"

"Hold your tongue," Martin said. "You will spare me any more of your performances if you know what is good for you, boy."

Sander lapsed into a sullen silence, extending his hand for the book. Martin reluctantly surrendered it to him.

Sander stared at it, running his fingers almost reverently over the ancient leather cover. As he opened the book, studying the strange writings, the boy's face lit up with a covetousness that was all too transparent.

"Well, boy?" Gautier prompted.

Sander turned back toward the stage to reply. "It looks genuine, monsieur."

"Then fetch it to me."

"No!" Martin clamped his hand upon Sander's arm. "Not until you release my daughter."

"I will as soon as I have the book. Master Naismith, bring it to me."

Before the boy could respond, Martin acted with lightning swiftness. Locking Sander in an iron grip, he unsheathed the boy's own dirk and held the blade to his throat.

Martin heard the intake of Sander's breath. Although the boy looked terrified, he maintained his grip on the *Book of Shadows*.

Martin snarled, "Let Meg go right now or I'll—"

He was interrupted by Gautier's mocking laugh. "Or you'll what, monsieur? Slit the boy's throat? I was tempted to do the same thing myself earlier. He means nothing to me. Go ahead and kill him. But if I don't have that book by the time I count to ten, you will see your daughter dangling lifeless from the end of that rope.

"One . . . two . . ."

Martin's brow beaded with sweat as Gautier began his count. He silently cursed himself, realizing he had rushed into this situation, ignoring Cat's warning. She had been right. He doubted that Gautier had any intention of allowing Martin or his daughter to leave this theater alive whether he surrendered the book or not.

"Three . . . four."

Martin's thoughts raced, weighing his options. He could only think of one thing to do: Thrust Sander out of his way, hurl the knife into the heart of the man looming over Meg, then race to save his daughter before Gautier got to her.

Martin wondered if he had the skill and speed to bring it off. He had to, he told himself. It was their only hope.

✦✦✦

Cat hung back, cloaked in the darkness of the upper tier of the theater. Drawing on a well of strength she had never known she possessed, she had managed the journey to the Crown. The night air had done much to clear her head, sharpen her senses.

The bandage threatened to slip over her eyes and Cat stripped it off. The whiteness of the linen could only serve to draw attention to herself, something that she had avoided by being otherwise garbed in black.

Keeping to the shadows, she observed the scene unfolding below her. Meg's plight made Cat want to roar with fear and rage. But she kept her jaw clamped tight while Martin held Sander hostage and Gautier began his relentless count.

The bastard was hidden somewhere offstage. One raven-haired brute guarded Meg. For all Cat knew there could be more men lurking in the wings, but she had no more time to assess the situation.

Martin's bow clutched in her hands, the huntress prepared to take the most difficult shot of her life. Cat drew from her quiver the arrow she had tipped with pitch. She lit it from the lantern concealed on the floor behind her.

"Five . . . six," she heard Gautier intone. "I am losing patience, Monsieur le Loup."

Cat's heartbeat quickened, but she knew she could not

afford to lose her nerve and panic. She nocked the flaming arrow into position, taking aim with careful deliberation.

She paused only long enough to offer up a silent prayer to the goddess Brigid and the good Mother Earth. Then she let the arrow fly.

It hissed through the air in a flaming arc, lodging itself in the rope suspended above Meg's head. Before anyone below had time to react, Cat hastened to fit another arrow to the bow.

At the same moment, Martin hurled Naismith from him. He flung the knife at the man guarding Meg. Jacques howled with pain. Cat loosed her second arrow, driving it straight through the man's eye.

Jacques sprawled to the floor, knocking over a lantern and Meg's stool. But the rope had given way, releasing Meg. With a tiny cry, she toppled to the stage.

Martin raced to his daughter, barely reaching her as Gautier emerged from backstage, drawing his sword with a furious hiss.

Martin scrambled to retrieve the sword from the fallen Jacques. He unsheathed it just in time to fend off Gautier's deadly assault.

As the two men fought, parried and thrust at each other, Cat reached for another arrow, waiting for a chance to unleash it at Gautier without hitting Martin. But she caught sight of something that filled her with more alarm. Either a spark from her arrow or the overturned lantern had set the rush matting strewn across the stage afire.

Fueled by the dry straw, the flames spread rapidly, threatened to consume all in its path and that included Meg.

Cat slung the bow over her shoulder and raced for the stairs, nearly tumbling down them in her haste to reach the pit.

Her hands still bound, Meg choked on the smoke, trying to inch her way to the edge of the stage, farther from the flames.

"Meg!" Martin cried. He was prevented from rushing to his daughter's aid by Gautier's blade. Martin barely avoided a lethal thrust.

Cat reached Meg's side and drew out her knife, slicing through the girl's bonds.

"Cat," Meg rasped, her eyes streaming, whether from relief or the rising smoke Cat could not tell.

Cat felt her own eyes sting, the acrid odor of burning rushes and wood invading her nostrils. But she hugged Meg close, reassuring the child as she pulled her farther downstage away from the flames.

"It's all right, Meggie. I'm here now."

"I—I knew you and Papa would come. But Sander—"

"Don't worry about him. No one shall harm you now."

Meg squirmed away from her. Coughing and sniffing, the child gasped out, "You—don't understand. He's escaping. With the book."

Meg gestured frantically at the opposite side of the theater. Taking advantage of the chaos erupting around him, Naismith skulked toward the exit, the book gripped in his hands.

Cat reached for the bow. She could not bring herself to shoot the boy down before Meg's horrified eyes. She did the only other thing she could think of, something that should have been done by a daughter of the earth eons ago.

Tipping another arrow with flame, Cat fitted it to the bow. Blinking her vision clear, she aimed and launched the arrow at the book, piercing it.

Sander screamed as the brittle ancient text erupted into flames. The boy might have been all right if only he'd dropped the book. As he sought to put out the flames, the fire caught his sleeve. Panicking, he flailed about, only making the situation worse.

His shrieks rent the air as the flames consumed him. Cat moved to shield Meg from the horrible sight, but the gesture was unnecessary.

The fire in the theater raged out of control, the air filling with a blinding haze of smoke.

"Cat!" Meg heard Martin roar. "Get Meg out of here."

Seizing Meg by the arms, Cat lowered Meg off the stage, commanding her to run. She glanced back frantically for Martin and was relieved to see him gaining the upper hand with Gautier.

Martin broke through the captain's guard, slashing open Gautier's face. He bellowed, dropping his sword. As Martin closed in for the kill, a third man whose presence had gone unnoticed rushed to the captain's aid.

Cat tried to call out a warning as the man drew his sword, but her throat was too clogged with smoke. Hurtling forward, she dove between Martin and his assailant.

She gasped with shock as sharp steel pierced her side. Before the man could stab her again, Martin was there, cutting him down. Cat reeled, collapsing to the stage. She could feel the warmth of her own blood oozing between her fingers. As the smoke thickened about them, she could hardly breathe.

She was dimly aware of Martin lifting her into his arms. She closed her eyes, weakly resting her head against his shoulder, feeling as though the two of them were hopelessly lost in some blazing inferno.

She would never know how he managed it, but somehow they were clear of the theater, away from the blistering heat and choking smoke.

As she dragged a gulp of clear cool air into her lungs, it was as painful as the wound burning in her side. Martin lowered her to the ground. She forced her eyes open to narrow slits.

The night seemed filled with chaos, the sound of shouts in the distance and thundering feet. The burning theater lit up the dark sky, drawing people from their beds and out into the street.

But Cat saw that Martin and Meg were safe and that was all she cared about. He tore off strips of Meg's petticoat.

As he sought to bind Cat's wound, she gasped his name. "Martin."

"Don't try to talk," he commanded her. "We are all safe, but we've got to get out of here. We left four dead men back at the theater and it's going to be cursed awkward offering explanations."

"Not so difficult," Cat croaked before she lost consciousness for the second time that day.

"They died of an evil thought."

Chapter Twenty-Two

MARTIN SPENT WHAT REMAINED OF THE NIGHT SLUMPED in a chair, keeping vigil over Cat as she slept. Exhaustion claimed him at last, and he dozed in fits and starts.

He was roused by the sound of a lark singing outside his bedchamber. Martin jerked upright, blinking and rubbing his eyes. After such a night of fire, violence, and hairbreadth escape, it seemed strange to wake to anything as normal as a lark's song and the sunlight spilling through the window.

He shoved to his feet, going to peer anxiously down at Cat. With Agatha's help, he had cleaned and bound her wound. She had lost a fair amount of blood, but if Cat took no infection, she should be well.

Martin touched his fingers lightly to her brow and was

relieved to find no sign of fever. She slept so deeply but that could just be evidence of exhaustion. Martin's throat tightened when he reflected how near he had come to losing her last night.

He had once been fool enough to imagine that it would be Miri Cheney's ethereal image that would haunt him to the end of his days. But if he lived to be a hundred, he knew he would never forget the sight of Cat silhouetted in the gallery, a fiery-haired warrior goddess clutching that bow in her hands.

She did not look quite so indomitable now, swallowed up in his bed, her hair tumbled across the pillow, her face pale and bruised, a rough line of stitches marring her brow. But Martin thought he had never seen any woman more beautiful.

There was so much he wanted to say to her when she awoke. So much he needed to tell her. But for a man who had always been so glib with words, he had no idea how he would even begin.

When he drew the coverlet up over her bare shoulder, Cat stirred at last. Her eyes fluttered open, the blue depths clouded with confusion.

"Martin?"

"Yes, I am right here and so are you." He caressed her cheek. "Thank the bon Dieu. I thought I might lose you."

"No, I am right here. Wherever here is." Her gaze roved about the room as she appeared to assess her surroundings. Lifting the coverlet, she stole a peek beneath and complained, "I am naked. And back in your bed again."

Perhaps that is where you belong, Martin was tempted

to quip, but his heart was far too full. Frowning, Cat sniffed at him.

"You smell like smoke."

"Er, yes. Your pardon, but after all that happened, I felt far too exhausted to bathe and change my attire."

"After all that happened," Cat repeated. Her eyes cleared as remembrance flooded back to her. She groaned.

"Oh, hell's kite. I burned your theater down."

"While saving my daughter's life, to say nothing of my own miserable hide. The theater is of little consequence as long as I still have all that is precious to me." Martin curled his hand about hers.

Either she did not understand him or she did not choose to do so. Cat drew her hand away.

"Meg," she murmured. "How is she?"

"Well enough, all things considered. When I last looked in upon her, she was asleep. A rather astonishing thing considering she now has an entire new set of horrors in her head."

Martin shook his head bitterly. "I was so arrogant when I took Meg away from her mother. I vowed I would do so much better by my daughter, keep her safe and protected. But I have turned out to be as bad a parent as Cassandra ever was."

"That is not true, Martin," Cat reproved. "You are being most unfair to yourself."

"No, you are the one I was unfair to. All those harsh things I said to you yesterday, blaming you for my own faults. I hardly know how to beg your pardon."

"You don't have to. You had every right to be angry

with me. I should have told you that Meg was still practicing the ancient arts, attempted to make you understand."

"Not an easy thing to do, my dear, when a man is deter-
mined not to listen. I want you to know that you have won.
As soon as you are well enough, we'll take Meg to Faire
Isle."

Cat regarded him sadly. "Oh, Martin, I didn't want to
win. I never wanted you to feel forced into this decision. I
had hoped that in time you would come to see that that
was best for her."

"I do see that. Perhaps a part of me always did." Martin's lips quirked in a rueful smile. "But I am a very selfish
man. Meg has been mine for such a short time. I found the
thought of sharing her with anyone unbearable, even the
Lady of Faire Isle."

Cat said nothing, merely stretched her hand out to him
in a gesture of comfort. Martin sank down on the edge of
the bed, gathering her hand in his.

"There is another reason that I have always been terrified of Meg having anything to do with the ancient learning. It is something that is difficult for me to admit even to
myself." Martin moistened his lips. "There have been times
when I have stood over my daughter, watching her sleep,
searching her face, terrified that I might see some trace of
her mother in her. That no matter what I might do, Cassandra would triumph in the end and Meg would become the
Silver Rose."

"That will never happen, Martin. Not with Ariane
guiding her."

"I am sure you are right. I pray that in time the whole
myth of the Silver Rose will be forgotten. How many lives

that cursed legend has already claimed and I fear it will have one more.

"Jane Danvers. I have no idea how to save her, Cat, short of telling the truth. But Meg is my daughter. I can't sacrifice her, even to spare Jane."

"We will think of something, Martin. Once we have Meg tucked safely back on Faire Isle." Cat pressed his hand.

Martin smiled at her gratefully, carrying her fingers to his lips.

Neither of them noticed the creak of the door or the retreat of the small figure who had been listening. Meg flattened herself against the wall in the corridor, pressing her hands to her lips.

She had only stolen downstairs to check on Cat, see how her wound was faring. Meg had never expected to be dealt such a sharp blow herself.

Papa . . . her own papa had feared that one day Meg might become like her mother, that she would fulfill the dark prophecy of the Silver Rose.

Meg's lips trembled, a tear stealing down her cheek. Now that he realized she had been hiding the *Book of Shadows,* he would be more convinced than ever.

Meg could only see one way of proving to him he was wrong, of bringing an end to the Silver Rose and saving Lady Danvers. Only one way . . . if only she could find the courage to do it.

❈❈❈

STILL DRAINED BY THE EVENTS OF LAST NIGHT, CAT HAD dozed off again. Martin seized the opportunity to clean himself up a bit. Stripped down to his breeches, he was splashing water over his bared chest when his bedchamber was invaded.

Mistress Butterydoor and Maude charged in, distraught and breathless, both women trying to talk at once.

"Oh, Master Wolfe, she's gone and it's all Maude's fault."

"'Tis not," Maude responded, bursting into tears.

"Indeed it is, you great blubbering fool. You were the one who helped lace her up in her finest gown."

"Well, h-how was I to know? After all the t-terrible things that happened to her yesterday, I t-thought she just wanted to look p-pretty."

"Idiot. If you had half a brain, you would have—"

Martin intervened, commanding them both to silence. "Now, Mistress Butterydoor, will you tell me in some coherent fashion that I can possibly understand what the devil is going on?"

"It is Mistress Meg. She has run off," Agatha announced dramatically while Maude wept into her apron.

"Don't talk nonsense, woman," Martin snapped. "After what she has just been through, Meg would be neither rash nor foolish enough to do such a thing. She is likely just out in the garden."

Her eyes filling with tears, Agatha shook her head and handed him a small folded note. Martin snatched it from her with mounting trepidation.

There was no mistaking Meg's handwriting. His daughter had a careful, labored script. As Martin scanned the brief lines, he swore.

"Sweet Jesu."

The uproar had disturbed Cat's rest. Wincing, she attempted to raise herself higher on the pillow as she asked anxiously. "Martin, what is it?"

He responded by reading aloud in a taut voice.

Papa,

I am sorry I have proved to be such a great disappointment to you. I have tried terribly hard not to become an evil sorceress like Maman and I don't want anyone else to be hurt because of my legend. There is only one way I can save Lady Danvers and that is to confess that I am the Silver Rose.

Forgive me and remember me always as your loving daughter,

Margaret Wolf

Martin could scarce read her signature, it was so stained with tears. He experienced an unmanly urge himself and had to swallow thickly.

Cat for once made no effort to conceal her emotion, her eyes welling as she exclaimed, "Sweet, brave girl!"

"Brave?" Agatha wailed. "My poppet has run mad. Is the child so determined to get herself hung?"

"That is not going to happen." Flinging the note down, Martin set up a frantic search for his boots. "I'll find Meg, stop her before she ever gets near Walsingham."

When he saw Cat struggling to rise, he commanded her to lie still. "You are in no condition to accompany me."

"I know that," she said. "But you've got to listen to me before you go rushing off. Stop and think, Martin. Meg knows nothing of Walsingham. If the girl has made up her mind to confess, there is only one person in London she would seek out and we both know who that is."

Martin froze, fearing that Cat was right. And if she was, it made it all the more urgent that he get to Meg in time.

※※※

THE PRESENCE CHAMBER AT WHITEHALL WAS THRONGED with courtiers and petitioners, all hoping to catch the eye of the queen as she returned from chapel. Any person presenting a well-dressed appearance could gain admittance to this outer chamber.

Meg had trailed in after a stout country knight and his wife, attempting to blend in with their flock of chattering daughters. Losing herself amidst the waiting crowd, she could only marvel at how brave Elizabeth must be, to parade boldly among her subjects after so many plots against her life.

Meg only hoped that she could match the courage of the queen she so admired. She feared that she had used up what small store she had possessed merely getting herself here. She shrank to the back of the crowded chamber, unable to see anything past the forest of shoulders and heads.

Her only intimation of the queen's approach came from the stirring of the crowd, caps being doffed, voices crying "God save the queen."

Meg's heart began to beat so fast she could scarce breathe. She stood frozen, overwhelmed by the prospect of at last coming into the presence of Queen Elizabeth and dread of what she was about to do.

Meg knew if she did not move soon, her chance would be lost. Gulping in a lungful of air, she fought her way forward through the sea of silk skirts and masculine legs clad in trunk hose. Ignoring the rebukes and protests hurled at her, Meg surfaced at the front of the crowd.

For a moment she felt almost blinded by a dizzying vision of a tall willowy woman who seemed all fire and gold, her costly gown embroidered with gems, the silk fabric fanning out over a wide farthingale.

Allowing herself no more time to think, Meg hurled herself forward and sank to her knees. She bowed her head, not daring to raise her eyes.

"God's death. Who is this?" Meg heard a musical voice exclaim.

"G-God save Your Grace. I—I crave—," Meg stammered, but she could not make herself heard above the hum of voices in the chamber.

A problem the queen did not have. "Silence," Elizabeth called out in a ringing tone.

Her Majesty was instantly obeyed, but to Meg that made everything worse. The chamber was now so quiet all she heard was the quickness of her breath, her pulse drumming in her ears. She was aware of every eye in the chamber trained upon her and she stared fixedly at the hem of Elizabeth's gown.

"There is nothing to be afraid of, child," the queen said. "Tell us your name."

"It is Margaret. Margaret Elizabeth Wolfe," Meg replied in a voice scarce above a whisper.

"Well, Mistress Wolfe. What would you have of your sovereign?"

Heartened by the kindness she detected in the queen's voice, Meg was emboldened to speak a little louder.

"God save Your Grace. I crave your ear . . ." Meg glanced upward and the rest of her carefully prepared speech fled from her mind.

Her jaw falling open, she studied Elizabeth, the queen at once so much more and so much less than Meg had expected.

Elizabeth carried herself with a regal bearing, a ruff circling her slender neck. She had an intelligent face, long and thin with a hooked nose and pointed chin. Her red curly hair was obviously a wig, her complexion layered beneath cosmetics to conceal the ravages of smallpox and time.

This Elizabeth appeared so much older and far more a mere mortal than the queen of Meg's imaginings. Except for her eyes.

Set beneath fine arched brows, Elizabeth's eyes seemed ageless, so bright and piercing that Meg blinked. It was like staring straight into the sun.

"Gloriana," Meg breathed, sending a ripple of laughter through the chamber.

Even the queen looked amused, but her smile bathed Meg in all the warmth of a summer's day.

"You may dispense with the flattery and come to the point, Mistress Wolfe," Elizabeth said. "To what end do you crave our ear?"

Meg moistened her lips and blurted out, "I came to beg you to free Lady Danvers."

The queen's smile fled. It was like watching the sun vanish behind the clouds. A murmur of unease circulated about the room.

"What is her ladyship's fate to do with you, girl?" the queen demanded.

"May it please Your Grace, I—I know she is innocent."

"And how would you know that?"

Meg's heart beat so hard with fear she felt she would faint. She swallowed hard and managed to tip up her chin bravely as she replied, "Because I am the one who should have been arrested. I am the Silver Rose."

※※※

MEG SAT UPON THE STOOL AS THE QUEEN COMMANDED HER, not daring to move, but her eyes darted about the room. She had fully expected to be arrested by this time and taken under guard to the Tower.

Instead she was bemused to find herself ensconced in a part of the palace where only a privileged few were accorded admittance—the queen's private apartments.

Despite the peril of her situation, Meg could not help but eagerly study her surroundings, the imposing bed designed with different colored woods and hung with draperies of painted silk, a silver-topped table, a jewelry chest ornamented with pearls.

With its tapestry-adorned walls and gilded ceiling, it was indeed a chamber fitted out for a queen. But it was a trifle gloomy because there was only one window.

How strange and sad, Meg thought, for a queen to only have one window that opened out onto the world. It was as though Elizabeth was a prisoner of sorts herself.

That impression only deepened as the gentlemen ushers closed the doors, shutting out the uproar Meg's announcement had produced.

The queen's ministers had been prepared to immediately drag Meg from Elizabeth's presence. Her courtiers had begged the queen to keep a safe distance until it could be determined if Meg were merely mad or something far more sinister.

The queen had imperiously ignored them all. Even commanding her maids of honor to leave her, Elizabeth had closeted herself alone with Meg.

Settling herself in a cushioned chair opposite, the queen studied Meg as curiously as Meg regarded her. Folding her elegant slender hands in her lap, Elizabeth abandoned the more formal tone she had employed in the Presence Chamber.

"Well, Mistress Silver Rose," she said. "It has been a long time since I received a magus at my court. Not since my unfortunate friend Dr. Dee was accused of sorcery and obliged to flee abroad. He was a most gifted mathematician and astrologer. One of the services he performed for me was determining the most auspicious day for my coronation."

"He chose well, Your Grace," Meg replied timidly. "Your reign has been a great success thus far."

"Humph, I see you know how to flatter as well as my courtiers."

"Oh, no! I am not always as honest as I would wish to be. But I would never lie to a queen."

"Why not? Everyone else does," Elizabeth said wryly. "All might have gone well with Dr. Dee if he had limited himself to astrology. But he is believed to have delved into necromancy, attempting to communicate with spirits and demons from the great beyond. Have you ever succumbed to such temptation?"

"Not yet."

Meg's frankness surprised a bark of laughter from the queen. "You strike me as being rather young to claim to be such a powerful sorceress. So tell me, where have you gained all your knowledge?"

Meg reluctantly told her, opening herself up as she seldom had to anyone, not even Cat. She told the queen all she had learned from the *Book of Shadows,* her days in France, the attempted uprising orchestrated by her mother.

The queen listened in fascination.

She exclaimed, "Your mother actually thought to make you the queen of France?"

"Yes, Your Majesty. But I never wanted to be."

"Such a wise child," Elizabeth said. "To be a queen and wear a crown is more glorious to them who see it than it is a pleasure to them who bear it."

"Everyone believes my mother was evil and perhaps she was. She was a witch. She would have torn an entire kingdom apart."

"Mine did," the queen said, so softly Meg scarce heard her.

Elizabeth was swift to turn the subject. "So you have come here to surrender yourself to save Lady Danvers. How very brave of you."

"I don't feel very brave at all," Meg confessed. "But it seems the only honorable thing to do. I pray that you will release her now that you know the truth."

Elizabeth slowly shook her head. "Lady Danvers may be innocent of witchcraft, but there seems little doubt her ladyship conspired with this Father Ballard in a plot against my life."

"No, Lady Danvers is loyal to you. I am sure of it.

When I looked inside her purse, she carried with her two treasures. One was her ave beads. The other was this." Meg delved inside her own purse to produce the small scrap of blue carpet.

"This was part of—"

"I know what that is. A segment of my coronation carpet." Elizabeth took the scrap from Meg. She fingered it for a moment, her eyes misting with memories while Meg continued to plead for Jane Danvers.

"Her ladyship is a devout Catholic, but she is your true subject. She may be disappointed that you were not able to do more to protect the Catholics in your realm, but she would never seek to harm Your Grace."

The queen returned the cloth to Meg. "How can you be so sure of that?"

"Because I did more than look in her purse. I—I looked into her mind."

"You can read minds?" Elizabeth asked incredulously.

"It is one of the first things I learned as a child from my first nurse, Mistress Waters. I am quite skilled at reading eyes. Usually." Meg flinched, remembering Sander.

"Can you read mine?" the queen challenged.

Meg felt that she hardly dared. But when the queen persisted, Meg peered into Elizabeth's eyes.

She frowned. It was not easy penetrating the queen's piercing gaze. Elizabeth's mind was like a labyrinth of chambers, rooms laden down with the thoughts, hopes, and dreams of an entire country. It was as though the real Elizabeth was lost somewhere down those twisting corridors.

Meg's brow furrowed as she delved deeper until at last she found the woman behind the queen. She shivered, overwhelmed by the suppressed emotions that poured into her.

"Oh! You—you are so strong and brave like my friend, Cat. But you are tired, and worn down as well. All you want is peace and neither your councillors nor your enemies will allow you to have it. You fear that soon you will be forced to take harsh, even cruel measures against—against your own cousin."

The queen drew back, looking startled. "You begin to convince me, Mistress Margaret. You are a witch."

"I am sorry, Your Grace." Meg faltered. "If I was too bold—"

"No, I asked you to do it." Elizabeth appeared unnerved, but intrigued as well. "Is that the full measure of your sorcery or can you do other things as well? Can you divine the future?"

"I have attempted to use a scrying ball, but—"

"Show me," the queen interrupted eagerly. Before Meg could protest, Elizabeth whisked over to her writing cabinet and produced a small glass globe.

But when she attempted to hand the scrying ball to Meg, Meg whipped her hands behind her back.

"Oh, n-no, Your Grace. I have never had much success in foretelling the future."

"Try," Elizabeth insisted. "At my behest, Dr. Dee often attempted to consult the ball and reveal to me my destiny. If you could accomplish this, I might be persuaded to grant your request and release Lady Danvers."

Meg accepted the ball reluctantly. "I am not very good at it. But I will try."

Not very good? She had never succeeded in using the

ball before. Meg turned the globe in her hands, remembering Sander's shameless boasts of how he had tricked people into believing he could do magic. Meg wondered if she dared do the same. But she did not believe she could deceive Elizabeth, not even to save Lady Danvers.

She sucked in a deep breath, staring into the crystal orb, straining harder to focus than she ever had before. She imagined her eyes as curved lenses like those she had fitted into the spyglass, probing the vast reaches of the heavens, drawing the stars ever closer, closer.

Pinpricks of light danced before eyes and then seemed to explode in an array of dizzying images, one after the other. But it was the last that caused Meg to shriek and fling the ball away from her.

She cowered back on her stool, trembling as the queen bent to retrieve the scrying glass. She placed it on the silver-topped table and asked, "What did you see, child?"

Nothing, Meg wanted to shriek.

"I—I saw that you will have a long and glorious reign. Your enemies will not triumph over you. You—"

"Don't lie to me, girl. Tell me the truth. It was no vision of my glory that caused you to blanch and tremble as though you'd seen your mother's ghost."

Cassandra's ghost . . . if the queen only knew. Meg sought to blot the last terrifying vision from her mind. She thought sorrowfully of the other one she'd had, the one that pertained directly to Elizabeth, and wished she could keep it to herself. But she saw that the queen was not to be denied.

She swallowed and then admitted, "I saw what you

dread the most. A—a woman about to be executed. Not Lady Danvers. An older woman in an old castle so far from here. She had a little spaniel hidden under her skirt when she laid her head upon the block. When the executioner swung his ax, the first time, he missed and—"

"Enough." Elizabeth leaped up from her chair. "You need tell me no more."

She strode away from Meg, her face averted as she stared out her lone window. A heavy silence fell.

"I—I am sorry, Your Grace," Meg said at last. "What I saw—it might not mean anything. My friend Cat always tells me the future is not written down anywhere. We make our own decisions."

"And sometimes those choices are forced upon us." When Elizabeth swung back to face Meg, something had shut down in her eyes.

It was not Elizabeth but the queen who spoke. "Well, Margaret Wolfe, you have convinced us. Lady Danvers shall be freed, but we must deliver you up to the person in our realm best suited to take charge of such a dangerous witch."

Meg's heart sank. She had experienced such an inexplicably strong connection with Elizabeth, she had hoped the queen might sense it and be induced to pardon her.

But she gave a brave nod. As she followed the queen from her apartments, Meg held her shoulders erect, trying not to quail as she wondered what sort of dread dungeon master or executioner she was about to be handed over to.

When they entered the antechamber and Meg saw the man awaiting her, she blinked in disbelief.

Martin le Loup had been pacing the small room like a caged wolf. He came to an abrupt halt as the queen entered with Meg trailing in her wake.

Never had Meg received such a stern look from her father. She cringed, feeling she might have preferred the dungeon master.

Martin sank to his knees before the queen, not giving Elizabeth a chance to speak.

"Your Majesty, I crave your pardon for my daughter. I know naught what Margaret may have said to you, but—"

"She has favored us with a most extraordinary tale, Monsieur le Loup."

Her father winced. "Meg possesses far too much imagination for her own good. The child—"

"Is one of the most remarkable young women we have ever chanced to meet," the queen cut in. "She has convinced us to set Lady Danvers at liberty."

Martin cast an anxious glance up at the queen. "And Meg herself?"

"We have decided to release her into your custody. We would strongly advise you to convey her to this Faire Isle as soon as possible."

The queen added wryly, "Besides being a remarkable girl, Margaret is also one of the most unnerving we have met. Therefore we think our English climate might not prove at all suitable for, er, such a rare French rose."

❦

WHITEHALL FADED IN THE DISTANCE AS THE BOATMAN PLIED his oars, the wherry gliding down the Thames. Martin wrapped his arm about Meg, holding her so tightly, she could barely breathe. She made no complaint, burrowing her face against her father's doublet.

"Are you angry with me, Papa?" She risked a glance up at him. "Am—am I to be punished?"

"I must admit, when I was racing to the palace, nearly out of my wits with fear for you, I did have a fleeting thought about switches." Martin did his best to look stern, but he finished up by pressing a fierce kiss to her brow.

"Mon Dieu, Meggie. You have got to stop slipping away from me. Don't you know that is my greatest fear?"

Meg's eyes filled with tears. "I am s-sorry, Papa. I know I have disappointed you. I have tried so hard to be all that you wanted me t-to—"

"Hush, mon ange. No father could be prouder of his daughter. What you did, going to the queen, risking your own life to save Lady Danvers, it was the bravest thing I have ever seen anyone do."

Meg blinked back her tears and regarded him hopefully. "Was I as brave as Cat?"

"I vow that you were. The pair of you women quite put me to shame." Martin smiled. Using his thumb he whisked away a stray tear that had trickled down Meg's cheek.

"I am the one who should be craving your pardon, child. Your mother . . ." He had to swallow before he could continue.

"I was wrong to forbid you to ever speak of her, wrong about a good many things. I despised what Cassandra did to you, trying to force you to fulfill her dreams, become the Silver Rose. But I treated you no better."

"Oh, no, Papa, that is not true," Meg tried to protest but Martin stopped her.

"I fear it is, petite. I also tried to mold your future to suit myself, transform you into an English lady."

"But it is a father's right to decide his daughter's future."

"Other fathers and other daughters, perhaps. But you are more remarkable than that."

"*We* are more remarkable," Meg said solemnly, laying her palm against his bearded cheek.

Martin caught her hand, curling her smaller fingers within his own. "My plans for you were wrong and perhaps a trifle selfish, but I swear all I wanted to do was keep you safe and happy."

"I am happy, Papa, as long as I am with you."

"For now, perhaps." Martin's smile was tinged with melancholy. "I know that will not always be so. I have no idea what future awaits you but I have no doubt it will be extraordinary."

"No doubt." Meg tipped her chin proudly. "After all, I am the daughter of Martin le Loup."

As her father laughed and hugged her close, Meg gave a contented sigh, feeling safe and loved. She was almost able to forget that final image she had seen swirling in the scrying ball. A disturbing vision that had had nothing to do with Elizabeth, but a far different queen.

Meg had seen Catherine de Medici upon her deathbed and much to her alarm, Meg had seen herself there as well, hovering over the Dark Queen, the witch blade clutched in Meg's hand. And somewhere in the distance, she fancied she had heard Cassandra Lascelles laughing in triumph.

Meg shivered and clung closer to her father, trying to

dispel the frightening vision, remind herself what Cat had often told her.

"Your destiny is in your own hands."

Meg wanted to believe that. When she returned to the house the first thing she intended to do was find her own scrying ball and shatter it into a thousand pieces.

Epilogue

THE NIGHT WAS COLD, THE GROUND HARD WITH FROST, BUT that did not stop the women of Faire Isle from gathering in vigil outside of Belle Haven. They lit candles and prayed for the safe deliverance of the Lady of Faire Isle.

The wee girl whose arrival had been so breathlessly awaited was coming into the world too soon. A night and a day had already come and gone and still the Lady labored to give birth. The older wise women amongst the crowd already shook their heads and mourned. Given Ariane Deauville's age and tragic history in childbearing, this delay could not be a good sign.

The window of Ariane's bedchamber was cracked open despite the chill in the air. A skilled midwife herself, Ariane had nothing but scorn for the customs of confinement that dictated a woman in labor be closeted in a gloom-ridden, stuffy chamber.

Despite the fresh air invading the room, Ariane's shift was soaked in sweat. As she was seized by another contraction, she gripped Cat's hand until her knuckles turned white.

"That's right, milady," Cat crooned. "Hold on tight. You are doing just fine."

Just fine? Cat flinched at the inanity of her own words. Ariane looked anything but fine to her, her eyes rimmed with exhaustion, her face as white as the bed linens.

Much as Cat loved her friend, she heartily wished one of Ariane's sisters had arrived to support her through this ordeal. Cat felt so helpless and inadequate. There was nothing that she would not have done for her chieftain, but this was one battle she could not wage for Ariane.

All she could do was offer Ariane her hand to clutch, try to infuse some of her own strength into the woman whose own ebbed a little more with each contraction.

Among all the island women, Cat would have thought that some skilled midwife could be found, but no one's knowledge rivaled Ariane's. The Lady had insisted that she required no attendants other than Cat, her husband, and her maid.

Justice Deauville looked as drained as Ariane, every spasm of his wife's pain mirrored on his rough-hewn face, even as he tried to offer encouragement.

"I can see the crown of our daughter's head, chérie. Just another push or two and your little girl will be in your arms."

Ariane sank back against the pillows, tears leaking from her eyes.

"Oh, Justice, I—I don't think I can."

Her giant of a husband looked ready to weep himself from fear and exhaustion, but he said, "Damn it, Ariane. Yes, you can. You have to. Cat, help her. Lift her up."

As the next contraction struck, Cat shifted her arm behind Ariane, supporting her into a sitting position. Ariane gritted her teeth, straining with the last of her will. She emitted a loud cry.

Somewhere beneath Ariane's shriek, another wail was heard, feeble at first, then growing lustier by the moment.

"I have her, chérie," Justice shouted. "I have our girl."

Both Cat and Ariane collapsed back against the pillows, laughing and weeping. Cat scarce paid any heed as Justice and the maid tended to cutting the cord, cleaning Ariane and the babe.

Cat hovered over her friend. Ariane seemed so spent and Cat knew the danger to the mother often came after the rigors of labor with the onset of fever. As Cat bathed Ariane's brow, she was heartened when Ariane opened her eyes, regarding Cat with her familiar clear gaze.

"My babe. I want to see my babe," she whispered.

Cat nodded, unable to speak past the lump in her throat. But when she hastened over to Justice to convey Ariane's request, Cat's heart sank.

She could tell from the grave expression on his face that something was terribly wrong. The babe who had cried out so lustily before had gone omniously still.

"My lord, what is amiss?" Cat hardly dared to ask but

somehow she found the courage. "Is something wrong with the child?"

Justice nodded, numbly. "The babe. The child Ariane risked her life for—and she will never have another."

Peeling back the blanket, he displayed the babe to Cat. She caught her breath.

Justice cast a stricken look. "What am I to tell Ariane?"

"The truth." Cat hunched her shoulders in a helpless gesture. "You can hardly conceal it from her."

Wrapping the blanket back around the babe, Justice shuffled to the bed. Ariane scooted higher on the pillows, stretching out her arms.

Justice flinched at the sight of the eager, expectant look on Ariane's face. Desperately, he sought for the words to prepare her.

"Ariane, there is something important I must tell you—"

"Tell me anything you like," she interrupted. "Just as soon as you give me my son."

Justice was so stunned, he nearly lost his grip on the babe. Somehow he managed to convey the babe to Ariane without dropping him.

As Ariane drew the child close, Justice sagged weakly down beside her on the bed.

"You—you *knew* it was a boy?"

"Oh, yes, I sensed that some months ago. Your son has often communed with me in the early hours of the morning. Mostly through lusty kicks on his part."

Her eyes glowing, Ariane peeled back the blanket, inspecting tiny fingers and toes. She gave a heartfelt sigh of satisfaction.

Justice continued to regard her in amazement. "And you don't mind that the child is a boy?"

"Why would I mind? He's beautiful." Ariane beamed at her son, cooing words that sounded like some ancient tongue. Or perhaps it was only that peculiar language that only mothers and babes could comprehend.

"But I thought you wanted a daughter so badly, to succeed you as the Lady of Faire Isle."

"All I wanted was a healthy child. Yours and mine. As for the succession, I can do as other Ladies of Faire Isle have done before me. Search out the right young girl and train her. I have plenty of time to do so now."

Justice smiled at her tenderly. Wrapping his arm about her shoulders, he drew Ariane and their new son into his strong embrace.

Ariane pulled down her shift and set the boy to nurse. He latched eagerly onto to Ariane's nipple, delighting both his parents with his vigor.

Justice pressed a kiss upon Ariane's brow. "While our son was communing with you, did he ever happen to mention his name?"

Ariane peered deeply into her son's unfocused blue eyes.

"Leon," she pronounced softly. "His name is Leon, our young lion."

THE NIGHT THAT HAD BEEN SO SOLEMN ERUPTED WITH WILD rejoicing. The Lady of Faire Isle was safely delivered of a son. The wine flowed, bonfires were lit. Fishermen, housewives, and young maidens alike all danced with madcap abandon, capering about the flickering flames.

Martin le Loup hung back, observing the merriment from beneath the shadows of a huge oak. Happy as he was for Ariane and Justice, he was content to observe the celebrations from a distance, wistfully watching Cat as she linked hands with the other women, laughing and dancing wildly about the bonfire. Even old Agatha Butterydoor joined in, hopping about and brandishing her cane.

Out of all of Martin's household, only Agatha had been brave enough to face the channel crossing and the prospect of living in a foreign land.

She had declared fiercely that nothing or no one would separate her from her wee poppet, certainly not a parcel of Frenchies. And if Agatha could accustom herself to Mistress Cat and her strange Irish ways, the old woman was confident that she would not be daunted by anything.

And indeed for a woman who had never been farther from London than Southwark, Mistress Butterydoor had adapted remarkably well to Faire Isle. She was even learning to speak French, albeit with an accent that often caused Martin to cringe.

He summoned up a half-smile as he watched Cat and Agatha prance about the flames, even though he felt closed outside of the celebrations, of the entire world that comprised Faire Isle. He had never been entirely comfortable on the island, finding it entirely too narrow and solitary.

The important thing, he told himself, was that Meg seemed happy here. But it had been difficult to watch her these past few weeks becoming more and more absorbed in Ariane's teachings, caught up in the life of the island. His daughter seemed to be growing up and away from him at far too great a rate.

When she sought him out in the garden, he thought that Meg looked so much older, even though she wriggled beneath his arm, nestling against his side in quite the old way.

"Isn't it wonderful, Papa? About the Lady of Faire Isle's new babe?"

"Wonderful," Martin stooped down to deposit a kiss atop Meg's head. "So you are quite pleased with your new home?"

"Oh, yes. Cat was right. Faire Isle is an amazing place. You can feel the ancient magic pulsing everywhere, even in the trees." Meg wriggled away from him to caress her fingers along the trunk of the tree. "You see? Try it for yourself."

To oblige her, Martin stroked the oak's trunk. "Feels like tree bark to me."

Meg laughed and shook her head at him. "I love you dearly, Papa. But you are so hopelessly obtuse sometimes about a good many things."

"I realize I was wrong when I tried to force you to deny your gifts as a daughter of the earth. I believe I have apologized on several occasions."

"I am not talking about your blindness in regards to me. I am speaking of Cat. I know you adore her and you are certainly adept at courting a lady. So why haven't you gone down upon your knee and declared yourself by now?"

"Perhaps because I am afraid of getting my ears clouted," Martin retorted. He added in a quieter tone,

"Cat does not love me, no matter how much you or I might wish it."

"Yes, she does," Meg insisted with an impatient stamp of her foot.

"What have you being doing? Reading her eyes?"

"It so happens I have, but any dolt could see how much she adores you. She is just far too proud to tell you so." Meg splayed her hands upon her hips, leveling a severe look at him.

"The question is, Papa, what are you going to do about it?"

✦✦✦

CAT STRODE ACROSS THE MEADOW, MOONLIGHT SHIMMERING over the frost-struck grass, the earth crunching beneath her feet. The sounds of the revels left far behind, she drew in a deep breath, relishing the quiet to gather her thoughts.

She reflected back to when she had first left the island at the beginning of summer to carry out the mission Ariane had given her. Things had turned out so much better than Cat had had reason to hope at the time.

Ariane was safely delivered of her babe, the coven of the Silver Rose destroyed, Meg safely lodged on the island. With the *Book of Shadows* gone, it seemed unlikely that even the Dark Queen would have reason to pursue the child.

Cat was now back on Faire Isle, exactly where she had so longed to be. Why then had she often found herself so restless and beset with melancholy?

She did not have to wrack her brain too hard for an answer to that. Martin. Cat could tell that he was not comfortable residing here on Faire Isle any more than Jane Danvers was.

Exiled from England, her ladyship had joined them on the journey to the island, a sorrowful figure in the black mourning Jane had donned in memory of her brother. The mystical atmosphere of Faire Isle clearly made Lady Danvers uneasy.

She intended to move to Paris, where she had friends among the other Catholic exiles. It would not surprise Cat if Martin volunteered to escort her. Jane's tragic situation was exactly the sort of thing to appeal to Martin's romantic notions of chivalry.

Expecting the parting to come, Cat had done her best to detach herself from Martin, reclaim the heart that she had given him. Thus far she could not congratulate herself on her success.

The crackle of a twig alerted her to someone's approach. She came about to find Martin striding toward her.

Her heart did its familiar foolish dance, but she sought to quell the emotions that flooded her at the mere sight of the man.

"Martin." She managed to greet him with a friendly, but cool nod. "So you felt the need for a little quiet too?"

"The revels do appear likely to go on until morning." He smiled. "But they all have reason to rejoice. A young Lord of Faire Isle is not born every day."

"Everyone is glad to see our Lady safely delivered of a healthy boy. But the child will never be the lord of this island. Only a woman has ever ruled this island and thus it will remain. Ariane will still have to find a successor."

Cat hesitated before adding, "There is a good chance she will choose Meg. The child is so extraordinary."

She watched Martin, uncertain how he would react to the prospect. But he replied, "I would be very proud if Meg were chosen. It would be a great honor. Cassandra always insisted Meg was destined to become a leader among wise women. Perhaps her prophecy will come true in a way she never imagined."

"And what of the destiny of Martin le Loup?" Cat asked, striving to keep her voice light as though the answer was of no import to her. "I suppose you will be off on some new adventure, seeking another damsel in distress. Perhaps Lady Danvers will serve your turn. She still seems in great need of rescue."

"Perhaps she does, but some other man will be obliged to do it. I have quite enough on my hands rescuing you."

"Me?" Cat snorted. "What do you imagine I need rescuing from?"

"Your stubborn Irish pride. I fear it may prove enough to do us both in." Martin took a step closer, planting his hands on his hips, his boots square upon the ground. "So you expected me to just go riding off into the sunset? Well, I can be just as stubborn as you. I am going nowhere until you tell me."

"Tell you what?"

"That you love me."

Cat gasped, making a great show of spluttering with indignation. "Where did you get a damn fool notion like that?"

"From Meg. She said she read it in your eyes."

"The impertinent little vixen." To her dismay, Cat felt

her cheeks fire so hot, she doubted even the shadows of night would be enough to hide it.

"Tell me!" Martin persisted. "Is it true? Do you love me?"

Cat squared off with him in belligerent fashion, arms akimbo, imitating his stance.

"Mayhap I do. What of it?"

"This," he growled, seizing her in his arms, crushing his mouth against hers.

Cat struggled to break free before he reduced her to a state of melting helplessness with the fire of his kiss.

"No," she panted. "You—you need not feel sorry for me just because I was fool enough to go and fall in love with you. I won't be the object of your chivalry."

"Chivalry be damned. I am completely besotted with you. Can't you see that? What sort of wise woman are you?"

"One who has never been all that good at reading eyes." Cat reared back, trying to search his face, scarce daring to believe. "I am not in the least like Miri Cheney or Jane Danvers. Some sweet gentle beauty that you—you could—"

"Worship from afar?" Martin quirked his brow. "You yourself told me that was not what I needed. What I need, nay, what I want is . . ."

Martin smiled at her and quoted her own words back to her. "A woman who knows how to get right down there, thick in the muck of life, sweating and fighting beside me, nurturing, loving, and protecting each other to the end of our days."

"Oh." Cat swallowed and said gruffly, "Well, I suppose it is possible that woman could be me."

"More than possible, *petite chatte*. Of complete certainty."

Martin gathered her back in his arms and this time Cat surrendered to his embrace without a murmur. They simply held each other thus for a long time under the vast canopy of the night sky.

Martin was the first to break the silence, exclaiming suddenly, "It's gone."

"What is?"

"The comet."

Cat lifted her face and peered upward at the moon and stars, the heavens no longer disturbed by any ghostly phenomenon.

She gave Martin an indulgent smile. "You are just now noticing that? The thing disappeared days ago."

"You mean after plaguing us for all these months, it vanished just like that?" Martin asked in disbelief. "Maybe the comet was a portent of something."

"Of what?"

"I don't know. Maybe it announced the birth of Ariane's babe or—or an event even more earthshaking, you agreeing to be my wife."

Cat tipped up her chin challengingly. "I don't recall agreeing to that."

"You will," Martin replied with a trace of his old arrogance. "Maybe the comet heralded our union, a love that will be the stuff of legends, outlasting the moon, the stars."

"And maybe it was only a comet." Cat laughed and dragged his mouth down to hers for another lusty kiss.

Author's Note

The comet that trails across the sky throughout this novel blazed entirely out of my own imagination. There was no such celestial phenomenon in the summer of 1586 when my story takes place. The emotional impact of the comet and the reactions of my characters are drawn from records of comet sightings throughout history.

Much of this novel deals with one of the many plots against the life of Elizabeth I. The Babington conspiracy was as complex and devious as the mind of the queen's spy master, Francis Walsingham. For the purposes of fiction, I was obliged to condense and simplify the details of the plot. Martin le Loup's participation in uncovering the conspiracy and the theft of the portrait are entirely my own creation.

The painting, itself, is not. The conspirators were indeed foolish enough to sit for the portrait which eventually aided in their capture. The Babington portrait is one of those marvelous tidbits of history, far better than anything a writer could invent.

About the Author

SUSAN CARROLL is an award-winning romance author whose books include *The Bride Finder* and its two sequels, *The Night Drifter* and *Midnight Bride,* as well as *The Painted Veil, Winterbourne,* and most recently, *The Dark Queen* and *The Courtesan.* She lives in Rock Island, Illinois. Visit Susan Carroll's website at www.susancarroll.org.

About the Type

The text of this book was set in Life, a typeface designed by W. Bilz, and jointly developed by Ludwig & Mayer and Francesco Simoncini in 1965. This contemporary design is in the transitional style of the eighteenth century. Life is a versatile text face and is a registered trademark of Simoncini S.A.

Don't miss these three captivating novels in the

DARK QUEEN series

by Susan Carroll

The Dark Queen
On sale April 2005

Set in Renaissance France, a time when women of ability are deemed sorceresses; when France is torn by ruthless political intrigues; and all are held in thrall to the sinister ambitions of Queen Catherine de Medici—Ariane Cheney, Lady of the Fair Isle, must risk everything to restore peace to a tormented land.

The Courtesan
On sale August 2005

Skilled in passion, artful in deception, and driven by betrayal, she is the glittering center of the royal court —but Gabrielle Cheney, the most desired woman of Renaissance France, will draw the wrath of a dangerous adversary—the formidable Dark Queen.

The Silver Rose
On sale February 2006

France is a country in turmoil, plagued by famine, disease, and on the brink of a new religious war. In the midst of so much chaos, Miri Cheney must face a far greater evil—a diabolical woman known only as The Silver Rose.

Published by Ballantine Books • Available wherever books are sold